D1598447

Lutosławski and his music

Lutosławski
and his music

STEVEN STUCKY

Assistant Professor of Music
Cornell University

CAMBRIDGE UNIVERSITY PRESS

Cambridge
London   New York   New Rochelle
Melbourne   Sydney

Published by the Press Syndicate of the University of Cambridge
The Pitt Building, Trumpington Street, Cambridge CB2 1RP
32 East 57th Street, New York, NY 10022, USA
296 Beaconsfield Parade, Middle Park, Melbourne 3206, Australia

First published 1981

Printed in Great Britain at the University Press, Cambridge

British Library Cataloguing in Publication Data
Stucky, Steven
Lutosławski and his music.
1. Lutosławski, Witold
I. Title
780′.92′4   ML410.L965   80–40982
ISBN 0 521 22799 2

Contents

Preface

Witold Lutosławski's rise to international prominence has introduced a distinguished body of music into Western cultural life. It is
gratifying that nowadays his most celebrated compositions, those
produced since about 1960, are frequently performed and widely
appreciated, together with a handful of earlier works. To most admirers of Lutosławski's art, however, the details of his life, the impact of
political and cultural developments in Eastern Europe on his career,
and the aspects of his musical language linking his earliest compositions to his latest have remained all but unknown; and it is this
unhappy circumstance which prompted the present study. His recent
achievement can be properly understood only in this wider context,
and it is my hope to have contributed to such an understanding. Thus
I have devoted considerable attention in these pages to Lutosławski's
music written before 1960 not only because this music deserves study
in its own right, but also because it allows us to appreciate his late
style as the summation of a lifetime of patient, determined effort
under frequently adverse conditions.

Of necessity the biographical account offered here is mainly a
chronicle of Lutosławski's public transactions. There remain regret-
table *lacunae* in our knowledge of his life, particularly for the period
before 1937 and the years spanned by the Second World War.
Moreover, I have been constrained by the conviction that to pry into
the personal life of a man who places a high value on his privacy
would amount to indecent curiosity. Even so, the material I have been
able to assemble may prove valuable as a background against which to
view Lutosławski's growth as an artist. I have approached his creative
life in terms of four style periods: the works leading to the First
Symphony, completed in 1947; the functional music, much of it
connected with Polish folklore, written between 1945 and 1954; a group
of transitional works in which salient features of the late style emerge;
and the mature production in which the technique of limited aleatorism is used, beginning with the *Jeux vénitiens* of 1961. Stylistic
periodization is, admittedly, a risky and often artificial proposition,
and as a technique of historiography it has begun to fall into some

disrepute among musicologists. But in the case of Lutosławski the events of his life have so decisively influenced his musical development that the four-period view I have adopted seems rather clearly indicated and may make more easily comprehensible the course of his creative work. Since *Jeux vénitiens* the evolution of Lutosławski's style seems to me so seamless that I have not sought to impose on the more recent works any further division.

Analytical and critical discussion of the earlier works is scattered throughout the four biographical chapters. Chapter 5 is intended to serve as an introduction to Lutosławski's style since 1960. The technical apparatus and the generalizations about Lutosławski's compositional procedures and aesthetic stance presented there will, I hope, prepare the reader to make sense of the summary discussions of the individual late works gathered in the final chapter. The late works are treated partly in terms of rather technical analysis. This approach will probably gratify those composers and theorists who have a professional curiosity in such matters. There is a more fundamental reason for taking this approach, though; for if music is indeed a nonrepresentational art, if its 'meaning' is expressible only in purely musical terms, then the very stuff of which music is made is the only solid basis on which to found an appreciation.

The composer was kind enough to discuss with me the analysis of some of his earlier works; we were not able to discuss the later works in much detail together. In any case, I have not felt bound by his views; the analytical remarks in the present study represent my own views, and I am responsible for any flaws they may contain. The style of the musical analysis offered here is frankly eclectic; although I have borrowed freely from the methods of modern theorists and from Schenker, my aims in discussing Lutosławski's works are pragmatic, not theoretical, and I believe that mixed means in analysis are, in general, likely to produce more useful results than is the doctrinaire application of a single theory. Moreover, my analytical remarks arise not out of the métier of the professional theorist but rather out of the admiration that I, as a composer, feel for the achievements of a genuine master. Though it is notoriously difficult to do, I have tried at least in a modest way to proceed from the truism that a work of art ought to imply its own methods for analysis and its own standards for criticism. Above all, I hope to have avoided that false analysis which Edward Cone has called 'prescription': the far too common practice of adopting in advance a consistent theoretical outlook and then arranging the musical evidence to fit the theory.

The present study would not have been possible, of course, without the help of many people; I regret that I can mention only a few. I am especially grateful to Mariola Górska and Jeff Cooper for assisting with thorny translation problems. The support of the Friends of Music at Cornell University and especially of George Winter and John Hsu made possible my first meeting with Lutosławski in April 1977; that of the National Endowment for the Humanities, Washington, DC, made possible a visit to Warsaw in June 1979. I must also thank Alina Sawicka-Baird and K. Nowacki of the staff of the Union of Polish Composers, Leslie Caplan of Magnamusic-Baton, Inc., and Robin Boyle of Chester Music, all of whom provided materials which would not otherwise have been available. Musical examples from the works of Lutosławski are quoted with the kind permission of the composer and by arrangement with Polskie Wydawnictwo Muzyczne (Cracow), Chester Music (London), and Moeck Verlag (Celle). I am grateful to Clare Davies-Jones, Rosemary Dooley, and Penny Souster of Cambridge University Press for their sympathetic advice. Most especially I wish to thank Witold Lutosławski and his wife, Danuta, for the warm hospitality they displayed when I visited them in Poland, for their generosity in sharing unpublished materials and information with me, and for their unfailing kindness and encouragement. To my family I cannot adequately express my thanks for their patience and support over many years, and especially to my wife, Melissa, for countless hours of typing, retyping, and proofreading beyond the call of duty.

S. S.

Appleton, Wisconsin
February 1980

1 The early years: Lutosławski to 1948

On the eve of the First World War Poland was, despite her thousand-year cultural history, a stateless nation, the victim of the territorial ambitions of her neighbors to the west, south, and east. The partitions of 1772, 1793, and 1795 and the 'fourth partition' effected in 1815 by the Congress of Vienna had divided the ancient kingdom of Poland among Prussia, Austria, and Russia. Borne on the tides of nationalism and socialism rising throughout Europe, and fired by the memory of such outrages as the Russian massacre of the Warsaw suburb of Praga in 1794 and by the specially Romantic spirit for which Poland was famous, her patriots had again and again mounted futile insurrections during the nineteenth century. Now, as Europe approached a war which would embroil all three of the occupying powers, Poland braced herself for the inevitable fact that the war would be fought on her soil, while at the same time many Poles saw in the approaching conflict yet another chance to assert the right of their homeland to independent statehood. Such was the world into which, on 25 January 1913, the composer Witold Lutosławski was born in Warsaw.

The composer's father was, indeed, in the thick of nationalist politics. Józef Lutosławski had been born 28 March 1881 to Franciszek and Paulina (née Szczygielska) Lutosławski at the family estate at Drozdowo, near Łomża on the river Narew northeast of Warsaw. The family were influential and highly educated members of the *ziemiań-stwo* (landed gentry). Józef's older brother Wincenty, a distinguished philosopher and a prolific writer on a variety of subjects, was best known abroad for pioneering a modern method of literary style analysis through which he established the chronology of Plato's writings.[1] Wincenty Lutosławski's wife, Sofía Pérez Eguía y Casanova, was a noted Spanish poet and novelist. Brother Jan was an editor and agricultural writer; Kazimierz (pseudonym Jan Zawada), a priest and physician; and Marian, a mechanical and electrical engineer prominent in politics.[2] The family were musical as well; Józef's father was an amateur violinist, his mother played piano, and an aunt, Karolina Bohomolec, was a fine pianist who had studied with César Franck.

1

As a child at Drozdowo Józef displayed a sensitive, dreamy nature and showed considerable musical talent. In 1898 he finished *gimnaz- jum* in Riga; later he studied agriculture at the Zurich Polytechnic Institute. He is supposed to have studied piano with Eugène d'Albert, though precisely when and where are a mystery. In 1903 he moved to London, where in addition to studying political science he served as foreign correspondent for the Warsaw journal *Gont* (The Shingle), an organ of the National Democratic Party. He returned to Poland in 1905, and in 1908 he settled at Drozdowo, where for a time he devoted himself to managing his parents' estate.

As a student in Zurich Józef had fallen in love with a remarkable young woman, Maria Olszewska, a fellow student of his brother Kazimierz at the university medical school. Born in 1880, Maria was, like Józef, a member of the *ziemiaństwo*. Her father owned a large estate in Podolia, an area of the Ukraine which had once been part of the medieval kingdom of Poland and where most of the land remained in Polish hands. (Tymoszówka, the birthplace of composer Karol Szymanowski, was nearby.) Olszewski was a mathematician and taught in the (thoroughly russified) schools of the area, and he must have been a somewhat liberal thinker, for he took the unusually progressive step of sending his daughters to university abroad. When Józef Lutosławski took Maria Olszewska home to Drozdowo for the first time, the fact that she was a university student – and, what is more, a medical student – provoked some astonishment. After Zurich, Maria attended universities in Berlin and Cracow, since it was con- sidered fashionable to change schools frequently. In 1904, Maria having won her degree as a physician, Józef returned from London and the couple were married. Together they went back to London where their first child, Jerzy, was born later the same year.

Once settled back at Drozdowo in 1908, Józef became more and more deeply involved in the affairs of the National Democrats (ND, or Endecja). Under the leadership of Roman Dmowski, the Endecja had by 1905 become the strongest bourgeois party in Poland and thus the chief adversaries of the country's strongest leftist party, the Polish Socialist Party led by Józef Piłsudski. Dmowski and his followers sought to foster nationalism but opposed insurrectionary tactics; seeing in Germany and Austria-Hungary the greatest threats to Polish autonomy, they sought to improve relations with tsarist Russia and to enlist Russian support for Polish independence. After the outbreak of the world war and the occupation of most of Poland by troops of the Central Powers, many Endecja leaders went to Russia, both to con- tinue their political activities and to organize Polish military units to fight on the side of the Entente. Among them were Józef Lutosławski and his brother Marian. When Józef went to Russia in August 1915 he left behind Maria and three sons (a daughter had died in infancy): Jerzy, the eldest, would become an engineer; Henryk, born in 1909, would become an agronomist; and Witold, the youngest, would be a composer.

In Russia Józef was among the leadership of the ND's Ognisko (Watchfire) group and served on the executive committee of the Polish Interparty Union. At the same time he was commander of the Polish League of Military Preparedness, and it was his military activity which ultimately brought him into conflict with the Bolsheviks. To the rightest ND a Bolshevist Russia was, of course, anathema, and in practice Polish troops in Russia had found themselves engaged principally in resisting Red forces. Allied-held Murmansk in the far north became in 1918 the potential port of evacuation for Polish soldiers as well as the base for British, French, and American expeditionary forces against the Bolsheviks. Józef and Marian Lutosławski angered Red factions by helping to plan for Polish evacuation and by cooperating in a revolt of Polish officers and soldiers in Murmansk. Marian was arrested on 23 April 1918, and Józef was arrested two days later; the brothers were charged with counterrevolutionary activities and forgery of diplomatic papers. As a prisoner Józef wrote an impassioned nationalist tract entitled *Chleb i ojczyzna* (Bread and the Fatherland), dated 'Moscow, Butyrsky prison, 28 May 1918'. The Lutosławski brothers were arraigned in August. On 5 September – several days before they were to be tried – they were led to the village of Vshekh-Shvyatskoye outside Moscow, and there, with a large group of fellow prisoners, they perished in a mass execution.

As a legacy Józef Lutosławski left not only his book, published in Warsaw posthumously; to his youngest son he had also bequeathed his love for music. Among the composer's earliest memories is that of his father's playing Beethoven and Chopin 'very musically'. By 1919 Maria Lutosławski had settled again in Warsaw, and there at the age of six the young Lutosławski demanded of his mother that he be given piano lessons. He was driven, he recalls, 'by an inner desire which has been with me ever since I was aware of the world around me'.[3] Immediately he began to study with Helena Hoffman. At the same time, since the Warsaw household saw a great deal of music-making and received a steady stream of musical visitors, he began as a very young child to absorb a rich musical culture at home. Already the impulse to compose was strong in him; he and his brother Henryk played at being composers, and Witold began to improvise seriously. The lessons with Hoffman continued for two years, until the family

4 The early years: Lutosławski to 1948

moved back to Drozdowo. There, at the age of nine, the young composer wrote out his first fully notated piano piece.

At eleven, Lutosławski returned to Warsaw to enter the Stefan Batory gimnazjum, and he now resumed serious piano study, this time with Józef Śmidowicz (1888–1962), a concert pianist and prestigious teacher at the Chopin College of Music. Until now he had been raised on a steady diet of Chopin and Beethoven, but at eleven Lutosławski had his first encounter with modern music: Karol Szymanowski's Third Symphony, op. 27 (Pieśń o nocy [Song of the Night], 1914–16). He describes himself as 'dazed' by the experience and remembers, 'Afterwards I ran home and spent days trying to recapture those sounds at the piano. For weeks I could think of nothing but this work.' One can easily imagine the powerful impression this symphony might have made on a precocious young musician, with its large and colorful orchestra augmented by tenor soloist, organ, and chorus, its exotic orientalism, its mystical Persian text, and its sensuous harmonic language.

In 1926 Lutosławski became a violin pupil of Lidia Kmitowa (1888–1967), an excellent teacher who had studied with Joseph Joachim and who later played with the Polish Radio Quartet and with her own Kmita Piano Trio. He studied with Kmitowa for six years and progressed as far as the Bach solo sonatas, Mozart concertos, and the Franck sonata. He was still composing as well, and in 1927 he produced two sonatas for violin and piano which he recalls as 'terribly naive' pieces bearing the imprint of Grieg and early Debussy. It was also in 1927 that Lutosławski's family decided that he should enter the conservatory in Warsaw. He attended the conservatory for only a year, though, since with this additional burden it proved impossible to keep up his regular schoolwork at the gimnazjum, composing, and practicing the violin.

On leaving the conservatory in 1928, Lutosławski applied to Witold Maliszewski for composition lessons, taking with him a new Poème for piano written under the influence of Skriabin's late style, which sufficiently impressed the teacher that he accepted the fifteen-year-old composer immediately. Maliszewski (1873–1939) was the composer of four symphonies and numerous works in the other standard genres, including opera. A student of Rimsky-Korsakov at the St. Petersburg Conservatory from 1898 to 1902, he wrote at first in the neoromantic Russian manner, influenced by his teacher and Glazunov. In his later works he developed a strongly nationalistic (i.e., Polish) style. Maliszewski served as director of the Odessa Conservatory from 1908 to 1921, when he came to Warsaw.

Under Maliszewski's tutelage Lutosławski wrote his first publicly performed composition, *Taniec chimery* (Dance of the Chimera, 1930), which he played two years later at a conservatory concert. From the same period date his earliest orchestral compositions: a Scherzo (1930) and in 1931 an incidental score for the play *Harun al Raszid* by Janusz Makarczyk. A reorchestrated version of the music for *Harun al Raszid*, given in 1933 by the Warsaw Philharmonic Orchestra under Józef Oziminski, was the composer's first orchestral performance, although in later years he discounted its importance, preferring to cite the 1939 première of a more mature work, the Symphonic Variations, as his début.

In 1931 Lutosławski passed his final *gimnazjum* exams and enrolled at Warsaw University to study mathematics. In 1932, when Maliszewski was appointed professor of composition at the Warsaw Conservatory, Lutosławski entered his class there. On Maliszewski's advice he dropped his study of the violin and joined the conservatory piano class of Jerzy Albert Lefeld (1898–). For a year he tried to continue both the mathematics courses at the university and his studies at the conservatory, but in 1933 he left the university to devote all his time to music.

By his own account Lutosławski was an indifferent student of tonal harmony and counterpoint, not for lack of ability but for want of interest. Maliszewski taught these subjects rather cursorily anyway, preferring to devote more attention to the study of form. Lutosławski recalls that his teacher was a demanding taskmaster: 'Maliszewski instilled in the student a rigorous attitude toward one's materials and a sense of responsibility for every note one wrote. He was merciless in ferreting out the haphazard and illogical.'[4] Unfortunately little of Lutosławski's work from the conservatory years has survived to testify about his early development. As a student he produced a three-movement piano sonata and two songs in 1934, and in 1936 a double fugue for orchestra and *Prelude and Aria* for piano. He also wrote music for three short films in 1935–6, in which he experimented with creating sound-track montage effects. Of these works only the piano sonata is extant, and it remains in manuscript.

The style of the piano sonata reflects both the excellent training in classical form the young composer had received from Maliszewski and his early and strong attraction toward French music. Thus the first movement is in clear sonata form, and it opens with a first theme whose figurational texture recalls, perhaps, the Ravel *Sonatine* (ex. 1.1). This opening passage also gives early evidence of Lutosławski's postimpressionist love of harmony as color and his habit of juxtaposing synthetic scales with tonal harmony to achieve such coloristic ends. Here the coloristic accessory is the symmetrical

1.1   Theme 1, first movement of Piano Sonata (mm. 1–7)

octatonic scale – what Messiaen would later call the second of his
modes of limited transposition – in m. 6 (ex. 1.2). The sonata is highly
eclectic as well; and the Russian musicologist Lidia Rappoport, who
is at pains to claim for Lutosławski a Russian musical heritage, may be
right to find in the second theme of the first movement an echo of
Glazunov or Borodin (ex. 1.3). Rappoport judges the second movement to be more independent stylistically and the finale to be uneven
in quality and stylistically diverse.[5]

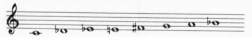

1.2   Abstracted scale, Piano Sonata

1.3   Theme 2, first movement of Piano Sonata

Lutosławski earned his diploma as a pianist in 1936, after four years' study with Lefeld. For his composition diploma in 1937 Maliszewski required that he write an examination piece, and for this purpose Lutosławski produced two requiem movements in the conservative style his teacher expected. The Requiem aeternam movement for chorus and orchestra was never performed and has since been lost, but the Lacrimosa for soprano and orchestra survives in manuscript and has been published in a transcription for voice and organ. An unassuming piece of about three minutes' length, it retains a certain quiet charm even now. The chains of parallel triads and seventh chords and the pliant, sensitively wrought vocal line of the first section again suggest the influence of the French (ex. 1.4); the hushed, devotional character of the music recalls, at least in spirit, the Fauré Requiem. Like Fauré, too, are the quasi-modal harmonic progressions, the avoidance of the leading tone, the steady, stepwise bass, and the consistently good contrapuntal sense of the individual lines. A middle section contrasts in key and melodic material and departs from the diatonicism of the opening, introducing at its climax colorful fragments of a whole-tone scale.

The musical culture that awaited Lutosławski upon his graduation in 1937 was largely an unsympathetic one. The great achievements of the early twentieth century in most of Western Europe remained beyond the ken of the Polish public. Le sacre du printemps had yet to be heard in Poland. Audiences and critics were stubbornly conservative. In this unfriendly environment, only Karol Szymanowski offered the young composers of Lutosławski's generation inspiration and guidance.

Szymanowski occupies a curiously ambiguous position in the history of Polish music. He was born 6 October 1882 in Tymoszówka, the Ukraine. He studied briefly in Warsaw with the progressive composer Zygmunt Noskowski (1846–1909), a pupil of Moniuszko and composer of the first Polish symphonic poem, Step (The Steppe, 1896); but he remained essentially self-taught, continuing to absorb a great variety of influences throughout his career. Early in life he developed the friendships with pianist Artur Rubinstein, violinist Paweł Kochański, and conductor Grzegorz Fitelberg that were to make possible the propagation of his music, particularly abroad. In 1905 Szymanowski and four other Noskowski pupils – Fitelberg (1879–1953), Ludomir Różycki (1884–1953), Apolinary Szeluto (1884–1966), and, perhaps the most promising, Mieczysław Karłowicz (1876–1909) – banded together as Młoda Polska (The Young Poland), with the goals of modernizing Polish music along European lines, as symbolized by Richard Strauss, and working for

1.4 *Lacrimosa* (mm. 1–12)

the performance of their music and the recognition of their countrymen. Młoda Polska itself was short-lived, but Szymanowski's sense of
a personal mission to rescue Polish music from provincialism
remained strong.

The customary division of Szymanowski's works into either three
or four style periods is prompted by the successive waves of foreign
influence which affected his music. He began under the spell of
Chopin and Skriabin, later was influenced by Brahms, Reger, and
Strauss, still later by Debussy, Ravel, and Stravinsky, and by a fascination with Middle Eastern culture (as in the Third Symphony and the
opera Król Roger [King Roger, 1918–24]). Frequent travels to destina-
tions as diverse as England, the United States, Russia, and North
Africa surely contributed to this extraordinarily cosmopolitan
stylistic mélange. Ultimately he succeeded in finding an idiom at
once personal and national in the works of the thirties, many of which
were influenced by folk materials (e.g., the ballet Harnasie [The
Highland Robbers], the Fourth Symphony, the Stabat Mater, and the
mazurkas for piano).

To the end of his life, though he never fully shook off his own
romantic temperament, Szymanowski remained receptive to the anti-
romantic trends in Europe, and he urged younger Polish composers to
look to the West, and especially to France, for new aesthetic ideals.
Despite his continued failure with the Polish public, or perhaps partly
because of it, he was, at his death in 1937, a figure of immense
authority to his younger colleagues. He had fought their battles for
them, bringing Polish music into the twentieth century virtually
single-handed; and, although his own music remained tied, ultimately, to the past, he made it possible for younger Poles to look to the
future. Stefan Jarociński writes:

If any historian of music tried to trace a logical line of development in Polish
music in the first three decades of the XX century . . ., he would be amazed at
the inexplicable gap which would naturally yawn between the works of
Paderewski, Karłowicz or Różycki, and the works of those composers whose
talents matured in the years between the two World Wars. It is precisely
Szymanowski's, and only Szymanowski's work, that fills up the gap supply-
ing the missing link between the two periods . . .

Since in Poland [the musical] revolution had its bearing solely and exclusively on Szymanowski's music, and genuinely took place only in him (as he
alone made up nearly half a century of our cultural lag), the new composers
came, as it were, to a tilled field. They missed the period of Sturm und Drang
of new music, because they had inherited it all through the experience of
Szymanowski in his music.[6]

Lutosławski had, as we have seen, encountered the powerful stimulus
of Szymanowski's Third Symphony at an early age. He had met the

older man but once, briefly in Riga in 1935. As a conservatory student it was the orchestral scores of Debussy, Ravel, and early Stravinsky which had most strongly attracted his admiration, and it was those composers more than Szymanowski himself who shaped the young composer's outlook as he now embarked on his career in the climate Szymanowski had prepared. As Szymanowski had urged his younger compatriots to do, Lutosławski now looked to France and began laying plans to study in Paris with one of her famous pedagogues, Boulanger or Koechlin.

After graduating in 1937 Lutosławski was conscripted into the Polish army for one year's service, during which he was trained in radio communications. Afterward he resumed performing, including playing his sonata over Polish Radio, and in 1938 the *Lacrimosa* was given by soprano Helena Warpechowska and the Warsaw Philharmonic Orchestra, conducted by Tadeusz Wilczak. His most important activity during this period, however, was work on his first important composition, the Symphonic Variations, completed in 1938. He had begun the piece in 1936, working on his own to pursue a more modern style than his teacher could accept:

[Maliszewski] belonged to the Russian school, had studied with Rimsky-Korsakov and was not interested in modern trends. For example, he regarded Szymanowski as a talented composer who 'degenerated' in the middle of his career and developed in the wrong direction. It was inevitable for us to gradually come into an ideological, or rather aesthetic conflict – as private people, however, we remained on good terms. I showed him my *Symphonic Variations* which I had started to compose a year before the end of my studies, but had written completely independently, without his help. He declared openly that he did not understand it. I prepared the harmonic analysis of the piece – and he said: 'Now we talk a common language, now I understand it. But that does not mean that I like it. For me your work is simply ugly.' He added that if I developed along these lines, he would not be able to give me advice. – He was a wise and sincere man. He did not say the piece was bad, he just remarked that he did not like it. I respected him highly for that, after all my style was completely alien to him.[7]

And well might Maliszewski have been perplexed, for the variations are a far cry from *Lacrimosa* and the Piano Sonata. Though this was not Lutosławski's first orchestral composition, it was the first in which he gave free rein to his developing harmonic and coloristic impulses.

The Symphonic Variations were broadcast in April 1939 over Polish Radio in Warsaw and first publicly performed at the Wawel Festival in Cracow on 17 June 1939 by Grzegorz Fitelberg and the Polish Radio Symphony Orchestra. The interest and sympathy of Fitelberg, who had done so much to advance Szymanowski's career, was indispensable to Lutosławski in 1939. Fitelberg was widely traveled (he had been Diaghilev's conductor in Paris, for instance) and was himself a composer; and it was he alone among Polish conductors who championed the cause of young composers and exposed them to performances of contemporary music from abroad. As an *enfant prodige* Lutosławski had been confident of his own talent, but now, thrown into an inhospitable musical environment and groping uncertainly toward modernism, he was tormented by self-doubt and severely self-critical. 'Nowadays', he has said, 'it is difficult to imagine in what an unfriendly environment everyone worked then, how little chance contemporary music had in Poland at that time.'[8] But Fitelberg recognized Lutosławski's genius, and he is reported to have announced after the première of the Symphonic Variations, 'Listen, this is a real master! . . . You have to be born a musician to write this way. His scores . . . are a pleasure to hold in one's hand: it's not just notes, it's music!'[9] This kind of encouragement from so influential an artist helped Lutosławski through a very difficult period.

It is in the Symphonic Variations that Lutosławski's ambivalent attitude toward Szymanowski comes most clearly to light. He could not help admiring the late composer's pioneering efforts in Polish music, nor could he escape wholly the attraction of Szymanowski's opulent sound world; but at the same time he was put off by the extreme emotionalism infusing much of Szymanowski's music and by its stylistic bonds with postromantic music, never fully effaced. The new musical spirit emanating from the West, the spirit of neoclassicism represented in various guises by Stravinsky, Roussel, Ravel, even by the *Neue Sachlichkeit* of Hindemith, had gained the ascendancy among young Polish composers (Polish neoclassicism can be dated from about 1926, the year of Stanisław Wiechowicz's symphonic scherzo *Chmiel* [Hops]). We can only speculate about the relation of Lutosławski's earlier orchestral music to Szymanowski; but in the variations only isolated harmonic touches and perhaps a hint of Szymanowskian orchestration (itself largely derivative of French and Russian models and Strauss) remain.

The composer confirms that he had by this time joined the general reaction against Szymanowski, but he points out a single chord at the beginning of the first variation which strongly recalls Szymanowski, not only in its whole-tone content but in register and scoring as well (see the last measure of ex. 1.5). But this chord is an anomaly in the variations, where elsewhere the rule is a kind of pandiatonic harmony emphasizing thirds, as in the setting of the theme (ex. 1.5), or a harmony emphasizing tertian polychords, some of which may be

1.5   Theme of the Symphonic Variations (mm. 1–11)

explained with enharmonic reinterpretation as altered eleventh and
thirteenth chords (ex. 1.6). In a few instances (e.g., mm. 92, 204–5) one
finds streams of dyads or triads progressing in contrary motion, but
real, sustained polytonality of the kind found in Milhaud (or even in
Szymanowski's First Quartet) is absent.

The use of polychords, the prevalence of rhythmic and melodic
ostinati, the concertante use of smaller groups from the orchestra
alongside richly scored passages for the entire ensemble: these and
other characteristics point to the principal influence on the Symphonic Variations, the Stravinsky of the Russian ballets. Rappoport

1.6   Isolated chords from the Symphonic Variations

argues that the work lies in the Rimskian tradition as transmitted by Maliszewski and professes to find the theme itself imbued with Slavic accents.[10] Western listeners are unlikely to perceive anything terribly Slavic about this theme, however; and what Russian character the variations betray has been derived more from Stravinsky than from Lutosławski's immediate teacher. The composer himself calls the influence of early Stravinsky obvious.

The orchestra Lutosławski calls for is essentially that of *L'oiseau de feu* and *Petrushka*, not *Le sacre*: triple woodwinds; standard brass; standard percussion augmented by xylophone, glockenspiel, harp, celesta, and piano; and strings. The piano plays an especially prominent role (as it will do in virtually all the composer's orchestral works), adding color here, there reinforcing an accent, elsewhere lending a brittle edge to the woodwinds. Lutosławski's command of the orchestral palette is little short of astonishing for a twenty-five-year-old composer of such limited experience; the mastery of color, balance, and instrumental idiom which distinguishes the more familiar Concerto for Orchestra is essentially already in place, nearly twenty years before. A wide range of orchestral textures is explored, from motoric toccata-like writing of immense rhythmic vitality, anticipating the third movement of the Concerto for Orchestra, to the quasi-impressionist episode of variation 7.

Formally the nine-minute work is divided by tempo and character changes into four larger sections: the theme and first variation, variations 2–5, variations 6 and 7, and an extended coda which serves as a kind of finale and includes a reprise of the theme. In addition, the technique, so frequent in Brahms, of basing a variation as much on the preceding variation as on the theme itself serves to pair variation 2 with 3 and again variation 6 with 7 (see table on p. 14).

The presence of a well-developed fugato in the coda is evidence of Lutosławski's early and persistent contrapuntal bent. A three-voice exposition (mm. 204–15), complete with countersubject, is followed by a developmental episode in which fragments of the subject and other material derived motivically from the original theme appear alongside augmentations of the head-motive and of the complete subject (mm. 222–30) and an inversion of the subject (slightly altered) in the trumpet (mm. 234–9).

A clear tonal center is usually obvious to the ear, and tonality is given a purposeful structural role. The complete theme in its original form or in transformation is presented only in E 'major': at the beginning, at the work's midpoint (variation 4, m. 96, transformed), and at the final reprise. Even the traditional dominant function is exploited: the coda begins with a tonic six-four (with the addition of the major seventh, literally $1\frac{4}{3}$), followed at m. 205 by the dominant triad as the heart of a polychord; and the dominant pitch returns in the bass, still unresolved, to underlie the reprise of the theme. In a sense, then, the coda may be seen as a highly elaborated cadential progression, in which the entire fugato section is but an interruption, the ultimate resolution v–ı in the bass being filled in by passing motion (ex. 1.7).

Symphonic Variations: Structural Synopsis

Mm.			
1–11	Theme		*Andante*
11–29	Variation 1		*Tempo I.* Thematic fragments stated antiphonally
30–46	Variation 2		*Allegro.* Toccata based on motive *a*
47–95	Variation 3		*Stesso movimento.* Variation of 2 in compound time
96–123	Variation 4		*Poco più mosso.* Lyrical transformation of the theme
124–51	Variation 5		[*Più mosso.*] Opening motive in quavers; continuation of orchestral texture of 4
152–77	Variation 6		*Adagio.* New melody based on motive *a*
178–200	Variation 7		*Andante.* Melody from 6 extended using motive *b*
201–46	Coda, part 1		*Allegro non troppo.* Fugato; subject head-motive based on motive *a*, continuation derived partly from motive *b*
247–57	Coda, part 2		*Subito poco meno mosso.* Restatement of theme
258–60	Coda, part 3		Codetta

If the Symphonic Variations lack real originality and stylistic integration, these shortcomings are at least partly compensated for by the sensitively controlled harmonic language, accomplished use of the orchestra, and rhythmic vitality they display. One wonders whether, had not political events intervened, this work might not have made Lutosławski's name known abroad much earlier. In the event, the variations were to be the last important work he would finish for almost ten years. He worked briefly in 1938 or early 1939 on a *Suita kurpiowska* (Kurpian Suite) for orchestra, based on folk materials from the Kurpie district northeast of Warsaw, but he became dissatisfied with the project and abandoned it. Then Lutosławski was mobilized in the summer of 1939 and assigned to command a military radio station attached to First Army headquarters. On 1 September Hitler invaded Poland.

Lutosławski was stationed first at Cracow, then near Lublin in eastern Poland where he was taken prisoner by the Germans:

I escaped after eight days, and walked four hundred kilometers to Warsaw. That experience has left a lasting impression on me ... The real shock, however, was caused by the fact that we had lost the war so soon. The only thing that [later] 'comforted' me was that it had lasted even shorter in France. I was informed of everything at the radio station.[11]

1.7   Harmonic reduction of the coda of the Symphonic Variations

When the composer arrived in Warsaw in December 1939, he found conditions under the occupation particularly harsh for authors, artists, and teachers. Jan Szczepański has estimated that 35 per cent of the Polish intelligentsia were lost in the war, explaining that 'in a deliberate attempt to destroy the very roots of Polish national life, the occupation forces set out to exterminate first of all the educated stratum, which could have provided the nation with resistance leadership'.[12] Lutosławski's older brother Henryk was executed in a Soviet concentration camp in 1939 or 1940. It has been estimated that in Warsaw alone at least 150 musicians perished,[13] among them the pioneering twelve-tone composer Józef Koffler (1896–1943), a pupil of Schoenberg. Lutosławski himself had some narrow escapes in the capital.

Polish music had been driven underground. In Lutosławski's words:

When the Nazis entered Warsaw, Polish music stopped. After the Jews and gypsies, we Slavs were hated most by them. They took over the orchestras, kept most of the Polish musicians, but German conductors and repertory were imported. Poles boycotted their concerts but we arranged clandestine meetings in rooms, daring imprisonment to play chamber music or premiere some of our things.[14]

Warsaw's cafés (kawiarnie) provided virtually the only public forum for Polish soloists, and it was in such establishments that Lutosławski was forced to make his living for the next four and a half years. He appeared occasionally as a soloist or as accompanist for such artists as the violinist Eugenia Umińska, the soprano Ewa Bandrowska-Turska (with whom he premièred in 1941 his Two Songs of 1934), and the mezzo-soprano Janina Godlewska. Most of his playing, however, was done in collaboration with his old conservatory classmate, composer and conductor Andrzej Panufnik. The Lutosławski–Panufnik piano duo played first at the kawiarnia Aria, which was associated with the Polish Radio, and later at the theatrical café U Aktorych (Among the Actors). Ultimately they settled at the Sztuka i Moda (Art and Fashion), popularly 'SiM', on Królewska Street, where their regular concerts attracted a following. Their repertoire consisted not of light café music but rather of arrangements of serious works on which the two composers collaborated, embracing a variety of musical styles. Among the pieces they adapted were Bach organ toccatas, works of Mozart and Brahms, Strauss waltzes, Ravel's Bolero, excerpts from Carmen, and music of Debussy and Szymanowski. One of these arrangements, made by Lutosławski alone in 1941, was published after the war as Wariacje na temat Paganiniego (Variations on a Theme of Paganini). Being the better pianist, he designed the first pianist's part for himself and the easier second part for Panufnik. According to Lutosławski it is typical of the pieces on which they collaborated. Of the roughly two hundred such pieces they concocted together, all but the Paganini Variations perished in the Warsaw Rising.

It is ironic that the Paganini Variations – a mere by-product of Lutosławski's wartime café playing – have achieved a prominent place in the duo-piano repertoire and have become by far the composer's most frequently recorded work. And it is curious that many pianists and listeners apparently assume that Lutosławski's Paganini Variations, like those of Brahms (op. 35), Rakhmaninov (op. 43), Blacher (op. 26), Ginastera, Rochberg, and others, are an original treatment of the famous theme. In fact, the piece represents only a transcription, albeit a highly imaginative one, of Paganini's own set of variations from the twenty-fourth caprice for solo violin; and as such Lutosławski's version is closer in genre to that in Liszt's Grandes études de Paganini (1838, revised 1851) for solo piano or to Szymanowski's transcription for violin and piano (op. 42, 1918) than to the newly invented variations of Brahms or Rakhmaninov.

The variations follow closely the Paganini model. In each, the original violin line is translated ingeniously into the keyboard idiom. The *bariolage* of Paganini's second variation becomes a showy flourish of chromatic neighboring chords, for example, while the parallel thirds and tenths of Paganini's sixth variation are set by Lutosławski in canon, with the thirds in the second piano accompanied by their inversion in parallel triads in the first piano. Even the alternating arco and left-hand pizzicato of variation 9 are imitated in the piano with the help of scattered sforzati. Whereas the Paganini original gives no tempo indications after the initial *Quasi presto*, Lutosławski uses a succession of five tempi to support a variety of character changes and thus to strengthen the work's structural profile. He dispenses with Paganini's finale, which consists simply of arpeggiations of the cadence formula I–V/IV–IV–V⁹, replacing it with a grandiose restatement of the theme followed by a brief figurational codetta.

Polyharmony between the two keyboards is frequent, often involving triads whose roots lie a tritone apart (see, for example, mm. 9–14 and 155–70). Tonality (though not always the original A minor) remains a clear force, and traditional dominant-tonic cadences are common. The dominant is most often represented by a polychord superimposing the Neapolitan (lowered II) and dominant functions.

Though circumstances had thwarted Lutosławski's intent to study in Paris, in the Paganini Variations he approached in spirit and style the experience of those countrymen who had reached that great cosmopolitan source of neoclassicism. Owing in part to its café origins, this work is as close as the composer ever came to that glittering Gallic superficiality, to the deliberate if slightly ironic evocation of salon and dance-hall one finds in Satie, Milhaud, and Poulenc. Symbolically, when in 1977 a series of concerts was organized in Poland to commemorate the fiftieth anniversary of the Association des Jeunes Musiciens Polonais à Paris, the Lutosławski Paganini Variations were performed alongside works by Szałowski, Perkowski, and Tansman (all Paris-trained Poles), Poulenc, Ravel, and Milhaud.

Between 1942 and 1944 Lutosławski composed resistance songs, as did many other composers, in response to appeals from the Polish Underground. Because of the obvious danger such songs were generally circulated anonymously or bearing pseudonyms; but after the war five of Lutosławski's songs were published under his name as the first volume in the series *Pieśni walki podziemnej* (Songs of the Underground Struggle). Naturally the vocal lines are kept melodically and rhythmically simple, and each song is cast in simple stanza-plus-refrain form. In these respects they rather resemble mass songs. The piano accompaniments, on the other hand, even though they are tied closely to traditional functional harmony, are occasionally rather adventurous. Even in popular songs we find Lutosławski experimenting with manipulations of pitch material: in the third song, for example, he uses a scale containing a major third, raised (Lydian) fourth, and lowered sixth and seventh degrees. Four of the songs are marches; more attractive is the single love song, no. 4. Musically this is the most overtly Polish of the songs, set in mazurka rhythms and again employing the Lydian raised fourth characteristic of some Polish folk music.[15]

Of more immediate import for Lutosławski's musical development than either the Paganini Variations or the resistance songs were the Two Etudes for piano (1940–1) and the series of small woodwind pieces the composer wrote during the war. Aside from the café transcriptions, the piano études were the composer's first creative undertaking upon his return to Warsaw after his capture and escape, and they tell us a great deal about his thinking at the time, bridging as they do the gap between the Symphonic Variations and the First Symphony. These two études were to have been part of a projected set modeled after those of Chopin, and the C tonality and rising broken-chord figure of the opening of the first make deliberate allusion to Chopin's C-major étude, op. 10, no. 1.

The classical formal habits Lutosławski displayed in the Piano Sonata and the Symphonic Variations remain intact in the études. Both are in clear ternary form (plus coda in the second); both employ as structural underpinning more or less traditional tonal schemes in which the middle section offers tonal contrast, the original tone center returns with the reprise of the first part, and conventional tonal adjustments permit the last section to remain close to the main tone center. Indeed, the second étude even includes a deceptive cadence on the lowered submediant (here E-flat, the tonic being G) in m. 68, where the opening measures of introductory accompaniment pattern return; the tonic harmony is withheld until the return of the principal thematic figure in the right hand three measures later. (This kind of noncoincidence of tonal and material recapitulation has direct models in the mature sonata style of the Classical era.) Organization around tone centers in the études is reserved mainly for such structural roles; between cadences the harmonic nature of the music is largely a product of its linear-contrapuntal unfolding in a freely chromatic environment.

The pitch language of the études represents a considerable advance over that of the Symphonic Variations and reveals a number of characteristics which hint at the composer's future development. Of particu-

lar interest is Lutosławski's experimentation (especially in the first
étude) with various kinds of tetrachords – major, minor, whole-tone –
and the use of a synthetic scale identical to Messiaen's mode 6,
comprising two major tetrachords disjunct by a semitone, i.e. the
tetrachord (2–2–1) and its transposition at the tritone (ex. 1.8). It is
significant that this construction hinges on the tritone, for the interval
itself and the pair of tritone-related perfect fourth/fifth dyads implied
by the two tetrachords play central roles in both the linear and vertical
aspects (ex. 1.9). The tritone does, in fact, serve in a limited way as a
polar opposite to the tonic, but it never assumes quite the structural
importance of a surrogate dominant, as sometimes happens in Bartók.

The other principal harmonic interval is the perfect fourth (fifth),
which pervades both études linearly and vertically and upon which
many of the cadences are built. Example 1.10, an excerpt from the
middle section of the first étude, shows how perfect fifths in conjunction with the various kinds of tetrachords treated sequentially are
used to build melodic lines. Note especially the way whole-tone
tetrachords alternate with the other types, and, leading to the
cadence, the use of the entire scale formed by the disjunct major
tetrachords.

1.8   Abstracted scale and derived dyads, Two Etudes

The bustling, muscular character of the études owes something to
the spirit of neoclassicism, as does a texture that fairly bursts with
sequences, ostinati, and pedal points. With only a few exceptions, the
rhythm remains rather square. But in the handling of pitch these
pieces marked for Lutosławski a conscious attempt to expand his
technical resources as a composer. The manipulations of tetrachordal
segments, in particular, seem frankly (if modestly) experimental,
although due to Lutosławski's sense of discipline that experimentation remains subservient to tidy formal construction.

In 1941 Lutosławski began work on a symphony, and he had
finished the first movement by the summer of 1944. In the meantime
he wrote between 1943 and 1944 a series of thirty contrapuntal pieces
– ten canons for two clarinets, ten canons for three clarinets, and ten
pieces for oboe and bassoon – in which he strove to master a style of
atonal harmony based on a freer use of the twelve chromatic pitches.
At the same time these studies served to test ideas for the First

1.9   a. Etude no. 1 (mm. 64–7); b. Etude no. 2 (mm. 1, 23)

1.10   Etude no. 1 (mm. 23–8, right hand)

Symphony, and some of their materials were in fact to resurface in that work.

With the outbreak of the ill-fated Warsaw Rising, launched on 1 August 1944 by the underground Home Army (Armia Krajowa, AK), Lutosławski fled with his mother to Komorów, a few miles outside the capital.[16] There they would spend the winter of 1944–5, crowded together with other displaced relatives in a house owned by one of the composer's uncles. Lutosławski took with him the manuscript of the symphony in progress, but most of the prewar works he left behind were destroyed in the fighting. Huddled in the attic at Komorów, Lutosławski kept working on the development of his musical language, pursuing the severely disciplined logic of the contrapuntal wind studies to produce a three-movement Trio for oboe, clarinet, and bassoon. Like the contrapuntal studies, the trio was an experiment. 'I . . . was trying to find my bearings in the world of free tonality', the composer recalls. 'I chose wind instruments because my research into pitch, rhythm, and the organisation of sound could be carried out in the simplest way with their help.'[17]

After the failure of the Warsaw Rising, in which at least 150 000 Poles were lost, the Nazis resumed their campaign to reduce the capital to rubble and to exterminate her inhabitants. But early in 1945 Polish and Soviet forces succeeded in regaining Warsaw and driving the German army back to the Oder and Neisse rivers. On 1 February 1945 a provisional Polish government was set up, with Warsaw as capital, and in the spring the Lutosławskis returned to the devastated city.

With the end of the war, the composer faced uncertain prospects for supporting himself while he resumed work on his still unfinished First Symphony. Thus he attached himself to the Polish Radio, for whom he would produce over the next several years great quantities of functional music of various sorts: children's songs, music for small orchestras, incidental music for radio plays. B. M. Maciejewski reports that Lutosławski even wrote popular songs and light music for the radio under the pseudonym 'Derwid'.[18] Such utilitarian music, though he attached no artistic importance to it, would be his principal source of income for the next fifteen years or so. In addition to his work for the radio, he produced music for stage plays;[19] scores for the documentary films Odrą do Bałtyku (To the Baltic on the Oder, 1946) and Suita warszawska (Warsaw Suite, c. 1947); for the newly founded Polskie Wydawnictwo Muzyczne (Polish Music Publisher, or PWM) in Cracow the Melodie ludowe (Folk Songs, 1945) for piano solo and Dwadzieście kolęd (Twenty Carols, 1946) for voice and piano; and, for the Warsaw publisher Edition Czytelnik, Trzy kolędy (Three Carols, 1945) for soprano, unison chorus, and chamber ensemble.

In 1945 it was by no means clear to most Polish musicians that Witold Lutosławski would become the outstanding composer of his generation. Others – Panufnik, for example – seemed more promising. Moreover he was competing for attention with the ranks of older, established composers, both traditionalists still following in the footsteps of Wagner, Strauss, and Szymanowski, and neoclassicists like Tadeusz Szeligowski (1896–1963), Bolesław Szabelski (1896–), Piotr Perkowski (1901–), and Artur Malawski (1904–57). But as the country's concert life and musical institutions were gradually rebuilt,

Lutosławski's name came little by little to the fore. The Union of Polish Composers (Związek Kompozytorów Polskich, or ZKP) was founded at an All-Poland Composers' Congress in Cracow, 29 August–2 September 1945, replacing the prewar Association (Stowarzyszenie) of Polish Composers. Lutosławski was elected secretary–treasurer of the board of directors. He remained a member of the ZKP leadership until 1948, and he represented Poland at the International Society for Contemporary Music (ISCM) festivals of 1947 (Copenhagen) and 1948 (Amsterdam).

Among the earliest postwar performances of Lutosławski's serious works were the première of the Woodwind Trio at the Festival of Contemporary Polish Music in Cracow, September 1945; a performance of the Symphonic Variations in Paris in December 1946 (his debut abroad); and performances of the Symphonic Variations in Cracow on 3 and 17 October 1947, under the baton of Walerian Bierdiajew. In reviewing the trio, Stefan Kisielewski shrewdly appraised both the thirty-two-year-old composer's present stage of development and the promise of his gifts:

It is unfortunate, as always, that the work of his which was performed must be viewed in a special light as 'unrepresentative'. But in his slow, methodical effort to gather his materials and, as it were, to focus intense light on his musical tinder, can he not yet have kindled a work of synthesis, a work in which at long last he could give full expression to his 'credo'? Closest to answering this description would be the Symphonic Variations – a pity they were not performed at the festival. The Trio is a laboratory piece, a composer's étude displaying certain of the elements from which Lutosławski constructs his work: an almost scientific rigor with respect to form and a world of sound combinations which is personal, absolutely individual, grounded in a fundamental, if not yet fully understood, necessity. This personal harmonic world encourages me to see in Lutosławski a composer who might create works of the highest importance for the development of contemporary music.[20]

Meanwhile the young composer gained his first public exposure as a conductor. Impressed by Lutosławski's skill at conducting his own film scores, Grzegorz Fitelberg in 1946 invited Lutosławski to conduct his Polish Radio Symphony Orchestra, based in Katowice. The composer agreed somewhat reluctantly. Since he had once prepared rehearsals of Haydn's 'Oxford' Symphony with the Warsaw Philharmonic when Witold Rowicki, the orchestra's regular conductor, was called away, that was the work he chose for his conducting debut in Katowice. But although he would continue to conduct his own music for the radio from time to time, not until 1963 was Lutosławski to begin in earnest to conduct publicly.

In 1946 Lutosławski married Maria-Danuta Dygat-Bogusławska,

daughter of the architect Antoni Dygat and his wife Jadwiga (née Kurowska), and sister of Stanisław Dygat, a well-known author of satirical novels and short stories. Lutosławski and his bride set up housekeeping in a small, noisy flat in the Warsaw suburb of Saska Kępa, on the east bank of the Vistula. The Lutosławskis were to live there for more than twenty years; the composer's mother lived with them until her death in 1967. The marriage produced no children, though Mme Lutosławski has a son, Marcin Bogusławski (now an architect living in Norway), by her first husband.

In 1947 Lutosławski's First Symphony, the work whose first movement he had spirited out of Warsaw three years earlier, was finally completed. Again it was Fitelberg who supported the composer's cause, conducting his radio orchestra in the first performance on 6 April 1948 in Katowice and repeating the work at the Cracow Festival on 15 June. Fitelberg's role was not lost on those critics sympathetic to new music. Zygmunt Mycielski praised the sixty-nine-year-old conductor for his

unusually accurate and enthusiastic performance of Witold Lutosławski's symphony. I say 'enthusiastic' because Fitelberg put into the première of this work as much understanding, effort, and intensity as he did into introducing Karłowicz or the Third Symphony of Szymanowski. It is extraordinary, the vitality of this man who manages to infuse in a work written today as much life as he put into new works in the days when he first set foot on the concert stage.[21]

The First Symphony, seven years in the making, is a work of culmination, the largest and most impressive achievement of Lutosławski's early years. In this work are revealed more clearly than ever before both the assorted stylistic influences shaping the composer's language and the magnitude of his own talent; for against the lingering traces of Stravinsky, Debussy, and Ravel, against the newer influences of Prokofiev and Roussel, there begins at last to emerge a distinctive, personal voice. It is a fervent, dramatic work, vividly colored and charged with moments of powerful emotion. Reviewer Roman Haubenstock declared Lutosławski's First the first genuine symphony in Poland since Szymanowski's day. 'It seems to me', he wrote, 'that today only Lutosławski is endowed with that great gift – the gift of expressing things which are inexpressible in words, things so great as to be at times almost overwhelming – the gift that destines a composer to be a symphonist.'[22] Mycielski asserted that this first fruit of Lutosławski's maturity had thrust him into the first rank of Polish composers. In the view of Stefan Jarociński, the First Symphony embodies the 'universal aspirations of Polish postwar music, which sought a synthesis between a contemporary musical language and elements of native tradition'.[23]

On the other hand, for Stefan Kisielewski, an early and persistent admirer of Lutosławski's talent, the work was a failure in which the many splendid details were lost in an excessive display of technical skill. Kisielewski criticized the work as an aberration in Lutosławski's development, declaring it to be marred by 'a sort of general extravagance of taste, a lack of simplicity in the overall sensory design, a tendency toward hyper-variability of texture, [and] a deficiency in the emotional element, caused perhaps by excessive intellectualism, perhaps too by the great consciousness of technique'.[24] Kisielewski's disappointment may be ascribed partly to his own quite conservative tastes, but in at least one respect he identified a genuine problem: namely, that the sheer complexity of Lutosławski's orchestral sound threatens to obscure what is fundamentally a quite direct musical argument. This is especially noticeable in the first movement, where the scoring relies too heavily on the thickening of contrapuntal voices in parallel fifths, triads, or seventh chords and on the principle of heterophonic doubling. The almost garish atmosphere created in the orchestra by such means may be what prompted Jarociński to label the work 'fauvist'.[25]

As regards both harmonic organization and contrapuntal texture, the results of Lutosławski's wartime exploratory works for winds are to be observed throughout the First Symphony. Canon has become the prevailing mode of discourse. Each movement has a clear tonal center (respectively D, E, A, and D), but these centers are simply poles exerting influence chiefly at structural points, while in foreground harmonic detail the composer has won considerable independence from the vestiges of functional harmony that remained in the Symphonic Variations. The dissonant linear intervals – sevenths and tritones – which characterized the woodwind studies now dominate the melodic style of the symphony as well. Although tertian polychords of the sort we have seen in the Symphonic Variations remain a part of the harmonic vocabulary, there is a new and – for the composer's developing harmonic style – very significant interest in vertical symmetries. The work opens with an eight-note chord whose nearly symmetrical construction in thirds points to the harmonic style the composer was to perfect some ten years later (see ex. 1.13).[26] Example 1.11 gives other instances of symmetrical harmonic structures from the first and fourth movements.

As in earlier works, so too in the symphony are tone centers established not only by emphasizing consonant dyads or triads at structurally significant points, but also by approaching such consonances by

1.11   Isolated harmonic structures from the First Symphony

way of carefully planned bass lines, often by stepwise motion.
Example 1.12a gives the principal bass pitches of the first movement
up to the establishment of D-flat at the beginning of the second group;
1.12b shows the approach to the recapitulation. True polytonality
remains rare, although in the opening of the finale's first theme
(mm. 2–5, 86–9) the centers D and E-flat are counterposed over a span
of several measures.

Lutosławski's sense of form was still deeply traditional, shaped by
the thorough training he had received from Maliszewski and by his
love for the masters of the Viennese Classical period and for Brahms;
shaped, too, by the example of the 'French Brahms', Albert Roussel,
whose last and best orchestral works (especially the Third Symphony
and the Sinfonietta) he took as models of twentieth-century symphonic form.

1.12   Simplified bass lines from the first movement of the First Symphony

The first movement is in clear-cut sonata form. It opens stridently with the eight-note chord and a pandiatonic D-major cadence; the first theme which follows is not an extended melody but rather a collection of rhythmic and melodic motives whose contrapuntal development will constitute the principal business of the movement (ex. 1.13). Theme 2, in D-flat, begins as a lyrical melody but itself quickly gives way to motivic fragmentation (ex. 1.14). The form of the movement is orthodox: exposition with two distinct key areas; development in which the motives of theme 1 are worked out in imitative counterpoint and theme 2 is restated in the 'wrong key' and briefly developed; recapitulation in which the second group is transposed to fit the principal tone center, D; and coda. The recapitulation restates all of the material of the exposition in its original order except the first appearance of theme 2, which has occurred near the end of the development, and the materials of mm. 14–24, which are reserved to serve a new purpose in the coda.

1.13 Introduction and theme 1, first movement of the First Symphony (mm. 1–7)

1.14   Theme 2, first movement of the First Symphony (mm. 25–32)

First Movement: Structural Synopsis

Exposition

Mm.	1–2	Introduction
	3–9	Theme 1 (D)
	10–15	Theme 1 dissolves to transition
	16–24	Transition
	25–32	Theme 2 (D-flat)
	33–9	Theme 2 in canon
	40–54	Transition
	55–7	Codetta

Development

58–67	Part 1: fugato on theme 1
68–95	Part 2: development of theme 1 with stretti
95–104	Part 3: theme 2 restated and developed (B-flat)
105–12	Retransition (D pedal and approach to cadence)

Recapitulation

113–19	Theme 1 (D)
120–4	Theme 1 dissolves to transition
125–33	Theme 2 in canon (D)
134–8	Transition
139–41	Codetta

Coda

142–53	Part 1: transition material from m. 16, head-motive of theme 1, and cadence from mm. 14–15
154–9	Part 2: fragments of theme 1 and cadence on D

True to the classical pattern, the first movement organizes its dramatic structure about a single paramount event, the arrival of the recapitulation and re-establishment of the principal tone center at m. 113. Here Lutosławski resorts to an archaic harmonic trick he had already used in the second piano étude, the deceptive cadence on the

lowered submediant (see ex. 1.12). Clearly this is intended as the most
forceful occurrence of the movement, for the composer, typically,
reserves for the downbeat of m. 113 the single highest dynamic marking in the piece, *sfff*. (Hence Rappoport has the 'culmination' slightly
early in placing it at m. 105.)[27]

Canon pervades the texture, and not only in such obvious places as
the canonic statements of theme 2 (mm. 33–9 and 125–33) or the
fugato section of the development (mm. 58–67) and subsequent stretti
(e.g., mm. 70–2). In the passage at mm. 105–8, over a rhythmic canon
pitting the trombones against the rest of the orchestra are imposed
isomelically a rectus pitch canon between first trumpet (doubled by
third clarinet) and third trombone, and two different cancrizans
canons between the violins (doubled by high woodwinds) and first
and second trombones.

The second movement, *Poco adagio*, is ternary in form, with the
music of the first section returning briefly as an interlude in the
second, thus:

Mm.	1–31	A
	32–59	B
	60–6	A′
	67–81	B′
	82–119	A″
	120–8	codetta

Here in the first theme is the kind of long and fully developed melody
which the first movement lacked (ex. 1.15); while the brooding
accompaniment in low strings recalls the first movement of Bartók's
Music for Strings, Percussion, and Celesta, especially when treated
canonically (ex. 1.16). The sardonic, slightly grotesque theme of the
middle section seems to reflect the influence of Prokofiev (ex. 1.17).
Lutosławski adapted this material from one of the experimental
canons for three clarinets, and, according to Rappoport, it is related to
the slow movement of the Wind Trio as well.[28] Upon its return the first
theme is transformed from melancholy ballad into anguished, relent-

1.15   Theme 1, second movement of the First Symphony (mm. 4–12)

1.16   Second movement of the First Symphony (mm. 12–15)

1.17   Theme 2, second movement of the First Symphony (mm. 38–40)

less dirge, rising over an implacable, Stravinskian ostinato to climax in m. 114 with a depth of emotion nothing in Lutosławski's earlier music has led us to expect.

Nor is the third movement, the putative scherzo, a particularly light-hearted affair. This large rondo alternates a macabre scherzo theme (a), *Allegretto misterioso*, with a bittersweet waltz (b), until against a background of scurrying figures (c) the brass intrude with terrifying brutality (d):

Mm.	1–24	a	
	25–53	b	
	54–80	a'	
	81–120	b'	A
	121–50	c	
	151–92	d	B
	192–200	c'	
	201–30	a"	
	231–75	b"	A'

Rappoport interprets the turbulent middle section as an evocation of the war. In Soviet symphonic jargon this is an *episod nashestviia* ('episode of invasion'), a phrase deriving from the traditional interpretation of Shostakovich's Seventh Symphony ('Leningrad'). Rappoport even detects in the brass theme an echo of the sequence *Dies irae*.[29] All of this is firmly disavowed by the composer.

The explosive, toccata-like finale was, according to Lutosławski, modeled directly on the large sonatina form (i.e. sonata without development) which Brahms chose for the finales of his first and third symphonies. Here the composer has largely dispensed with traditional sonata rhetoric, inasmuch as the opposition of tonalities no longer plays a crucial role in propelling the work along, nor does the return of the opening theme (in the proper 'key') function as a dramatic goal. The climax occurs instead much later, near the end of the second group in the recapitulation.

Fourth Movement: Structural Synopsis

Exposition

Mm.	1	Introduction
	2–13	Theme 1, part 1
	13–21	Theme 1, part 2
	22–33	Transition, part 1
	34–42	Transition, part 2
	42–50	Theme 2, part 1
	51–66	Theme 2, part 2 (note motive from theme 1, part 2, in accompaniment)
	67–76	Development of theme 2, part 1
	77–84	Codetta (four-note groups derived from theme 2)
	85	Retransition (= m. 1, introduction)

Recapitulation

	86–94	Theme 1 (part 1 only)
	94–115	Transition, part 1 (a new version, but based on the same motives)
	115–27	Transition, part 2
	127–35	Theme 2, part 1
	136–56	Theme 2, part 2
	156–73	Development of theme 2, part 1, with climax at m. 169
	174–81	Interlude based on theme 2, part 1

Coda

	182–5	From codetta
	186–91	From theme 2, part 2
	192–3	From introduction

As in the first movement, the theme groups are posited principally as motivic sources (see ex. 1.18). Here each group is associated on its first appearance with a different section of the orchestra. Theme 1 is entrusted to the woodwinds (m. 4), and indeed its style suggests that it

1.18   Thematic material of the finale of the First Symphony: a. theme 1, part
1 (mm. 5–7); b. theme 1, part 2 (m. 15); c. transition, part 1 (mm. 22–4); d.
theme 2, part 1 (mm. 42–5)

originated in the woodwind sketches; an associated and rather Bartókian idea first appears in the first violins (m. 15). The transition
material is announced by the brass, loosely in canon at the distance of
a single quaver (m. 22). Theme 2 includes three separate ideas: a brief
lyrical line first played by solo violin (m. 42), sequential groups of
four quavers in the strings (m. 45), and a motto of repeated staccato
quavers (m. 49).

The climax of the finale is prepared by pealing antiphonal brass set
against staccato chords in the rest of the orchestra and leading to an
immense polychord (m. 169, ex. 1.19). Then, by an inspired stroke of
orchestration, the polychord dissolves magically into a quiet inter-

1.19   Finale of the First Symphony (mm. 168–74)

lude based on theme 2 and its (free) inversion, followed by a final headlong rush to the cadence on D.

The First Symphony's favorable critical reception and Fitelberg's enthusiastic sponsorship had by 1948 brought national attention to the thirty-five-year-old Lutosławski. But although this work gave compelling evidence of the young composer's talent, it cannot be counted an unqualified artistic success, since the diverse stylistic elements which coexist in it fail to achieve complete integration. The composer's own dissatisfaction with the First Symphony was due not only to its continued dependence on external models, but also to its reliance on a moribund tonal language that he found increasingly alien and confining:

It is interesting that it was while composing the *First Symphony* . . . that I first felt that I was in a cul-de-sac, I could not develop in that direction any more, I had to create something new for myself . . . The piece was written in a sort of post-tonal idiom, which should be considered as one of the final stages of the dismantling of the tonal system, giving no prospects of development.

The musical world up till then had been too much linked to tonal music and was at the same too chaotic from the point of view of the future . . . When saying 'chaotic' I had in mind a style (very 'fashionable' in the 1930s) which consisted of the remnants of tonal music with 'false notes'. I have always hated that kind of music and felt a very strong need of a new order.[30]

The First Symphony, then, closes the composer's formative years. But the usual description of this first period as 'neoclassic' is clearly deficient. The term itself is notoriously problematic; it has been applied to a diverse body of European and American music of the twenties, thirties, and forties whose works bear any number of essentially different relationships to the past, and not simply to the Classical or Baroque eras. (Perhaps we should adopt in its place 'neo-tonal', as Eric Salzman has suggested.)[31] In Lutosławski's case 'neoclassic' is doubly inappropriate, since so simplistic a label does not begin to account for many facets of a distinctive musical personality which is already manifest.

The symphony stands as symbol of a preparatory period for the composer, embracing the salient characteristics of all of his earlier music. Those traits include the eclecticism of a composer still absorbing a multitude of Eastern and Western Europen influences, and still in that respect a 'student' composer; an adherence to tonality, weakened and complicated but still structurally meaningful; a preoccupation with contrapuntal texture; a fascination with and impressive mastery of the coloristic resources of the modern orchestra; a devotion to classical form and a gift for persuasively shaping musical materials; a pronounced dramatic musical personality; and a tendency to build up large forms by combining small motivic particles. Yet, although the symphony ends one line of development, it is easy with benefit of hindsight to perceive in this work many of the seeds of Lutosławski's later styles, and we are not surprised to realize that the Concerto for Orchestra is only three years away.

Yet even as Lutosławski's First Symphony was being heard for the first time in April 1948, forces had been set in motion that were soon to make of it a symbol of a very different kind.

2 The dark years: 1949–54

From the very beginning the postwar government in Poland was dominated by factions with close ties to the Soviet Communist Party. For a time the government included both pro-Communists, led by Władysław Gomułka, and anti-Communists, led by Stanisław Mikołajczyk. But in January 1947, when national parliamentary elections were held, it was clear that Mikołajczyk had lost the power struggle, and Gomułka's Communist–Socialist coalition, claiming that it had won an eighty-per cent majority in the voting, set about remaking the country as a Socialist state. Gomułka soon had difficulties of his own, however, for Poland remained under heavy political pressure from her eastern neighbor, and by mid-1948 Stalin had resolved to replace the independent-minded Gomułka and his 'Polish road to socialism' with a more tractable regime. By 1949 the process was completed: Gomułka was stripped of power, Bolesław Bierut was installed as head of the Party, and the dismal atmosphere of Stalinism – the 'cult of personality' – enveloped Poland and Eastern Europe.

This was the political situation in Poland when, on 10 February 1948, the Soviet Communist Party's Central Committee published the infamous resolution 'On the Opera *The Great Friendship* by V. Muradeli', attacking 'the cult of atonality, dissonance, and disharmony . . . confused, neuro-pathological combinations that transform music into cacophony, into a chaotic conglomeration of sounds'.[1] None of the leading Soviet composers was spared. Miaskovsky, Khachaturian, Shebalin, Kabalevsky, Shostakovich, Prokofiev: each was singled out for vicious criticism. A 'new order' in Soviet music was publicly ratified at the All-Union Congress of Composers convened in Moscow, 19–25 April 1948.

The debate addressed the situation of the Soviet artist in terms of the struggle between 'formalism' – 'the separation of form from content' – and 'Socialist realism'. The latter term was coined in 1932 and was at first applied only to literature; Maksim Gorky was declared its founder, and *partiinost'* (party-mindedness) its backbone. Officially the term signifies, according to the *Great Soviet Encyclopedia*, 'the artistic method whose basic principle is the truthful, historically

34

concrete depiction of reality in its revolutionary development, and whose most important task is the Communist education of the masses'. But in practice both terms proved extraordinarily vague and thus marvelously flexible as polemical weapons. When in 1936 the Stalin lieutenant Andrey Zhdanov led an attack against musical modernism (beginning with the famous condemnation of Shostakovich's opera *Lady Macbeth of Mtsensk*), 'formalism' was broad enough to take in the slightest sign of Western decadence or unnecessary complexity: expressionism, neoclassicism, serialism, 'fauvism', 'cosmopolitanism'. Prokofiev is supposed to have remarked that 'formalism is sometimes the name given here to that which is not understood on first hearing'.[2] Socialist realism, on the other hand, demanded 'positive social content', clear national feeling, mass appeal – in short, a return to nineteenth-century Russian program music. The 1948 scandal, again incited by Zhdanov, was essentially a continuation and intensification of the antimodernist campaign of 1936, which the war had interrupted. Now Stravinsky was castigated as the most horrifying example of all that was wrong with Western music – though even reactionary Western composers like Menotti and conservatives like Barber and Britten were cited as shamefully formalist.

The furor over formalism quickly spread to the new Socialist states of Eastern Europe. In Poland the question had arisen in the ZKP as early as 1947,[3] and by 1948 it was being widely discussed in the press.[4] In May 1948 the Russians convened a Second International Congress of Composers and Musicologists in Prague in order to press their views on their neighbors. The declaration adopted in Prague on 29 May called for composers to renounce 'extreme subjectivism' in favor of expressing the 'aspirations of the popular masses and progressive ideals of contemporary life' and to turn away from cosmopolitanism towards nationalism. Composers were urged to cultivate the 'concrete' genres – opera, oratorio, cantata, mass song – and to take their inspiration from folk art. The musicologist Zofia Lissa signed the statement on behalf of the Polish delegation.[5]

Zhdanov's Polish counterpart, vice-minister of culture Włodzimierz Sokorski, wasted little time before emulating the Soviet example. He organized a conference of composers and critics in the little town of Łagów Lubuskie, 5–8 August 1949, where he promulgated the new guidelines calling for music 'expressing Socialist content in a national form'. In his opening remarks Sokorski criticized the *Symfonia olimpijska* (Olympian Symphony) of Zbigniew Turski. The late works of Szymanowski – *Stabat Mater, Harnasie*, the Fourth

Symphony, the mazurkas – he found acceptable, but he condemned Szymanowski's earlier 'experimental' compositions. Zygmunt Mycielski, president of the ZKP, defined for the assembly the composer's duty to create a Polish music by rejecting international styles. Interspersed among the ideological discussions at the conference were concerts followed by collective criticism.

Lutosławski's status at Łagów was somewhat ambiguous. He was, on the strength of the First Symphony, clearly a 'cosmopolitan' composer, and he had already been dropped from the ZKP leadership in November 1948. The situation he saw developing depressed him deeply, since he genuinely feared that serious musical life in Poland was dead forever. At Łagów he spoke only once, at the very beginning of the discussion, to suggest that the assembly settle on a definite agenda; this was to be his last public utterance in the meetings of the ZKP until 1957. Lutosławski's works were barely touched on in the discussions. Jan Maklakiewicz characterized Lutosławski's *Melodie ludowe* as 'atrocious' but praised his Tuwim songs for children; Professor Lissa defended the composer, stating that 'Comrade Lutosławski . . . in her opinion had already matured to the realism of today.'[6] The tide was running against Lutosławski, however. Later in 1949 his symphony, the fruit of seven years' painstaking labor under the most unfavorable conditions, became the first eminent work to be officially censured as formalist and removed from the repertoire. The state prizes for music, first presented in 1950, went to Grażyna Bacewicz, Tadeusz Szeligowski, Stanisław Wiechowicz, Alfred Gradstein, and Tomasz Kiesewetter, all of whom were praised for having used folk music in their work.

But Lutosławski was not alone in opposing the new policy. Although many composers had indeed turned to nationalism after the Nazi occupation in reaction against the years when even playing Chopin had been forbidden, it was another matter when a government ministry undertook to dictate a national style. As Stefan Jarociński writes: 'The proposition of composing music inspired by folklore was neither new nor harmless in itself but it was growing absurd when it was married with the demand of returning to functional harmony and to the major-minor system, in a word, to the musical language of Moniuszko.'[7] Polish composers had had no experience with Party interference, as had the Soviets. The new policy, commonly shortened to *socrealizm* in Polish, was especially galling because, having been imported from Poland's traditional enemy to the east, it was quite foreign to the predominantly Western European traditions of Polish art. Some composers dutifully produced propaganda cantatas, but not all. Some simply stopped composing; Włodzimierz Kotoński, for example, turned temporarily to ethnomusicological research. But some of the leading talents, including Lutosławski, Szabelski, and Malawski, stubbornly refused either to give up composing or to compromise their artistic integrity.

Sokorski tried to persuade Lutosławski to write something on the order of *Pesn' o lesakh* (Song of the Forests, 1949), Shostakovich's embarrassingly naive oratorio glorifying a Russian reforestation project, but of course he refused. Still, the composer had to make a living. Since there was no longer a place in Polish concert life for pieces like the First Symphony, and since Lutosławski had neither a faculty position nor private pupils, the only source of income left to him was to continue producing functional music commissioned by the radio, PWM, and the schools. 'I never wrote anything that would have complied with the official requirements, but I was not averse to the idea of composing pieces for which there was a social need. (Children's songs, and so on.)'[8] Thus the works of the next several years form a separable period in Lutosławski's creative life by virtue of their almost exclusively utilitarian character. The styles of these works are indeed relatively simple, but their simplicity was dictated by their function as *Gebrauchsmusik*, not by official decree.

Meanwhile there was an inner aspect of Lutosławski's compositional life as well, as he continued, mainly in private but using the utilitarian works to test his experiments when possible, to develop his own more advanced musical language. The full implications of these labors were to become apparent only later, after 1956; but a single abstract piece in the composer's experimental tradition did reach the concert stage: the Overture for Strings of 1949. Fitelberg, touring Czechoslovakia, conducted the first performance with the Prague Radio Symphony Orchestra on 9 November 1949. Because of the stigma attached to the First Symphony, the overture was to remain unheard in Poland for many years.

In texture and general atmosphere, the Overture for Strings brings to mind the Bartók *Divertimento for Strings* (written ten years earlier) and gives the first clear evidence of Lutosławski's growing interest in Bartók after the war. The work manifests a freer interpretation of closed form than we have previously seen. There is a concise exposition with an introduction, three groups of thematic material (mm. 7–27, 28–44, and 45–58), and even a cadence of sorts (mm. 57–8); but, in the manner of the finale of the First Symphony, development takes place continuously from the first measure. There is no full recapitulation, although elements of the exposition reappear near the end of the work, reordered and truncated. The first theme returns only as the basis of a short coda (mm. 168–88). Rhythmically, the overture represents a modest advance in its extensive use of mixed meters. Accent patterns remain uncomplicated, however; there is no polymeter and very little in the way of polyrhythm.

As regards pitch, the overture lies squarely in the tradition of Lutosławski's experimental sketches. Though it is a short work – four or five minutes – it must have cost the composer considerable effort, for its pitch content is the result of the continuous manipulation of a variety of interrelated cells at the most minute level. The aim was to achieve a logical and thoroughly integrated style of pitch organization without recourse either to tonal organization or to existing atonal systems. For this purpose Lutosławski returned to synthetic scales, now used in a much more thoroughgoing fashion. Both themes of the first group and the closing theme (third group) of the exposition are derived from the eight-note mode comprising two tetrachords of (2–2–1) construction, disjunct by a semitone, which we first encountered in the first of the piano études (ex. 2.1). Notice the strong likeness linking theme 2 and the closing theme of the overture with the material of theme 1 of the First Symphony finale. For 'tonal' contrast a second eight-note scale, this one comprising only semitones and deriving from the opening gesture of the introduction, is used for the second group – theme 3 (ex. 2.2). But having thus succeeded in creating a coherent, consistent, and largely atonal language for the work, the composer somewhat spoils the effect by tacking on a quite out-of-place G-major ninth chord at the end.

It would be a mistake to take too seriously the functional music by which Lutosławski supported himself and his family from the war's end until about 1960, for clearly he himself did not take these works to be serious artistic statements. So little importance did he attach to them that many of the manuscripts have disappeared, and it is no longer possible to establish their chronology with any precision nor even to say with any certainty how many children's songs were produced or how many incidental scores written for radio dramas. Still, the calibre of imagination the best of Lutosławski's functional pieces display is very high. As with the arrangements of Irish, Welsh, and Scottish folk songs which both Haydn and Beethoven made in great quantities for British publishers, so too in this case an examination of such music ought to reveal something of interest about the composer.

Indeed, the earliest of the folklore-related pieces, Melodie ludowe (Folk Songs, 1945) for piano and Dwadzieście kolęd (Twenty Carols, 1946) for voice and piano, show that Lutosławski's Gebrauchsmusik was rarely divorced entirely from his current technical investigations

2.1 Overture for Strings: a. abstracted scale; b. theme 1 (mm. 6–18); c. theme 2 (mm. 19–23); d. closing theme (mm. 45–6)

2.2 Overture for Strings, theme 3 (mm. 28–31)

into the craft of composing. Both works were commissioned by PWM. The twelve Melodie ludowe are drawn from apparently unpublished collections by Jerzy Olszewski, and they represent several regions of Poland: Silesia, Podlasie (east of Warsaw), the Sieradz (northwest of Warsaw), Łowicz, Cracow, Kurpie, and Mazury. The twenty kolęda melodies are taken from several collections of Michał Mioduszewski and Oskar Kolberg.[9] Both works set the simple diatonic tunes to more complex accompaniments displaying many of the stylistic features which inform the more serious works with which they are contemporary: chromatic enrichment of diatonic linear frameworks, colorful 'escaped chords', occasional bitonality, imaginative use of pedal points, linear and harmonic patterns generated by manipulating small motivic cells, tall tertian chords, synthetic scales like the octatonic and whole-tone.[10] Whereas the Melodie ludowe are easy enough for young pianists, the accompaniments of the Kolędy are rather more elaborate; and on the whole this collection is the more varied and interesting, despite the fact that the melodies are even more conventionally tonal and metrically regular than those of the Melodie ludowe.

Kolędy – Christmas songs found over a wide area of Eastern Europe (called kolendy in Bohemia, colinde in Rumania, koliadky in Russia) – are in fact not true folk songs at all. The Polish repertory originated in the sixteenth to eighteenth centuries when texts celebrating the Nativity in both Latin and the vernacular were sung to popular Polish dance tunes, to foreign dances (the Ukrainian kolomyika and Russian cossack dances, sarabandes, minuets, Ländler, etc.) transmitted from court, or to existing religious melodies (sequences, tropes, Latin songs). The Polish kolędy are much more dependent on the major–minor tonality of Western art music and much less complex rhythmically than, for example, the Rumanian carols collected by Bartók in Melodien der rumänischen Colinde (Weihnachtslieder).[11]

For the most part Lutosławski avoided the best-known tunes. An exception is the tune of no. 10, 'Lulajże, Jezuniu' (Sleep, Little Jesus), which Chopin had incorporated, slightly altered, in the middle section of his B-minor Scherzo a century earlier. Lutosławski gives the tune in E-flat major but harmonizes it in C major, first with parallel triads over a dominant pedal, then with whole-tone tetrachords over a tonic-dominant double pedal. The fourth carol, 'Jezus malusieńki' (Tiny Jesus), demonstrates that even in a work of such slight import, and using the simplest of materials – the succession of triads evoking mystic wonder, the modest heightening of dissonance in the second half, relaxing with marvelous ease to the cadence – Lutosławski could achieve artistic results of the highest order. Example 2.3 gives the

2.3 'Jezus malusieńki' (piano only), with hypothetical bass reduction

music of the song complete and a reduction showing the linear framework of the bass.

Lutosławski has remarked that his model in folk-music settings was Bartók, not Szymanowski. But if we compare the *Melodie ludowe* to similar pieces by Bartók for young players – say the two volumes of *For Children* (1908–9, revised 1945), based respectively on Hungarian and Slovak folk tunes – we find remarkably little in common. *For Children* is perhaps not an apt comparison, for the Bartók pieces are directed toward rather less advanced players than those of Lutosławski. But even if we choose instead the *Improvisations on Hungarian Peasant Songs*, op. 20 (1920), there remain distinct and fundamental differences. Bartók's aim was to derive a setting which depended for its harmonic values on the characteristic melodic intervals and modal degrees of the tune itself;[12] hence, for example, the pentatonic harmonizations. Lutosławski, on the other hand, began with a repertoire of melodies altogether less exotic both rhythmically and modally. Moreover, he maintained a deliberate distance from the folk material he used, never identifying spiritually with it as did Bartók nor feeling any urge to do so. Lutosławski's involvement with folklore was a purely practical matter of making a living, nothing more. Thus his settings are much less personal, and they reflect a harmonic language which has more in common with his own earlier tonal music than with folk music. Further, the styles of singing and playing required are only the 'normal' ones of Western European art music. There is no imitation of peasant vocal ornaments, for example, nor of folk instruments (as with Bartók's cimbalom-like piano writing).

As with the Melodie ludowe and Kolędy, Lutosławski's series of songs for children began even before the formalism scandal of 1948–9. He entered the field in 1947 with two sets of songs on texts by Julian Tuwim (1894–1953). As with the folk miniatures, the composer did not expect to establish a whole series of such pieces, but when events forced him to fall back on this genre he produced a large quantity of songs for children between 1950 and 1954 and a few more in 1958–9. Lutosławski's catalog lists forty-one children's songs, counting individual songs in sets and cycles but excluding alternate versions, but the total number actually written may be somewhat higher. Of the forty-one known songs, ten are on texts by Tuwim and another nine on texts by Lucyna Krzemieniecka (1907–55). Some were written for publication by PWM, but the larger number of unpublished songs for solo voice or children's chorus and orchestra were intended for broadcast over the Polish Radio. Typically the radio would send a text to the composer by messenger and he would dash off a musical setting, sometimes spending as little as half an hour at the task.

Probably the best of the children's songs were the 1947 Tuwim songs, published in two sets: Sześć piosenek dziecinnych (Six Children's Songs) and, a short while later, 'Spóźniony słowik' (The Belated Nightingale) and 'O panu Tralalińskim' (About Mr Tralaliński) as a set 'dla dzieci małych i "dużych"' (for children little and 'big'). The first six were subsequently (1952–3) arranged by the composer for children's choir and orchestra and for mezzo-soprano and orchestra; the last two, for solo voice and orchestra. Tuwim was prominent as a poet, humorist, and translator; and like Iłłakowicz, another poet who has interested Lutosławski, he was involved with futurism and expressionism around 1920 as a member of the literary circle 'Skamander'. All the children's texts Lutosławski used are from a collection Tuwim published in 1938. The 1947 songs achieved an early and persistent popularity in Poland, becoming so well known that Grzegorz Michalski claims that 'the youngest generation of modern Polish composers owe their first encounter with music to Witold Lutosławski'.[13] His music for children brought him the Music Prize of the City of Warsaw on 9 December 1948.

The song cycle Słomkowy łańcuszek i inne dziecinne utwory (Chain of Straw and Other Children's Pieces) requires soprano, mezzo-soprano, flute, oboe, two clarinets, and bassoon. As published, the cycle

combines an original instrumental introduction and six songs based
on folk melodies, written for radio broadcast in 1950, with an original
set of variations ('Słomkowy łańcuszek') on texts by Krzemieniecka,
written and broadcast in 1951. The cycle is full of musical text-
painting designed to appeal to young listeners. Grandmother's stub-
born goat is depicted in no. 3. In each of the variations in the 'chain'
which closes the cycle, the theme remains unchanged while the
accompaniment varies to represent in turn the children, the farm-yard
pump, a rosebush, the dog, a flower, and the cow (with appropriate
mooing by the bassoon). Two similar song cycles on children's texts,
Wiosna (Spring) and Jesień (Autumn), were also written for the radio
in 1951.

Rather similar to the children's songs, though perhaps even simpler
in style, are the Dziesięć polskich pieśni ludowych na tematy
żołnierskie (Ten Popular Polish Songs on Soldier's Themes) of 1951,
arrangements of traditional melodies for men's chorus a cappella,
commissioned and published by the Polish army; a number of mass
songs composed 1950–2; and another set of soldiers' songs in manuscript (1953). Both genres have more sociological than musical significance. The mass songs, comprising a published set of seven
(1950–2) and an unpublished 'Towarzysz' (Comrade, 1952) for mixed
chorus and orchestra, include love songs, marches, and soldiers'
songs; some of their texts deal with such tender subjects as a construction project and a new steel mill. A 1954 article on these songs by the
Polish musicologist Elżbieta Dziębowska is typical of the polemics
of the time. Dziębowska complains that the resistance songs
Lutosławski had composed during the war were too difficult:

Lack of contact with the listener during the years of the occupation caused the
composer, working in isolation, to use too sophisticated a musical language,
which prevented these works from gaining mass popularity. Consequently,
despite their great artistic merits, these songs missed those for whom they
were intended and were performed [instead] . . . by professionals.[14]

Though Dziębowska exaggerates the difficulty of the resistance
songs, she is naturally happier with the even simpler language of the
mass songs.

During this period PWM commissioned other works for educa-
tional use, including Trzy utwory dla młodzieży (Three Pieces for
Young People, 1953) for piano, notable for its closing march, a clev-
erly done homage à Prokofiev; Cztery melodie śląskie (Four Silesian
Songs, 1954) for four violins (an arrangement of the last four of
the Melodie ludowe); and Zasłyszana melodyjka (An Overheard
Tune, 1957) for two pianos. In 1953 Lutosławski produced for Polskie

Nagrania, the Polish recording company, a set of *Dziesięć tańców polskich* (Ten Polish Dances) for chamber orchestra to be used in the schools.

A number of minor occasional pieces from these years may also be mentioned here. The song 'Lawina' (The Snowslide, 1949) for soprano and piano won second prize in a competition for songs on texts of Aleksandr Pushkin organized in honor of the 150th anniversary of the poet's birth. In 1951 Lutosławski wrote a short *Recitativo e arioso* for violin and piano as a gift to Tadeusz Ochlewski, then director of PWM. (This piece was later transcribed by the Polish–Swedish violinist Bronisław Eichenholz for the violino grande, a five-string instrument with a range encompassing the ranges of the traditional violin and viola designed by the Swedish luthier Hans Olof Hansson.) In 1954 Lutosławski made an arrangement of Polish dances under the title *Dmuchawce* (Dandelions) at the request of a folk-dance troupe, and the same year he provided four fanfares for the second Festival of Polish Music.[15]

Lutosławski's relations with his colleagues, some of whom we must consider collaborators in the emasculation of modern Polish music, continued to be uneasy, but his prestige was sufficient that in 1951 he was restored to the executive board of the ZKP. The same year he visited the Soviet Union, where he met a number of leading composers including Khrennikov and Khachaturian, and on his return he reported his impressions in the monthly *Muzyka*. From 27 September to 5 October 1952 he attended a contemporary music festival and composers' conference in East Berlin; his review of the event for Polish readers devoted particular attention to works by Hanns Eisler, Fidelio Finke, and Paul Dessau.[16]

The year 1953 saw the deaths of both Stalin and Prokofiev in Russia. The same year in Poland Lutosławski lost a supporter and friend of long standing when Grzegorz Fitelberg died on 10 June at the age of seventy-three. Fitelberg had been responsible for the first performances of the Symphonic Variations, First Symphony, Overture for Strings, *Mała suita*, and *Tryptyk śląski*. The younger man eulogized the great conductor in the pages of the weekly *Przegląd kulturalny* and in *Muzyka*.[17]

All of the larger, better-known folkloric works Lutosławski created during the years 1950–4 were, like the many smaller ones, occasioned by functional needs. *Mała suita* and *Tryptyk śląski* were for the radio, *Bukoliki* and *Preludia taneczne* for PWM. As the contrapuntal studies and the trio for woodwinds had served as sketches for the First Symphony, so in these functional works can we see Lutosławski hammering out new and subtler ways of employing folk materials, techniques which would make possible the only middle-period work of symphonic proportions, the Concerto for Orchestra:

the whole series of 'functional' pieces which I wrote based on folk themes gave me the possibility of developing a style which though narrow and limited, was nevertheless characteristic enough . . . I thought at the time that this marginal style would not be entirely fruitless and that despite its having come into being while I was writing typical 'functional' music, I could possibly make use of it in writing something more serious. A suitable opportunity for putting this into practise soon turned up. This was in 1950. The director of the Warsaw Philharmonic Orchestra, Witold Rowicki, asked me to write something especially for his new ensemble. This was to be something not difficult, but which could, however, give the young orchestra an opportunity to show its qualities. I started to work on the new score not realizing that I was to spend nearly four years on it . . . A work came into being, which I could not help including among my most important works, as a result of my episodic symbiosis with folk music and in a way that was for me somewhat unexpected.[18]

Mała suita (Little Suite) was written within about two weeks in 1950 to fulfill the radio's request for a piece for a small orchestra of the sort that plays light music. Thus it occupies a genre midway between popular and concert music. In 1951 the composer made a slightly longer version for larger orchestra. The folk melodies are from the village of Machów, near Rzeszów, east of Cracow; Lutosławski heard them at a festival of Polish folk music. These melodies are presented practically unaltered as themes, but in the manner of the Concerto for Orchestra they are also subjected to subtle rhythmic transformations and made to yield motives which form the basis for textural elaboration. Lissa identifies the theme of the third movement, 'Piosenka' (Song), as the folk song 'Zapalcież mi popioły' (Light the Ashes for Me), and she notes that the finale, 'Taniec' (Dance), is of the type known around Rzeszów as a *lasowiak* (forest dance).[19]

The *Tryptyk śląski* (Silesian Triptych, 1951) for soprano and orchestra is based on texts and melodies of Silesia drawn from the collections of the ethnologist Jan Stanisław Bystroń (1892–). Its three movements form a little program of distinctly popular cast. A peasant girl, ecstatically in love in the first movement, is discovered in the second abandoned and grieving:

> Ah! the spring gushes in these wells,
> But ah! my sweetheart drinks at another.
> He drinks at another and wants me not.
> Oh! my heart knew it, my heart knew.

The third movement finds her again jocular, feeling well rid of the foolish boy and congratulating herself on having preserved her virtue.

Stylistically Mała suita and Tryptyk are twins. Moreover, the direct connections between these works and stylistic devices of the Concerto for Orchestra, on which Lutosławski was working simultaneously, may be traced quite concretely. Polymetric effects created by overlaying rhythmic patterns of different lengths are common, as in the first movements of both the suite (mm. 74–83, 104–15) and the triptych (mm. 54–63), where $\frac{3}{8}$ melodies are set against $\frac{5}{8}$ accompaniment patterns; or in the second movement of the suite, where the duple-meter folk theme is notated in $\frac{3}{4}$ and accompanied by three-beat patterns. The stepwise duplets (m. 28) and the pounding, Sacre-like quavers (m. 53) of the first movement of the suite will be echoed in the first movement of the concerto (respectively mm. 64 and 56); the contrabass gesture which closes the Hurra polka of the suite will likewise end the Capriccio notturno of the concerto. The quintuplets at m. 29 in the second movement of the triptych resemble the sextuplets of the concerto's passacaglia (m. 499). Polyharmony, long an element of Lutosławski's tonal language, remains prominent; and the gradual accretion of polychords which opens the suite presages the first movement of the concerto; while the oscillating major and minor triads in the horns in the second movement of the triptych will also figure in the third movement of the concerto (m. 455 in violas, cellos and horns.)

Ironically these very works which Lutosławski regarded as inconsequential, as peripheral to his real work as a composer, were received in Stalinist Poland as models of realism. The authorities awarded Lutosławski second prize (no first prize was given) for mass songs in 1950; first prizes for Tryptyk śląski and for mass songs in December 1951; a State Prize, class II, in 1952, again for the triptych; and on 1 June 1954 a Prime Minister's Prize for the children's music. The composer was taken aback: 'the authorities . . . mistakenly believed that I had composed [functional music] to obey the guiding principles. That was another shock because I realized that I was not writing innocent, indifferent little pieces, only to make a living, but was carrying on artistic creative activity in the eyes of the outside world.'[20] It seems likely that the government was exploiting the functional nature of Lutosławski's work in the early fifties for the propaganda value of displaying one of Poland's most eminent composers as if he were cooperatively practicing socrealizm.

Zofia Lissa, generally an admirer of Lutosławski's music, was not always reliable as an observer of the works themselves. (She believed, for example, that the Overture for Strings was a serial piece, a notion which the composer has refuted.)[21] But because of her position as the leading Marxist spokeswoman among Polish musicologists her opinions were influential. Lissa's enthusiasm for *Mała suita* and *Tryptyk śląski* prompted her to welcome Lutosławski back into the fold in 1952:

Nothing is more foreign to [Lutosławski] than opportunism, internal compromise, or chasing after cheap effects and easy success. These psychological attributes have meant that the rate at which he has matured to the postulates of our time has been perhaps slower than in some other composers and that this process has taken place against many obstacles, but that at the same time it is profound and is producing results of greater consequence than with other composers. We recall that several times Lutosławski was criticized by our home-bred vulgarizers, who did not understand the complex nature of the processes taking place in the psyche of our creative intelligentsia. That these processes were neither easy nor straightforward is attested by the fact that they occurred only with difficulty even among Soviet composers . . . [Witness] the complicated creative path of Shostakovich.[22]

Bukoliki (Bucolics, 1952) for piano, the best of the works leading to the Concerto for Orchestra, received less attention at the time. This five-movement suite is more difficult than *Melodie ludowe* or *Trzy utwory* (the composer himself gave the first public performance, in fact, in December 1953), but still quite possible for students of intermediate accomplishments. Each of the movements is based on folk tunes of the Kurpie forests taken from the collection by Father Władysław Skierkowski (one of the many musicians who was murdered in Nazi concentration camps). But these are no mere settings of folk songs. The borrowed material is developed motivically and combined with newly invented material so smoothly that there is no effect of quotation. *Bukoliki* marks a further advance in rhythmic subtlety as well, developing more fully the possibilities hinted at in the First Symphony and partly explored in the earlier functional works. Polymetric effects are particularly striking in the first and third movements. The harmonic and melodic pitch language embraces a variety of styles – diatonic tonality (no. 1, mm. 1–28; no. 3, mm. 15–23), bitonality (no. 1, mm. 29–45),[23] folk-song-derived modality (no. 2, mm. 10–13; no. 4) – and synthetic scales are used. A passage from the third movement includes one such scale (see mm. 29–33 in the example). The use of contrametric patterns in this movement affords an attractively supple rhythmic character; the example illustrates the foreshortening of pattern lengths propelling the music toward a cadence (ex. 2.4). In 1962 the composer transcribed *Bukoliki* for viola and cello for publication by PWM.

The most important work of Lutosławski's middle period and

2.4 *Bukoliki*, no. 3 (mm. 29–44)

surely the greatest achievement of those bleak days in Polish music is
the monumental Concerto for Orchestra. The composer spent four
years on the score, beginning in 1950 with Rowicki's suggestion that
he write something for the new Warsaw Philharmonic Orchestra and
finishing only in 1954. Rowicki conducted the première in Warsaw
on 26 November 1954, and the work was a huge and immediate
success both among the public and within the musical establishment.
Stefan Jarociński's review in *Przegląd kulturalny* is typical of the
enthusiastic reception accorded the concerto. Jarociński notes tact-
fully that not everyone had liked the First Symphony, that some had
thought Lutosławski, like Ravel, a 'watchmaker' who worked best in
smaller forms. But in Jarociński's view the Concerto for Orchestra
settles once and for all the question of Lutosławski's mastery of the
large form and establishes him unequivocally as the country's leading
composer.[24] The work led to a second State Prize, class I, and the
Order of Labor, class II, on 22 July 1955. It is the only piece from the
middle period which the composer still considers important, and the
only one he still includes on his own concert programs.

The Concerto for Orchestra is no less brilliantly colored than the
First Symphony. But if the symphony was marked by youthful
extravagance, the concerto, completed only seven years later, reveals
an artist in complete control of his powers. The work represents a
synthesis of the experience gained in the folk miniatures – one listener at the première called it '*Mała suita* to the tenth power' – with
aspects of the serious side of Lutosławski's development, the side
largely hidden from the public since the symphony. It falls into three
movements, which, though they are adorned with titles borrowed
from the Baroque era, depend in fact on eighteenth- and nineteenth-

century conceptions of form. The opening Intrada serves as an introduction for the whole cycle, but it has none of the march-like character historically associated with the term. Similarly, the Passacaglia which begins the finale, though it does occur over a ground in triple meter, has nothing further in common with neoclassical (i.e., neo-Baroque) conceptions of form but rather with postromantic. This third movement – Passacaglia, Toccata e Corale – is longer than the first two combined; and, in contrast to the classical model in which the center of gravity lies in the first movement, here the finale bears the dramatic weight of the whole cycle. This was Lutosławski's first experiment with shifting the resolution of musical tensions toward the end of the large formal cycle – remember that even the finale of the First Symphony is rather less earnest – and Lissa reports that the composer labored long and hard over the finale, reworking some portions again and again until he was satisfied, apparently *before* commencing work on the first and second movements.[25]

It is easy to suppose that Lutosławski's Concerto for Orchestra must have been deeply influenced by the well-known Bartók work of the same name. Lutosławski had indeed come under Bartók's influence in the late forties, and it is difficult to believe that his love for that composer's music did not filter into his own concerto. But aside from the obvious coincidence that both composers' works contain a chorale, one can search in vain for clear traces of Bartók in the actual musical text of the Lutosławski concerto. What is in fact more interesting and more significant is the crucial *difference* between the methods of the two composers. In Bartók's œuvre there are many unabashed arrangements in which the character of quoted folk songs is carefully preserved; and in later works there develops a musical language in which, as Halsey Stevens writes, 'the composer employs neither folk melodies nor imitations of folk melodies, but absorbs their essence in such a way that it pervades his music'.[26] Lutosławski adopts neither method. Instead, folk songs and dances are mere raw material from which he fashions not only themes but also the tiny motivic fragments of which to build up an elaborate contrapuntal edifice. Folk tunes are never simply quoted: they are radically transformed, manipulated, made to serve the composer's artistic vision. This approach makes possible a style which is at once so demonstrably 'national' as to be politically unassailable, yet modern enough and personal enough to burst the bounds of *socrealizm*. It permits the composer to be master, not slave, of folklore.

Appropriately, the folk sources are all from Masovia (the region around Warsaw). Eight of these source melodies are shown in example 2.5.[27] Lutosławski's unorthodox method of extracting his

2.5　Folk sources for the Concerto for Orchestra

material from folklore contributes to a high degree of thematic unity among the three movements. Another force unifying the cycle is the intentionally systematic tonal scheme linking the movements in a chain of third-relations (ex. 2.6).

2.6   Principal tone centers of the Concerto for Orchestra

The Intrada has a ternary structure in which the middle section has five subdivisions:

m.	1	A
	40	B
	42	C
	64	B′
	75	C′
	100	B″
	124	A′

Despite the appearance of arch form, however, the effect is cumulative and highly directional rather than symmetrically balanced. The form seems to gather substance as it goes, so that B′ is longer and more intense than B; C′ bears an analogous relation to C; and B″, longer still than B′, forms the climax of the movement.

Theme 1 transforms a simple Masovian folk tune from the village of Czersk (no. 5 in ex. 2.5) into a vigorous statement capable of supporting symphonic argument (ex. 2.7). The counterpoint to this theme is concocted of two folk-song fragments (nos. 6 and 7 in ex. 2.5). Over an F-sharp pedal point, theme 1 enters imitatively on the successive tonics D, A, E, B, and F-sharp (all minor). Thus the entire texture expands upward by perfect fifths as the first section progresses, and in this way the pedal gradually acquires four additional pitch classes (plus F-sharp, replicated at the top of the cycle). Upon the return of

2.7   Theme 1, first movement of the Concerto for Orchestra (mm. 2–9)

this material at m. 124 the process is inverted, not tonally but texturally. The F-sharp pedal is now positioned in the highest register of the
orchestra (piccolo, celesta, and violin artificial harmonic), and the
theme's entrances on the tonics, D, A, E, B, and F-sharp now spell a
series of descending fourths as the texture expands from the top
downward (ex. 2.8). The dramatic function of A is likewise inverted in
A′. Whereas the opening section served to build tension, introducing
the central section where the climax is approached and resolved, A′
occurs after the climax has come and gone; it is an epilogue softly
echoing the opening but devoid of its aggressive urgency, balancing
thus the sustained intensity of everything which has come before by
its sustained calm.

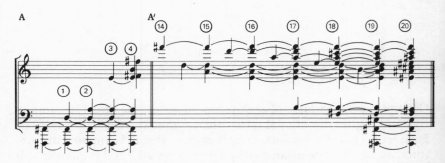

2.8   Harmonic reduction of the first and third divisions of the first movement
of the Concerto for Orchestra

Theme 2 (the B sections) is also derived from folk song (no. 1 in ex.
2.5), and this folk song serves as one of the chief vehicles of thematic
unity, furnishing also the second theme of the toccata and other
material. The material of the C sections – falling minor sixths in
marcato dotted crotchets and pounded quaver chords – is wholly
original.

The second movement, Capriccio notturno e Arioso, may be compared in structure to the traditional scherzo–trio–scherzo pattern:

m.   173   A ⎫
     237   A′⎭ Capriccio notturno
     311   B   Arioso
     343   A″   Capriccio notturno

where each occurrence of A is a fully developed part-form of six
sections, including a codetta which on its final appearance is
extended to serve as coda to the entire movement. Unlike the traditional trio, the Arioso is not tonally independent, for it falls midway

in an ongoing tonal process which gives overriding tonal coherence to the whole movement (ex. 2.9).

2.9   Tonal centers in the second movement of the Concerto for Orchestra

The scherzo music has been compared to the nocturnal scherzi of Mendelssohn (*A Midsummer Night's Dream*) and Berlioz (the 'Queen Mab' scherzo in the *Romeo and Juliet* symphony); like them it is a *tour de force* of delicate orchestration. The opening idea is perceived as no more than a blurred line of string color, so quickly does it pass by. Yet embedded in this line is a turning chromatic motive whose potency transcends the opening gesture to permeate the shimmering orchestral textures of the fourth, fifth, and sixth sections of A. The second section of A, on the other hand, has nothing to do with this motive but derives instead from folk song (no. 8 in ex. 2.5). (See ex. 2.10.) The reprises of A are formally quite strict, but their scoring is varied and resourceful. Note, for example, how the harp-and-strings accompaniment on the first two appearances of the codetta (mm. 224–35 and 295–306) is translated into percussion terms on the third playing (mm. 394–417). Indeed, one of the most interesting aspects of this movement is the way in which orchestration and the exploitation of register and timbre are, more than simply window-dressing, active participants in the shaping of form.

2.10   Second movement of the Concerto for Orchestra (mm. 189–93)

The broad trumpet theme of the Arioso, made the more stirring by the hammered interjections of the rest of the orchestra, presents the most radical transformation of a folk source in the entire concerto. The original folk song, 'Przedzierzgnę się siwą gołębicą' ('I'm Turning into a Gray Dove'; no. 4 in ex. 2.5), is distorted beyond audible recognition (though the intervals are preserved). What is more, it is thoroughly dismembered. Lutosławski uses only the first half of the folk melody for his theme. Later in the Arioso section, however, he returns to its last four measures for the material just preceding the movement's climax (m. 331). The passage in question consists entirely of the folk-derived melodic motive, the chromatic turning motive from the beginning of the movement (inner voices), and an octatonic scale generated as a series of (2-1) trichords (bass) and deriving from the oboe and clarinet in m. 316 (ex. 2.11).

The task of the vast finale, the main movement of the concerto, is to summarize, unify, and finally resolve the dramatic tensions of the much shorter first two movements. Though the last movement bears three titles – Passacaglia, Toccata e Corale – it is actually in two large parts: the opening passacaglia, which serves as an extended introduction, and the toccata, in the course of which the chorale is twice interpolated. The ground theme on which the passacaglia is based is adapted from yet another folk song (no. 2 in ex. 2.5). The ground is heard eighteen times, although on the first and last playings it is reduced to a skeletal version comprising only the principal pitches ($\hat{1}$, $\hat{3}$, and $\hat{5}$ in D major). Over the course of the passacaglia this theme gradually migrates upward from the lowest to the highest register. It begins in the lowest reaches of the orchestra, on D^1; octave doublings are added until at m. 490 (the tenth playing) it is heard in six octaves, D^1 to d^3. Beginning with the eleventh playing the lower octaves are gradually removed, until the ground remains only in the top register.

There are twelve variations. As the ground systematically expands and then contracts again with respect to register, the material of the variations undergoes similar though not identical processes of growth and decline in several parameters: register, dynamic, textural density, and tempo. The complex interaction of these aspects of the music with the gradual passage of the ground from one extreme of register to the other produces the dynamic profile of the passacaglia, a profile whose peak comes at the beginning of variation 11 (m. 540). The variations rarely begin or end with ground statements, but rather they remain out of phase throughout most of the movement. Thus variations 1–5 are each eight measures long, but each begins in the sixth measure of the ground; variation 6 lasts nine measures and variation 7, ten. The two elements intersect at the beginning of variation 8 (m. 498) – the moment at which the ground begins to contract from its six-octave spread, and the spot where the passacaglia is divided psychologically (if not arithmetically) in half by virtue of the return of Tempo I, the crotchet rest on the first beat of the measure setting off the arrival of a new statement of the ground, and the dramatic entry of the strings with a new variation on the next beat. Variation 8 then occupies ten measures, and the ground and varia-

2.11   Derivation of the Arioso theme in the second movement of the Concerto for Orchestra (mm. 311–16 and mm. 327–31)

tions do not coincide again until variation 10 (m. 530), preparing the
climax in m. 540.

The toccata which follows as the main body of the movement
exposes and develops two principal thematic ideas (both transformations, in turn, of earlier material). After a short introduction signify-

ing the dominant of F-sharp, theme 1 enters as a new version of the ground theme from the passacaglia (or a new version of the original folk-song source). Theme 1 is imitated three times, ascending by perfect fifths until a cadence on E-flat minor is reached at m. 597. The second theme, which follows immediately, is a new transformation by intervallic contraction (e.g., major third replaced by minor third) and by rhythmic alteration of the second theme of the first movement. The chorale is inserted following the long second group, and if this were a sonata it would seem to serve as a kind of closing theme for the exposition – though it will return near the end of the work in a very different function. The chorale itself is newly invented, but its accompanying counterpoint, first given to solo flute, is descended from a folk song (no. 3 in ex. 2.5). Once introduced, this counter-melody figures prominently throughout the rest of the movement.

In fact the composer does think of the toccata as being in sonata form. We may accept his notion of the form only with reservations, for it is a sprawling piece which dispenses with some of the most basic conventions of the sonata. There is no recapitulation in the ordinary sense, and the unequivocal re-establishment of the principal tone center, F-sharp, does not occur until deep in the coda, at the triumphal reprise of the chorale. Instead of a recapitulation we find a long coda, really a second development presenting metrical trans-formations of theme 1 and omitting any clear statement of theme 2. This account of the form may be summarized thus:

Toccata and Chorale: Structural Synopsis

m.   563   Introduction, establishing dominant of F-sharp

Exposition

570   Theme 1 (transformation of passacaglia theme); imitative entries in F-sharp, C-sharp, G-sharp, E-flat minor
597   Theme 2, part 1 (transformation of theme 2, first movement)
614   Closing material based on motives of theme 1
623   Theme 2, part 2 (transformation of theme 1 in B-flat, C-sharp minor)
643   Retransition
668   Reprise of theme 2, part 1 (head-motive only); subsidiary climax (dissolves into transition)

Chorale

681   Three statements: woodwind (E-flat), brass (E-flat), strings (A-flat)
726   Dissolution

Development

736   Section 1: based on contrapuntal figures from theme 1
788   False retransition (like introduction); dominant pedal (C-sharp)

802 Section 2: transformation of theme 1, plus chorale counter-
     melody
834 Transition based on chorale countermelody

Coda (Second Development)

852 Section 1: transformation of theme 1 in compound time;
     development of motive from theme 2
876 Section 2: transformation of theme 1 in triplets; development
     of motive from theme 2
903 Section 3: preparation for reprise (dominant-surrogate har-
     mony); figures based on theme 1
922 Section 4: reprise of chorale in F-sharp (principal tone center);
     subsidiary climax
939 Section 5: based on mm. 736ff.
949 Section 6: F-sharp returns in the bass; principal climax

The development techniques are varied and sometimes imaginative.
Besides simple metrical transformations of theme 1, less obvious uses
of the material demonstrate the extent to which the orchestral texture
is permeated with thematic substance. Note, for instance, the first six
pitches of theme 2 (first and third movements) partitioned as two plus
four between strings and horns (mm. 885–7, 891–3). Even the washes
of orchestral color near the end of the work reveal the head-motive of
theme 1 in their individual instrumental parts.

The dynamic profile of the finale – which in this work we may
interpret simplistically by comparing levels of loudness – in a sense
recapitulates and gives final resolution to the individual profiles of
the earlier movements. The first and second have each peaked at
about two thirds their length. The passacaglia represents a steadier,
more continuous rise to a climax very near the end. The toccata, on the
other hand, has a number of climaxes and in its second half a succession of several individual rises whose cumulative momentum is
meant to carry through the final climax from the chorale reprise to the
end, rounding off not only the movement but the work as a whole.

Is the Concerto for Orchestra, finally, an artistic success? Not without qualification. There are distinct disappointments, as for example
the gratuitous resolution of the last harmony in the first movement to
a tonic major seventh chord, which seems as out of place here as was
the ninth chord tacked onto the end of the Overture for Strings. A
more serious problem is that the design of the finale is carried out
imperfectly. The two developments of the toccata – everything, that
is, after the first chorale – may well be too long and too sectional to
carry off convincingly the composer's intended drive to the ultimate
climax at the end of the movement (though it must be admitted that
among recorded performances the composer's own reading comes
nearer succeeding in this regard than any other – especially in making

convincing the necessary acceleration after rehearsal number 92).
The attempt is no less significant for its flawed execution, however,
for the idea of shifting the dramatic crux of a multi-movement cycle
away from the first movement and towards the end of the last and then
managing a carefully controlled and long-sustained ascent to a
single most important climax is a problem which would occupy
Lutosławski again in future years, and he would come to solve it
brilliantly.

The musical style of the Concerto for Orchestra was, of course, hardly
up to date for 1954 by foreign standards; at the same time Lutosławski
was finishing the concerto, Carter was beginning the Variations for
Orchestra, Boulez was completing *Le marteau sans maître*, Varèse
was writing *Déserts*, Stockhausen was producing *Elektronische
Studie Nr. 2* and the *Klavierstücke* series. But the highly characteristic tonal style which had evolved in Lutosławski's functional music
from the *Melodie ludowe* and *Kolędy* through the works of the early
fifties, and which achieved its fullest expression in the concerto, is
not simply irrelevant in the broad context of his career. The concerto
shows unmistakable connections with the past, it is true: specifically,
it is bound to *Mała suita* and the *Tryptyk* by quite concrete details of
style and substance. But in the light of Lutosławski's subsequent
development we can see quite clearly that a number of traits essential
to his later style are already represented in the concerto. Among these
characteristics are the shift of dramatic weight later in the formal
cycle; the role of register, timbre, and texture as formal determinants;
the strong sense of music as drama; the cultivation of a 'blurred
toccata' style (Capriccio notturno); the utter mastery of the orchestra
and acute sensitivity to instrumental and harmonic color as expressive values; and above all the construction of large forms through the
accretion of the smallest motivic building-blocks.
     After the completion of the Concerto for Orchestra in 1954,
Lutosławski undertook one final project based on folklore. PWM had
asked him for an easy instrumental work for student performers. At
first a set of ten pieces for violin and piano was projected. At the same
time, however, the composer was sketching a work for clarinet and
piano, and in the end it was this composition which he completed and
gave to the publisher under the title *Preludia taneczne* (Dance Preludes). The original version was later reworked twice: for clarinet,
harp, piano, percussion, and strings in 1955 (the version best known
today), and in 1959 for the Czech Nonet (woodwind quintet plus
violin, viola, cello, and doublebass).
     The five-movement *Preludia taneczne* is based on folk songs from

northern Poland, but the precise source of the folk material is uncertain. As with *Bukoliki* and the Concerto for Orchestra, however, what has been borrowed has been so seamlessly woven in that nothing seems extraneous. *Preludia taneczne* is a meticulously crafted, rather Bartókian little piece whose harmonic style leans heavily on synthetic scales and related polychords (though each movement conveys a clear tone center: E-flat, F, B-flat, G, and E-flat). Polymeter between the clarinet and accompaniment is frequent, and here at last it is notated as such, with separate time signatures and barlines which do not coincide.

The principal interest of this work is not technical, however, but biographical; for Lutosławski called it 'my farewell to folklore for an indefinite period',[28] and it thus draws to a close the most difficult and least rewarding chapter of his life. The years 1949–54 may appear to be nothing more than a pointless detour in the composer's career, imposed by odious forces quite beyond his control and leading nowhere. But in fact he spent even the blackest period marshalling his creative resources for the future. Ludwik Erhardt has correctly seen that for Lutosławski the utilitarian works

were exercises in the possibilities of sound and instrumentation. Exploration of interesting rhythm problems was wedded to a feeling for form, a subtlety of tone colour and a sense of musical humour to create a recognizable foretaste of the Lutosławski style . . . On balance, however, the years 1949–54 spelled for Lutosławski (as for Malawski) a standstill in his development, but marked an accumulation of technical resources which was to explode in the mature brilliance and innovation of his subsequent œuvre.[29]

Looking back a few years later, Lutosławski himself characterized his existence in Stalinist Poland for an interviewer this way:

My work in recent years frequently had a dual nature: alongside my studies toward a new language were works in which I used methods I knew well, techniques I had already mastered. Some of my works, therefore, I freely characterize as a 'makeshift', . . . I wrote as I was able, since I could not yet write as I wished . . . As for the psychological effect of such a dichotomy (a perilous subject, this!) – I survived it somehow, despite the fact that inwardly I was far from comfortable. I rejoice that I can speak of this now in the past tense.[30]

3 The years of transition: 1955–60

Poland's artistic community had languished in a curious sort of cultural vacuum under the Stalinist government of Bierut since 1949. Polish musicians, though conversant with recent developments in the music of the Soviet Union and other Eastern European states, were quite literally cut off from the West at the very moment when the most radical changes within the European avant-garde were transforming the nature of new music. In the West, Stockhausen, Boulez, and Nono emerged as international figures. The cult of Webern arose. *Musique concrète* was born, and the first electronic studios were established. Messiaen and his students in Europe and Babbitt in America experimented with extending the serial principle beyond the realm of pitch. In New York, John Cage consulted the *I Ching* to produce *Music of Changes*, and Earle Brown explored graphic notation. And all the while Polish composers labored on in profound and stultifying isolation.

With the death of Stalin in March 1953, the Soviets embarked on the period of relative tranquillity known as 'the Thaw' (after Ilja Ehrenburg's novel of the same title), and in Poland composers began to sense a very gradual relaxation of the aesthetic canons enforced by the Bierut regime. Among composers and other artists it became possible, little by little, to speak out against the excesses of *socrealizm*. In the ZKP dissatisfaction with the status quo was unexpectedly dramatized in the summer of 1954 by the defection to England of Andrzej Panufnik, who had been prominent in the union's affairs for several years;[1] and in the General Assembly of the ZKP that year the prevailing cultural policies were openly criticized. In 1955 the moderate Kazimierz Sikorski was elected president, and Zofia Lissa withdrew from the union's leadership to devote herself to scholarly pursuits. On 4 June of that year the membership heard Zygmunt Mycielski describe with remarkable candor the unhealthy state of Polish music:

At this point I must state emphatically that unfortunately we exist in a world which is closed and, practically speaking, isolated from the artistic life around us. Even the many official visits, congresses, and assemblies which a few (generally only virtuosos and concert artists) attend do not help much.

60

That is not genuine artistic contact. Artistic contact means a concert life in which the programs include the most recent music from around the world; it means easy access to publications and the exchange of the best soloists and conductors; it means travel for youth, who should not be expected to do without contact with experienced critics and working professionals, whether they be in the Soviet Union, the popular democracies, or the West. Our country is becoming a backwater where it is impossible for us to imagine how or what is being written and played abroad . . .

And what a decade it has been the world over! Therefore it is essential that we be included in that world and not isolated, for isolation is always bad for art, and for young people is but a provocation. The young will always flock to the unknown, to anything that has the air of the forbidden. Only a more informed, open, courageous comparison of our own achievements and aspirations with those of others can satisfy this natural craving and allow us to respond soundly or, as the case may be, to resist . . .

To criticize and oppose that which is unknown is something the politician may be able to do now and then, but it is beyond the province of the artist.[2]

Outside artistic circles, too, forces were gathering which threatened the Polish government's grip on the country. Although the events leading to the revolution of October 1956 are too complex to be recounted thoroughly here, a brief summary is in order. Many factors had conspired to produce intense dissatisfaction among all segments of the society. A dismal economic record under state planning, the ruthless methods of Bierut's secret police (Bezpieka), the traditional anti-Communist and anti-Russian biases of Poles in general, and the unshakeable allegiance of the vast majority of the population to the Church – these and other forces had by 1955 produced a volatile mood throughout the country. An emboldened press became increasingly critical; Antoni Słonimski's 'Poetic Manifesto' and especially Adam Ważyk's 'Poem for Adults', both published in the summer of 1955, played an important role in preparing the revolution of the following year. De-Stalinization was already proceeding in Moscow when Bierut died unexpectedly on 12 March 1956. The same month, the Nineteenth Culture Session in Warsaw was the occasion for vehement attacks on Socialist realism by writers and literary critics. An armed uprising protesting government policy broke out in Poznań on 28 June 1956, leaving forty-eight dead and hundreds wounded. By the time the Eighth Plenum of the ruling Polish United Workers' Party's Central Committee began on 19 October 1956, an extraordinary level of excitement ran throughout Polish society, and it was clear that only substantial liberalization could avert a full-scale revolt and inevitable armed intervention by the Soviets. Władysław Gomułka, only recently released from house arrest and rehabilitated in Party circles, was therefore invited to take over the leadership of the country. The accession of Gomułka and the ensuing climate of relative freedom which prevailed, albeit briefly, under the new regime constitute the second great watershed in mid-century Polish cultural life, the 'Polish October'.[3]

Although the Gomułka government soon retreated from some of the reforms Poles had come to expect, the creative intelligentsia managed to maintain a degree of independence unknown in the other Socialist states, thanks both to the high prestige traditionally accorded this class in Polish society and to the international prestige their efforts were earning for their country. Artists of all sorts seized the opportunity to reclaim their independence and to learn about new developments in Western Europe and America. As a result Poland quickly assumed a vanguard role among the nations of Eastern Europe in the arts and letters, particularly in film, theater, and music.

The year 1956 was an epoch-making date for Polish music, dividing its postwar course into two distinct stages. As if a dam had burst, an astonishing flood of pent-up creativity from Polish composers rushed to meet the flow of Western scores, books, and recordings which now resumed. The names not only of Lutosławski and his generation – Bacewicz, Serocki, Szabelski – but of a number of younger composers as well, led by Penderecki, Górecki, Kilar, and Baird, quickly became known in the West. But if modern music was to succeed in Poland, an audience had to be created for it. The principal weapon in this campaign and the abiding symbol of the changing climate for musicians became the international festival known as 'Warszawska Jesień' – the Warsaw Autumn. First proposed in 1955 by the composers Tadeusz Baird and Kazimierz Serocki, the festival was inaugurated in the fall of 1956 under the sponsorship of the ZKP. That first festival presented twentieth-century 'classics' still unknown to the Polish public – works of Stravinsky, Schoenberg, Berg, Bartók, and others – as well as music by Polish composers, including Lutosławski, who was represented by *Mała suita* and the Concerto for Orchestra. Already at the second Warsaw Autumn in 1958 (for it was originally planned as a biennale) the works of Webern, Boulez, Berio, Nono, and Stockhausen were added, along with twelve-tone serial pieces by Serocki, Górecki, and Kotoński. The experience was as invigorating for the public as it was for composers:

The fact that music is no longer written (allegedly to meet social demand) by order of a ministerial institution has brought forth during the last few years many valuable works which have aroused interest and discussion. I know many people who have no direct contact with musical circles, but who nevertheless know what the composers are working on. And it was those people who had been impatiently awaiting the publication of the scores of

Funeral Music by Witold Lutosławski, the *Four Essays for Orchestra* by
Tadeusz Baird, and inquiring about the date of the first performance of . . . the
Symphonic Variations by Grażyna Bacewicz.[4]

The combination of receptive audiences and an energetic group of
local composers made the Warsaw Autumn a forum for the newest in
international music and made the Polish capital an important center
of contemporary music – a development which would have been
unthinkable a few years before. Musical life revived on other fronts as
well. During 1957 a national committee was established to cooperate
with UNESCO's International Music Council, and the Polish section
of the ISCM was revived; the semimonthly *Ruch muzyczny* (Musical
Movement) resumed publication; several young composers attended
the Darmstadt summer course; and the Polish Radio experimental
studio was founded under the direction of Józef Patkowski.

When the ZKP gathered in the spring of 1957 for its ninth General
Assembly, the members symbolically chose Witold Lutosławski as
moderator of the meeting. On 9 March Lutosławski, who had kept
silent for eight years, opened the discussion by observing that,
although some serious problems remained, there was now cause for
hope:

For our meeting for the first time in a long while takes place in an atmosphere
of real creative freedom. No one here will persecute anybody for so-called
formalism; no one will try to prevent anybody else from expressing his
aesthetic views, regardless of what individual composers may stand for.

Then, speaking from bitter personal experience:

When I look back today from the perspective of eight and a half years on the
'famous'[5] conference in Łagów in 1949, when Polish musical creativity was
openly attacked, it gives me chills just remembering that horrible experience.
In fact it is difficult to conceive of a more absurd hypothesis than the idea that
the achievements of the past several decades should be abandoned and that
one should return to the musical language of the nineteenth century. And yet
they tried to convince us of this thesis. Not only that, they sometimes tried to
launch epigonic, sterile works, at the same time barring the way to the concert
platform for original, creative efforts. We all know that what happened was
caused by people to whom the very idea of beauty is utterly foreign, people
who do not care about music unless one can pin to it some kind of little story
or legend.

The period of which I speak may not have lasted long, for as a matter of fact
it passed a couple of years ago, but all the same it was long enough to do our
music immense harm. The psyche of the creative artist is an incredibly
delicate and precise instrument. Thus the attack on that instrument, the
attempt to control it, caused not a few of us moments of severe depression.
Being completely cut off from what was happening in the arts in the West

played likewise a considerable role in that dreary experiment we were subjected to.

Have we shaken off our despondency? Do we have enough enthusiasm for
new creative explorations? Certainly. Still, our situation is by no means an
easy one. Each of us faces the problem of discovering his own place in that
chaos which the art of our era represents. The problem is sharply drawn for
those of us who, after an interruption of several years, have renewed contact
with Western European music. We don't all have here a clear view of what is
happening in this music, of where it is leading. But I believe it is only a
question of time before we will not only acquire a clear view of the situation
but will play a positive and a not inconsiderable role in it.

I can feel optimistic on account of the fact that today we breathe an
atmosphere of true creative freedom. And that is the first, the indispensable
condition for the development of all art.[6]

Lutosławski was one of the composers for whom the stylistic and
aesthetic issues were 'clearly drawn', and the next several years were
to be a time of transition for him, leading to a genuine crisis of style
and ultimately to the development of a radically different musical
language. The prolific year 1954 had seen, in addition to Preludia
taneczne (the 'farewell to folklore'), the completion of the Concerto
for Orchestra, four children's songs, a folk ballet scene, four fanfares,
and the arrangement for four violins of four of the Melodie ludowe.
Suddenly the composer fell silent for two years, producing only the
chamber orchestra transcription of Preludia taneczne in 1955 and
nothing at all in 1956, for it was during these years that he was slowly
working out the details of a mature and personal style of organizing
pitch which would make possible his greatest works.

Meanwhile Lutosławski maintained a busy public life. For the first
time since 1948 he was able to travel outside the Communist bloc
countries. As a critic he attended the Sibelius festival in Helsinki in
1955 and the Mozart festival in Salzburg in 1956 (21–23 January). As a
composer he became increasingly active in the ISCM, together with
Grażyna Bacewicz representing Poland at the 1958 festival in Strasbourg. In June 1959 he served on the jury of the ISCM festival in Rome,
where he heard Agon, Improvisations sur Mallarmé, and works by
Nono, Nilsson, Clementi, Rochberg, and Castiglioni. Lutosławski
already admired Webern for his 'discovery of a sound world of
microscopic dimensions, in which, lightning-like, the briefest musical expression is forged through powerful personal experience'. But
he disliked intensely the endless cantatas by Webern's 'frequently
incompetent, vulgar disciples' which dominated the festival programs, and he hoped that as Debussy had been rescued from the
Debussystes, so would Webern be delivered from post-Webernism.[7] 'I
felt very sad and lonely', he remembers, 'for if music was going to

develop like that in the future I would be left completely on my own . . .'[8]

But the style which during these years was gradually taking shape in Lutosławski's sketches was not so much a response to or a reaction against these renewed contacts with Western music; rather it was the continuation of his dogged search for a means of expression wholly his own. The same force which had prevented his being satisfied with the Symphonic Variations or the First Symphony or the Concerto for Orchestra now impelled him during the 'silent' years 1955–6 to perfect the first stage of that new language. In the works of transition – the Iłłakowicz songs, *Muzyka żałobna*, and the Three Postludes for orchestra – are revealed, one by one, individual traits of style which would finally coalesce to produce the mature style of the 1960s.

The first step in this transition was the completion in 1957 of Five Songs on texts of Kazimiera Iłłakowicz, for mezzo-soprano and piano, begun in 1956. A version for mezzo-soprano and chamber orchestra followed in 1958. The importance of this work in Lutosławski's development is often overlooked; Lidia Rappoport's monograph, for example, omits it altogether in favor of an extended discussion of *Muzyka żałobna*. But in the critical matter of harmonic organization it is the Iłłakowicz songs which mark the turning-point by exhibiting the salient feature of Lutosławski's mature harmonic practice: the consistent use of harmonic aggregates comprising all twelve pitch classes, employed for their expressive and coloristic values. Every other parameter is reduced to the bare minimum of complexity here so that the composer can concentrate more intently on developing this new harmonic style.

Four of the songs are dedicated to Nadia Boulanger in honor of her seventieth birthday. Lutosławski had first set the poetry of Iłłakowicz in 1934; now from her *Rymy dziecięce* (Rhymes for Children, 1922), he chose short juvenile poems – 'Morze' (The Sea), 'Wiatr' (The Wind), 'Zima' (Winter), 'Rycerze' (Knights), and 'Dzwony cerkiewne' (Church Bells) – whose simple emotional content permitted concise settings emphasizing landscape and atmosphere over textual exigesis. Thus, in marked contrast to earlier works, the texture is largely static and homophonic, and the polymetric complexities of *Bukoliki* and *Preludia taneczne* are abjured in favor of a simple, lyrical style of declamation. In his program note for the 1960 Warsaw Autumn, Lutosławski discussed his sudden preoccupation with the vertical dimension of his music:

As far as I am concerned it would be impossible to write even the smallest composition without carefully considering the purely sensual reaction to the vertical and horizontal arrangement of the sounds. It is for this reason that I greet skeptically the assertion that harmony as an element of musical creation has disappeared; what is more, I believe that it is only now that we are liberating ourselves from the conventions of the tonal system that we can comprehend all the wealth of harmonic possibilities available in the chromatic scale.

These problems (quite unpopular today) preoccupied me particularly while I was writing the Five Songs. . . I put aside everything else in this work to concentrate solely on the expressive and coloristic possibilities of twelve-tone chords in their manifold variations – whence the homophonic texture, the traditional, static rhythm, and finally the choice of 'infantile' texts calling for a simplified, lapidary musical interpretation.[9]

The roots of this new harmonic practice are of course plain to see in Lutosławski's lifelong predilection for rich polychords of as many as nine notes (Symphonic Variations, First Symphony). But only about 1955 did he begin to experiment with the expressive possibilities of actual twelve-note chords. As a result of his inveterate habit of sketching abstract studies, he must have amassed a considerable collection of such chords, as can be seen from the great number and variety of them in the Iłłakowicz songs and the almost schematic ways in which they are set out.

The individual morphology of chords in the songs reveals a very large number of constructions which will recur again and again in the later music, and many of the processes by which these chords are generated and manipulated find their archetypal expression here. In the first song, 'Morze', for example, a twelve-note aggregate derived through the superimposition of a series of fifths on a series of thirds, and producing a symmetrical structure containing (with one brief exception) only interval classes 1 and 3, is unfolded over the space of twenty-one measures.[10] Both the limited interval-class content and the very gradual accretion of the aggregate in time are highly characteristic. Later (m. 40) another chord is restated at five transpositional levels, falling by semitones, a procedure which presages, for example, *Mi-parti* (1976). Near the close of the first song (m. 47) the first chord reappears transposed ($t = 11$). The pitch content of the entire song may be reduced to chords of only three types, represented by x, y, and z in example 3.1.[11]

The second song, 'Wiatr', partitions the twelve tones into tetrachords of three types – (2-1-2), (2-3-2), and (1-1-1) – which through transposition maintain a fully chromatic aggregate harmony (ex. 3.2a). Note that the first tetrachord generates a twelve-note chord containing only two interval classes (1 and 2), the second only three (1, 2, and 3), and the third only one (1). Later in the second song the total chromatic is stated as the three possible mutually exclusive tetrachords (3-3-3) ('diminished seventh chords', ex. 3.2b), a device

3.1   Harmonic reduction of 'Morze'

3.2   Isolated harmonic structures from 'Wiatr', segmented to show their derivation

which will return in *Paroles tissées* (1965) and elsewhere. The final harmony is a symmetrical construction in which are embedded two transpositions of the opening tetrachord (2-1-2) (ex. 3.2c). Whereas the vocal line of the first song was dependent on the harmonic background, selecting melodic pitches from the available harmonic repertory at any given moment, in the second song the voice is considerably more independent as regards pitch choice. Here the sung lines are organized according to motives inherent in the harmonic background – the (2-1-2) and (1-1-1) tetrachords, for example – but often not coinciding so systematically with the prevailing pitch-class collections of the accompaniment.

The voice is independent also in the third song, 'Zima', where it spins out melodic arcs emphasizing interval classes 1 and 3 and related motivically to the opening section of the first song. The accompaniment, on the other hand, consists entirely of a single twelve-note structure (and its transpositions) comprising the four mutually exclusive augmented triads, a sound whose harmonic 'coldness' provides a wonderfully apt evocation of winter. The fourth song, 'Rycerze', uses only two types of twelve-note collection. The first, spelled as complementary white-key and black-key hexachords, appears in two different gestural contexts (ex. 3.3). The second is again explicitly partitioned into 'diminished seventh chords', which at the close of the song lie in three distinct 'voices' which converge on one another through systematic transposition: the topmost element downward by perfect fourths, the middle downward by whole steps, and the lowest upward by semitones (ex. 3.4).

3.3   'Rycerze' (mm. 159, 169)

3.4   'Rycerze' (mm. 193–7)

The final song, 'Dzwony cerkiewne', is again fashioned from the only two harmonic aggregates. The first comprises several distinct subsets appearing gradually over the course of eighteen measures (ex. 3.5a). Here the effect is of pealing church bells ringing in the distance, bells of various sizes and timbres, some tinny, some luminous, some deeply resonant. The total agglomeration is never transposed. The second half of the song, from m. 224, presents a second static construct, likewise untransposed to the end, comprising four trichords (1-1) disposed symmetrically except for occasional octave transferences in the uppermost trichord (ex. 3.5b).

3.5   Harmonic reduction of 'Dzwony cerkiewne'

The instrumental resources of the second version of the Iłłakowicz songs (1958) afforded Lutosławski considerable enhancement of the text-painting effects of the piano version. String glissandi are used discreetly in 'Wiatr' to make the wind sound even more impetuous, to make the winter landscape even icier in 'Zima'. The fusion in 'Morze' of a static harmonic texture with the gently lapping wave sounds of the original piano version (now augmented by both harps) is more successful with the strings providing a truly legato, attack-less background, and the addition of the harps, two cymbals, and tam-tam is especially effective in the depiction of the church bells of 'Dzwony cerkiewne'. The chamber version shows the beginnings of an attempt to wed specific harmonic colors to particular instrumental groupings. Thus the first song employs strings, harps, and piano; the second adds percussion; the third uses only strings playing *sempre pianissimo e non vibrato*; and the fourth is set entirely for harps, piano, and percussion, exploiting the attack characteristics of these instruments. The first half of the final song, marked *soave*, uses only strings and harps while the text describes the bells as 'singing'; when in the second half the bells thunder angrily (*rude*), piano and metal percussion are added. The relationship between the structural use of timbre groups and the form-articulating role of harmonic processes in the songs is undeniably crude by comparison with Lutosławski's later achievement, but it is not different in kind.

The growing mastery of pitch demonstrated in the Iłłakowicz songs was not immediately apparent to the public, since the first performance was to take place only somewhat later. A more immediate effect was made by *Muzyka żałobna* (Music of Mourning) for string orchestra, completed early in 1958. The work required a full four years to germinate; Lutosławski began sketching it as early as 1954, after the conductor Jan Krenz suggested that he write a piece commemorating the tenth anniversary of Bartók's death (1955). *Muzyka żałobna* thus was in progress at the same time as the Iłłakowicz songs; but it is rather different from that work as regards both technical procedures and significance for the composer's development. Whereas the songs bear directly on Lutosławski's late style, *Muzyka żałobna* is both a more radical departure of Lutosławski and at the same time more closely bound up with his style of the early fifties. In this sense the work is pivotal, and certainly as regards the external aspect of Lutosławski's career its immediate success in Europe was of the greatest importance. But its distinctive feature, the application of limited serial techniques in quite novel ways, is an experiment he has never really repeated, and in this sense Edward Cowie is right to call the work a 'diversion' from the main stream of the composer's stylistic evolution.[12]

The work's four sections group themselves into a ternary arch: in the center a development section (the Metamorphoses) with its culmination (Apogeum), flanked by a Prologue and Epilogue which constitute the actual mourning music referred to in the title.[13] The Prologue unfolds as a series of isorhythmic canons on a *talea* of seventeen durations occupying twenty-three beats (ex. 3.6). Six successive canons are played out on this rhythmic theme, with the first canon in two voices, the second in three, the third in four, the fourth in six, and the fifth and sixth in eight voices.

3.6   Rhythmic theme (*talea*) of the Prologue, *Muzyka żałobna*

The pitch material is supplied by an invariant twenty-four-note *color* comprising a twelve-member series and its inversion at the tritone (ex. 3.7). Every canonic voice uses either this untransposed version or its transposition at the tritone. The singular construction of this series by alternating interval classes 6 and 1 (tritone and semitone) is particularly appropriate in a work dedicated to Bartók, since pitch motives juxtaposing tritone and semitone are important in that composer's music (e.g., Fourth String Quartet). But it is important to note that Lutosławski did not attempt a deliberate stylistic homage to Bartók in Muzyka żałobna; if there are traces of Bartók's influence or stylistic coincidences, they were present in Lutosławski's own language long before 1954. This particular tritone-plus-semitone construction, for example, had fascinated Lutosławski for a very long time; it appears in the Two Etudes, the Paganini Variations, the First Symphony, the Overture for Strings, and other early works. In Muzyka żałobna its purpose is to produce a harmony devoid of thirds, i.e. including as simultaneities interval classes 0, 1, 2, 5, and 6, but excluding 3 and 4. Beginning with the fourth canon, interval class 4 (but never 3) does occasionally occur vertically (compare, for example, violin IV and cello II in m. 17), but the aural effect of a great, gray mass of shifting tritones and fourths is not disturbed. Combined with the steady expansion of the texture upwards and continuous growth in the dynamic level, the canonic opening, which seemed at first abstract and impersonal, acquires an inexorable momentum of its own and becomes, finally, utterly gripping. An intense emotional result has been achieved through primarily intellectual means.

3.7   Pitch theme (color) of the Prologue, Muzyka żałobna

The composer recalls that, having planned in general this method of achieving the emotional tenor of the Prologue, he then made no fewer than eight complete versions of this section in a single day. In the version which has survived in the finished work, the color is heard 4 times (96 pitches). Where the fifth color statement would begin (m. 29, first cello and contrabasses), the sixth talea statement (in progress) is interrupted after only 11 durations (5 × 17 = 85 + 11 = 96). A new process now begins. A four-voice augmentation canon using only the pitches B and F (the first two notes of the basic series) played at four speeds is succeeded by an eight-voice stretto in which the original series is imitated at the tritone (P-0, P-6). Then the augmentation canon is inverted both texturally and intervallically and is followed by the inversion of the stretto (I-6 now imitated by I-0), and finally by the augmentation canon restored to its original configuration and now extended:

Prologue: Synopsis

m.	1	Rhythmic canon 1 (two voices)	p
	6	Rhythmic canon 2 (three voices)	mp

11	Rhythmic canon 3 (four voices)	mf
16	Rhythmic canon 4 (six voices)	quasi f
21	Rhythmic canon 5 (eight voices)	f
26	Rhythmic canon 6 (incomplete; eight voices)	f (basses added)
29	Augmentation canon, rectus (four voices)	ff
33	Stretto, rectus, on P-0, P-6 (eight voices)	mf
37	Augmentation canon, inversus (four voices)	ff
41	Stretto, inversus, on I-6, I-0 (eight voices)	mf
45–58	Augmentation canon, rectus (four voices, gradually reduced to one)	ff to pp

The existence of a twelve-tone series underlying these operations has given rise to the widespread but quite erroneous notion that *Muzyka żałobna* inaugurated a 'serial period' in Lutosławski's work. In fact neither in this work nor since has the composer ever adopted 'classical' twelve-tone technique, and he has made explicit his own view of the subject:

[my technique] has nothing in common with either twelve-tone technique or with serial music. The only common trait is the 'chromatic whole.' I consider serial music to be a phenomenon of the first order in the history of music. But that method has led to effects which are absolutely foreign to me, and this is why it is difficult for me to believe that I could one day draw close to it. To tell the truth, everything I write lacks any connection with the Viennese tradition (Schoenberg, Webern).[14]

Schönberg's principles were among other things intended to replace functional harmony. I have never been interested in that goal. The use of a row had to serve a difficult purpose: to create a special kind of harmony. . . In reality, then, *Funeral Music* has very little to do with twelve-tone music.[15]

The Metamorphoses are constructed according to quite different and very complicated processes uniting diatonic and chromatic musics in a way which is analogous to the union of diatonic themes with chromatic harmony and counterpoint in the Concerto for Orchestra. The composer has confessed that he felt a bit at sea in his suddenly acquired stylistic freedom, and that retaining the old diatonic-chromatic principle from earlier works was a way of easing the transition. The music progresses through the dialectical interaction of three textural elements: a principal melodic line determined quite strictly by the logic of a precompositional scheme, and in which the actual 'metamorphosis' of pitch material from the Prologue takes place; a freely composed subordinate melodic line; and a 'harmonic continuo'

(Lutosławski's term) which is freely composed but which follows roughly the rule of complementarity (i.e., pitch classes are seldom duplicated from one chord to the next).

In the twelve metamorphoses the specialized serialism of the Prologue becomes the basis for an even more idiosyncratic (and utterly un-Viennese) procedure. The principal line of each metamorphosis is based on one complete statement of the basic series. The first uses the series at its original pitch level (on F; t = 0); each succeeding metamorphosis transposes the series down by a perfect fifth. Thus the second begins on A-sharp (t = 5), the third on D-sharp (t = 10), and so on. To each pitch of the basic series are then added pitches of a diatonic mode comprising two conjunct tetrachords (1-2-2), i.e. a 'Locrian' scale, in which semitone and tritone are naturally prominent (ex. 3.8). This procedure gives the composer a collection of twelve modal pitch segments beginning on the twelve pitch classes of the series from which to construct the melodic line. The segments are, of course, ordered according to the original series, but each segment is internally unordered, so that the series pitch which begins it does not necessarily appear first. The first metamorphosis adds only one modal pitch to each series pitch, but later metamorphoses add more and more pitches until, from metamorphosis VII on, each segment contains all seven pitches of the mode.[16] Excerpts from the principal melodic line are analyzed in ex. 3.9 to illustrate their construction according to modal segments. (The modal segments are bracketed, the order numbers of the original series pitches are circled, and only those voices contributing to the principal melodic line are shown.)

3.8   Scale, Metamorphoses, *Muzyka żałobna*

The relation of the three textural elements – principal and subordinate lines and harmonic continuo – is a complex one. At first the three are kept distinctly, audibly separate; e.g., in metamorphosis I the principal line is in the violas, the subordinate line in the double-basses, and the harmonic continuo in the violins. But as the work gathers density and complexity, these three elements begin to interpenetrate each other registrally and in terms of orchestration until it becomes impossible to distinguish them by ear, as illustrated in ex. 3.10.

The subordinate line for each metamorphosis begins some measures

Metamorphosis I, mm. 65-72 (t = 0; 1 pitch added)

Metamorphosis IV, mm. 101-7 (t = 3; 3 pitches added)

Metamorphosis VI, mm. 129-34 (t = 1; 5 pitches added)

Metamorphosis XI, mm. 215-17 (t = 2; 6 pitches added)

3.9 Excerpts from the principal melodic line of the Metamorphoses, *Muzyka żałobna*

before the principal line sets in. This constant overlapping is only one of the factors which combine to create enormous directional tension as the Metamorphoses section progresses. Another is the character of the principal line itself: the additive process by which its pitches are generated, the progressive rise in dynamic level, and the continuous increase in rhythmic activity from minims to semiquavers. The other elements support this rise in tension. The subordinate line passes from diatonic to largely chromatic and undergoes a rhythmic transformation similar to that of the principal line. The harmonic continuo begins 'consonantly', emphasizing interval classes 2 and 5, and becomes increasingly dissonant, finally emphasizing all-interval chords; at the same time it thickens from dyads (metamorphosis I) to trichords (metamorphosis III) and pentachords (IV) to hexachords. The confluence of all these processes of growth produces an aggregate dynamic profile which rises steadily to culminate in the Apogeum. An important stage in this process is reached at metamorphosis VII, where simultaneously the circle-of-fifths trans-

3.10 Muzyka żałobna (m. 218)

position scheme of the basic series reaches its midpoint, the tritone (t = 6); all six modal pitches are added to each melodic segment for the first time; semiquavers appear for the first time; and all six interval classes are used in the harmonic continuo. All of this is summarized in the table on p. 76.

The goal of the Metamorphoses section and the climax of the work is the Apogeum, a tremendous outcry of grief and protest that fairly shudders in its intensity. Here twelve-note chords appear for the only time in the work. They are of two sorts, founded on the two basic intervals of the piece: widely spaced chords in which the tritone is prominent, and dense clusters of semitones.[17] The chords of the Apogeum contract gradually to the unison A that begins the Epilogue's poignant unison statement of the basic series (t = 4).

The Epilogue then approximately reverses the order of the Prologue in a shortened version: augmentation canon (inversus) on pitches B and F in four voices, stretto on I-6 in seven voices, augmentation canon (rectus) in four voices, and a succession of isorhythmic canons in eight, six, four, and two voices. Here the *color* for the isorhythmic

Metamorphoses: Synopsis

Mm.	No.	Principal Melodic Line — Pitch level of series; transposition	No. pitches in modal segments	Prevailing rhythmic value	Subordinate Line — Mm.	Harmonic Continuo — Prevailing interval classes
65–76	I	F; t = 0	1 + 1	♩	59–72	2, 5
77–85	II	A♯; t = 5	1 + 2	♩	72–82	2, 5
86–100	III	D♯; t = 10	1 + 3	♩	84–93	2, 3, 4, 5
101–13	IV	G♯; t = 3	1 + 3	♩	94–108	2, 3, 4, 5
113–28	V	C♯; t = 8	1 + 4	♪	108–20	2, 3, 4, 5
129–40	VI	F♯; t = 1	1 + 5	♪	121–36	2, 3, 4, 5, 6
142–56	VII	B; t = 6	1 + 6	♪	137–50	1, 2, 3, 4, 5, 6
157–69	VIII	E; t = 11	1 + 6	♪	150–62	1, 2, 3, 4, 5, 6
169–93	IX	A; t = 4	1 + 6	♪	163–84	1, 2, 3, 4, 5, 6
194–214	X	D; t = 9	1 + 6	♪	183–205	1, 2, 3, 4, 5, 6
215–25	XI	G; t = 2	1 + 6	♪	205–21	1, 2, 4, 5, 6
226–33	XII	C; t = 7	1 + 6	♪	222–33	1, 2, 5, 6

canons is the inverse of that used in the Prologue, i.e. I-6 followed by P-0. The work ends with solo cello, still playing the *talea* and *color*, twice interrupted by ghostly echos (actually six-voice stretti on pitches 15-19 and 20-4 of the *color*) in the violins and violas. The solo cello repeats the last four notes of I-6, then the last three, finally a lone A-sharp and E punctuated by silence. Thus the Epilogue, rather than duplicating the atmosphere of the Prologue, performs a very different dramatic function – as indeed it must do following the explosion of the Apogeum. It is an echo of the work's despairing tone, an expression of quiet sadness and ultimately, in the solo cello, of resignation.

Jan Krenz and the radio orchestra gave the first performance of *Muzyka żałobna* in Katowice, 26 March 1958, and the work was repeated at the second Warsaw Autumn in September. The response was extraordinary. For Jarociński the work was confirmation of Lutosławski's pre-eminence among Polish composers. Rather pointedly (in view of Lutosławski's recent treatment in his own country) Jarociński wrote:

I daresay it is time at long last to realize that not since the days of Szymanowski has there been in Poland a composer who could so deeply understand his own strivings, who could with such courage and determination attack the most difficult musical problems of his age, and who could equal Lutosławski in artistic achievement. One would have to be dull-witted and have film over one's eyes or envy in one's heart not to see what calibre of creative artist is this who now dwells among us.[18]

Foreign critics were no less favorably impressed. *Muzyka żałobna* was widely acclaimed as the outstanding work at the 1958 Warsaw Autumn, and for many it was the first clear indication that Polish composers had escaped the Soviet sphere of cultural influence and were 'setting themselves far different tasks than providing catchy tunes for the proletariat'.[19]

The work was performed in Minneapolis, Boston, Cleveland, and other American cities in 1959 and at the twenty-second Venice Biennale the same year. In February 1960 a concert of twentieth-century Polish music given for the participants at the first International Musicological Chopin Congress in Warsaw included, besides *Muzyka żałobna*, the First Violin Concerto (1916) of Szymanowski, Baird's *Four Essays* (1958), and Serocki's Sinfonietta for two string orchestras (1958). In 1961 the work was given in London (the Proms), Utrecht, Paris ('Domaine musicale'), Strasbourg, Prague, Berlin, and Basel, and the composer's international reputation was growing quickly.

The formidable impact *Muzyka żałobna* had on other composers around 1960 was due in part to the historical situation. Fascination with Webern-inspired serialism had begun to pall, and chance techniques and theater music had arisen as rivals to it. The undogmatic and humanistic modernism of *Muzyka żałobna* and other Polish scores, such as Baird's *Four Essays*, must have seemed an attractive alternative. *Muzyka żałobna* cannot have seemed up-to-date by comparison with Stockhausen's *Zyklus*, Varése's *Poème électronique*, Nono's *Coro di Didone*, or Boulez's Third Sonata. But Lutosławski's authentic originality and his successful mastery of complex organizational means in the service of powerful emotional expression made an immediate and strong impression. And as the other countries of Eastern Europe began (somewhat later than Poland) to 'thaw', their composers were stimulated by the Polish example. Péter Várnai reports that as Hungarian composers began to abandon folklorism they were especially influenced by *Muzyka żałobna* and the Baird *Essays*, which 'infiltrated' Hungary immediately.[20]

Lutosławski's career prospered in other ways as well. On 15 January 1959 he received the annual prize of the ZKP, and in May of that year he shared first prize for *Muzyka żałobna* with Baird (*Four Essays*) in the Tribune Internationale des Compositeurs of UNESCO. On 16 August he was elected to the executive council of the ISCM; in September he served on a composers' competition jury in Liège, and in October he attended the Donaueschingen festival.

Meanwhile the works of the folklore period spread abroad; the Concerto for Orchestra, for example, was performed in Cleveland in 1958 and in New York on 1 January 1961 to generally favorable reaction. (Not everyone liked the work, though; a New York critic wrote that 'its materials are flimsy, its form distended, and its style turgid and rhetorical'.)[21] In Poland the First Symphony was rehabilitated in May 1959. The same year Lutosławski joined the organizing and program committees of the Warsaw Autumn. The first version of the Five Songs was given its first performance by Krystyna Szostek-Radkowa on 25 November 1959; and the same artist, joined in Katowice by Krenz and the radio orchestra, gave the première of the orchestral version on 12 February 1960. In June of 1960 Lutosławski was in Cologne for the annual ISCM festival, where he was elected vice-president. In September he attended a composers' conference in Dubrovnik, and in October he judged the Reine Marie-José competition in Geneva. On 18 January 1961 he became president of the Polish section of the ISCM.

The remaining composition of the transition period has a curiously circuitous history. Lutosławski began work on an orchestral postlude in 1958 and by 1960 had substantially completed it. By 1959 the idea had grown to a four-movement symphonic cycle: three short movements followed by a larger finale which would resolve the tensions aroused by the inconclusive character of the earlier movements – precisely the plan, incidentally, which he was to realize with signal success in the *Livre pour orchestre* of 1968. The second and third movements were written in 1960, and sketches for the finale were under way when Lutosławski abandoned the project. For although he had made great strides in handling pitch organization, solutions to some rhythmic and formal questions still eluded him. At this stylistic impasse the three largely completed movements were shelved, and the sketches for the fourth lay unused until in 1966 he incorporated them in the Second Symphony. When in 1963 the International Red Cross invited the composer to contribute a composition to its centenary celebration, he returned to the manuscript of the original postlude, retouching it slightly. The Postlude, subtitled *Per humanitatem ad pacem* for the occasion, was first performed in Geneva's Grand Théâtre on 1 September 1963, by Ernest Ansermet and the Orchestre de la Suisse Romande, along with two other works honoring the centenary, Frank Martin's *Inter arma caritas*, a short piece for orchestra, and Benjamin Britten's *Cantata Misericordium*. It was published separately in 1964 and performed in Warsaw in May of that year under Jan Krenz. Subsequently the composer resurrected the other two movements, the whole was performed in Cracow on 8 October 1965 conducted by Henryk Czyż, and the set was published together in 1966 as Three Postludes.

The Three Postludes are altogether a less satisfactory work than the Iłłakowicz songs or *Muzyka żałobna*; indeed they reveal rather clearly the sort of stylistic problems which caused the composer to abandon the fourth movement in 1960. Postlude no. 1 is performed occasionally; the second and third are almost never heard. Lutosławski has called the cycle a 'farewell' to the orchestra, explaining: 'At that time I had already realized that the symphony orchestra has no prospects for further evolution, that its heyday had long since passed.'[22] In fact he has since written seven works for large orchestra, seven more farewells. But the Postludes are certainly retrospective in character. Each movement is somehow connected with an earlier work: the first with 'Morze' from the Five Songs, the second with the 'blurred toccata' style of the Capriccio notturno in the Concerto for Orchestra, the third perhaps with the First Symphony (especially the first episode of the postlude with the transition music of the symphony's finale). But there are many signs pointing to the future as well. The blurred toccata style of the second postlude develops that of the Concerto for Orchestra in the direction of the second movement of

Jeux vénitiens; the association of small groups of instruments with characteristic intervals in the first postlude presages the first movement of the Second Symphony; the formal experiment in the last postlude points the way to the finales of Jeux vénitiens and Livre pour orchestre.

The most successfully realized movement is the first. There are three sections: a static opening; a transitional crescendo, climax, and rapid falling off; and a static close. A kind of 'harmonic continuo' based on three different models of pitch generation – systematic but not serial – underlies the whole. As in Muzyka żałobna, the character of this harmonic continuo is carefully controlled so as to shape the emotional direction of the music; thus the first section is 'consonant', the transitional crescendo much less so, and the climax 'dissonant'. The first section's harmonic background, in the strings, consists of two complementary hexachords, each of which can be derived as a series of perfect fifths. At each appearance, each hexachord is stated in two symmetrical arrangements, the second derived by octave transfer. One complete statement of the two hexachords in the strings constitutes a kind of harmonic color occupying thirteen measures; this color occurs three times. Rhythmically this harmonic background is expressed through four playings of a ten-measure talea.

Above this seemingly static continuo appears a succession of four phrases of intervallically constructed melodic fragments (unrelated to the strings' harmony) given to four instrumental groups in turn: oboe and piano (seconds), mm. 2-11; trumpet and harp (thirds), mm. 12-21; piccolo, flute, xylophone, and celesta (tritones and minor ninths), mm. 22-31; and finally clarinet, bass clarinet, and piano (perfect fourths and fifths), mm. 32-41. Each of these instrumental groups plays a ten-measure talea:

In the second section of the movement the brass take over the harmonic function, while the thematic semiquaver rhythms are transferred to the percussion. The brass present a set of more dissonant symmetrical hexachords which are not complementary but rather share a small number of invariant pitch classes. The harmonic succession is constructed vertically according to a scheme of progressively contracting interval classes:

i.c.   5   6   5   4   3 | 5 | 3
       6   5   4   3   2 | 3 | 2
       5   6   5   4   3 | 5 | 3
       6   5   4   3   2 | 3 | 2
       5   6   5   4   3 | 5 | 3

The strings interrupt at m. 54 with a new version of their fifths-
derived hexachord (enclosed in the rectangle above). By contrast,
then, the harmonic material of the climax and closing section is
generated entirely through semitone 'clusters'. The harmonic background of the entire movement is sketched in example 3.11.

3.11   Reduction of the harmonic background of Three Postludes, no. 1

The four instrumental groups of the first section return in the last,
but their phrases are now presented simultaneously instead of in
succession. Moreover, although for each instrument the small semiquaver figures of the original *talea* remain intact, the rests between
them have been altered so as to grow progressively longer for each
instrumental group according to a precisely arithmetic regime:[23]

	duration of rests, in semiquavers								
oboe	8	4	9	6	4	6	6	24	9
trumpet	10	6	13	10	10	12	14	32	19
piccolo, flute	12	8	17	14	16	18	22	40	29
clarinet, bass									
clarinet	14	10	21	18	22	24	30	48	39
	(+2	+2	+4	+4	+6	+6	+8	+8	+10)

Thus transformed, the four *talea* statements combine to form a sort of mensuration canon yielding a phrase of ten measures for the oboe, fifteen for trumpet, eighteen for piccolo and flute, and twenty-three for clarinet and bass clarinet. It is typical of the later works of Lutosławski that he should construct so careful an arithmetic scheme governing a rhythmic process, and that what at first blush might appear coldly calculating is in fact motivated by purely musical intentions. Here the effect the composer was after was a comparatively dense beginning as the canon commences at the beginning of the final section followed by a gradual rarefaction of texture, until at last the bass clarinet is left to finish the movement alone. It is as if, having exhausted all its energy in the middle section, the work trails off into silence.

Lutosławski's predilection, as in the Concerto for Orchestra, for employing texture as a form-articulating element takes on in the Three Postludes a more radical guise, what Butsko has aptly called 'textural thematicism'.[24] All the qualities of musical textures – register, registral spread, timbre, microrhythmic character, etc. – are called into play to function in place of traditional thematic processes. The third postlude, though it includes episodes of traditionally thematic cast, is perceived fundamentally as a succession of contrasting textural blocks, each with its own characteristic tempo, scoring, and rhythmic profile. After ten such episodes have been stated in full, they are stated again, now shortened and fragmented; yet again, reduced to two bars each; and finally reduced to one bar each. Throughout the movement the onset of each new section is marked by a fortissimo orchestral chord, staccato. This first explicit attempt by Lutosławski at a formal (i.e., macrorhythmic) accelerando of the type we shall meet again in the works of the sixties remains an interesting failure, but it does show with striking clarity that the composer was but a short step from the world of *Jeux vénitiens*. Nordwall has characterized the Postludes, and especially the third, thus:

The composer makes three increasingly ambitious but equally fruitless attempts to make headway, and finally lets them become an increasingly affirmative emphasis of the nonaffirmative and unfinished and finally impossible – a private documentation of a profound stylistic crisis.

... The merciless contraction of the music [in the last movement] has in it something inhumanly mechanical: it is no organic process, but can be seen as the result of outside pressure. The title 'Postludes' does not appear to need any particular motivation, and this movement is placed quite rightly at the end of the work like a brutally formulated final comment on an irrevocably concluded style period.[25]

'Unfinished and finally impossible', indeed. For in 1960 Lutosławski set out on a very new artistic adventure.

4 The years of maturity: 1960–79

What caused Lutosławski to break off work on the Three Postludes in 1960 was a chance encounter with the music of John Cage through a radio broadcast:

It was in that year that I heard an excerpt from his *Piano Concerto* [i.e., *Concert for Piano and Orchestra* (1958)] and those few minutes were to change my life decisively. It was a strange moment, but I can explain what happened.

Composers often do not hear the music that is being played; it only serves as an impulse for something quite different – for the creation of music that only lives in their imagination. It is a sort of schizophrenia – we are listening to something and at the same time creating something else.

That is how it happened with Cage's *Piano Concerto*. While listening to it, I suddenly realized that I could compose music differently from that of my past. That I could progress toward the whole not from the little detail but the other way round – I could start out from the chaos and create order in it, gradually.[1]

There was no question of imitating the Cage *Concert*, a work in which the sequence, number, and even the character of events is indeterminate: Lutosławski remains to this day philosophically opposed to music in which the composer surrenders direct control of the musical material or the form. Indeed on rehearing the *Piano Concert* later he reacted quite differently. But that first hearing served as a catalyst, and in that moment the composer grasped the solution that had been eluding him: the introduction of a limited degree of freedom in realizing the rhythmic physiognomy of polyphonic textures.

The breakthrough work with which the third major style period commenced was *Jeux vénitiens* (1960–1). The conductor Andrzej Markowski had asked for a chamber-orchestra piece to take to the 1961 Venice Biennale. Always a slow worker, Lutosławski completed only a preliminary version of the first, second, and fourth movements in time for the festival; these were played in Venice's Teatro la Fenice on 24 April 1961 by the Chamber Orchestra of the Cracow Philharmonic under Markowski. Over the summer Lutosławski revised these movements and finished the third, and the final version was conducted by Witold Rowicki at the Warsaw Autumn, 16 September 1961.

Since 1958 *Muzyka żałobna* had brought the composer considerable attention abroad; with *Jeux vénitiens* his position among the world's leading composers was confirmed. During the first half of 1961, for example, more than thirty performances of major works took place abroad. The composer was invited to lecture at the Zagreb Festival of Contemporary Music, where he spoke (in French) on 19 May 1961 on 'The Evolution of Contemporary Musical Language'.[2]

As the result of a telephone invitation from Aaron Copland, in the summer of 1962 Lutosławski made his first visit to the United States, where he spent a busy and fruitful three months. For eight weeks he conducted the composition course at the Berkshire Music Center (Tanglewood) in western Massachusetts. For the course Lutosławski prepared a cycle of four formal lectures: an introduction summarizing historical developments since the nineteenth century, a discussion of rhythmic problems in new music, an address on the problem of constructing large-scale form in the twentieth century, and an explanation of his own approach to pitch organization and harmony in the context of limited aleatorism. He met many American composers that summer at Tanglewood, including Iain Hamilton, Lukas Foss, Leon Kirchner, Irving Fine, and Arthur Berger. After Tanglewood Lutosławski traveled for four weeks under the sponsorship of the International Institute for Education, visiting many of the centers of musical activity in the US. His itinerary included Los Angeles, San Francisco, and Minneapolis; he also visited the electronic studio at the University of Illinois, where he met Lejaren Hiller, and the Columbia–Princeton Electronic Music Center, where he met Milton Babbitt. In New York Lutosławski saw two distinguished émigrés, poet Kazimierz Wierzyński and composer Michał Kondracki, and, best of all, he met the seventy-nine-year-old Edgard Varèse.

While he was abroad Lutosławski received the prize of the Polish Minister of Culture and Arts, class I, 22 July 1962. The same year the composer was again honored by the Tribune Internationale des Compositeurs, this time for *Jeux vénitiens*. The new work had its American première on 14 December in Minneapolis. In 1963 Lutosławski was elected to the Swedish Royal Academy of Music. In August of that year, at the invitation of William Glock of the BBC, he lectured at Britain's Dartington Summer School of Music. While in Britain he gave a talk over BBC Radio entitled 'Is It Music?'[3] In November 1963 Lutosławski took first prize in an international competition sponsored jointly by UNESCO's International Music Council and the

Gesellschaft der Musikfreunde, Vienna, for a Danish State Radio Orchestra recording of the Concerto for Orchestra.

A number of foreign commissions were by now being offered to Lutosławski. The town of Hagen in West Germany commissioned an orchestral work as early as 1962; several years later *Livre pour orchestre* would result. In 1963 the composer accepted a commission from the Koussevitzky Foundation, though nothing ever came of this one. By this time Lutosławski had also accepted a Swedish Radio commission for his String Quartet, and he was already planning a work for the tenor Peter Pears. But the first of the new commissions to be completed was the work requested by Slavko Zlatić and the Zagreb Radio Choir to be performed at the 1963 Zagreb Biennale. Lutosławski had begun in late 1961 (after finishing the revised *Jeux vénitiens*) to plan the general shape of the work; by 1962 he had chosen the poetry and at Tanglewood began to write out in detail the first movement of *Trois poèmes d'Henri Michaux*.

The finished work calls for twenty-part chorus of solo voices and orchestra of winds, two pianos, harp, and percussion; two conductors are required. At the première on 9 May 1963 Zlatić conducted the chorus while the composer conducted the orchestra, making his first appearance in this role for nearly twenty years. *Trois poèmes* was an overwhelming success, winning Lutosławski new admirers among foreign critics; one British writer thought the work displayed 'a talent of exceptional calibre which dwarfed most of the novelties at Zagreb'.[4] Lutosławski again lectured at the festival, talking about the recent trends in Polish music, and he participated in a panel discussion with Gunther Schuller, Luigi Nono, and Alois Hába, finding himself in the awkward position of defending Cage against attacks by the other panel members. *Trois poèmes* was repeated at the Warsaw Autumn in September 1963, and for a time it became the composer's most famous piece. Visiting Poland with Stravinsky in 1965, Robert Craft took the work to be 'Polish music's current pop-modern display piece'[5] – whatever that may mean.

Lutosławski continued to take an active part in the leadership of the ISCM. He was re-elected to the executive board at the festival of June 1963, held in Amsterdam; in January 1964 he served on festival juries in Copenhagen and Rome. That summer he again taught at Dartington. He continued to accumulate honors: for the 1963 Warsaw Autumn recording of *Trois poèmes*, a jury consisting of composers Luciano Berio and Leon Kirchner and critic Alfred Frankenstein awarded Lutosławski the Koussevitzky Prix Mondial du Disque on 27 May 1964; and on 22 July 1964, the twentieth anniversary of the Polish People's Republic, he received the State Prize for music, class I.

He was by this time traveling extensively for performances of his music, and sometimes conducting, as at the French première of *Trois poèmes* in November 1964. In January 1965 he visited Prague for the Czech première of the same work and made a great impression there.

Lutosławski composed his only string quartet in 1964 to satisfy a commission from the Swedish Radio celebrating the tenth anniversary of its concert series 'Nutida Musik'. His recently developed technique of aleatory counterpoint was to be applied here in its purest form; in fact, the composer originally planned to prepare parts only, since the players are independent of each other much of the time, making the traditional score format meaningless. Since it is Lutosławski's habit to attack a new composition at its most difficult point, the longer and more complex second movement was ready first, in November; and the introductory first movement was in the hands of the LaSalle Quartet, to whom the first performance had been entrusted, the following month. The LaSalle, accustomed to playing contemporary works from score, complained when none was forthcoming. Finally, after considerable correspondence on the subject, the composer agreed to provide a study score of sorts. His wife, Danuta, whose architectural training made her an excellent draftswoman, has done most of his copying in recent years, and it was she who pasted together strips cut from the individual parts to make a sort of score in which each independent voice is enclosed in a rectangular 'box'.

Lutosławski met the members of the LaSalle Quartet in a Helsinki hotel room a few days before the première to coach them on the new work. But when they played through it for him, he found that they had already understood his intentions perfectly. The performance in Stockholm on 12 March 1965 was a great success, 'the most significant contribution not only to this anniversary celebration but to the New Music generally'.[6] While in Stockholm Lutosławski lectured in the composition seminar of the Royal Academy on his technique of aleatory counterpoint.[7] The LaSalle repeated the Quartet later that year at the Donaueschinger Musiktage and at the Warsaw Autumn. In the years since, this piece has established itself firmly in the repertory, despite the fact that the uncompromising nature of its musical language places it among the least readily accessible of his recent compositions.

Lutosławski had been working at the same time on Peter Pears's commission, a proposal he had accepted eagerly on account of his admiration for the great English tenor. As he had done before with the Michaux poems, the composer turned for a text to French, his first foreign language and the only one he feels close enough to to set to music. (Indeed, this state of affairs is only natural among educated Poles of Lutosławski's generation, since, as in prerevolutionary Russia, French was still the language of culture and the expected 'first language' during the composer's gimnazjum days.) After reading through a large quantity of poetry, he chanced on the perfect text for his purposes, Jean-François Chabrun's 'Quatre tapisseries pour la Châtelaine de Vergi', from which he fashioned Paroles tissées, a four-movement work for harp, piano, percussion, strings, and voice — not a song cycle in the traditional sense, but a chamber work in which the voice is an equal participant. Lutosławski conducted Pears and the Philomusica of London in the première at the Aldeburgh Festival, 20 June 1965. The work was scheduled for Warsaw Autumns of 1966, 1967, and 1968, but each time the work had to be withdrawn because of difficulties with Pears's schedule. Ultimately a different soloist, the Belgian tenor Louis Devos, sang the Polish première at an all-Lutosławski concert on 16 February 1968, with the composer conducting.

At the invitation of Mario di Bonaventura, the composer made his second visit to the United States to spend two weeks at the Congregation of the Arts at Dartmouth's Hopkins Center in July 1966. There he heard performances of many of his works, including the Concerto for Orchestra, Muzyka żałobna, the String Quartet, and Paroles tissées (sung by Robert Jones). Afterward he went to Austin for a short seminar at the University of Texas; and in New York he received the Alfred Jurzykowski Foundation prize and heard the Concerto for Orchestra performed in Carnegie Hall by the American Symphony Orchestra.

The composer was now being offered more commissions than he could accept. He wanted the freedom to pursue his creative course independent of external pressures and so began accepting only those commissions which coincided with his own aims at any moment. Following Paroles tissées he planned to write a large symphonic work, his first since the Concerto for Orchestra, and thus readily agreed when the Norddeutscher Rundfunk of Hamburg proposed that he write a work to celebrate the one-hundredth concert of its series 'Das neue Werk'. Lutosławski set to work in the summer of 1965, nearly twenty-five years after beginning the First Symphony, on the second (and more challenging) movement of a two-movement Second Symphony. Not atypically, though, he was unable to complete the entire piece in time for the scheduled première on 18 October 1966. Still, he was reluctant to default on his promise to the Norddeutscher Rundfunk and so allowed the completed second movement, 'Direct', to be performed as an independent piece by the radio's orchestra, with Pierre Boulez conducting. He wrote afterwards (1967), that

the warm reception accorded the piece by the Hamburg audience and by those who had come to the gala concert from many parts did not however relieve my deep sense of regret that I was able to present merely part, merely the torso, of my work and therefore did not give the audience a full picture of what I had undertaken to do.[8]

The first movement, 'Hésitant', was finished the following spring. The composer conducted the first complete performance as part of an all-Lutosławski program in Katowice on 9 June 1967 and conducted it again at the eleventh Warsaw Autumn that fall. The German première of the entire symphony took place only in 1968, in Baden-Baden under Ernest Bour.

Honors continued to be proffered from all quarters. The Freie Akademie der Künste in Hamburg elected Lutosławski an honorary member during his visit there for the first performance of the Second Symphony finale and on 16 October 1966 awarded him its annual *Plakette*, citing his role as a 'bridge' between old and new musical styles and his leadership in the reconstruction of musical life in postwar Poland. The composer addressed the academy on the problems of combining historical and analytical studies with creative activity.[9] In 1967 he received the Gottfried von Herder Prize from the University of Vienna, and in August of that year he was given the Léonie Sonning Prize in Copenhagen 'in recognition and admiration of his mastery as a composer, which is a source of inspiration to the musical life of our age'. The award was presented at an all-Lutosławski concert as part of the Royal Danish Festival of Music and Ballet celebrating the 800th anniversary of Copenhagen's founding. In 1968 he was made an extraordinary member of the Akademie der Künste in West Berlin, and in May of that year he collected for the third time the first prize of the Tribune des Compositeurs in Paris, for the Second Symphony.

In matters of pitch choice and the control of rhythmic texture, Lutosławski's style was by now firmly established. Although he tried to make each work somehow 'new', he did have a sort of repertoire of pitch procedures and a secure mastery of his own harmonic language, and his conquest of the new technical domains of limited aleatorism and aleatory counterpoint was complete. His restless musical intellect turned during the sixties to exploring new conceptions of musical form – a subject which had long fascinated him, but which could now claim more of his attention. When in 1968 he took up the long-standing orchestral commission from the town of Hagen, he took the opportunity to revive the formal scheme he had tried and abandoned in 1960 with the Postludes. He decided to write a suite of independent symphonic movements of varying lengths and characters, a *Livre pour orchestre* in the tradition of the Baroque clavecin *livres* and *Orgelbüchlein*. The creative momentum established during work on the Second Symphony carried the composer quickly through the preparation of the new work, and the finished *Livre* has much in common, particularly in its final *chapitre*, with the preceding work. But the composer realized on completing the piece that its four 'chapters' were not nearly so unrelated as he had planned: 'my instinctive sense of form sometimes makes itself felt against my wishes . . . When I finished it, it was much too organized, against my will, and the title no longer corresponded to the character of the piece . . . I asked those who commissioned the work to change the title but it was too late – [the concert program] was already printed.'[10] The première was given on 18 November 1968 by the city orchestra in Hagen, conducted by Berthold Lehmann. The composer recalls the modest circumstances: 'the orchestra prepared with great care but fought with obvious difficulties. Practically nobody knew of the event, only those who were present.'[11] A Lutosławski première is an event bound to attract attention, though, even when it takes place outside the well-worn festival circuit, and critics did not neglect the Hagen performance. Horst Kniese called *Livre* a 'masterpiece',[12] and other reviewers were similarly lavish. Shorter, more concentrated, and more immediately appealing than its companion piece, the Second Symphony, this work quickly became one of Lutosławski's most frequently performed pieces. The Warsaw Autumn program for 1969 included the Polish première under Jan Krenz, and Krenz's recording of the work with the National Philharmonic of Warsaw won the Grand Prix du Disque of the Académie Charles Cros, presented in Paris in 1970 by Jacques Duhamel, the French minister of culture.

In 1968 the Lutosławskis finally were able to leave their cramped, noisy flat in the Saska Kępa district of Warsaw for a comfortable and private home of their own in Żoliborz, a more elegant section north of central Warsaw, not far from the New Town. Meanwhile the composer continued to travel extensively in Europe as conductor and lecturer. In early March 1968 he visited London to lecture and to attend the British première of the String Quartet. That summer he conducted a four-week composition course at Aarhus, Denmark. The following year Skrowaczewski conducted the Second Symphony in New York and Philadelphia and *Trois poèmes* was performed in Dallas and Chicago. The British première of the Second Symphony was also given in 1969 by the Royal Liverpool Philharmonic Orchestra in London. That year Lutosławski toured Holland, Norway, and Austria conducting his music, and late in the year he directed a series of concerts in Paris. In 1970 he attended the ISCM festival in Basel, where the String Quartet was performed. A reviewer on this occasion described the Quartet as 'a masterpiece, as is everything released to the public by this man who creates his art slowly and with enormous care'.[13]

Lutosławski had been considering a work for solo instrument or voice and orchestra, a 'real concerto', since at least 1968. The idea had been suggested by the Russian cellist Mstislav Rostropovich, who approached the composer in Warsaw while on a concert tour:

several years ago – I don't recall now exactly when – Mstislav Rostropovich urged me to write a cello piece . . . In order to encourage me to write this concerto, he said, 'I can't guarantee I will play it well, but I certainly will play it very often.' At one of our later meetings, Rostropovich played especially for me Britten's [First] Suite for Cello. He wanted to make me familiar with his playing, which in the setting of a private home was something quite different from a concert. Then he asked me to play him my compositions on the tape recorder. I put on the tape of *Paroles tissées*. While listening to this piece he studied the score intently and at the end said, 'I would like to play such music,' and after a moment of reflection, 'I would like to play *this* music.' That gave me a lot to think about. Then he added a very significant statement: 'I am still young as an artist, and I have already played the entire cello repertoire; now I would like to play such music as I have never played before.' That is probably why he became interested in music written by me. Because everything he had in his repertoire – as far as contemporary music is concerned – was indeed very different from the music I write.[14]

For some time, however, the pressure of other commitments prevented Lutosławski's beginning work on such a concerto. In 1968 the Royal Philharmonic Society in London, with financial support from the Calouste Gulbenkian Foundation, commissioned the composer to write an orchestral work. The society had in mind a symphonic composition in the manner of the Second Symphony and *Livre pour orchestre*, but the composer suggested instead the cello concerto he had been waiting to write, and the sponsors proposed to engage Rostropovich for the first performance. The composition took all of 1969 and part of 1970. Though there was no collaboration between composer and cellist as the work took shape, the concerto was written with Rostropovich's gifts and temperament constantly in mind: 'obviously during the work on this piece the prospect of its being performed by an artist so almighty not only in his own field, but in general – for I regard him as one of the greatest musicians of our century – was an enormously stimulating factor for me'.[15]

Lutosławski sent the work to Rostropovich page by page as it progressed, with explanations couched largely in extramusical terms of the work's dramatic scenario, in which the cellist and the orchestra confront each other as adversaries. This concept appealed strongly to Rostropovich, and he developed a deep identification with the dramatic persona represented in the solo part.

The day before the première Lutosławski met with critics and musicologists at a 'press conference' held at the Polish Cultural Institute in London. The première of the Cello Concerto was given on 14 October 1970 by the Bournemouth Symphony Orchestra, conducted by Edward Downes, in London; the work was repeated the next day in Bournemouth and the following day in Exeter. At the première, Sir Arthur Bliss presented to the soloist the Royal Philharmonic Society's gold medal. As he had been earlier with the LaSalle Quartet and with Peter Pears, so with Rostropovich the composer was blessed with a performer who displayed not only a supreme technical command of the work, but also a profound understanding of the composer's intentions:

It is hard to find suitable words to describe this experience, for Rostropovich is an artist about whose keen intelligence, musicality, and technical capabilities not only as a performer on the cello but as a great and gifted artist a separate study would be required. And here again genius is alloyed with modesty. Some time later I received a letter from him, in which he let me know about receiving a recording of the concerto's première. He commented on this performance, 'In the future I will play this piece a hundred times better.'[16]

Rostropovich was scheduled to repeat the concerto in Moscow on 27 May 1971 and at the fifteenth Warsaw Autumn, 19 September 1971, but political events intervened. On 31 October 1970 – just after the première – Rostropovich sent a defiant letter to the editors of four influential Soviet publications, protesting attacks on the writer Aleksandr Solzhenitsyn, who had been named a Nobel laureate on 8 October. Needless to say, the letter was never published in the Soviet Union, but it did appear soon afterward in the West. In the text Rostropovich recalled the official attacks on Shostakovich and other composers in 1948, and he boasted that he had not taken part in the later vilification of Boris Pasternak, despite pressure to do so. He ended boldly:

I know that after my letter there will undoubtedly be an 'opinion' about me, but I am not afraid of it. I openly say what I think. Talent, of which we are proud, must not be subjected to the unjust assaults of the past. I know and like the works of Solzhenitsyn. I believe he has the right through his suffering to write the truth as he saw it, and I see no reason to hide my attitude toward him at a time when a campaign is being launched against him.[17]

The Soviet government retaliated swiftly for this affront, relieving Rostropovich of his position at the Moscow Conservatory, forbidding him to travel abroad, and even forcing some concerts at home to be cancelled. In the meantime a number of talented young cellists – among them Heinrich Schiff, Siegfried Palm, Roman Jabłoński, Erling Blöndal Bengtsson, Wolfgang Boettcher, Andrzej Wróbel, Roman Suchecki, Natalia Gutman, and Miklós Perényi – have taken up the Lutosławski concerto with considerable success. Rostropovich himself resumed playing the work after his travel restrictions were lifted, as, for example, in Minneapolis on 13 and 14 January 1972. But not until 13 December 1972 did he give the Russian première with the USSR Radio and Television Symphony Orchestra, conducted by Gennady Rozhdestvensky; and on that occasion, with the composer present in the Great Hall of the Moscow Conservatory, the work received a huge ovation. Yet, despite the concerto's success with the Russian audience, not a single review appeared in the Soviet press, a circumstance which Rostropovich attributes to his friendship with Solzhenitsyn.[18]

In December 1970 Lutosławski was back in London to participate with Sven-Erik Bäck, Cornelius Cardew, and Alexander Goehr in a composers' panel discussion sponsored by the Park Lane Group and moderated by John Manduell. An observer reports that Lutosławski was 'the most sensible and restrained speaker' present.[19] In 1971 the composer once again visited the United States, to accept an honorary Doctor of Music degree from the Cleveland Institute of Music. The festivities included two concerts of his music under the aegis of the Cleveland Contemporary Arts Festival (Second Symphony, Livre, Iłłakowicz songs, Preludia taneczne in the 1959 nonet version, String Quartet, Paganini Variations) and on 2 June an address to the graduating class.[20] Other honors in 1971 included the Prix Maurice Ravel, awarded by a distinguished French jury which included Messiaen and Dutilleux, and a special prize ad honorem bestowed by the president of France. That year he also visited East Berlin to be installed as a corresponding member of the Deutsche Akademie der Künste, and while there he conducted a concert of Muzyka żałobna, the Iłłakowicz songs, and the Second Symphony.

Lutosławski gave up teaching after the 1968 Aarhus summer course. He has never, in fact, taught regularly on any faculty or privately; and he came to feel that even short summer courses were inappropriate for him, since, as he puts it, 'I am not a good teacher,

Mstislav Rostropovich with Lutosławski in Moscow, December 1972 (from the composer's collection)

teaching is not my profession. I have not got the necessary knowledge either, for a good composition teacher has to know all the existing techniques while I have only concentrated on mine. I have spent years in developing my own musical language and have had no energy left to carefully study the efforts of others.'[21] He still accepted occasional invitations to lecture, however, and at such times spoke most often about aspects of his own musical language and philosophy of music. Mario di Bonaventura invited Lutosławski to attend for a second time the Congregation of the Arts in Hanover, New Hampshire, as composer-in-residence and lecturer, and commissioned a new work to be performed there. The composer chose to fulfill this commission with a work for thirteen solo strings; it is uncertain precisely when the commission was offered him, but he seems to have begun the piece in 1970. The finished composition, Preludes and Fugue, was ready in 1972; in the interval, though, the Dartmouth festival had failed for financial reasons, and the composer's projected fourth trip to America was cancelled. Instead the première was given by di Bonaventura and the Chamber Orchestra of Radio-Televizija Zagreb at the Steirischer Herbst festival in Graz on 12 October of that year.

On 17 October came the Austrian première of the Cello Concerto at the ISCM festival, also in Graz. Rostropovich was supposed to perform, but the Soviet authorities had once again forbidden him to travel. In his place an unknown German cellist only nineteen years old, Heinrich Schiff, was engaged. Before the start of the Graz festivals, Schiff met Lutosławski in Zagreb for several days of coaching. At the performance in Graz, the young cellist created a sensation; he has since played the Lutosławski concerto a great many times, and he and the work have grown famous together.

Lutosławski spent an increasing portion of his time traveling about to conduct his own works. He had begun conducting publicly at the first performance of *Trois poèmes* in 1963 in Zagreb, but, as we have seen, that was not his first experience on the podium:

Conducting itself was not quite new for me, for I had conducted my own incidental music as a student, before the war, and after the war I also appeared on Polish radio. I developed my technique myself although I had studied several handbooks . . .

Naturally it is indispensable that one should have talent for conducting. I think I have a certain gift for it; some people seem to take me more seriously since I have had success as a conductor as well. I only conduct my own works, and initially decided to do it to prove not only to others but to myself as well that the new kind of music-making required by my compositions was quite possible to conduct.[22]

My latest works contain several new proposed solutions in the realm of orchestral performance. This has to do with the function of the conductor, both during rehearsals and concerts, as well as the work of the members of the ensemble. There are comparatively few conductors perfectly at ease with what my scores contain in this respect. More numerous are those who look askance at the conductor's role required by my scores, a role more like that of a stage-manager or call-boy than a true performer. For this reason I often prepare new works and conduct them myself. In order to prove to myself, to the musicians, and possibly to other conductors who might be interested that the manner of playing and conducting proposed in my music is possible, serves a definite purpose, and moreover is the only way of achieving that purpose. Apart from this, conducting my own works affords a really inestimable advantage as regards enriching my skills as a composer.[23]

The composer's activities as conductor were well received. One critic wrote that 'Lutosławski is a remarkable interpreter of his own works for orchestra, a conductor who combines precision with imagination and who exercises a sovereign control over the orchestra';[24] another compared him to Hans Rosbaud, 'whose gestures came from sheer love of the music, and for whom the orchestra played con amore'.[25]

Among the cities where the composer conducted concerts of his music were Amsterdam in 1971 and Bydgoszcz, Leipzig, and Edinburgh in 1972. His Leipzig concert (18 April) with the local radio orchestra included Muzyka żałobna, Livre pour orchestre, and the Iłłakowicz songs, sung in German by the fine young mezzo-soprano Roswitha Trexler, daughter of composer Georg Trexler. So taken was the composer with her performance that he invited her to record the songs with him for Wergo. Lutosławski conducted his First Symphony at the sixteenth Warsaw Autumn, 16 September 1972. On 20 January 1973 Lutosławski and the London Sinfonietta performed Preludes and Fugue (the British première), Paroles tissées, Jeux vénitiens, and Muzyka żałobna in London's Queen Elizabeth Hall. While in London he wrote a strong letter to the editor of the Times praising the Sinfonietta's playing and expressing concern over the orchestra's financial difficulties.[26] Other 1973 appearances included Bucharest, Witten, Aldeburgh, Amsterdam, the Hague, Vienna, and Düsseldorf. The Warsaw Autumn presented Polish premières of both Preludes and Fugue and the Cello Concerto, with Schiff as soloist and the composer conducting. In 1974 came the French première of the Cello Concerto with Siegfried Palm as soloist and Gilbert Amy conducting.

Although Lutosławski's own concert programs emphasized his recent works, especially Preludes and Fugue, the Cello Concerto, Livre, and Paroles tissées (often with Pears), he used some of his older music as well: Muzyka żałobna, the Iłłakowicz songs, and even the First Symphony. Except for the Concerto for Orchestra, though – a work he was by now reluctant to conduct – he had nothing suitable for closing concert programs. Thus he sketched during 1973–4 a short orchestral work to be called A maiori . . ., intended both to meet this programming need and to satisfy a commission from Zubin Mehta. But as always his own severest critic, Lutosławski was dissatisfied with the work and shelved his sketches. At the same time – at least as early as March 1973 – he was collecting ideas for another orchestral composition, commissioned by the Concertgebouw orchestra. He continued a full conducting schedule as well, appearing in 1974 in Stockholm, Gothenburg, Cluj (Rumania), Wrocław, East Berlin, Warsaw, and Oslo; during 1975 in Cracow, West Berlin, Lucerne, Warsaw,

Mannheim, Dresden, and London; and during 1976 in Copenhagen, Vienna, and Warsaw.

In 1975 Rostropovich invited some ten composers to contribute works for a celebration of the seventieth birthday of the Swiss conductor Paul Sacher in 1976. For this occasion Lutosławski wrote a lighthearted *Sacher Variation* for solo cello. The work contains two opposing sorts of music: wistful, tentative playing using the pitches B-flat, D-flat, A-flat, G, F-sharp, and F, and – emerging gradually until it dominates the piece – the forthright theme based on the six letters of Sacher's name: E-flat, A, C, B, E, and D. Even the humorous cadence which closes the piece spells out the Sacher hexachord (ex. 4.1). *Sacher Variation* is an attractive, if inconsequential, little piece. But it is a not altogether welcome product of fame that even a composer's minor efforts will be played and discussed with great seriousness; and since its first performance by Rostropovich on 2 May 1976 the *Sacher Variation* has been performed frequently, especially by Heinrich Schiff. Schiff gave the British première at the Edinburgh Festival on 6 September 1977; the American première was given the following year by the young American cellist Paul Tobias.

4.1 Conclusion of *Sacher Variation*

Most of the year 1975 was devoted to a one-movement piece for baritone and symphony orchestra entitled *Les espaces du sommeil*, on a text by Robert Desnos. The piece resulted, indirectly, from a recital of Hugo Wolf songs given in Warsaw by Dietrich Fischer-Dieskau and Svyatoslav Richter on 2 October 1973. For Lutosławski that program was 'an unforgettable experience'. When the composer and the singer met after the recital they discussed the possibility of Lutosławski's writing a work for baritone, and soon afterward the composer began to search for a text for the purpose. He read through a quantity of German poetry without finding anything that suited him. When he happened on a recording of Fischer-Dieskau singing Debussy and Ravel songs and discovered that his French is superb, the composer was delighted to fall back on his favorite language and settled quickly on Desnos's prose poem. Lutosławski planned the vocal part around Fischer-Dieskau's voice, making careful notes on his range in the Brahms Vier ernste Gesänge, the title role in Wozzeck, Jokanaan in Salome. The completed Les espaces was ready late in 1975, but because of Fischer-Dieskau's heavy schedule the première could not occur until 12 April 1978, in Berlin, as part of a concert in which the composer also conducted the Berliner Philharmoniker in Jeux vénitiens and the Second Symphony. Lutosławski and Fischer-Dieskau repeated this program on 25 February 1979 in Amsterdam with the Concertgebouw orchestra. They were to have given the British première in London on 9 November 1978, but Les espaces had to be removed from the program when Fischer-Dieskau fell ill. Ultimately it was the English baritone John Shirley-Quirk who gave the first London performance at a Prom concert, 30 July 1979, with the composer conducting the BBC Symphony Orchestra. Fischer-Dieskau gave the first Paris performance in October 1979 with the Orchestre de Paris.

A number of honors came to Lutosławski during the seventies. In January 1973 he received the annual ZKP prize for a second time, largely on the strength of the Cello Concerto. On 30 June 1973 the senate of Warsaw University conferred on Lutosławski an honorary doctoral degree. After a presentation speech by Zofia Lissa, the composer addressed the assembled dignitaries on 'The Aim of Art', comparing Debussy's views of the purposes of music with those of the Polish philosopher and aesthetician Stanisław Ignacy Witkiewicz.[27] Afterward the Wilanowski Quartet performed his String Quartet. On 9 October 1973 the Finnish Wihuri Foundation awarded Lutosławski its Sibelius Prize in Helsinki. Following the award ceremony the composer conducted the city orchestra in Livre pour orchestre. Also in 1973 he was elected a corresponding member of the Bayerische Akademie der schönen Künste, Munich. In the spring of 1974 Lutosławski traveled to Chicago to receive an honorary Doctor of Fine Arts degree from Northwestern University.

On 29 April 1974 the United States ambassador to Poland, Richard T. Davies, presented the composer with a diploma naming him an honorary member of the American Academy of Arts and Letters and the National Institute of Arts and Letters, at a ceremony in the American embassy in Warsaw. The actual investiture was held in New York on 24 May in Lutosławski's absence. The president of the academy, Richard Wilbur, read a well-meaning but inaccurate citation:

Since the 1950s, Witold Lutosławski has been the leader of a most distinguished school of Polish composers, active as part of the Union of Polish Composers, in Polish musical publications, and with the 'Warsaw Musical Autumns' festival and the Radio Council. But with the performance and recording of *Trois Poèmes d'Henri Michaux* and his *Symphony No. 2*, he has achieved an international eminence. He has broken from the rigidity of serialization into a freer and more expressive style.[28]

Lutosławski thus became the first Polish musician so honored since Paderewski, joining a roster of honorary members which includes Boulez, Britten, Chávez, Ginastera, Malipiero, Menotti, Messiaen, Paz, Sauguet, Ravi Shankar, Tippett, and Xenakis.

Lutosławski visited Britain in 1975 to accept yet another honorary doctorate, this one from the University of Lancaster. On 6 May at the first concert of the university's Spring Festival 1975, he and Bryden Thompson conducted the BBC Symphony Orchestra in the Symphonic Variations, *Muzyka żałobna*, and *Livre*. Lutosławski lectured the next day on 'The Large Form in Contemporary Music'. The presentation of the degree on 8 May was followed by a concert including the Paganini Variations, String Quartet (played by the Sartori Quartet), and *Trois poèmes*, with the composer and Edward Cowie conducting the university chorus and orchestra. In July 1975 Lutosławski lectured at the international Jeunesses Musicales seminar in Toruń, discussing his own methods of composition. In 1977 he received an honorary doctorate from the University of Glasgow. The composer was elected an honorary member of the Royal Academy of Music, London, in 1976; an honorary member of the Guildhall School of Music and a corresponding member of the Académie des Beaux Arts, Paris, in 1978. In 1977 he was decorated at home with the Order Budownych Polski Ludowej (Order of the Builders of People's Poland).

As a conductor Lutosławski had already made several recordings of his music for the Polish label Muza when in 1972 he made his first recording for a foreign firm, a reading of *Paroles tissées* with Pears for Decca. In December 1974 the composer and Rostropovich recorded the Cello Concerto in Paris for EMI; this recording earned the Koussevitzky Prix Mondial du Disque for 1976 (Lutosławski's second). Soon afterward the composer and EMI embarked on a project to record new performances (with Polish ensembles) of all his major orchestral pieces, including three pre-1956 works: Symphonic Variations, the First Symphony, and the Concerto for Orchestra. The tapings were done in two or three sessions of about a week each. The resulting six-record set, issued in 1978, won the twelfth annual International Record Critics' Award, presented at the Yehudi Menuhin Festival in Gstaad, Switzerland, the following year.

Mi-parti, the Concertgebouw commission which Lutosławski had begun sketching as early as 1973, was completed in 1976. The composer conducted the première in Amsterdam on 22 October 1976 on a program with the First Symphony, *Paroles tissées*, and the Cello Concerto (Schiff). Late in the same month he lectured in Munich to the Bayerische Akademie der schönen Künste.

Lutosławski made his fifth trip to the United States in 1977 for appearances with the Saint Louis Symphony Orchestra on 1 and 2 April. He conducted *Paroles tissées* (with Pears as soloist), *Livre*, and the Concerto for Orchestra. He spent 3 and 4 April at the Cincinnati College Conservatory of Music, where he participated with the LaSalle Quartet in a lecture-recital of his String Quartet, conducted a rehearsal of *Muzyka żałobna*, and informally addressed students and faculty. The same year he attended the International Violoncello Competition at La Rochelle, France, where the required compositions for the finalists were his own concerto and those of Shostakovich and Dutilleux. He served on the contest jury with Berio, Dutilleux, Xenakis, and others; and he conducted the Radio Hilversum orchestra when Rostropovich performed his concerto.

Mi-parti was repeated on 31 August 1977 at the thirty-first Edinburgh Festival, with Bernard Haitink conducting the Concertgebouw orchestra. Appropriately, the work was placed on the program between two works of Debussy. The composer himself conducted the Polish première at the Warsaw Autumn, 17 September 1977, and the Swiss première in Basel on 21 October. Haitink conducted the London première with the London Philharmonic Orchestra on 5 December, after which Paul Griffiths pronounced the work 'a superbly cogent essay' and 'Lutosławski's most perfectly balanced achievement to date'.[29] The first American performance was given in Chicago on 16 December, with Daniel Barenboim conducting.

In January 1978 Lutosławski attended the Dublin Festival of Twentieth-Century Music as guest composer, along with his old duo-piano partner, Panufnik, and Peter Maxwell Davies, and on 13 January he conducted the Dublin Philharmonic Orchestra in the First Symphony, *Mi-parti*, *Muzyka żałobna*, and the Cello Concerto (Schiff). In June of that year the composer was the guest of the International Society for Music Education Pro Sinfonika in Poznań. On 22 July he received a State Prize for music, class I – his third.

Among the composition projects occupying Lutosławski during the late 1970s was a commission from the Chicago Symphony for a large orchestral work. He must have begun thinking about this work in 1976 or so, and by early 1977 he had decided to write a Third Symphony in four movements: Invocation, Cycle of Etudes, Toccata, and Hymn. The toccata movement, which was to bear the dramatic weight of the cycle, was completed late in 1977, but the composer decided he was not satisfied with it and put the symphony aside, pessimistic about ever finishing it. At the same time as he was working on the Third Symphony, Lutosławski was engaged in the more unlikely enterprise of recasting the Paganini Variations of 1941. A pianist friend, Felicja Blumental, had asked him to write something for piano and orchestra, and though he had neither the time nor the interest sufficient to undertake a large new work for this combination, he did oblige by reworking the old duo-piano piece for her. He made the orchestration at odd moments during 1977 and 1978, to save time working on score paper on which his wife had already glued the piano part of the 1941 version. Since the duo-piano version was a bit short to serve as a concert piece with orchestra, Lutosławski expanded it by repeating each section (save the theme itself and variations 10 and 11), with the soloists and orchestra exchanging roles for the second playing of each variation. Otherwise he made very little change in the musical substance. Blumental gave the first performance of the new version in Miami on 18 November 1979, with Brian Priestman conducting the Florida Philharmonic Orchestra.

In the meantime the composer continued a full schedule of conducting. After leading the Polish Radio orchestra in a concert of his own music at the Flanders Festival in late 1978, Lutosławski conducted for the first time in the Soviet Union early in 1979. In Moscow and Leningrad he gave concerts of his own work, including splendid performances of the Cello Concerto by a young Russian cellist, Natalia Gutman. Gutman's playing and the enthusiastic crowds which greeted the composer made this first Russian tour a 'great thrill' for him. At the Warsaw Autumn Lutosławski conducted the Polish première of Les espaces du sommeil, with baritone John Shirley-Quirk as soloist, on 14 September 1979. In November 1979 he toured Japan for the first time, and in 1980 he visited Turkey and Australia.

The first important work completed since Mi-parti came as the result of Lutosławski's friendship with Rostropovich. When the cellist left Russia and in 1976 became music director of the National Symphony in Washington, he proposed that the composer write something for his new orchestra. The idea was immediately attractive to Lutosławski, but he postponed thinking seriously about it because of his involvement with the Third Symphony. Once that project had been laid aside, he took up the piece for Rostropovich in 1978 and finished it in May of the following year. The resulting cycle of five orchestral tableaux he called Novelette. Rostropovich conducted the première in Washington, 29 January 1980, and in the same concert played the Cello Concerto with the composer conducting.

The close of the 1970s found Lutosławski, now approaching the age of seventy, still leading a vigorous professional life on concert stages and lecture platforms, still closely involved in the affairs of the composers' union and the conduct of the Warsaw Autumn festivals, and still pursing any number of compositional projects. He sketches more or less continuously at his home in Warsaw, at a cottage in Norway, and even while traveling. He often works on several pieces at once. Sketches for a particular work may collect over a period of years, a fact that makes precise dating of his recent compositions a difficult task. 'I'm not a quick worker and I don't find it any joke to work to a particular date – I doubt if I will do it again', he said in 1971. 'It's a struggle for my ideas to get born. I hate to use such an unfashionable word but each piece, each idea must be the result of inspiration.'[30] Only after he has a well-developed formal–dramatic scheme in mind and has amassed a number of concrete musical ideas does he proceed with writing a score. When that stage is reached, he composes directly for orchestra, never in reduced score: 'I do not think in an abstract manner, as most 19th century composers. For example, Schumann's works could obviously have been orchestrated in different ways.'[31] He may have as many as five large works in progress at any one time. At the same time his old habit of doing theoretical studies persists; and after years of preoccupation with his harmonic language, he began in the mid-seventies to write melodic studies, the fruits of which are already evident in *Mi-parti*.

Given the zeal with which he guards the quality of his completed works, it would be foolhardy to predict which of Lutosławski's works in progress will be allowed to escape the confines of his studio. But among the most interesting prospects is Paul Sacher's commission for an oboe concerto, intended as a vehicle for the Swiss virtuoso Heinz Holliger. The composer described his plans for the work as early as March 1973:

The commission is for an oboe concerto, but I am fulfilling the artist's request and am including an obbligato harp part as well for his wife, Ursula Holliger. That coincides with my own plans, for I want to compose an aleatoric piece for polyphonic and monophonic instruments. In this work, chance will play a greater role than in the past. Although it may sound paradoxical, the piece is also going to be highly organized, but there might be greater differences between the various interpretations.

... Perhaps one might liken it to a sculpture out of liquid substance. This problem attracts me a great deal, I would like to extend the idea of a musical composition. It is not a question of wanting to change my compositional technique, I merely want to try out a new method. The first movement is going to be a short introduction, while the last will be a series of marches – it will start with a quick march, and end with a funeral march. The experiment concerns the second movement which will consist of short episodes. Only the beginning and the end will be given, within the movement the instruments will be free to choose the duration of occurrences. Primarily, it will be the pauses between the occurrences and the order of the particular sections that will be free. The movement will have to be composed in such a way that any section can be played together with any other.[32]

Lutosławski's viewpoint in his later years has remained remarkably youthful and forward-looking. Even the possibility of trying his hand at electronic music has engaged his imagination, though he speaks more wistfully than realistically of it now. He likes to reminisce about his early experiments with manipulating film sound tracks, and although since his student days he has not been directly involved in electronic composition, he has been an ardent supporter of the Polish Radio's electronic studio since its founding in Warsaw in 1957. In the late fifties he helped organize a series of electronic and instrumental concerts to introduce the Polish public to the new medium. And, though he calls the symphony orchestra his 'favorite instrument' and all his mature compositions have been written for conventional instruments, he has long contended that traditional instruments, which have not continued to evolve to keep pace with the changing demands of modern composers, must ultimately be replaced by something new. Though admittedly Lutosławski's montage attempts in the thirties were primitive by today's standards, 'nevertheless the fact that I had such thoughts so early proves that something in this field attracts me seriously. I don't know if and when I will manage to realize music of this sort, but at any rate it remains, if not among my intentions, then among my fantasies.'[33]

He has also spoken with keen interest of two other dreams: of creating an opera and of writing another large choral work, which would be his first since the *Trois poèmes* of 1963. As early as 1968 Lutosławski began mentioning the possibility of an opera and his hope that a collaboration with the Polish surrealist animator and film director Jan Lenica would produce a suitable libretto.[34] In 1970 he discussed the problems attending such an undertaking:

I must find a new convention – the old ones are dead – and a suitable libretto. Only *L'Enfant et les Sortilèges* fulfils my idea of what an opera can be like today. If a person sings instead of talks it's not natural. But an armchair – well that's different and credible. An opera must be anti-realistic. I want something surrealistic. A musical friend has lent me [Kenneth Grahame's] *Wind in the Willows*, a book I didn't previously know, and that may be the answer.[35]

Gradually Lutosławski's conception grew to encompass a stage work employing not only the traditional operatic means, but also film, lights, and other modern techniques. In late 1972 he mentioned that the collaboration with Lenica was continuing: on his trips to Paris the composer was meeting with the film-maker, who has made his home there for several years, to discuss the project.[36] But apparently the opera has never got further than the planning; like electronic music it remains, if not an intention, then an enticing fantasy. Of his hope to write another choral work, Lutosławski confided to Tadeusz Kaczyński:

For a long time I have thought about writing a vocal–instrumental work of large dimensions. I am not quite decided about the theme, because several texts might enter into consideration here. Once while I was still studying at the conservatory, I began to write a Requiem, which was not meant to be finished at that time; it was only fragments, which I had to present for the composition diploma. The idea of writing a Requiem has followed me throughout my whole life, and from time to time I think about it. I don't know yet whether the Requiem will be exactly this work to which I refer. I also know an unusually beautiful text of Henri Michaux that I might use for this purpose.[37]

Anyone observing from abroad the state of Polish music after the October 1956 turning-point might be forgiven for failing to predict Witold Lutosławski's subsequent rise to international prominence. On the evidence of those works likely to be known outside his own country – the Paganini Variations and the Concerto for Orchestra – it can hardly have seemed likely to an outsider that he would come to be considered the greatest composer Poland has produced since Chopin. Yet long before 1956 Lutosławski had mastered the expressive ends of his art, and there remained only the perfecting of technical means to make clear to us his artistic vision. Though he attained maturity as a composer only at the age of forty-eight (Jeux vénitiens), his late emergence as an important modernist was the result not of a sudden change in direction but rather of a protracted and single-minded struggle. Edward Cowie has aptly observed that

like Tippett, Gerhard and Elliott Carter, Lutoslawski is that most complex of creative phenomena, the so-called late developer ... Yet the essential dynamic in all these cases seems to have been the persistence from the outset of a vision so individual as to require years for the rethinking and elaboration of a commensurate technique in which to embody it.[38]

Lutosławski's adventurous spirit has earned the admiration of many. Olivier Messiaen recently expressed his opinion of the Polish composer in an interview:

I have had the opportunity to discover that he is a man of great culture and refinement and uncommon nobility. I am struck most of all by his generosity and goodness as a human being and by his extraordinary nature as a composer. I say 'extraordinary' because, although he began composing as a neoclassicist, he did not remain at that stage but instead has continued to develop more and more. If we compare his earliest compositions with his most recent ones, we can see how great a leap into the unknown he has made. This characteristic is quite rare. Most people as they grow older are merely confirmed in the traits of their youth; but Lutosławski grows more and more modern, and this seems to me quite extraordinary. What could reflect greater credit on a composer than that he prove himself so youthful in his later years?[39]

But no less striking than his late growth has been Lutosławski's concomitant refusal to join any fashionable 'school' or to pursue newness as an end in itself. As early as 1937 he warned that 'these days a composer wastes much of his creative energy on appeasing the restless appetite for "novelty" . . . He is not able to concentrate his efforts in any one direction for very long; he must always be creating something different, breaking radically from his earlier work. This dulls a composer's sensibilities.'[40] Lutosławski has avoided this trap, coolly spurning the trends: the avant-garde music theater, improvisation, music of chance, serialism, neotonal primitivism. This artistic independence and the fact that he never compromised himself during Poland's politically difficult years have combined to make Lutosławski as much a figure of moral authority to the present generation of Polish composers as Szymanowski was to an earlier generation.

Viewed against this background Lutosławski's supposed relation to the younger composers popularly imagined to comprise the 'Polish school' may be quickly laid to rest. By historical coincidence – the product more of political than of artistic developments – Krzysztof Penderecki and his generation came to the attention of Western musicians at the same moment as did Lutosławski, twenty years Penderecki's senior. The impact of the younger man's strikingly novel ideas and his fresh, youthful voice as a composer attracted immediate notice, and his works spread quickly in the West. Lutosławski, in many ways a more traditional composer (and certainly one less given to aggressive self-promotion), was for some time overshadowed, and outside Central and Eastern Europe his reputation has grown more slowly. But those who imply, as Antoine Goléa has done, that in his stylistic development Lutosławski merely followed Penderecki's lead[41] have neither compared carefully enough the music of the two men nor considered the chronology of their separate careers. The harmonic technique on which Lutosławski's third-period style is founded was worked out in sketches for the Five Songs and Muzyka żałobna beginning about 1954, when Penderecki was still an unknown conservatory student in Cracow. *Jeux vénitiens* appeared at about the same time as Penderecki's first international successes, *Ofiarom Hiroszimy: Tren* (To the Victims of Hiroshima: Threnody, 1959, rev. 1961) and *Fluorescences* (1961–2); but even a cursory glance at these scores makes clear that they can hardly have served as Lutosławski's inspiration. Lutosławski's String Quartet has nothing in common with Penderecki's First Quartet (1960); and his *Trois poèmes* antedates the *St. Luke Passion* by two years. In fact, despite their friendship and mutual admiration, the music of the two men shows remarkably little similarity. On the other hand, still younger Polish composers, notably Krzysztof Meyer (1943–), have recently been influenced by Lutosławski's achievement.

Lutosławski's considerable success with the public and the esteem he commands today among musicians may well prove ephemeral. Already he has his critics. Adrian Jack, for example, has called his music 'benumbing', 'calculated to the point of being not only effective but glib', and so easily comprehensible as to be 'a mere toy'.[42] Stanley Sadie's frequent characterization of the composer as a musical lightweight is similar (though it seems to measure Lutosławski against an ideal of musical profundity which belongs essentially to the nineteenth century and which the composer would surely reject as irrelevant).[43] But Lutosławski's life has given ample evidence of the strength of character and sureness of artistic purpose necessary to regard with equanimity both the blandishments of his 'fans' and the disparagements of his detractors.

In 1973 the composer described his goals as an artist by reading a passage from his notebook to an interviewer:

Artistic creative activity can be motivated by different aims. The most commonplace of these is the desire to attract the attention of others, to be popular, to earn money and so on. In my case, the main motive is the desire to give the most faithful expression of a constantly changing and developing world that exists within me. The question can be raised: am I only interested in what goes on in me and nothing else? Isn't this standpoint too introverted? My answer is: no. I have a strong desire to communicate something, through my music, to the people. I am not working to get many 'fans' for myself; I do not want to convince, I want to find. I would like to find people who in the depths of their souls feel the same way as I do. That can only be achieved through the greatest artistic sincerity in every detail of music, from the minutest technical aspects to the most secret depths. I know that this standpoint deprives me of many potential listeners, but those who remain mean an immeasurable treasure for me. They are the people who are closest to me, even if I do not know them personally. I regard creative activity as a kind of soul-fishing, and the 'catch' is the best medicine for loneliness, that most human of sufferings.[44]

5   Elements of the late style

Since 1961 Lutosławski has worked largely independently of the fashions of the European avant-garde, refining and extending a compositional technique which has produced, to use Bogusław Schäffer's phrase, 'stylistically the most independent works of modern European music'.[1] Certainly the elements of this style are not easily reduced to general formulations, for each new work has raised new problems and proposed new solutions; but the similarities between the works since 1961 outweigh their differences, and the continuing evolution of the late style has manifested a gradual, organic process of growth, not a series of radically new departures.

Bohdan Pociej once described Lutosławski's mature works in terms of four dominant tendencies:

First, the systematic tendency, which is a constant endeavour to achieve a system, to implement it, to increasingly find one's own personality in an individual system of composing.

Then the harmonic – and at the same time colouristic – tendency which has both an intuitive source (since it is born of a 'Debussyan' fascination with the pure sound and beauty of harmony) and an intellectual basis (since it is [grounded] in the systems of chords).

Next, the polychronic tendency, reflected as it is in a constant and intense inclination to organize 'parallel plots' in music; to split the composition into many interpenetrating levels and planes; and to fill musical space with multi-directional and multi-tiered motions.

Finally, the dramatic tendency expressing itself in conflict, confrontation, struggle – in the various vicissitudes of form.[2]

We have seen that each of these tendencies – systematic, harmonic–coloristic, 'polychronic', dramatic – has in fact been present in Lutosławski's music since long before 1961. We shall examine the mature works along lines similar to those suggested by Pociej (though in rather more concrete terms); but we must first come to terms with the question of the *systematic* aspects of Lutosławski's thinking, since this is a question which transcends the boundaries between various aspects of his style.

We have seen from the very beginning of Lutosławski's creative life

107

the tendency to generate and manipulate musical materials in systematic ways, from the synthetic scales of the Piano Sonata, Two Etudes, the Overture for Strings, and other works, to the disposition of harmonic structures according to vertical symmetries and methodical transpositions in the Five Songs and elsewhere, the elaborate precompositional schemes underlying *Muzyka żałobna*, and the mechanical approach to form in the last of the Postludes. This tendency is a manifestation of the composer's exceptionally precise mode of thought and his steadfast desire to exercise mastery over his materials. These qualities have prompted comparisons with Boulez, another composer whose early mathematical training has influenced his musical endeavors. But Lutosławski's music has never degenerated into mere numerology, as Boulez in *Structures I* and Stockhausen in *Formel* (both 1951–2) have been accused of doing. Mathematical processes have never assumed for him any symbolic significance. The composer has made explicit his attitude toward the place of system in music:

What is alien to me in Schönberg is the pre-eminence of the system over ear control. The latter is of course also present in his music, after all Schönberg was an outstanding musician. However, the system in his art assumes universal significance, and determines the composition of not just one work but a whole series of works. That never occurs in my case. I always work out new elements of a system for every new work which serves my musical imagination.[3]

I must emphasize that I am speaking of the listener undergoing a direct experience and not of [his] becoming aware of the actual organization of the musical material. I am thus on my guard against all experiments which would lead to a purely mathematical beauty in the arrangement of elements of musical work. This particular concept of beauty is known to all those who have ever come into contact with mathematics. I do not intend to negate its existence nor to deplore the delight it may give. However, I consider it to be a misunderstanding to realize this form of beauty in music. I do not wish to discern in all the mathematical and quasi-mathematical operations, to which a composer of today must turn, anything apart from that which it gives in its sound effect and consequently its psychological effect on the listener.

It seems to me quite extraneous to discern in numbers and their arrangement some factor of equal importance to the actual perception, and which might be supposed to have some value in itself even when it has no perceptible influence on the sound progress of the work . . .

In opposing the significance of numbers being raised above everything else in music in this way, I do not, however, consider all mathematical operations as being of no use whatsoever. On the contrary. I often turn to mathematics, or rather to certain simple mathematical processes, in my composing. However, in all such operations I try never to lose sight of my basic aim – which is to compose the particular aesthetic experiences of my listener.[4]

Lutosławski has admitted that he is by nature 'too systematic' but that he cannot seem to escape that trait. And he insists on the necessity of the 'irrational' in music, on the value of the 'slip of the pen'. He deliberately introduces such elements in his late works: the 'intermissions' in *Livre*, the climax of the fugue in Preludes and Fugue (completely unrelated to the thematic working-out of the rest of the piece), the irrelevant intrusion of the brass fanfares near the end of *Mi-parti*. The composer's determination to keep the systematic elements hidden below the surface of the music and his appreciation for the value of inspired illogic on the surface, in short his paramount concern for producing music capable of emotional, not only intellectual, communication, allow Pociej to conclude that 'for all its fine-wrought precision his music is the very antithesis of calculated, cerebral composition'.[5]

Against this background we may proceed to examine Lutosławski's late works in terms of four broad aspects of style: microrhythmic organization and the technique of limited aleatorism; pitch organization and the technique of aleatory counterpoint; the role of texture; and, synthesizing the other aspects, macrorhythmic organization, form, and drama.

Microrhythmic organization and the technique of limited aleatorism

The technique of applying a limited degree of chance in realizing the rhythmic aspect of music has acquired several names in the literature of twentieth-century music. Lutosławski calls it 'limited aleatorism' or 'controlled aleatorism'.[6] His own discovery of this method had a liberating effect:

[limited aleatorism] gave me the feeling of release from restraints which had hampered a serious development of my musical thought. I found a way in which to use sound combinations which had interested me for a long time according to the possibilities afforded by instruments played by living people. In this connection new horizons were opened up before me for the development of this new technique both in the immediate and distant future.[7]

György Ligeti credits Lutosławski with originating the technique. To Ove Nordwall's suggestion that it stems instead from the first version of *Apparitions* (1957), Ligeti replied that the appearance of aleatorism in his score is crude and primitive by comparison with the already refined and individual conception Lutosławski presented in 1961 in *Jeux vénitiens*.[8] Penderecki claims that in some of his very early pieces (presumably before 1960) he experimented with controlled aleatorism, and other composers – Stockhausen and Berio, for example – had introduced limited degrees of aleatorism before 1960. It hardly matters who first used the technique, however. It is Lutosławski who first produced distinguished artistic results with it and whose example in this respect has exerted a powerful influence in Europe and especially within Poland. All his works since 1961 have involved the technique to some extent, and Lutosławski's name has become so closely linked with it that he once complained about being labeled 'controlled aleatorist', as if singling out this one aspect of his work could suffice to describe it.

Lutosławski permits chance to function only at the smallest level of microrhythm, where the performer is sometimes allowed to play independently, expressively, as if he were a soloist. Chance is never allowed to affect pitch choice, form, dynamics, nor indeed any parameter but rhythm. All these other elements remain under the composer's strict control:

I am not, . . . even to the least extent, counting on the possible creative ability of the performers. I do not presuppose any improvised parts, even the shortest, in my works. I am an adherent of a clear-cut division between the role of the composer and that of the performer, and I do not wish even partially to relinquish the authorship of the music I have written.[9]

Thus Lutosławski's aleatorism fulfills precisely Werner Meyer-Eppler's classic definition: 'A process is said to be aleatoric (from Lat. *alea* = dice) if its course is determined in general but depends on chance in detail.'[10]

For Lutosławski aleatorism is a means, not an end. The goal is twofold: to accommodate the performer by restoring his interpretative role, and to realize specific textures of enormous microrhythmic complexity and variety. The first of these objectives represents a reaction against the unreasonable demands placed on performers in the fifties:

The very concept of 'collective ad libitum' can be considered a reaction of composer–performer to the often absurd demands which some composers have made of performers in the last few years. Such demands are the result of a completely abstract approach to music considered exclusively as a series of sound phenomena occurring in time. I consider such an approach to music as being flagrantly one-sided. I understand music not only as a series of sound phenomena but also as an activity which is carried out by a group of human beings – the performers of the piece. Each of these persons is endowed with many far richer possibilities than those which a purely abstract score demands. I want to include into the repertoire of compositional means that wealth which is presented by the individual psyche of a human being – the performer.[11]

. . . I hold the principle that compositions must be made as easy to perform as possible, despite the fact that this places an additional burden on the composer. For everyone knows how extremely difficult it is to write works easy to play without sacrificing something important. Nevertheless, I on my part do try to write simply not only because I firmly believe that music that is easy to play sounds better than difficult music, but also because in this manner I hope to have some part in helping musicians recapture the sense of pleasure that the playing of music can provide.[12]

The second objective, the achievement of rhythmic complexity, may be insured 'statistically' through the application of simple arithmetic operations to the rhythms of the individual parts. The opening section of the second movement of the String Quartet is an excellent example.[13] Here each of the four instruments plays a succession of fifteen rhythmic 'phrases', together creating an extremely dense and, for the listener, unpredictable mass of attack points. The constitution of these phrases is determined according to two different processes. All odd-numbered phrases are constructed of four groups of semiquavers, with a semiquaver rest separating the first group from the second and again the third from the fourth, e.g.:

There are four such series of semiquaver groups: 4 3 5 5 (shown above), 5 4 6 6, 6 5 7 7, and 7 6 8 8. In the eight odd-numbered phrases, this sequence of semiquaver series rotates twice through each instrument, as follows:

phrases:	1, 9				3, 11				5, 13				7, 15			
vn 1	4	3	5	5	5	4	6	6	6	5	7	7	7	6	8	8
vn 2	6	5	7	7	7	6	5	5	4	3	5	5	5	4	6	6
vla	5	4	6	6	6	5	7	7	7	6	8	8	4	3	5	5
vc.	7	6	8	8	4	3	5	5	5	4	6	6	6	5	7	7

The seven even-numbered phrases, on the other hand, are constructed of seven different combinations of duration values ranging from demisemiquaver to dotted minim. In each even-numbered phrase the four instruments play a similar but not identical pattern, e.g.:

phrase 6

vn I

vn 2

etc.

vla

vc.

The microrhythmic construction of this entire section is highly characteristic in the precision of its planning, the juxtaposition of rationality (odd-numbered sections) and irrationality (even-numbered), and the fact that the arithmetic process itself is inaudible, only its textural consequences being perceived.

Lutosławski has also used extensively what might be called polyagogics – e.g., simultaneous accelerando in one voice and ritardando in another – to create rhythmic complexity. For the same purpose he also employed genuine (i.e., notated) polymeter, but only briefly: it appears in the finale of *Jeux vénitiens*, in the first movement ('Pensées') of *Trois poèmes*, and, for the last time, in the first movement of the String Quartet.

It will be readily apparent that the technique of limited aleatorism obviates the need for complex rhythmic figures in the individual parts. Lutosławski's rhythms tend to be extremely simple as a consequence. Typical are a kind of mosaic construction of small rhythmic cells in only two or three duration values, often simply 'long' and 'short', and the use of accelerating and decelerating gestures. Irrational duration values are comparatively infrequent; where they do occur they are almost always in a metrical (not limited aleatory) context, and they rarely divide the beat into values smaller than the quintuplet.

Sections with meter, conducted in the traditional manner, are freely mixed in the late works with sections of ad libitum playing, where the conductor gives only an initial downbeat and sometimes left-hand cues for individual instruments. Choosing whether to notate a given passage metrically or not is a matter of most efficiently achieving the intended sound result. The decision often depends on the prevailing 'harmonic rhythm', since the faster the rate at which the harmonic background changes, the more precisely must the players be coordinated, hence the more useful meter becomes. But Lutosławski has acquired such mastery of the technique that he is able to control ad libitum passages very precisely and, conversely, to achieve complex, spontaneous-sounding effects in metrical passages; 'aleatory' and 'metrical' become thus regions of a single continuum, not two distinct styles, and it is often difficult for the listener to tell where one leaves off and the other begins.

Limited aleatorism gives rise to certain difficulties as regards notating time and coordinating the members of an ensemble. Lutosławski's solutions have evolved gradually. His attitude is essentially conservative: 'On principle, I avoid any new sign', he says, 'unless it is absolutely necessary'. In practice this attitude has produced a style of notation which is preponderantly traditional, with only a limited number of symbols peculiar to Lutosławski's usage. And since Lutosławski is opposed to new ways of playing traditional instruments, ways which he finds 'unnatural' and 'brutal' and which add only 'decidedly second-rate and marginal attributes' to the tonal repertory of these instruments,[14] he has no need for a battery of symbols specifying such effects. Over the years his notational habits have been refined and made more efficient by his experience as a conductor, especially as regards symbolizing graphically the synchronizing functions of the conductor. The traditional score format, in which vertical coincidence implies temporal simultaneity, of course falsifies the ad libitum sections, but in orchestral works Lutosławski has been forced to keep a version of the traditional score for want of a practical alternative. The study score of the String Quartet is more realistic, since it separates the individual parts graphically. But this is the only chamber work of the late period requiring no conductor; for larger ensembles this solution is unworkable. And we will recall that in the quartet the composer actually wanted to provide only parts but acquiesced in the making of a study score at the insistence of performers.

Some of the notational devices of Lutosławski's third-period scores are explained in example 5.1 (see p. 115).

Pitch organization and the technique of aleatory counterpoint

The number of twentieth-century composers who may be called great masters of harmony is conspicuously small, but Lutosławski must surely be counted among them. Pitch organization in both the horizontal and vertical planes is of fundamental importance in his music – he calls it the 'basic problem' – but especially important is the management of vertical aggregations, a subject which has preoccupied him since the Five Songs of 1956–7. For Lutosławski harmony is a musical element of vast expressive and coloristic potential, and in his love for this aspect he feels close to Debussy:

An important feature of Debussy's world of music is his sensitivity to vertical aggregations, and also the independence [from] functional thinking in determining the logical sequence of musical events. Schönberg's twelve-tone system was in my opinion a natural consequence of the functional system, and was born to replace it. Debussy's system of organizing sound shows that he was indifferent to functions – that is what I have in common with him.[15]

In 1961 Lutosławski pointed out his reliance on harmonic aggregates based on all twelve pitch classes, in a statement which remains as pertinent to *Mi-parti* as it was to *Jeux vénitiens*:

The fundamental unity of which I make use in my latest pieces is the vertical aggregation of all the notes in the scale – a phenomenon of harmonic nature. Practically, there exists, as we know, an infinite possibility of creating twelve-tone chords which are unceasingly new. However, my technique preoccupies itself primarily with harmonies which for me possess an expressive physiognomy, a special and characteristic colour and consequently, a peculiar structure. There are often striking [contrasts] between the different chords of twelve notes. The interplay of these constitutes, among other things, one of the fundamental principles of my technique. As you can see, this has nothing in common with either twelve-note technique or with serial music. The only common trait is the 'chromatic whole'.[16]

The twelve-note vertical aggregations which form the basis of the harmonic style appear in a number of roles.[17] In almost every movement of every work since 1960 such a chord appears at the dynamic climax. Elsewhere they appear as harmonically static backgrounds against which melodic foregrounds are played out, in the manner originating in the last of the Five Songs and the first of the Postludes; or as splashes of color, as in 'Wiatr'. The characteristic 'physiognomies' Lutosławski ascribes to such chords are the product simply of the sorts of harmonic intervals they contain. The expressive power of a single interval is enormous, even when that interval is removed from the context of triadic tonality; even though the major third and the perfect fourth differ only by a semitone, for example, the difference in their effect is immediately obvious to the ear of any musician, even if the tones of each interval be separated by several octaves. For the power of the individual interval to assert itself in a large and complex chord, however, the chord must be so contrived that the desired interval can dominate the sound of the whole. Thus the most distinctive of Lutosławski's twelve-note chords are those which are constructed so that only two or three different types of intervals (i.e., interval classes) exist between the vertically adjacent pitches.

This principle of limited interval-class construction is fundamental to understanding the harmonic language of Lutosławski's late works. In his view, all-interval chords (such as Nicolas Slonimsky's *Grossmutterakkord*) are by their very nature colorless, lacking clearly

SYNCHRONIZATION

In metrical music, vertical strokes aligning the noteheads but not passing through the staves replace traditional barlines in *Jeux*, *Poèmes*, and the Quartet (using broken lines), the Cello Concerto and Preludes and Fugue (using solid lines). *Paroles*, Second Symphony, *Livre*, and *Mi-parti* use conventional barlines.

In *Poèmes*, conductor's signal to begin an ad libitum section.

From *Paroles* to the present, conductor's signal to begin an ad libitum section.

From *Poèmes* to the present, traditional a battuta beats.

In *Mi-parti*, left-hand beats.

In *Jeux*, cues to individual sections.

In Cello Concerto, left-hand cues to individual sections.

In Second Symphony, *Livre*, Preludes and Fugue, and *Mi-parti*, left-hand cues to individual sections.

Break off the repeated passage immediately at the conductor's signal. Consistent since *Poèmes*.

At the conductor's signal play up to the next repeat sign (or rest, etc., usually specified) and then stop (or go on, etc., specified). Consistent since *Poèmes*.

DURATION AND ARTICULATION

Repetitions of the same pitch. Used occasionally in *Jeux*, consistently since *Poèmes*.

In *Jeux*, horizontal distance between noteheads corresponds proportionally to time interval between attack points.

In *Poèmes*, the shortest possible sounds. Horizontal distance corresponds to time between attack points.

In *Poèmes*, length of beam corresponds to duration, according to the scale 2.5 cm. = 1 second.

In *Livre*, time between attack points is proportional to horizontal distance, and the length of a beam represents duration. Scale is generally specified in the parts.

In *Livre*, solid beams indicate legato for woodwinds and brass; broken beams indicate tonguing. The length of the beams is proportional to duration.

From *Poèmes* to present, notation for the duration of glissando.

The length of fermate is often left up to the individual player. For strings, 𝄐 often equals one whole bow.

PITCH

Accidentals affect only the notes they immediately precede; read F-sharp, F-natural, B-flat, B-natural for all scores since *Poèmes*. Performance materials, however, include cautionary natural signs.

In *Livre* and Second Symphony, three-quarters tone flat, one-quarter tone flat, one-quarter tone sharp, three-quarters tone sharp, respectively.

In Cello Concerto, Preludes and Fugue, and *Sacher Variation*, three-quarters tone flat, one-quarter tone flat, one-quarter tone sharp, three-quarters tone sharp, respectively. (*Jeux*, *Poèmes*, *Paroles*, and *Mi-parti* do not use quarter-tones.)

In Quartet, one- and three-quarters tone sharp, respectively.

5.1   Inventory of notational devices

defined individuality. Chords containing only one interval class are
of limited usefulness, on the other hand, for purely practical reasons:
it is possible to construct such chords only from interval classes 1
(yielding a fully chromatic cluster or groups of clusters) and 5 (producing a 'chord in fourths' occupying four octaves plus a fifth or –
even more unwieldy – a 'chord in fifths' requiring six octaves plus a
fourth and challenging the register resources of even the symphony
orchestra). But chords containing two or three interval classes offer a
rich and flexible source of harmonic expression. Three general types
of such chords are especially prominent in Lutosławski: those
emphasizing interval classes 1, 5, and 6; interval class 2; and interval
classes 3 and 4.

Harmonic aggregates containing some combination of interval
classes 1, 5, and 6 produce a kind of harmony which Lutosławski has
described as 'icy' (*Mi-parti*, rehearsal number 40). The interval-class
array notated beside each chord in example 5.2 demonstrates that
such structures are often vertically symmetrical. Also common are
aggregates emphasizing interval class 2 and so arranged as to maxi-
mize whole-tone segments (ex. 5.3).

Aggregates emphasizing interval classes 3 and 4 afford a more
impressive range of expressive values, since they offer the possibility

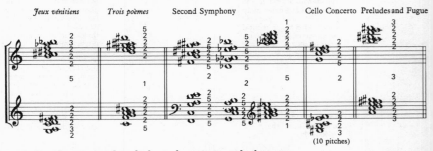

5.2   Twelve-note chords based on interval classes 1, 5, and 6

5.3   Twelve-note chords based on interval class 2

of embedding triads of various qualities or (very often) diminished
seventh chords in more complex structures, imparting to such structures a specially distinctive character (ex. 5.4). As we have seen,
Lutosławski's interest in this aspect of twelve-tone harmony extends
back to Five Songs and *Muzyka żałobna*, and it remains a very
important ingredient in his harmonic style to the present. The
examples demonstrate several characteristic procedures. Note the
consistent partitioning of the twelve tones into diminished seventh
chords in *Paroles tissées*; the passage quoted from continues in the
same vein for eight measures. The first of the chords extracted from
Livre pour orchestre demonstrates the idea of partitioning into
minor-third dyads separated by a constant interval (here the perfect
fifth), an approach Lutosławski has explored in a number of works.
The third chord quoted from *Livre* is the climactic harmony of the

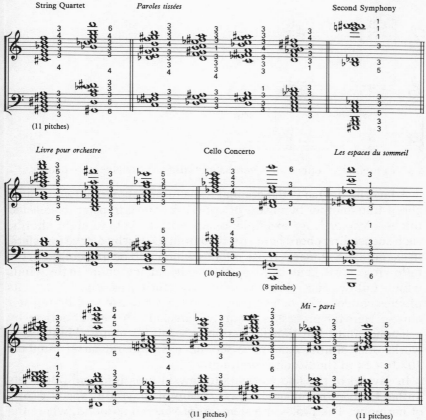

5.4   Twelve-note chords based on interval classes 3 and 4

entire work; the composer gives it a wonderfully 'consonant', affirmative sound by solidly orchestrating the perfect fifth which lies at the bottom and by keeping registrally and timbrally distinct the 'F-sharp-major/minor triad' and the 'F-minor seventh chord' above.

Lutosławski does have private methods of classifying twelve-note chords according to their musical effect, though we can only guess at some of the principles involved in his compositional choices. One such principle, however, may be illustrated by the two chords in example 5.5. Each is constructed (quite typically) in three layers of sound, and the interval content of the two is very similar. But for Lutosławski, the first of these chords is 'stable' and the second much more 'tense', because he believes that *sevenths*, of which there are a great many between the layers of the first chord, exert an attraction inward toward each other, while *ninths* (in the second chord) 'explode' outward, repelling each other.

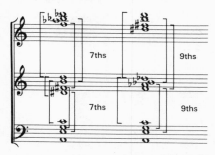

5.5   Comparative effects of sevenths and ninths in twelve-note chords

A favorite device is the gradual transformation of one twelve-note chord into another by means of applying octave transfer to selected pitches. *Mi-parti*, for example, opens with a cycle of eight chords, each succeeding chord being derived from the last by octave transfers. In example 5.6, x marks those pitches which will be transferred in the following chord. Later in *Mi-parti* the tall and 'icy' chord in the winds which follows the climax is gradually effaced as, one by one, its pitches converge by octave transfer to form a dense middle-register cluster. Here the process is so subtly managed as to pass unnoticed by a listener until the transformation is a *fait accompli*. Many other works offer similar examples: see, for example, rehearsal numbers 107 to 123 in the Second Symphony.

In several of the late works Lutosławski uses informal pitch sets (either twelve-tone or smaller) as a means of generating specific sorts of harmony. The procedure stems from *Muzyka żałobna*, where the peculiar series which provides the pitches of the Prologue and

5.6   Chord succession from the beginning of Mi-parti

Epilogue is postulated as a source of the grim 'thirdless' harmony that gives the mourning music its ineffable power. As in that earlier piece, the later works containing such sets are in no sense 'serial' music. The set does not play a fundamental structural role; it is subjected neither to the classical operations of twelve-tone technique (inversion, retrograde, retrograde-inversion) except transposition, nor to more abstruse permutations (rotation, multiplication, etc.); it is not used to generate series affecting other parameters (register, dynamics, rhythm, timbre); it does not persist for an entire work but rather is used only for special and quite limited purposes.

The first movement of the Second Symphony depends on several models of pitch generation, but that responsible for the opening 'march' in the brass is a twelve-tone set constructed solely of interval classes 2 and 5 and thus yielding, at least initially, predominantly 'consonant' harmony. (The same set influences some of the material of the second movement as well.) Lutosławski calls on a similar set (also of interval classes 2 and 5) in the fugue of Preludes and Fugue, where its purpose is to produce the placid, harmonically bland music of the episodes, against which the much more intense expositions of the fugue's six subjects (all based on interval classes 1 and 6) may stand in sharp relief. Similar 'series' emphasizing perfect fifths may be found in more limited applications in the third movement of Jeux vénitiens (piano) and in the last of the Trois poèmes (two pianos).

Two different sets are at work in Mi-parti. The first is a twelve-tone set which exists only as a precompositional construct; it is never stated in its entirety in the actual text. Instead Lutosławski uses as harmonic aggregates a number of unordered subsets (generally of five notes) drawn from this source set. On the other hand, the brass episodes (at numbers 24 and 28 and four measures after number 35) state linearly an unrelated nine-note set.

In several works Lutosławski has organized pitch by setting up two complementary (unordered) hexachords. This principle (inaugurated in simple form in the 'harmonic continuo' of the first of the Three Postludes) is detectable in the first and third of the Trois poèmes, the first chapter of Livre, some of the preludes and the end of the fugue (number 58) of Preludes and Fugue, and other works; and it is, of course, the whole point of *Sacher Variation*. A particularly frequent hexachord – deriving, in fact, from the *Muzyka żałobna* series – serves as the basis of thirdless harmony in three of the later works (ex. 5.7). Beginning at number 29 in the String Quartet this hexachord (apportioned in melodic dyads among second violin, viola, and cello) is systematically transposed until, at number 34, it produces its own complement. The same model is used as the basis of the double-reed refrains in the first movement of the Second Symphony and the brass interruptions in the Cello Concerto (e.g., rehearsal number 7).

5.7   Hexachord from String Quartet, Second Symphony, and Cello Concerto

   Though Lutosławski's vertical aggregates occur in metrical contexts, of particular interest is their management in moments of nonmetrical ad libitum playing through the technique of 'aleatory counterpoint' – the composer's term for the extension of limited aleatorism into the domain of pitch control. The composer, of course, chooses every pitch, and he relies on simple rhythmic calculations to insure that the harmonic result he envisions does in fact sound in every performance, despite the small rhythmic liberties given the players. At its simplest, the technique amounts to nothing more than realizing a preplanned chord by partitioning it among the players:

> If you take a twelve-note chord . . . , we can write down a passage that is based on the notes belonging to [it]. The different parts can play very complicated rhythms, . . . and yet play only the notes of that chord . . . This is the simplest way of organising pitch within an aleatoric section . . . It may occur that the chord never actually sounds in its entirety – it is supplemented by our memory and imagination.[18]

Clearly the resulting harmonic language is in no sense indeterminate, though Ove Nordwall falls prey to just such a misunderstanding when he claims that for Lutosławski 'harmony, in the usual sense of the word, becomes a mere by-product of a counterpoint which is aleatory'.[19] On the contrary, the complex foreground in Lutosławski's aleatory counterpoint represents the composing-out of a simple background structure – a situation strikingly like that which one finds in the 'harmonic counterpoint' of, say, Handel. The challenge to the composer is to take advantage of the textural and rhythmic benefits offered by limited aleatorism *without* relinquishing control over the harmonic result.

   The technique of aleatory counterpoint is put to more sophisticated uses as well. A frequent practice is to assign segments of a chord to specific instruments or families in such a way that the combined effect is modified by the character of the individual parts. The episode for three flutes, celesta, and tom-toms between rehearsal numbers 5 and 6 in the first movement of the Second Symphony is particularly instructive (in ex. 5.8 vertical alignment is irrelevant; tom-toms are omitted). Here the chord being composed out is a fully chromatic

5.8 Excerpt from flute-celesta episode, first movement of the Second Symphony (after no. 5)

cluster from a-flat¹ to a-natural², but the chord is partitioned in such a
way that each instrument plays only the 'consonant' intervals major
second, perfect fourth, and perfect fifth. Thus there are four diatonic
layers comprising together a chromatic aggregate and creating,
together with the timbre of flutes and celesta, the peculiar 'cold'
sound the composer was after. There is, moreover, an additional
peculiarity. All four instruments share the eight pitch classes C-natural
to G-natural; A-flat is reserved to flute 3, A to flute 2, B-flat to flute 1, and B
to the celesta. This tetrachord is then separated in register (the c³
octave), dynamic (*f*) and articulation (staccato) from the diatonic
layers to form a discrete acoustical layer that is fully chromatic.

We have already seen how harmony can be gradually transformed
using selective octave transfers. The technique of aleatory counterpoint provides another method for creating the illusion of gradual,
spontaneous change within a complex of pitches. In the opening
section of the second movement of the String Quartet, the composer's
calculated microrhythmic scheme, which we have already examined
(see above, pp. 111–12), is used not only to secure a particular rhythmic
texture but also to control pitch motion. The basic pitch gesture is
expansion outward from the initial unison e-flat¹ to a fully chromatic
cluster bounded by b-flat and a-natural¹, followed by contraction to
converge on unison e-natural¹, the entire process lasting fully a
minute in performance. The limits of this gesture describe one of the
fundamental pitch motives of the work (ex. 5.9). Lutosławski appor-
tions the individual steps in this process according to the fifteen
rhythmic phrases in each instrument in such a way that the four
termini are spaced equidistantly, i.e., unison e-flat¹ in phrase 1, arrival at b-flat in phrase 5, arrival at a¹ (hence completion of the twelve-
note cluster) in phrase 10, unison e-natural¹ in phrase 15.

5.9   Linear pitch gesture, opening of the second movement of the String
Quartet

Lutosławski resists attempts to describe his methods of organizing
pitch as a system or theory; to do so would be to shift attention unduly
from musical ends to technical means and would threaten to restrict
his freedom to be eclectic in approaching new problems as a composer. (Hindemith's example is cautionary.) He has remained averse
even to discussing publicly the details of individual works. But there
is patently a sort of core of basic techniques on which he has relied
steadily since *Jeux vénitiens*. The works themselves, however, have

displayed a continued refinement of technique and, unmistakably, a growing serenity in the harmonic character of Lutosławski's music. His acceptance of consonances as useful harmonic material was explicitly 'announced' on the first page of the Second Symphony. In the succeeding works, *Livre pour orchestre* and the Cello Concerto, there are even passages which seem close to implying tonality, and triadic allusions are important to the exceptional beauty of *Mi-parti*. We may expect this remarkable harmonic language to develop even further, for Lutosławski has vowed to continue his search for

> purity and beauty of tone in relation to harmony and the manner in which the instruments of the orchestra are used . . . [though] I certainly do not identify the beauty of tone with a return to the tonal system or even with the supremacy of the [triad] over other chords.
> . . . My greatest concern at present is pitch and the development and enrichment of methods and procedures connected with it. This, I believe, will be clear to anyone who will compare my latest compositions with works written in 1961.[20]

Texture

Edward Cowie has observed that 'the desire to work directly with the most brilliantly coloured sound objects, rather than through traditional musical discourse, may be inferred from Lutosławski's earliest works, but only after a protracted struggle was he able to achieve the novel means of articulating such materials with the immediacy he commands today . . . '[21] Certainly his consummate mastery of the orchestra and of the techniques of limited aleatorism, coupled with his sensitivity to timbre and harmonic color, have made it possible for the *wizja dźwiękowa* or *obraz dźwiękowy* (sound vision or image) to emerge as an important element in Lutosławski's style. Stephen Walsh has called his music 'texturally some of the most absorbing to have emerged from the 1960s', while adding the reservation that 'whether it can stand its ground in terms of solid musical content – a point on which doubt has been expressed – remains to be seen'.[22] Both Cowie and Walsh view texture in Lutosławski's music as an end in itself, a pure sensual value, as if his music had been suddenly reduced in 1961 to a single foreground dimension. In fact, however, textural complexes, individually fascinating and rich in detail though they may be, are most often elements contributing to a larger design. Far from replacing traditional musical discourse, as Cowie has it, Lutosławski's textural complexes have become participants in it.

Lutosławski treats textural units in a way analogous to the treatment of individual linear voices in traditional music, making it possible to speak of textural (and timbral) homophony and polyphony.

The finale of *Jeux vénitiens* offers a concrete demonstration of a polyphony of textures, in which almost twenty distinct textural groups are engaged in a kind of contrapuntal free-for-all. In the rather similar scheme of the final postlude, written only the year before, the textural 'themes' had been static blocks which simply succeeded each other with mechanical regularity. Now the textural themes have become active participants – 'voices' – in a polyphonic dialectic, a sort of textural stretto.

The notion of a whole group of instruments fused by their harmonic and rhythmic organization, register, and timbre into a separable textural entity functioning as would a single polyphonic voice recurs in many of the works of the sixties, originating perhaps in the second postlude. The opening of the third chapter of *Livre pour orchestre* provides an especially clear illustration of the technique. This idea is at its most consequent in the composer's most thoroughly contrapuntal work, the fugue of Preludes and Fugue; here each of the six subjects is exposed by what the composer calls 'bundles' of lines, each bundle comprising from two to five instruments playing the same pitches heterophonically to create a complex but unified voice.

The fact that the several variables of texture may be subjected to change either singly or in combination, at varying rates of speed, and so on, makes texture an extraordinarily flexible expressive vehicle. Thus Lutosławski is concerned not only with juxtaposing or superimposing interesting textural and timbral complexes but also with organic processes of growth within a single textural component, producing (by analogy with thematic transformation) textural transformation. The first chapter of *Livre* is an essay in such transformations. The opening string gesture, which 'flows' within the narrow registral ambitus bounded by a^1 and e^2, provides the germ for a development in which texture itself is the subject. The strings proceed to explore in quick succession the multifarious possibilities of expanding and contracting their registral space, of filling it densely or sparsely, evenly or with denser 'lumps' of sound floating within, and of making these changes both very quickly (e.g., one measure before 102) and very slowly (102–3). From number 106, three new texture blocks vie briefly with the strings for our attention: the brass (playing, in fact, their own version of the legato string texture); percussion; and a group containing contrabassoon, tuba, piano, and pizzicato contrabasses. And with what exquisite workmanship are these textural complexes called into being; how subtly are they elaborated, with what lapidary care is each detail set in place. This movement alone ought to be enough to refute the hasty but all too common identification of Lutosławski with the textural 'blocks', the 'bands of sound' in

works of the sixties by Penderecki and even Górecki, works whose
textural qualities seem by comparison crude and obvious. It would be
more apt to compare the 'sound visions' of Lutosławski's mature
œuvre to the Mikropolyphonie of György Ligeti, with its painstaking
construction and astonishingly rich and elegant aural result.

Several kinds of texture in Lutosławski's late music recur often
enough and are associated with sufficiently characteristic melic,
rhythmic, or instrumental traits that it is useful to describe them as
conventional types:

1. The cantilena, almost exclusively for strings and played ad
libitum, is important in a number of works: the String Quartet
(*funèbre* section at number 45), *Paroles tissées* (numbers 87–9), the
Second Symphony (from number 123), *Livre* (final chapter, to number
419), the Cello Concerto (slow movement), Preludes and Fugue (prelude 3 and fugue exposition 1). *Mi-parti* ends with a long, slowly
ascending cantilena line for twelve solo violins.

2. A technique that might be called, paradoxically, 'monophonic
polyphony' is used for all the episodes of the fugue in Preludes and
Fugue and the brass episodes in the mid-section of *Mi-parti*, and
traces of the technique may be seen as early as *Livre*. In such a passage
each pitch stated melodically is sustained as harmony following its
attack; the composer speaks of 'notes of dual function' having both
linear and vertical significance. Thus in *Mi-parti* a monophonic framework of individual attack points yields an apparently polyphonic
texture of six voices, and in the fugue the same procedure produces the
illusion of as many as thirteen voices. In the manner of traditional polyphony each performer's line is strongly individualized through its
rhythm, but here the combined parts form but a single succession of
melodic pitches.

3. The 'blurred toccata' style, deriving from the second movement
of the Concerto for Orchestra and the second postlude, is found in
Jeux vénitiens, second movement; *Paroles tissées*, third movement;
Livre, third movement; and Preludes and Fugue, preludes 1 (letter E)
and 2. This is a special application of the notion of a bundle of lines
acting as a single voice.

4. 'Mobiles', as Lutosławski has described sections of the String
Quartet, are passages of collective ad libitum in which the parts
contain discrete repeated fragments. The aural result is analogous to
the visual effect when a mobile of Alexander Calder is viewed from
different angles. The relation of part to part and part to whole is
constantly changing, familiar fragments of sound returning in ever-
new contexts. The quartet is full of this kind of thing – the music at
rehearsal number 3 is a splendid example – and similar effects occur

in many other works, including the third (at letter D) and fifth (letter G) preludes.

5. Sound visions of harmonic and rhythmic stasis are rather infrequent and are reserved for special dramatic situations. Examples include number 43 in the String Quartet and letter K in the seventh prelude.

Macrorhythm and form: music as drama

The whole arsenal of Lutosławski's technical procedures is mobilized to create an aesthetic experience for the listener:

The main purpose of a piece of music is that it should be experienced by the listener. Consequently [it] follows that a work of art is a complex phenomenon, the main part of which – according to the design of its purpose – is to play on the human mind . . .
. . . I understand the process of composing above all as the creation of a definite complex of psychological experiences for my listener, the fulfilment of which is on the whole extended throughout the greater number of performances of the same work.[23]

Lutosławski asserts that he always trys 'to compose the *perception* of a work, not only the notes', to compose the 'particular aesthetic experiences' of his ideal listener, who in reality is the composer himself, 'the one listener about whom I really know something'.

Clearly Lutosławski depends on the expectation–resolution or implication–realization model of perception, so firmly entrenched in the traditional Western ways of making and receiving the musical experience, in contriving to elicit affective response.[24] But to the extent to which the traditional conventions of musical practice are moribund, the composer must create in each work his own new conventions (he calls them 'once-only conventions') by which listener responses are conditioned. To take a simple example, the octave C figure interjected on eight occasions in the Introductory Movement of the String Quartet establishes a convention of predictable formal articulation that, when breached on the ninth appearance (rehearsal number 12), allows the listener to infer something about the formal moment. In *Livre pour orchestre*, Lutosławski has described the use of the interludes (*intermèdes*) and the means by which the fourth *chapitre* is introduced as constituting a deliberate psychological 'trick' whose effect depends on another such once-only convention.

Consistent with Lutosławski's insistence on retaining control over the musical experience and with his aversion for situations in which the composer abdicates his traditional responsibility for the finished musical product are his antipathy for open-form compositions and his commitment to a renewal of the closed form. Certainly there is no question of reviving archaic forms of the eighteenth and nineteenth centuries, but rather of seeking new methods to exploit the underlying bases of musical perception on which those forms were founded. For Lutosławski the twofold existence of the closed form – as a process in time and as an architectonic object out of time – is crucial:

Such a form owes its existence to the ability of the listener to remember the music he has heard and to integrate its individual sections while he listens so that after he has heard the composition (no matter how many times) he is [capable] of perceiving it as an idea that, like a painting or sculpture, exists outside the limits of time . . .

Thus the closed form is a complex phenomenon, for it is based on the concept of a dual role that time can play in a musical composition. The composition evolves in a given period of time, it is true, but once it has been performed it begins an independent existence of its own in the consciousness of the listener due to the faculties of memory and to the ability of the listener to integrate impressions. Unrestricted by time, the composition can be conceived in its entirety in one brief moment.[25]

In the 1930s Maliszewski taught Lutosławski form in the nineteenth-century Russian manner, as he himself had learned it as a student in St Petersburg. According to Lutosławski his teacher's method was to describe music in terms of four rhetorical 'characters' – introductory, narrative, transitional, and concluding – and in terms of formal function (so that it is possible, for example, to have a passage that is narrative in character but transitional in function). Lutosławski's own early works, especially the First Symphony, represent his application of Maliszewski's principles to produce forms belonging in spirit to the nineteenth century; and in the years since he has even adapted the same approach when confronting new music by composers of the avant-garde. Presumably there was some study of the works of eighteenth- and nineteenth-century masters with Maliszewski; it is likely Maliszewski had learned a good deal about Haydn from Glazunov. We know that when he taught Lutosławski in Warsaw he rarely discussed modern music. At any rate the younger man developed an admiration for Brahms and Haydn early on and even modeled the form of the finale of his First Symphony on the practice of Brahms. Even in recent years Lutosławski still speaks of taking lessons from Haydn, Mozart, and Beethoven in the construction of large-scale form and in the art of leading the listener through a piece of music.

The composer sees himself as belonging, with Stravinsky, Bartók, Varèse, and Messiaen, to a musical lineage of which Debussy is patriarch. But it is telling to note that none of the composers

Lutosławski admires in formal matters is French (save Albert Roussel, whom he admires mainly for the Germanic approach to form in his late works). In this decisive respect he does not belong to what Robert Sherlaw Johnson has called the 'anti-symphonic tradition' linking Debussy and Messiaen but rather falls squarely in the Austro-German symphonic tradition of the closed form, in which goal-directedness is central to the musical experience. His synthesis of these opposing traditions is, assuredly, not unique; other composers (e.g., Honegger, even Bartók himself) have effected the *rapprochement*, each in his own way. In Lutosławski's best works this synthesis has made it possible to present sonic tableaux of sometimes stunning beauty and yet to conserve that sense of directionality which lies at the heart of the Western musical tradition.

Musical structure is intimately bound up with the hierarchical organization of rhythm. Though any such structural hierarchy generally involves several levels – indeed, if we follow the notion of 'form' all the way down to the relations between individual sounds, we are apt to find ourselves juggling an unmanageable number of levels – we can make a start at describing the rhythmic nature of musical structure by distinguishing between the general concepts of *microrhythm* and *macrorhythm*. Microrhythm describes what we commonly understand by the term 'rhythm': the relationships in time between individual sounds and small groups of sounds; while macrorhythm describes the relationships in time between whole sections of music. The control of macrorhythm is perhaps Lutosławski's most important means of creating coherent large-scale form.

Many of Lutosławski's works appear to be highly sectional: the String Quartet, the final chapter of *Livre*, the Fugue, and *Mi-parti*, for example, all seem to comprise a large number of fairly short and quite discrete musical statements. The problem facing the composer of such a work is analogous to that faced by composers of the Classical era: namely to create at the highest level of structure what Kurt Westphal has called a *Verlaufskurve*,[26] a single compelling arc of musical motion transcending periodicity. One of Lutosławski's typical solutions is to construct a sort of macrorhythmic accelerando, in which discrete sections succeed each other at closer and closer intervals, not unlike the progressive reduction of phrase lengths in some Beethoven development sections as they approach the recapitulation. The method allows Lutosławski, as it were, to lead the listener by stages to a musical climax. It is a procedure he first attempted in the last postlude, then with greater success in the finale of *Jeux vénitiens*, in the String Quartet, and in the Second Symphony. The method is perhaps clearest and most compelling in the finale of *Livre*, where (from rehearsal number 419) a rich variety of vividly contrasting textural episodes appear one after the other, each one shorter than the last. The rapid succession of sound images has the effect of cinematic intercutting – a technique whose use in music, it has been pointed out, originates not in Central European but rather in Franco-Russian music. What is original in *Livre* is the fact that the macrorhythmic accelerando is continued until at last macrorhythm (the beginnings of sections) merges with microrhythm (notated quavers, beginning at number 439). How masterfully managed is this transformation, and how far Lutosławski has come in his treatment of macrorhythm, may be demonstrated by comparing this work with the less effective first and last movements of *Jeux vénitiens*, written seven years earlier.

The end of *Livre* demonstrates another of the composer's characteristic concerns: the desire for a natural (and original) means of leaving the climax. The method used here is much like that in the String Quartet and the Second Symphony. Lutosławski has described it thus:

> The building up to a single climax in the music is of course nothing new; what is perhaps my original contribution – and I think it is important for the understanding of my music – is the *way out* of the climax. This is closely bound up with my technique of 'aleatory counterpoint': gradually the music rises to a sort of (apparently) traditional climax, there is a definite high point . . . ; suddenly one of the musicians and then others and still others realize, as I imagine, that 'there is no use continuing it any more,' and they start playing something else, each one going his own way. The musical culmination is collective, the way out of the climax is individual.[27]

Typical as well is the overlapping of sections. Even as the brass players in *Livre* one by one give up playing, the strings have already begun the *ppp* harmonies which prepare the epilogue, much as in the symphony four solo celli and four solo basses begin a quiet epilogue even while the other instruments are yet engaged in a futile attempt to end the work on a note of triumph.

Microrhythm also functions importantly in the creation of directional motion. What Pociej calls the polychronic tendency in Lutosławski's music is evident in the second movement of the Second Symphony, where the superimposition of musics moving at different speeds sets up a tension which demands to be resolved and which makes possible the gradual transformation of character that prepares the climax of the work.

The relation between the creative artist and the potential consumers of his art – a delicate subject in Socialist societies, where it cannot be raised without evoking memories of the Stalinist era – has concerned Lutosławski deeply. His statement on the subject, a paper entitled 'The Composer and the Listener' which he read at a seminar on music criticism in Warsaw in 1964, has been widely reprinted and translated, and the opinions he expressed there remain valid for him today. While holding that the highest aim of the artist is 'to give the truest form to what he has to communicate to others', Lutosławski is at the same time skeptical of artistic methods which purport to aim at providing some service for listeners. Indeed any Soviet or Eastern European composer in our century would seem to have good empirical grounds to be dubious about the artistic results of composing music by attempting to guess at the tastes and desires of some concrete public. Lutosławski holds that, on the contrary, it is only by following the dictates of personal artistic conscience that a composer may hope to strike a genuine response among fellow human beings.

It is his desire to 'communicate' by organizing aesthetic experience for himself and, by extension, for others, which motivates Lutosławski's commitment to formal schemes whose broad outlines are simple, direct, and unambiguous. As a result the skilled listener – which is to say the listener practiced in concentrated listening to the repertory of the main stream of Western art music, but not necessarily expert at twentieth-century music – ought to take away from his first encounter with a work by Lutosławski a clear impression of the work's formal plan, its climax and dénouement. This is not to suggest, certainly, that repeated hearings will fail to reveal deeper, more complex layers of meaning, but simply to say that the basic shape of a work is likely to be simple enough to be grasped immediately.

The composer's distinctive contribution to the evolution of the closed form is his rethinking of the proper place of dramatic and emotional weight in the large-scale cycle. He was led to his solution, he says, by his own experiences as a listener, noting that he often grew tired of concentrated listening when hearing large-scale pieces whose most serious music fell in the first movement or was distributed throughout the work. In contradistinction to the Viennese Classical cyclic sonata, in which the first movement usually bears the greatest dramatic weight, or the sonata of Brahms or Mahler, in which that weight is likely to be shared by the outer movements, Lutosławski adopted a scheme in which the early sections are lighter in weight and a single important climax is reserved for a place very near the end. We might style this conceit 'end-accented form'. We have seen that such a plan was attempted as early as the Concerto for Orchestra, and apparently the aborted original plan of the Three Postludes was similar. In the sixties this design was made explicit, above all in the two-movement works String Quartet (Introductory Movement, Main Movement) and Second Symphony ('Hésitant', 'Direct'). In both works the function of the first movement is engaging (*angażujący*) the listener's attention through an apparently aimless juxtaposition of contrasting episodes, that of the second fulfilling, consummating (*spełniający*) the implicit promise of purposeful musical motion.[28] Most of the other late works manifest a similar end-accented construction, if less obviously. In *Jeux vénitiens*, *Livre pour orchestre*, and Preludes and Fugue the early movements are short, incomplete fragments, and the longer finale consummates the musical action. Even the opening monologue, the series of orchestral episodes, and the cantilena of the Cello Concerto cannot stand alone but require the dramatic confrontation and resolution of the last section to make a satisfying whole. Similarly, while the opening phrases of *Mi-parti* are very beautiful in their own right, they are essentially static; they create no formal urgency. The subsequent 'development' section is given the task of creating and satisfying dramatic expectation. The end-accented plan has not much affected Lutosławski's vocal music, on the other hand, since in *Trois poèmes d'Henri Michaux*, *Paroles tissées*, and *Les espaces du sommeil* it is the text that decisively influences musical structure.

Lutosławski's tendency to shape his musical materials in dramatic ways has in the last several works become even more pronounced. The music is often most easily understood in terms of dramatic scenarios, and the composer himself is prone to rely on such description. In many works individual instruments or groups are treated almost theatrically, as if they were the *dramatis personae* in a scenario of unfolding actions and emotions. For example, Lutosławski has described as a 'subplot' the cellist's pizzicato chords beginning each section from number 35 to number 38 in the String Quartet; when suddenly this subplot takes over the action briefly at number 39, the other three instruments are 'taken aback' and respond with a puzzled phrase at number 40. We also know that the composer sent explanations of the Cello Concerto to Rostropovich before the première, expressed in literary and dramatic language, describing a 'duel' between soloist and orchestra in which the cellist is 'attacked' by small groups of instruments and finally appears defeated, only to rise phoenix-like in triumph at the end of the work. It should be pointed out that such instrumental characterization as a formal resource is not a new idea with Lutosławski. Ernest Bloch made the cellist in *Schelomo* (1915–16) a sharply drawn persona, and instrumental characterization is central to Elliott Carter's second (1958–59) and third (1971) string quartets, as well as his Double Concerto (1961) and Piano Concerto (1966). Nor does this practice lie wholly outside the Austro-Germanic orchestral tradition, as witness the soloists in Richard Strauss's *Don Quixote* (1897), the snare drummer in Carl Nielsen's Fifth Symphony (1921–2), and the solo flutist and roguish bass trombonist in the same composer's Flute Concerto (1926).

The ease with which Lutosławski's musical conceptions can be translated into dramatic language points to the essential characteristic of his art: its profound humanity. The mature works show how completely he has understood the art of the Classical composers he so admires, composers whose sonata forms Schlegel likened to textless operas because they create in purely musical terms their own – unuttered and unutterable – texts.[29] But to speak of dramatic scenarios is indeed to *translate* from the sphere of language into the very different sphere of music, and to translate very imperfectly. Lutosławski is careful to point out that he does not attach extramusical meaning to his music, and that he resorts to metaphorical description only because music cannot successfully be described in its own terms. He is fond of quoting Debussy's remark to Ernest Guiraud in 1889 that 'music takes over where words fail; music is made for the inexpressible'. Rarely, indeed, is the drama of his music so earthly, so susceptible of anthropomorphic programmatic interpretation, as in the Cello Concerto. Rather Lutosławski bids us confront directly a universe which lies beyond the powers of ordinary language. The drama played out in his art is a cosmic drama, awakening in us, as Stefan Jarociński has observed of Debussy's music, the 'nostalgia for another world'.

6   Notes on the late works

Jeux vénitiens

It may very well seem arbitrary to select *Jeux vénitiens* as the one work marking the onset of the mature period in Lutosławski's creative life. The work can hardly be said to signal a violent change of direction, since in most respects its style very closely resembles that of the Three Postludes, which occupied the composer immediately before; the changes in Lutosławski's style around 1960, as throughout his career, were not revolutionary but evolutionary. On the other hand, the work seems experimental, tentative, and imperfectly realized by comparison with *Trois poèmes*, completed two years after. But Lutosławski himself dates his first maturity as a composer from *Jeux vénitiens*, for it is here that limited aleatorism makes its first appearance (hence the 'games' of the title, signifying nothing more than that there are moments of collective ad libitum).

The work is scored for a chamber orchestra of twenty-nine soloists: seven woodwinds, three brass, four percussionists, harp, piano (four hands), and twelve solo strings. The four-movement cycle includes three orchestral miniatures, each rather simple in formal structure, and a somewhat longer and much more complex finale – the end-accented formal plan – though here even the finale is on a rather small scale, since the entire cycle requires only thirteen minutes to perform. Instrumentation plays an important role in defining the contrasting characters of the individual movements: the first and second are founded on the contrast between the strings and the others; the third is for solo flute supported by the remaining woodwinds, harp, and piano; and only in the finale does the entire ensemble finally come together en masse. Ad libitum sections stand side by side with traditional a battuta playing: the first movement uses both, the second is exclusively a battuta (except for the piano part near the end), the third is exclusively ad libitum, and the finale again uses both styles of playing.

The first movement repeatedly juxtaposes two radically different kinds of music. The sections marked in the score A, C, E, and G present a lively, extrovert woodwind texture; these alternate with sections B, D, F, and H, which comprise soft, static clusters in the strings. The beginning of each section is marked by a single stroke in the percussion – the same device used in the last movements of the Three Postludes and *Livre pour orchestre*, and much like the formal articulations in the String Quartet as well. The seemingly mechanical succession of A- and B-type sections throughout the movement is given a sense of direction by the fact that to the former is added on each reappearance a progressively larger contingent of wind and percussion instruments. Moreover the macrorhythmic structure is so contrived that, in general, the sections of both types become longer and longer as the movement proceeds. An exception is section F, which lasts only two seconds. Its presence is a psychological trick, confounding listener expectation; in context it is not heard as an independent section but rather attaches itself to E and G to make one long division of the form:

A	12 seconds	woodwinds
B	27 seconds	strings
C	18 seconds	woodwinds, timpani
D	21 seconds	strings
E ⎤		woodwinds, timpani, brass
F ⎥	32 seconds	strings
G ⎦		woodwinds, timpani, brass, piano
H	39 seconds	strings
Codetta	*c*. 7 seconds	percussion

Seen in this light, sections E-F-G serve as the culmination of the A-type music, H as the culmination of the B-type music. The isolated percussion strokes at the end (echoing the form-articulating role of the percussion throughout the movement) make a kind of codetta, though its effect is not affirmative but inconclusive, since in dramatic terms nothing has 'happened'.

Contrast between the non-string and string sections is expressed in several musical dimensions: timbre, register (widely spaced v. narrowly confined), microrhythm (very active v. almost completely static and collective ad libitum v. a battuta), dynamic (moderately loud v. very soft), articulation (variegated v. undifferentiated). Beyond these obvious points, however, is another, more subtle, means of reinforcing the contrast: harmony. This first movement furnishes a concrete demonstration of Lutosławski's conviction that harmonic structure can exercise a powerful influence on form. The sections for winds and percussion employ a symmetrical twelve-note chord in the woodwinds dominated by interval class 2. When later the brass and piano join this texture, they together complete a second twelve-note collection, also symmetrical; the brass portion, which fills a gap in the center of the original woodwind chord, uses only interval class 1, while the piano, which adds notes at both extremes of register, uses interval classes 3 and 4. The resulting twenty-four-note chord reached in section G has the diffuse character of all-interval harmony; any sense of well-defined harmonic individuality present in the woodwind's original whole-tone collections has by this time been destroyed by the contributions of the brass and piano (ex. 6.1). This transformation in harmonic character is no less important in making formal sense of the recurring A-type sections than are the addition of instruments increasing the density of the texture, the expansion in total register, and the lengths of the individual sections.

6.1 Harmonic content of sections A, C, E, and G in the first movement of *Jeux vénitiens*

The contrast with the harmony of the string sections could hardly be more pronounced. Sections B, D, and H each represent a fully chromatic cluster spanning a perfect fifth. During the course of a section each cluster is gradually transposed by means of a series of octave transfers; most such transfers are easily followed, since they are marked by special dynamics and articulation in the individual string parts. The cluster harmony of these sections uses only eleven pitch classes; E-natural is reserved for use in a solo stratum set off from the harmonic background by register, dynamic, and articulation. Only at the very end of section H is the pitch E reconciled to the prevailing harmonic language, when it is sustained and is joined by D-sharp to form the closing dyad of the movement (ex. 6.2). On the other hand, section F, which as we have seen only *seems* to belong to the succession of static string passages, consists of a single chord whose intervallic structure relates it not to B, D, and H but rather to the A-type sections (specifically to the piano part in section G).

The second movement, a brief scherzo delicately orchestrated and

6.2   Basic harmonic motions of sections B, D, F, and H (*Jeux vénitiens*)

played very softly throughout, recalls the 'blurred' style of the second movement of the Concerto for Orchestra and the second Postlude. As in those earlier works, scurrying semiquaver figures produce a 'night-music' effect. The structure of the scherzo, like that of the first movement, is based on the alternation of only two different styles of texture. Thus the form may be represented simply as *a b*, with two variations added – *a b a′ b′ a″ b″* – again reminding us of the Concerto for Orchestra scherzo.

The material we are calling *a* belongs exclusively to the strings and consists of tiny fragments stated antiphonally between two contrapuntal voices, punctuated by the briefest of silences. Each 'voice' is really a bundle of three or four individual string parts. As the section progresses some four or five little phrases are discernible, their limits defined by the vertical 'width' of each fragment stated by the voice-bundles, ranging from one to six semitones. Leaving rhythm aside, the effect of the opening might be rendered as shown in ex. 6.3. Notice the symmetrical arrangement of intervals in the second phrase.

Vertical width of each voice-bundle:

6.3   Schematic reduction of the opening of the second movement of *Jeux vénitiens*

The *b* material proper (winds, mallet percussion, harp) begins at m. 30; but as early as m. 9 it has begun to contest the strings for center stage, first as isolated single notes, then as attacks coming closer together until they coalesce to form the *b* texture at m. 30. Unlike the *a* texture, which is characterized by many short rests, *b* is continuous, and the pitches are so arranged that the total chromatic is always sounding. Measures 30–6 can, in fact, be reduced to a succession of some six or seven twelve-note chords; it seems likely that at some stage in the composing these chords must even have been written out.

The harmonic rhythm (the rate at which chords change) is extremely fast, however, and it even accelerates toward the end; at the same time the registral space occupied expands downward by more than two octaves, from e-flat^2 (the lowest sounding pitch in m. 30) to B-flat (m. 36).

On its second appearance as *a'*, the string material has expanded from less than two octaves in register to exactly four octaves, but it has also been shortened from twenty-nine to eighteen measures. As before, the winds and percussion begin gradually to enter the texture, until at m. 55 they emerge alone as *b'*, now grown from seven to twenty-eight measures. Toward the end of *b'* the strings return with isolated pizzicato notes, mimicking the single notes of the winds earlier on. From all this it will be seen that the structure of the scherzo is not merely additive, as it may at first have appeared to be; it is instead progressive, for the *b* sections are gradually displacing the *a* sections as the principal material. The process may be said to culminate at m. 83, after the strings have been reduced to an accompanimental role, when the piano enters for the first time to punctuate the formal boundary with clusters encompassing the entire keyboard (achieved by depressing the keys using long cardboard cylinders).

What remains has the character of a coda. The final appearance of the strings with *a''* is the shortest of all, only nine measures. During this time the drums – five tom-toms, tenor drum, and three timpani – enter gradually with isolated single notes, just as the winds and later strings have done previously, until at m. 93 they present an unpitched version of *b* accompanied by staccato clusters in the piano.[1] (Recall that the scherzo of the Concerto for Orchestra also includes such a 'translation' of earlier material into the percussion.) Three measures of *b* material restored to the woodwinds complete the movement. It is worth noting that the roles of timbre, registral control, and instrumental characterization in shaping this movement bear eloquent witness to the essential continuity of Lutosławski's art; for they remind us that his new style in *Jeux vénitiens* did not spring full-grown ex nihilo but rather is intimately connected to the style of the Concerto for Orchestra and other early works.

The third movement of *Jeux vénitiens*, both the simplest and the most successful of the entire work, was the only movement not performed at the Venice Biennale in 1961; Lutosławski finished it later that year. It is a slow movement in the form of a recitative for solo flute, and the solo writing is highly expressive, sometimes virtuosic, and very beautiful indeed. The form is in a single continuous part, the solo flute describing a single arc from the lowest register of the instrument at the beginning to the highest at the end while at the same time producing in dynamics a long crescendo, climax, and short decrescendo.

The three groups of supporting players – woodwinds with harp, piano, strings – all contribute to this basic crescendo–decrescendo shape as well; but they also support the form in more complex ways. Together the woodwinds and harp create a kind of harmonic continuo, the six woodwinds sustaining what is for the most part a five-voice texture of overlapping long notes while the harp adds splashes of faster notes, all of this according to the following principles:

1. the total chromatic is partitioned as seven pitch classes in the harp (for obvious physical reasons) and five in the woodwinds; the content of the partitioned collections changes from time to time, but their size and their complementary relationship remain constant;

2. these pitch classes are deployed in a pattern of gradually expanding registers, reaching the widest registral expanse at the end of the movement; and

3. important structural pitches in the solo flute melody do not sound simultaneously in the harmonic continuo, except between the two flutes from letter U to the end.

The pitches of the piano part are generated quite differently, namely by repeating again and again the 'series' of descending perfect fifths (G, F, C, . . . E-double-flat = D, A-double-flat = G), also in a gradually widening registral distribution. What is more, the distribution of register is controlled in such a way that the right hand ascends at the same rate as does the solo flute line, allowing the pianist to reinforce all the soloist's important structural notes (e.g., f-sharp^2 at letter E, g^3 at letter I), while the left hand descends at about the same rate as do the bass notes of the harmonic continuo, reinforcing the general contour of the 'bass line'. In this way the pianist mediates between the continuo and the soloist.

The strings are quite independent of all this, except that they do support in their own way the basic crescendo-decrescendo shape of the movement. They enter occasionally to comment on the proceedings, on each occasion stating briefly a single twelve-note chord. There are a total of fifteen such chords in the course of the movement, and the rate at which the strings' entrances occur (i.e., the strings' macrorhythm) accelerates toward the climax at letter Q and then slows again to the end. The registral space occupied by the string chords is very wide at first, then collapses inward to dense middle-register clusters at the climax, and finally expands outward to its widest point at the end. Example 6.4 summarizes the changes in register of the soloist and all three elements of the accompaniment for the sake of comparison.

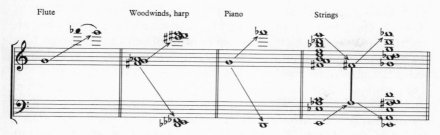

6.4   Registral ambitus in the third movement of *Jeux vénitiens*

To the reader who has endured patiently these descriptions, the technical means at work in the third movement and the kinds of precompositional decisions which produced them may seem abstruse and even mechanical. But written language provides us with poor substitutes for aural experience. In this exquisite little piece, as in others, Lutosławski's only object can have been the sounding result; and although it is unlikely that any but the most obvious technical features will be audible to the listener, the artistic result could only have been achieved by relying on technique. For Lutosławski artistic ends may justify systematic means, but never the other way round.

Although each of the first three movements does have elements of 'development' – the gradual augmentation of the orchestra in the first, the progressive variation of material in the second, the shaping of the third by register and dynamic – each of them is essentially an independent sonic tableau; none is 'symphonic' in character. In Lutosławski's formal scheme, the success of the entire cycle must hinge on the longer, more symphonic, more obviously directional fourth movement. The first three movements have required of the listener no great exertion or involvement; the finale demands concentrated listening.

We may distinguish four principal divisions in the form of the finale: an introduction, an approach to the climax and the climax itself, a period of subsidence after the climax, and an epilogue. The introduction presents the idea on which the construction of the whole movement depends: overlapping statements of radically contrasting blocks of texture. Here there are only two: a static twelve-note chord (first in the strings) and a mobile 'sound image' of considerable microrhythmic complexity (first in the winds). The microrhythmic complications are achieved here by introducing polyrhythm (this is, in fact, the prototype for the opening passage of *Trois poèmes d'Henri Michaux*); the metrical 'beat' is one second of time, but the individual parts have duple, triple, and quintuple subdivisions of this beat. In this way the effect of collective ad libitum may be achieved through metrical playing, allowing precise control of both rhythm and harmony. Contrast between the static and mobile textures is, as might be expected, not only rhythmic but harmonic; each statement of the former gives a static twelve-note chord in tritones and perfect fifths, each statement of the latter a composed-out twelve-note chord in semitones. As the introduction ends, the mobile texture (now transferred to the strings) is gradually taken over by *sf* accents (again foreshadowing *Trois poèmes*).

The piano interrupts this introductory passage abruptly to announce that the central business of the movement has begun. A succession of vividly differentiated textural 'themes' now appears in four orchestral groups – woodwinds, brass, piano (four hands), and strings – overlapping each other more and more closely in an accelerating polyphony of textures. Each texture is played in collective ad libitum; the conductor indicates only the entrances of the various groups. The overlapping textures are a fine example of what Lutosławski has called *wielowarstwowość* (multilayeredness) and what Pociej calls the 'polychronic tendency', a technique motivated by the realization that limited aleatorism tends to produce static textures. It is the conflict between layers, as well as the ever-quickening pace at which new ones are introduced, which produces musical tension – indeed, which produces what may be called a sonic brawl among the four groups of the orchestra.

Three stages in the macrorhythmic accelerando may be discerned. In the first stage, beginning at letter a_1 (p. 33 in the score), the macrorhythm (i.e., the interval between successive entries) contracts from five seconds to three; in the second (from a_2, p. 37), from three seconds to one; and in the third (from a_3, p. 40), from one second to less than half a second. Towards the end of this process it is necessary to reintroduce meter in order to control the rapid succession of entrances; thus macrorhythm has been transformed into microrhythm. By this point it is no longer possible to distinguish by ear the contributing textural themes as they enter; they have merged into a dense mass of sound.

The climax to which all of this has been leading comes at letter G in the form of two explosive outbursts of ad libitum playing in the winds and strings, framing a central episode of violent clusters in the piano spanning the entire keyboard. The percussion then enter alone in a *fff* attempt to continue the climax, playing a three-part rhythmic canon in augmentation. It is no use, though; celesta, harp, and piano enter soon afterward, softly arpeggiating twelve-note chords, and in the end the percussion give way and quiet prevails. A subdued epilogue follows, in which, as if startled at the fury they have produced, four orchestral groups – woodwinds and celesta, harp and lower strings, brass and vibraphone, and piano and upper strings in harmonics – play faint reminders of the kinds of textures which created the cataclysm.

The form of the entire movement may be summarized thus:

1–53	Introduction (a battuta)	11 macrorhythmic events in c. 53 sec.
a₁–F	Polyphony of textures (ad libitum)	Total c. 87 sec. First stage: 9 events in c. 34 sec.; second stage: 14 events in c. 28 sec.; third stage: 36 events in c. 25 sec.
G–I	Climax (ad libitum)	c. 29 sec.
101–45	Subsidence (a battuta)	c. 45 sec.
J–end	Epilogue (ad libitum)	c. 32 sec.

Having examined *Jeux vénitiens* in some detail, we may return to the question of what place this work occupies in Lutosławski's evolving œuvre. As striking as its connections with his earlier music may be, even more interesting are the many techniques which would in future works provide the basis for great artistic achievement. *Jeux vénitiens* is truly a seminal work for the composer. But though its plan is sound – essentially the same plan would produce seven years later a masterpiece, *Livre pour orchestra* – one has the inescapable impression that the composer, not yet fully master of his new technique, failed to make good the promise of that plan to fashion a convincing musical statement. Despite its many strengths, chief among them the magical third movement, *Jeux vénitiens* retains the air of a brilliantly conceived but imperfectly executed experiment.

Trois poèmes d'Henri Michaux

Henri Michaux, the enigmatic French poet and sometime painter, was born 24 May 1899 in Namur, Belgium, of bourgeois parents. Even as a child Michaux was strangely resistant to the world around him and withdrawn. After school he worked for a while as a sailor, then returned to Paris and in 1922 began writing seriously. At first Michaux's work attracted little attention and even less sympathy. The surrealists tried to claim him as one of them, but he rejected any such entanglements and remained an intensely solitary figure. It was not until 1941, when André Gide published an appreciation entitled

Découvrons Henri Michaux, that Michaux began to reach a larger audience. In 1956 he discovered the drug mescaline; he devoted the next several years almost exclusively to describing his experiences under the influence of this drug and other hallucinogens.

Among the hallmarks of Michaux's literary works are a sense of alienation from the world and even from the self and a disconcerting blurring of the line between internal and external aspects of being. Gide observes that Michaux 'excels in making us feel intuitively both the strangeness of natural things and the naturalness of strange things'. His free verse, prose poems, and prose are written in an idiosyncratic style characterized by odd syntax, invented words, slang terms, and peculiarly elliptical constructions, but characterized as well by surreal imagery of great beauty.

Michaux is enthusiastic about music, dance, and painting, precisely because they are more direct, more immediate modes of expression than is verbal language. His own approach to poetic language and structure has many points of tangency with music;[2] perhaps it is this musical quality which has attracted composers to Michaux's work. Boulez turned to his poetry in *Poésie pour pouvoir* (1958), and Lutosławski, already making sketches toward a vocal–instrumental work in 1961, found in the early poems of Michaux three short texts that suited his musical purpose exactly.

Trois poèmes d'Henri Michaux was Lutosławski's first choral composition (excepting functional music in the 1950s) in nearly thirty years, and the approach to text-setting he adopted here was thus a radically new one for him. Though the composer is a sensitive reader, careful never to violate the spirit of the poetic text, in this work he sometimes treats words and even individual phonemes as abstract sound values. There is no preoccupation with linguistic particles as musical material or with the structure of speech as subject matter (Berio, Gaburo, Babbitt, Nono, J. K. Randall); it is just that Lutosławski is more concerned with creating sound images compatible with Michaux's poetic images than with providing for a clearly enunciated reading of every word of text in performance. He also introduces, in the second movement, speaking, whispering, shouting, and murmuring for the singers; though these techniques were hardly innovations in the early 1960s – think of Milhaud's *Les Choéphores* (1915) – they too were new for Lutosławski.

In the succession of works begun by *Jeux vénitiens*, *Trois poèmes* is the first unequivocal artistic success. The technique of limited aleatorism is pushed even further here – indeed in this work and the next, the String Quartet, is to be found the highest proportion of ad libitum playing in any of the composer's scores – and it is done more subtly and with a surer hand than in *Jeux vénitiens*. Nothing seems experimental here; every note contributes to an elegantly simple but profoundly affecting musical experience. Much of the effect depends on the creation of extraordinarily fluid texture, especially in the chorus, and for this reason many of the rhythmic values are notated only approximately. (With minor exceptions, this is the only work of Lutosławski's in which this is true.) So independent are the chorus and orchestra from each other that each requires its own conductor. There are two scores, one for chorus with a reduction of the orchestral parts and the other for orchestra with the choral parts reduced. Both scores repay close study, for the meticulous reductions (which were done by the composer himself) constitute a short course in Lutosławski's methods of organizing pitch.

The three movements present three distinct moods: skeptical contemplation, violent activity, reflective resignation. The text for the first panel of the triptych, 'Pensées', pessimistically describes human thoughts as 'an indistinct sea', 'shadows of shadows,/ashes of wings', 'strangers in our houses', 'dusts which distract us and scatter our life'. Only in the third of the four short stanzas does the poet present briefly a more animated image:

> Thoughts in a wondrous swimming,
> that glide into us, among us, far from us.

Malcolm Bowie has described the poem as 'a flickering vision of the mental field: with shadow and sudden illumination, expansions and contractions, energies which surge and fade. The poet's mind wanders over his mind's wanderings.'[3]

Lutosławski's setting is faithful not only to the imagery of the poem but even to its structure. Each of the four stanzas is treated separately, with caesuras isolating one from the next; each is preceded by an orchestral introduction establishing mood and illuminating the poetic images. In addition, the sense of closure created in the poem when the last stanza returns to the pessimistic tone of the first is reflected plainly in the music by a return to the opening texture and even the opening harmony.

The orchestra opens with a fluid, almost featureless texture of twelve-note chords, an 'indistinct sea' of sound evoking the poem's first line. It is noteworthy that in the first and fourth stanzas the microrhythms of the individual parts, which in other Lutosławski scores would likely be strongly profiled, are instead deliberately rendered uninteresting, the better to reflect the poet's tone. Here the woodwinds and brass achieve their bland texture through simple polyrhythm of just the sort that begins the finale of *Jeux vénitiens*; and as also happened in that movement, the texture is gradually invaded by *sf* accents. When the chorus enters it produces a similarly indistinct texture, and the pitches produce a fully chromatic cluster, with the upper half (d-flat¹ to g-flat¹) assigned to the women, the lower half (g to c¹) to the men.

The other stanzas are rather similarly constructed. The second, like the first, is begun in the orchestra (number 34); only the woodwinds play, using little fragments of repeated staccato notes to represent the 'shadows of shadows', 'ashes of wings'. For the third stanza (number 85) the woodwinds are joined by keyboard percussion in a suddenly busy texture of rapid notes summoned up by the image of 'swimming' thoughts. The brass and woodwinds recreate the opening texture (though not at first the opening pitches) to introduce the fourth stanza (number 143), and when the chorus enter at number 154 ('étrangères en nos maisons') they are given the same cluster, g to g-flat¹, with which they began. The chorus finish the movement alone, fading away while repeating widely dispersed syllables of text like particles of the dust that 'scatters our life'. No better proof than the quite old-fashioned text-painting of the first movement could be adduced for the proposition that, although Lutosławski prizes the abstracted *sounds* of poetic language in the musical fabric, his first expressive goal is to illuminate the *sense* of the text.

The atmosphere of the second poem, 'Le grand combat', is very different. The text describes a savage physical battle between two unidentified men, urged on by a crowd of bloodthirsty onlookers and ending in death for one of the combatants. This grisly scene is made the more compelling by Michaux's grotesquely suggestive neologisms; the violence done to the language intensifies the physical violence it describes, at the same time removing the whole scene from the realm of everyday experience to a garish, irreal other world. Richard Ellman's translation captures the spirit admirably:

> He embowerates and enbacks him on the ground,
> He raggs him and rumpets him up to his drale;
> He praggles him and libucks him and berifles his testeries;
> He tricards him and morones him,
> He grobels him rasp by rip and risp by rap.
> Finally he enscorchorizes him.
>
> The other hesitates, espudates himself, unbrines himself, twisses and ruins himself.
> He'll soon be done for.
> He mends and immarginates himself . . . but in vain
> The hoop which has rolled so far falls.
> Abrah! Abrah! Abrah!
> The foot's collapsed!

The arm's broken!
The blood's run out!
Dig, dig, dig,
In the pot of his belly there's a big secret
You neighborhood shrews who cry into your handkerchiefs;
We're amazed, we're amazed, we're amazed
And we watch you
We others, we're looking for the Big Secret too.[4]

Given a speaking chorus and an orchestra dominated by the battery,
the composer is able to surpass even the poet in recreating this scene.
Using only the poet's lines, Lutosławski creates through the chorus an
effective picture of the gathering crowd, its growing excitement, its
strident exhortations to 'Dig, dig, dig', and its dispersal, still mum-
bling in undertones, after the spectacle has run its grim course. For
much of this movement it is given to the women (the 'neighborhood
shrews', one supposes) to depict the noise of the crowd by reciting
different lines of text simultaneously, while the men give a straightforward, unison reading of the poem in its proper order. All this is
interrupted at number 17 by a long, ferocious battle in the percussion.

The second division of the text, marked by the onset of coarse
flutter-tonguing in the low brass (number 22), depicts the rising
agitation of the bystanders. The climax for the chorus comes at
number 52, where they set up a fierce commotion by reading the first
sixteen lines of text simultaneously; the orchestra follows at 53 with a
furious climax of its own.

Teresa Błaszkiewicz has pointed out in this second movement an
example of the simple arithmetical procedures Lutosławski often
relies on to insure microrhythmic complexity. After number 48 the
orchestral instruments are given the following sequences of rhythmic
patterns (expressed in numbers of semiquavers); in each part, the
successive patterns are shortened or lengthened according to a consistent scheme:[5]

		increment of change:
piccolo 1	15, 12, 9, 6	−3
piccolo 2	6, 8, 10, 12	+2
flute	9, 8, 7, 6, 5, 4	−1
clarinet 1	6, 9, 12, 15	+3
clarinet 2	12, 10, 8, 6	−2
clarinet 3	4, 5, 6, 7, 8, 9	+1
glockenspiel	4, 8, 12, 16	+4
xylophone	16, 12, 8, 4	−4
piano 1	7, 14, 21	+7
piano 2	21, 14, 7	−7

Notice that there are actually only five discrete patterns operating here; each is accompanied by its inverse, so that piccolo 1 and clarinet 1 form a complementary pair, glockenspiel and xylophone another, etc. The reader is invited to discover similar rhythmic procedures elsewhere in this movement (including the choral parts).

After the central cataclysm of the second movement, the third, 'Repos dans le Malheur', comes as an almost complete relaxation of tension. With one crucial exception, the whole third movement is soft. The mood of fatalistic resignation communicated by the music is suggested by the Michaux poem, an apostrophe to sorrow in which the speaker (one can never be sure in Michaux whether the first person is the poet himself) embraces misfortune as man's future, his true mother, the limit of his existence. The speaker surrenders utterly to sorrow:

> In your light, in your fullness, in your dread,
> I abandon myself.

The musical form of the third movement rests on a simple line of four structural pitches leading upward from D-flat to F-sharp (ex. 6.5), elaborated in wonderfully subtle ways. Each of the structural pitches generates one section of the form, representing respectively lines 1–7, 8–10, 11, and 11–12 of the poem. Each section begins with an announcement by solo harp of the structural pitch, and in each case this is followed by harmonies expanding outward from this central pitch. In the first two sections the harmonic elaboration begins with the two pianos weaving a delicate web of sounds subtly emphasizing the organizing role of the structural pitches. Example 6.6 illustrates the way in which D-flat, the structural pitch at number 2, serves as a pivot connecting successive statements of the total chromatic (the example represents pitch classes, not specific registers). Notice also that the twelve-tone 'rows' are paired; in each pair the second twelve notes are the retrograde of the first twelve.

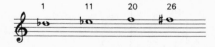

6.5   Basic pitch gesture of 'Repos dans le Malheur', *Trois poèmes*

The movement culminates with the arrival of F-sharp, the last of the four structural pitches, at number 26. Just before, the chorus have sung an eleven-note harmonic aggregate excluding F-sharp. The harp announces the missing pitch; softly the chorus intone 'dans ton horreur' on F-sharp; suddenly the orchestra explodes into F-sharps in six

6.6 Piano parts (reduced) at no. 2 of 'Repos dans le Malheur', *Trois poèmes*

octaves, shuddering convulsively, again, and yet again. In the quiet context this is an electrifying moment, a master stroke of surprise. Obviously the arrival of the F-sharp fulfills the basic motion underlying the work, and obviously it provides a dramatic event about which we, as listeners, organize our perceptions. But there are symbolic meanings here as well. Can it be fortuitous that the pitch class F-sharp, with its historical tritone implications, is reserved for the word 'horreur'? And are not these last, dreadful spasms in the orchestra one last vestige of human will, resisting for a moment longer the awful reality of the human condition, before dissolving at last in surrender?

One final, piquant technical detail. When finally the singers do surrender from their unison F-sharp – 'Je m'abandonne' – the texture flows downward to C-sharp, producing the same chromatic hexachord in the same register that was assigned to the women in the first and last stanzas of 'Pensées'. Now, however, the complementary hexachord, G to C, is given not to the men but to the two pianos: G, G-sharp, A in piano 1, and B-flat, B, C in piano 2. What is more, as these two trichords are played over and over again they are subjected to a symmetrical pattern of changing registers, a pattern that in turn is symmetrically disposed above and below the chorus. It is not likely that the details of this operation will be grasped by ear, but the resulting effect will be unmistakable: a profound calm, a sort of cosmic equilibrium in which man is at peace with himself in an uncaring universe.

String Quartet

Throughout his life Lutosławski has devoted very little attention to chamber music, and since 1961 only one work small enough to be performed without conductor has appeared: the String Quartet of 1964. The composer regarded the prospect of writing a quartet with some concern, since the transparency of the medium and the limited timbral and polyphonic capabilities of the four instruments would test the soundness of his new methods to the fullest. The finished score presents both limited aleatorism and the methods of managing pitch in such pure forms that it offers an ideal place to study these techniques. Although the quartet is perhaps more difficult for the listener than most of the other late works, it will reward both the persevering listener and the analyst handsomely.

As Joachim Hansberger has pointed out, the use of limited aleatorism in the quartet allows Lutosławski to take advantage of quasi-improvisational, soloistic playing even in ensemble contexts. There are cadenza-like passages characterized by short phrases of expressive profile, frequent rhetorical pauses, abrupt changes of character, written-out accelerandi, and so on.[6] Even so, the work depends for its originality neither on novel treatment of the instruments nor on novel ways of playing them. There is no electronic amplification, no tapping on instrument backs, no bowing behind the bridge, no scordatura. The number of special technical possiblities exploited is small and, by 1964, thoroughly conventional: the mute, occasional quarter-tones, playing without vibrato, natural and artificial harmonics, glissandi, occasional multiple stops, tremolo, bowing sul ponticello, pizzicato—the repertoire, roughly, of the Bartók quartets. It is not sound effects that make Lutosławski's quartet compelling but musical substance: the projection of pitch and gestural relationships on both foreground and deeper levels and the projection of a powerful formal structure.

Most of the time the four players are relatively independent of each other. Only now and then (e.g., sections 5, 10–11, 43–4) is there a true score in which vertical alignment on the page signifies rhythmic synchronization. Elsewhere a system of signals and cues, some of them rather elaborate, is necessary to allow the performers to begin and end each section together.

The quintessential expressions of Lutosławski's end-accented formal conceit are to be found here and in the Second Symphony, his only two-movement works. The quartet's first movement ('Introductory') was designed, the composer says, 'to create a sort of low pressure, after which the very substantial Main Movement will seem inevitable; whereas the character of the Main Movement makes it impossible to listen casually'. In Lutosławski's view, this formal plan should prevent a long work from being psychologically tiring; it should make the quartet seem shorter than its twenty-four minutes.

The two movements are continuous, with the first movement functioning as one division of an overall four-part design:

Introductory Movement (c. 8½ min.)	I. The work's textural and motivic materials are set forth, but in fragmentary fashion; the succession of events seems arbitrary, capricious.
Main Movement (c. 15 min.)	II. 'Development' (c. 7 min.). Sustained, purposeful activity, followed by developmental sections referring to earlier material, leading to III. Climax (c. 5½ min.) in three parts: Appasionato, chorale, *funèbre*. IV. Coda (c. 2½ min.). Fragmentary sections like those of the first movement.

In a rhythmic hierarchy, these four divisions would constitute the deepest level of macrorhythm. At least three additional levels can be defined: the macrorhythm of *groups* of sections united by function, texture, character, etc.; the macrorhythm of individual *sections* (in general, these correspond to the rehearsal numbers in the score); and the microrhythms of the individual parts, both alone and collectively.

The opening monologue of the first violin presents the two basic pitch motives that shape much of the material throughout the work: chromatic segments of various lengths (x) and the conjunction of tritone and semitone (y) (ex. 6.7).[7] (Notice that, disregarding the repeated g^1 at the beginning, this sequence of sixteen pitches divides neatly in half, the second eight being merely a transposition – or transposed retrograde – of the first eight.) Even with only four players, however, the usual kinds of twelve-note harmonic collections are also important, and since they are so easily isolated in the text of the quartet, we ought to investigate their use in some detail. The material of section 7 illustrates a typical partitioning of the total chromatic among the four voices (ex. 6.8); here only eleven pitch classes are represented, since throughout much of the first movement C-natural is reserved for a special role. Elsewhere, as in section 14, the total chromatic is partitioned so as to produce 'consonant' melodic patterns for each voice, lending a special character to the sounding twelve-note chord (ex. 6.9). In sections 29–34 the second violin, viola,

6.7 Opening of the String Quartet

6.8   Pitch class distribution in section 7 of the String Quartet

6.9   Pitch class distribution in section 14 of the String Quartet

and cello share hexachords producing thirdless harmony (see ex. 5.7, above). At the climax of the work, the Appasionato (section 42), comes a succession of harmonic collections, the principal features of which are summarized in example 6.10.

In the quartet Lutosławski used quarter-tones for the first time; glissandi (which had already appeared in the finale of *Jeux vénitiens*) are important here too, though only in the second movement. It is important to understand, though, that neither of these devices has the slightest influence on the principles of pitch organization. There is no attempt here to work out a microtonal harmony, as Alois Hába, Harry Partch, Ben Johnston, and others have done. For Lutosławski, quarter-tones and glissandi only embellish the twelve chromatic pitch classes. Clear examples of the former are in sections 1 and 9, of the latter in sections 24–8.

6.10   Summary of the harmonic content of section 42 of the String Quartet

The most characteristic microrhythmic gestures of the quartet are of two sorts: simple but irregular groupings of short and long values, and the gestures of accelerating and decelerating. The first of these is illustrated nicely by the first violin in section 2, a passage whose athletic demeanor, limited melodic repertory, and mosaic construction in units of two and three semiquavers are potent reminders of the extent to which Stravinsky has put his stamp on the music of our century (ex. 6.11). The accelerating–decelerating gesture recurs throughout the work in many guises. In passages of collective ad libitum it helps create complex microrhythmic textures through

6.11 String Quartet, section 2

polyagogics; in section 24, for example, all the parts display the pattern (with interposed semiquavers), but in conflicting forms:

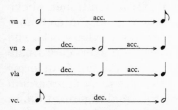

We have already examined above (pp. 111–12) the arithmetically controlled microrhythm of one section of the quartet. One additional example will serve here. In the third portion of the work's climax, the large cantilena section marked *funèbre* (number 45), each of the four instruments is assigned a series of short phrases. Each such phrase carries out three functions: establishing a main note (at first f-sharp[1]; later f-natural[1], e[1], and so on); making a descending glissando; and finally sustaining g (the open string for everyone but the cello). At the very end of the passage the only pitch class that has not been used, A-flat, is supplied. The combined effect of these independent phrases in the four instruments is to create a long, chromatic descent over a recurring g (in effect a pedal point) requiring fully two minutes to complete (ex. 6.12). The three principal functions carried out by each phrase may be seen as an ordered set of gestures (*a*, *b*, *c*), where *a* signifies the main note, *b* the glissando, and *c* the sustained open G string. Four different duration values, equal to two, three, four, and five crotchets, are associated with these gestures. The series of durations is mapped onto the set of gestures as follows:

	vn1			vn2			vla			vc.		
gesture:	*a*	*b*	*c*	*a*	*b*	*c*	*a*	*b*	*c*	*a*	*b*	*c*
duration:	3	2	4	5	3	2	4	5	3	2	4	5

This is only part of the story, however. There are two additional complications: a melisma in quavers and semiquavers is inserted following most of the main notes, and these melismas are themselves subject to systematic control; and during the course of the section the four main duration values are redistributed among the instruments.

6.12   Basic pitch motion, section 45 of the String Quartet

Though the four-part view of the overall form mentioned above seems simple enough, it represents only a broad, general plan whose details come clear only with repeated hearings of the work. The system of cues and signals by means of which the players coordinate their actions required that the composer conceive the music in terms of a great many sections, most of them quite short. By comparison with most of the late works, this sort of microformal organization, in turn, makes unusually heavy demands of the listener, but at the same time it creates the opportunity for unusually rich and varied musical experiences within the broad four-part scheme.

The end-accented formal plan requires that the first movement seem tentative, unstable, inchoate. Thus we are given a succession of contrasting sections, largely unrelated to each other (though it is possible to see numbers 10–11 as a kind of arco analog to the pizzicato texture of number 5). The prevailing dynamic in each section, moreover, is relatively soft; the highest marking in the movement is *quasi f.* Beginning with section 3, the pitch class C-natural is systematically excluded from the harmonic content of each section (except for two very brief appearances within section 10, p. 16 in the score); C functions instead as an articulating gesture separating one section from the next. As the movement progresses, the return of the octave C figure begins to seem predictable and even mechanical. Then, at number 12, the whole ensemble erupts in an extended statement of octave C's. This, clearly, is no ordinary sectional articulation of the kind we have come to expect. Is it an announcement of some sort? Is the work ending? The octave C's disintegrate into a four-note chord (pitch motive x), which is repeated at greater and greater intervals of time, as if the music were 'running down'; against this the cello plays a reminiscence of the opening monologue. We are left puzzled and dissatisfied. Unfulfilled expectations have been aroused by the mechanical repetition of those octave C's and by the repeated introduction and then abandonment of new types of texture.

The Main Movement follows without break and provides a resolution of the tensions generated by the uncertain quality of the Introductory Movement. Immediately there is a long passage of forceful, purposeful playing. Several groups of small sections follow. Numbers 14–23 are exclusively pizzicato; 24–8, with their texture of glissando and tremolo, recall the opening of the movement. Notice that the individual lines of sections 24–8 are permeated by pitch motive *y* and that each of these sections ends with a four-note *y*-chord. During sections 29–34 the texture is gradually invaded by a turning chromatic figure (*x*) that derives from section 8 in the first movement, until by the end of 34 the figure has taken over the texture completely.

A new stage in the 'development' section leading to the climax begins at number 35 with the cellist's *ff* chord pizzicato – the very same *x*-chord into which the octave C's of the first movement degenerated in section 12. The chord's identity is significant, for its reappearance heralds a succession of contrasting sections like those of the first movement. Psychologically the situation is now very different, though. In the first movement, every event was new to us; now, although there are pronounced contrasts between the character of adjacent sections, the music is full of references to previously heard thematic material (i.e., textures, melodic gestures, and rhythmic gestures like the accelerating-decelerating motive). What is more, there is now a strong sense of direction toward the climax, a sense created both by dynamics (each section represents a crescendo to *ff*) and by macrorhythm (each section is shorter than the last). As the octave C's constituted in the first movement a kind of subplot that finally broke through to the dramatic surface, so the cellist's recurring *x*-chords culminate in an outburst of such chords for the whole ensemble (section 39). We know from experience (section 12) and from context (constantly new textural mixes coming in shorter and shorter chunks) that section 39 is a landmark signalling the impending arrival of the climax of the work.

Christian Martin Schmidt has observed that the principal subject of Lutosławski's String Quartet is the relation of the individual performer to the total ensemble. In his view, the work may be seen as a progression from the independence of sound elements (especially in the first movement) to their 'fusion'. Schmidt finds the greatest degree of fusion at the climax, since in the middle portion of section 42 the individual voices are wholly submerged in a unified body of sound, each of them contributing three pitches to a fully chromatic cluster, c-sharp^1 to c^2. Hansberger describes the climax in rather similar terms, but for him the crux of the matter comes in the transition from the end of the Appasionato section (42) to the beginning of the chorale (44), for at this moment the opposing principles of independence and synchronization confront each other directly.[8] More broadly viewed, all three sections of the climax – Appasionato, chorale, and cantilena – stand together as a summation of the textural values of the quartet. Independence and mobile texture at the beginning and end of the Appasionato give way to homophony and stasis in the chorale; and these opposing tendencies are finally synthesized and reconciled in the *funèbre* section, where the four performers, playing independently, combine to produce a cantilena of enormous lyrical power. Lutosławski has remarked that the performance direction *funèbre* has no extramusical significance, but rather is meant solely to suggest the style of playing required. Even so, the *funèbre* music produces an astonishingly poignant, solemn, expressive impact that surpasses even the effect achieved at the beginning of the epilogue of *Muzyka żałobna*.

With the completion of the cantilena's long chromatic descent and the final unison A-flat, the main business of the String Quartet is done. The few remaining sections of music constitute a coda, in which the certainties attained in the climax dissolve once more into the uncertain atmosphere of the first movement. This method of ending the quartet is very much like the methods Lutosławski used in other works: *Muzyka żałobna*, *Jeux vénitiens*, the Second Symphony. There are quiet reminiscences of earlier events: the pizzicato gesture that began section 15 returns to open section 47 and 50; the turning *x* figure is recalled in 48; 50 is a clear restatement of 4; etc.[9] The cellist finishes the work on an inconclusive note echoing the end of the first movement.

The principal features of the second movement, including the decisive role played by dynamics, are summarized below:

Main Movement: Structural Synopsis

		'Development'
[First section]	*f*	
sections		
14–23	*mf–ff*	pizzicato
24–8	*f*	recalls first section of second movement
29–34	*p* ⋖	
35	*pp* ⋖ *ff*	⎡ x-chord sectional articulations;
36	*pp* ⋖ *ff*	fragments of earlier material,
37	*pp* ⋖ *ff*	recombined in various ways;
38	⋖ *ff*	⎣ macrorhythmic accelerando
39	*ff*	outbreak of pizz. x-cords (cf. section 12)
40–1	*pp* ⋖ *ff* *mf* ⋖ *ff*	

		Climax
42	*ff* *p*<*fff*>	Appasionato
43–4	*pp*	Chorale
45	*f*>*ppp*	Cantilena (*funèbre*)
		Coda
46	*pp*>*ppp*	⎡
47	*ppp*	recalls fragments of earlier textures
48	*ppp*	
49	*p*>*ppp*	
50	*mf*>*p*	⎣
51	*ppp*	cello recalls opening monologue and section 13 of first movement

Paroles tissées

As he set about planning a new vocal work for Peter Pears, Lutosławski already had a general idea of the sort of piece he wanted to write. Casting about for a text, he read dozens of volumes of French poetry before he chanced on the 1947 journal *Poésie*, where he found 'Quatre tapisseries pour la Châtelaine de Vergi' by an obscure writer named Jean-François Chabrun. He was delighted with this discovery, he has said, since 'besides its poetic qualities, this text lends itself exceptionally well to musical treatment. It would not surprise me if it turned out that, writing his poem, Chabrun had in mind combining it with music.'[10] Lutosławski wrote the poet asking that he suggest a shorter title for the musical work. Of the two titles Chabrun proposed, the composer chose *Paroles tissées*, even though he feels it does not quite match the music's qualities.

   Chabrun's original title refers to a metrical romance of the late thirteenth century, *La châtelaine de Vergi*. His four brief poems are verbal tapestries into which are woven recurring words, phrases, and surrealistic images, each time set in new contexts. For example, the opening line of the first poem, 'Un chat qui s'émerveille', returns as the second line of the second poem. Significantly, the word 'mort' appears in all four poems; so do fragments of the lines 'Le cri du bateleur et celui de la caille / celui de la perdrix celui du ramoneur / celui de l'arbre mort celui des bêtes prises' ('The cry of the tumbler and the quail / of the partridge and the chimney-sweep / of the dead tree and captured beasts'). The word 'ombre' returns frequently, as does the line 'une herbe qui s'éveille'. Fascinating as this motivic structure may be in the poem, however, Lutosławski did not choose to represent the recurring elements directly in the music (say as *Leitmotiven*). He reads the poem on another level:

It is difficult to talk about the poem's content, since it does not have an unequivocal 'plot'. But even though the sequence of images may at first blush seem unconnected, for me it has a concealed, inner logic. To be sure, it is not the logic of real events, but rather perhaps the logic of dreams. Despite the fact that from the point of view of realistic aesthetics the work seems absurd, one can see in it the outline of a kind of action, dramatic conflict, and calamity. And although the first line of the last poem reads, 'Sleep this pallor has reached us from far', it is abundantly clear to me that what is meant is the pallor of death.[11]

Indeed, though the characters of the romance never appear in Chabrun's *tapisseries*, the tragic end of the medieval knight and his beloved, the chatelaine, is reflected in the language of the third and fourth poems. It seems in the third that the chatelaine speaks directly ('ma peine'), while the fourth uses the first person plural and refers plainly to 'the lovers happy put to sleep so pale'.

Paroles tissées is a work of ripe maturity. The composer himself has noted that, as regards compositional technique, the music is retrospective in character; it represents a consolidation of several years' growth as a craftsman. The lessons of *Jeux vénitiens*, *Trois poèmes*, and the String Quartet combine to produce a beguiling sound world of rich, varied, fascinating textures that match perfectly the hypnotic effect of Chabrun's language. Critic David Murray has described the work as 'a little gem . . . The music is at once playful and exquisitely judged. Lutosławski has given loving attention to the seemingly hermetic imagery of the poems, and he has produced something curiously poignant and charming.'[12]

The structure of the poetic cycle fits neatly with Lutosławski's recent approach to musical form. The first two poems are brief and quiet; the third, much longer and quite agitated, is the basis for a musical climax falling fairly near the end of the cycle; the fourth, brief in length and resigned in tone, forms an epilogue (cf. *Trois poèmes*). The cycle is an integral whole; though the four poems are set as separate movements, they are to be performed without break (never as individual 'songs'). And though the tenor soloist is always clearly set off from the rest of the ensemble, the chamber orchestra is no mere accompaniment; all the performers are more or less equal participants. The tenor is required to sing in three styles: lyrical declamation on one or two pitches (in effect reciting tones), syllabic cantilena, and melisma. In the delicate timbral palette of *Paroles tissées* the harp and piano, both of which have been very important members of Lutosławski's orchestra ever since Symphonic Variations, are especially prominent colors, and they are very often allied with the tenor to form a distinct sound group against the seventeen strings.

Both the first and second movements are simple in structure and restrained in expression, and both are performed almost entirely in collective ad libitum. In the first, straightforward presentations of the text on reciting tones are interspersed among string textures made up of four twelve-note chords dominated by interval class 3 and separated by smaller clusters (ex. 6.13). The gentle, lullaby-like second movement is dominated by a duet between tenor and harp. The tenor begins alone with the first full line of text, set to an ascending line rich in whole-tone segments (ex. 6.14). There follows a succession of short cantilena phrases for the voice, each sung to a collection of between five and seven pitches. Most of these collections, like the opening phrase, contain prominent whole tones, and their melodic intervals are so arranged as to suggest an almost tonal orientation ('D major' in the first phrase, 'F minor' in the second, etc.) – though it is unlikely the composer would approve such an interpretation. The harp begins each little phrase by stating the operative repertory of pitches, and the tenor follows immediately in imitation. The effect of this quasi-canonic collaboration is utterly captivating. The pizzicato strings and the piano, meanwhile, contribute short, fragmentary phrases drawn mainly from the pitch classes not being used by the harp and tenor at the moment and suggesting the gently playful spirit of the text ('a cat that is wonder-struck', 'a shadow bewitches her'). The last two lines of the poem foreshadow the change in mood of the third poem:

> Speaking of wonders
> the shadow is torn in two

The tenor sings them alone to a variant of the opening solo phrase; when he reaches the final high F-sharp, the pizzicato strings do an admirable representation of the shadow that is torn in two.

Suddenly, unexpectedly, the third movement is loud and dramatic. Since the music's new character calls for rapid changes of harmony and vehement rhythmic gestures by the massed string orchestra, most of the playing is now a battuta. Given what we know of Lutosławski's

6.13 Harmonic summary of the first movement (strings only) of *Paroles tissées*

Quand le   jour   quand le jour a   rou-vert   a   rou-vert les branch-es du   jar-din

6.14   Opening of the second movement of *Paroles tissées*

reading of the 'Quatre tapisseries', his setting of the third poem would seem rather plainly to portray the chatelaine's horror upon discovering (mistakenly) that her knight has betrayed her love, her mounting hysteria, and finally the peace she gains in death. This little psycho-drama is, in a sense, played out twice, first in the extended passage for strings that ends in cataclysm at number 62, and afterward in the tenor.

One may plausibly read the middle portion of Chabrun's third poem in something like the calm, abstracted manner that characterizes most of the text. But Lutosławski has the tenor (from number 63) virtually shout these lines near the top of his range, giving the impression of an hysterical piling up of irrational images in a mind unhinged by grief. The true emotional climax comes not in the strings at number 62 but rather at 69, where the tenor reaches high B-flat on the crucial words 'ma peine' and then embarks on a long melisma – the first melismatic writing for the voice. This melisma is interesting, incidentally; its pitches form a twelve-tone series constructed entirely of interval classes 2 and 5 (cf. the Second Symphony, the Cello Concerto, Preludes and Fugue) in such a way that the second hexachord is the retrograde inversion of the first. Following this outcry of sorrow the soloist finishes the text of the poem in little fragments, growing ever softer until, at last, he repeats the melisma (or rather its transposed inversion or retrograde) very softly, alone.

It is worth noting that this movement provides another bit of evidence of the organic nature of Lutosławski's stylistic evolution. The means of creating gliding, sliding orchestral textures, which will distinguish the *Livre pour orchestre* three years later and lead some observers to see in that work the beginning of a new phase in the composer's development, are in fact already achieved here. The string textures from numbers 54 to 62 are equivalent, essentially, to the 'blurred toccata' style [Concerto for Orchestra, second postlude] with the natural enough addition of the glissando (String Quartet).

In the mournful final movement the tenor is allied exclusively with the strings, while the harp goes its own way, solemnly, implacably descending a peculiar seven-note scale while the others share the remaining five pitch classes. For the first time the soloist's part unites all three manners of singing: reciting, syllabic melody, melisma. The center of gravity in this fourth movement lies in the extraordinary setting of the lines

> the lovers happy put to sleep so pale
> the cry of the dead tree, of captured beasts,

in which the tenor's otherworldly cantilena, sung softly in an extremely high tessitura, is at once ecstatic and profoundly sorrowful. The accompanying ad libitum cantilena for sixteen strings, no less extraordinary in effect, recalls the *funèbre* of the String Quartet and foreshadows the second movement of the Second Symphony. As the tenor recites the closing lines, the strings intone the twelve-note chord that began the movement; the chord slowly collapses on itself through octave transfers until only a lone violist remains on f-sharp[1], roughly the midpoint of the original chord and the only pitch that has maintained its original register throughout.

Despite its modest scale, the refined poetics of *Paroles tissées* and the spellbinding web of delicate sound it weaves place it among the highest achievements of Lutosławski's art. And these very qualities remind us once more how closely that art is related, both in aim and in substance, to the sound world of Claude Debussy.

Second Symphony

If *Paroles tissées* represented a first summing up of style since 1960, a first plateau in development, in the next work Lutosławski set himself new challenges. The Second Symphony, completed two decades after the first, was the composer's first large-scale, purely orchestral work since the Concerto for Orchestra. (The Koussevitzky Foundation had commissioned a symphony in 1963, but it did not materialize.) As the String Quartet had tested his methods in the domain of chamber music, the Second Symphony provided their first real trial in the symphonic arena. The results have elicited mixed reaction. Many observers, especially in Poland, consider this work to be Lutosławski's masterpiece; others view it as a noble but not fully successful experiment.

Generally Lutosławski has avoided discussing publicly the analysis of his own music. In the case of the Second Symphony, however, we are fortunate to have his rather detailed remarks in published form.[13] It is impractical to offer here a detailed analysis of every aspect of so long and complex a score; but we can, at least, investigate the symphony's broader outlines and hint at strategies for deeper study.

Obviously the title 'symphony' cannot imply for Lutosławski any overt connection with the old symphonic forms; it means simply a large, serious work for orchestra. The form of the Second Symphony is a larger, more continuous version of the plan of the String Quartet: two movements, the first unsatisfactory ('Hésitant'), the second unfolding a musical argument that can lead to a satisfying conclusion ('Direct'). The construction of the first movement is rather like the old *rondeau*: a succession of contrasting episodes punctuated by a recurring refrain. The similarity to the structure of the Introductory Movement of the String Quartet is quite pronounced, although there the recurring element was simply the brief gesture articulating the sectional divisions. In the symphony the contrasts between episodes are even more vivid, given Lutosławski's tendency to paint with primary colors, i.e. to use the orchestra mainly by families of similar instruments rather than blending dissimilar timbres.

There are seven episodes, each for a different group of instruments. The first, for brass alone, has the character of an introductory fanfare or march. Three stages may be discerned. In the first the initially regular rhythm and 'consonant' harmony (at first, only the pitches e-flat¹, f¹, and b-flat) are gradually 'smudged' as, one by one, the players introduce new tempi and new pitches. The order in which new pitch classes are added is controlled by an informal twelve-tone set constructed exclusively of interval classes 2 and 5 (ex. 6.15). (It will turn out to be compositionally significant that one permutation of this series yields whole-tone collections: order numbers [0, 1, 4, 5, 8, 9] and [2, 3, 6, 7, 10, 11]). In the second stage (*meno mosso*, M.M. c. 105), the brass players achieve a bland, homogeneous texture devoid of accents; in the third, strong accents return and a general crescendo hints at the approach to some musical goal. Instead, however, the brass are interrupted by celesta and piano and, after a half-hearted attempt to reassert themselves, they disappear from the scene. The succeeding episodes are similarly interrupted. Each begins tentatively, eventually seems to gather momentum towards something continuous and concrete, but in the end is cut short and gives way to something new. All of this reinforces the hesitant, half-formed impression the first movement is supposed to convey.

The refrains contrast in every way with the episodes. They are all slow, while the episodes are generally lively; they are played by trios

6.15   Twelve-tone series underlying the opening of the first movement of the Second Symphony

of double reeds, instruments that never appear in the episodes; and, whereas a great variety of pitch-organizing principles may be found in the episodes, the refrains are restricted to a single hexachord whose construction guarantees thirdless harmony (see ex. 5.7). Harmonic color and instrumental timbre combine to give the refrains a plaintive, skeptical air, against which the futile attempts by other instrumental groups to sustain some concrete musical development stand in stark relief.

In addition to the two main pitch models exposed in the first movement – the series producing the introductory episode in the brass and the hexachord governing the refrains – a closer look at the text reveals a veritable compendium of Lutosławskian solutions to the question of partitioning the total chromatic. A few examples will have to suffice. At number 2, the piano combines two transpositions of the refrain hexachord, while the celesta has the three mutually exclusive trichords (4-4) (the 'augmented triads'). From number 15 to 16, the clarinets are confined to a single chromatic hexachord (C to F) dispersed among four octave registers. From 20 to 25, piano, celesta, and harp each maintain complementary chromatic tetrachords. At 34 the harp has a hexachord dominated by whole-tones (a construction first met in the first of the *Trois poèmes*), while the three flutes have the complementary hexachord, which is the retrograde inversion of the first. The rich variety of harmonic colors afforded by such an eclectic approach represents a quantum jump in style over the more limited techniques in *Jeux vénitiens* and even in *Trois poèmes*.

Both the last episode and the last refrain may be seen as the culminations of their respective roles in the form of the first movement. Aside from the introductory brass episode, episode 7 (beginning at number 32) is the only one that does not begin tentatively. Instead, without any pauses, there appears now a succession of different textures, each of them reminiscent of an earlier episode. (Compare the end of the first movement in the String Quartet, where the cello hints at a recapitulation of the opening music.) Finally these textural layers (the 'themes') are combined in the longest section of episode 7 (from number 35), with more and more of the orchestra joining in the textural polyphony as the music progresses. Episode 7 is like a developmental inventory of the movement's thematic material, and it would seem to the listener that the 'direct' music he has been promised has at last begun. But just as it seems that a successful music has been achieved and a climax is near, this final episode too is cut short; the percussion attempt to resume it, but it is no use.

The bleak atmosphere of the refrains has prevailed. The final refrain is, like the final episode, much longer than the others. It is, in fact, a series of ten refrains that grow shorter and shorter as they sink into the lowest registers of the orchestra. For the first time some of the phrases are assigned not to double reeds but to brasses. Perhaps it would be naively programmatic to suggest that the brasses, 'optimistic' at the movement's beginning, have in the end succumbed to the 'pessimism' of the oboes and bassoons; nevertheless the futility of what has gone before is clear, and the movement ends having whetted the appetite but not satisfied it.

There is no pause between movements, and the listener cannot even be sure precisely where 'Hésitant' ends and 'Direct' begins, since the tenth phrase of the closing refrain overlaps the entrance of the doublebasses that begins the second movement. But it soon becomes clear that the second movement will be everything the first was not. It is dominated at first by the string section, which took virtually no part in the first movement, and by slow, *cantabile* playing; it is continuous and purposeful, not sectional and tentative.

The composer has defined five stages in the growth of the second movement's form, though the music unfolds so continuously that their boundaries can be at best dimly perceived in performance.[14]

Stage 1	Number 101	a.	An expanding, 'languid', 'gummy' mass of sound at a slow tempo, from which emerges a massive cantilena texture;
	120	b.	a brief episode of lively music in the winds;
	123	c.	full-fledged cantilena in the strings.
Stage 2	123a		Cantilena in the strings contested by snatches of fast music played by small groups of winds; cantilena gradually infected by the faster tempi.
Stage 3	126		Fast tempo prevails; macrorhythmic accelerando.
Stage 4	135	a.	Metric notation for the entire orchestra; macrorhythmic accelerando merges with microrhythm; primitive unison rhythm emerges;
	151	b.	pauses and a 'contest of forces'.
Stage 5	153	a.	First attempt at climax, tutti ad libitum;
	154	b.	soft interlude;
	158	c.	second attempt at climax; dyad E-flat/F repeated 'with decreasing conviction' even as the soft coda begins.

Typically, the basic plan is clear-cut and direct, the details subtly elaborated. Its execution depends on familiar Lutosławskian techniques – multilayered textural polyphony (*wielowarstwowość*) and macrorhythmic acceleration – but the manner in which the music is gradually transformed during the second stage by superimposing radically different tempi is original and wonderfully effective.

The main methods of pitch organization in the second movement can be traced to the brass series of the first movement. In the first stage of the form, for example, as the string section expands upward from the doublebass opening, it gradually completes a twelve-note chord constructed, as was the series, entirely of interval classes 2 and 5. (The principal notes are embellished, as in the String Quartet, by quarter-tone auxiliaries and glissandi). When the strings achieve *f* and a real cantilena at number 106, it is with a new twelve-note chord, this one comprising the two whole-tone hexachords (also derived from the series). From 107 to 112 a third twelve-note chord takes shape little by little, reaching outward by interval classes 2 and 5 from an initial 'D-major' nucleus. Though other pitches are present as well (in the strings), the twelve *doubled* by the winds control the structure of the chord, giving it at once a complex and an exhilaratingly open sound (ex. 6.16).

6.16 Harmonic summary of nos. 101–12, second movement of the Second Symphony

The method by which the general tempo is now transformed is brilliantly conceived. Once the strings' cantilena has been firmly asserted, short, lively phrases are superimposed on it in stage 2. Generally these fast phrases grow longer, the pauses between them shorter. All of this erodes the authority of the slower cantilena music, which is itself gradually invaded by groups of fast notes (e.g. at number 123c). Finally, at 124c, the strings abandon any further attempt to maintain their cantilena; when they re-enter at 125, they have adopted the lively character the winds have insisted upon, with only faint reminders of the cantilena style remaining (the passages marked M.M. 150 in each player's part).[15] The third stage, in which the fast tempo reigns unchallenged, gives a succession of short sections of varying textures; the technique is rather like that used to approach the climax of the String Quartet, except that here one section overlaps another. Changing textures come faster and faster until, at number 135, it becomes necessary to introduce a common metrical pulse in order to regulate the onrushing flow of events (cf. *Jeux vénitiens*, *Livre*).

In the fourth stage the effects of the original pitch model are still evident, as witness the whole-tone segments in the strings at 135 and the brass chord at 138. Lutosławski is capable of ad hoc solutions as well, however; at 139 the violins and violas actually resort to the old eight-tone scale of the Two Etudes based on the tetrachord (2-2-1). Rhythmic values in the parts, meanwhile, continue to grow faster, and at the same time the pulse accelerates from crotchets at 150 to dotted minims at 90 (crotchets at 270) and finally to dotted minims at 110 (crotchets at 330). There gradually emerges a unison rhythm in hammered crotchets for the entire ensemble, still accelerating; the composer has called this rhythm 'deliberately primitive', and others have compared its elemental force to the *Sacre du printemps*. Suddenly the music stops short; there is a brief struggle between staccato playing in the winds and legato in the strings, another pause, another such contest; and we arrive at the climax of the work.

The first phase of the climax, at number 153, is played in collective ad libitum. It is as if the unanimity finally won in the metered section collapses into anarchy at the crucial moment. The twelve-note chord underlying the climax is of the type alternating interval classes 5 and 6, thus not of the type on which the rest of the movement has depended. Each player finishes his own climactic phrase independently with a three-note figure *tutta forza*. The strings finish first and drop out; as each wind player finishes, he joins a softly babbling texture in the background. Gradually this texture condenses in the middle register, gathers strength, and leads to an attempt at a second, more affirmative climax: the sustained dyad E-flat/F, a would-be 'tonic' recalling the opening notes of the first movement. But, as in *Jeux vénitiens*, an affirmative conclusion proves impossible. When the triumphal dyad stops, eight low strings are discovered already preparing the coda with *ppp* clusters. Four times the orchestra reasserts its E-flat and F, each time less confidently; in the end the low strings are left to finish the symphony alone. Against the continuing clusters, descending ever so slowly by octave transfer to the lowest registers of the celli and basses, two solo doublebasses play a timid duet using only the pitches G-flat, F, and E-flat and their quarter-tone neighbors (the remaining nine pitch classes are represented in the clusters), and the music dissolves into silence.

In many respects Lutosławski's Second Symphony is a brilliant achievement. There are passages of stunning harmonic beauty and of profound lyric power. The range and mastery of orchestral textures is unmatched in the music of any other composer. The slow rise of musical tension in the second movement reaches a searing intensity, and its progress is managed with such consummate skill that, despite its great length, it remains riveting throughout. And yet taken as a whole the symphony is less than satisfying. It seems, in retrospect, too long, because the proportion of hesitant to direct expression seems miscalculated. And the two climaxes, the first individual, the second collective but ineffectual, fail to bring about a conclusive resolution and so fail to keep faith with the grand artistic promise made.

Livre pour orchestre

Immediately after finishing the Second Symphony, Lutosławski took up another work for symphony orchestra, and many of the technical and expressive concerns that had occupied him there spilled over into the new work. In the tradition of the Concerto for Orchestra and the Second Symphony, *Livre pour orchestre* gives further proof of the composer's pre-eminence as master of the modern orchestra; students of orchestration would do well to make this score their textbook, as its composer once made the early ballets of Stravinsky his own. A highly charged work of dazzling inventiveness, ravishingly lush sound, and absorbing textural interplay, *Livre* makes a strong claim to be the best and most attractive piece Lutosławski has ever written. It has won an extraordinarily wide acceptance among conductors and audiences alike, and critics have been lavish in their praise. Reviewing a performance by the Philadelphia Orchestra, Royal Brown wrote that, although *Livre* uses effects 'that dominate the music of many of his contemporaries (such as Penderecki), it incorporates them in an instrumental context that is so sonorously inventive and so intriguingly structured that one has the impression of hearing not only these devices but indeed the entire orchestra for the first time'.[16]

The title is meant to suggest a suite of unrelated character pieces, by analogy with the French *livres* of the Baroque era. Lutosławski's suite movements are not static sonic tableaux expressing a single musical character, however, but rather brilliantly hued little pieces marked by mercurial temperament and capricious changes of direction. Owing to this hyperchangeable, nervous quality the composer has called them a distant echo of expressionism (though in other respects he has little sympathy for the expressionist music of the early twentieth century). There are four movements, or *chapitres*, separated from

A page from the autograph score of *Livre pour orchestre* (from the composer's collection)

each other by brief interludes of a simple, babbling texture designed to give the listener moments of relaxation from the more concentrated attention demanded by the main movements. The interludes are like *entr'actes*, and the conductor is encouraged to behave as he would between pieces, taking out his handkerchief, fidgeting with his watch, and so on. In a sense, the first three movements are only preludes; the fourth movement is as long as the other three combined, and it is the only one to establish large-scale continuity and to achieve a climax. This end-accented formal arrangement bears a close resemblance to the original plan of the Three Postludes and to the structure of *Jeux vénitiens*, as well as to the introduction–consummation scheme of the String Quartet; but in *Livre* this plan is for the first time carried out flawlessly.

The structure of each of the first three movements is simple. The first movement may be viewed as three ample phrases, each devoted to exploring various versions of the same general textural idea. In the first phrase this characteristic texture is given to the strings; only at the very end is it transferred to the brass, who are then interrupted by an irrelevant aside in the percussion, piano, contrabassoon, tuba, and basses. In the second, the strings resume their statement forthrightly, but it is almost immediately transferred to the brass, who develop it at length. This phrase, too, is interrupted by the percussion. The last phrase finds the strings again with an extended version of the thematic texture, now played very slowly; the piano adds a little postscript.

Several things about this first movement are striking. It is written almost completely in metrical notation, to be conducted in the traditional manner, and it signals in fact a general trend towards meter in the works that will follow it. There is no overriding harmonic system organizing the pitches, but rather a variety of techniques (a very few twelve-note chords, many smaller chords of various types, partitioning into chromatic hexachords, etc.). Nor is there a characteristic melodic gesture or microrhythmic physiognomy. Rather the subject is texture itself – a texture of extraordinarily liquid quality made to glide continuously by means of glissando and quarter-tones, a stream of texture, now shallow, now coursing in deeper channels, now rushing ahead, now collecting in quiet pools of sound, now agitated, now tranquil. It is difficult to imagine more persuasive evidence for the thesis that, in the hands of a composer of subtle and sophisticated skills, the qualities of texture can take on thematic substance no less compelling than the more traditional thematic materials of melody, rhythm, and harmony.

The formal organization of the second movement is more diffuse. It divides into two roughly equal parts, the first passive and almost mechanical in effect, the second active and variegated. The first part presents a gentle, rustling texture in the strings (reminiscent of rehearsal number 5 in the String Quartet). Microrhythms are restricted to five different patterns filling the minim beat:

At first these patterns are strictly ordered in the individual parts so as to form a rhythmic canon; later their order is freely changed, patterns are repeated, etc. Even in this context, where pitches would not seem to matter very much, Lutosławski has taken care to control the harmony quite intricately. The twelve-note chords on which the string parts are based are in a constant state of flux, one dissolving rapidly into another by means of octave transfers. Each such chord, however, has roughly the same effect, since all are based on combinations of interval classes 2, 3, and 5. To the pizzicato background is added gradually a glittering, gamelan-like sound in the percussion doubling pitches of the strings' twelve-note chords; in the midst of all this comes a brief, premature intrusion of the sort of music that will begin the second part. The second part proper (from number 206) contrasts strongly with the first not only by virtue of timbre, register, and articulation, but also because of pitch organization. In the first of three sections comprising the second part of the movement, pitches are organized in freely deployed chromatic tetrachords; thus interval class 1 has taken over from 2, 3, and 5 as the controlling factor. The second section of the second part (from number 207) uses a variety of diatonic and chromatic collections; the final section is based on a contracting regime of twelve-note chords against which single pitch classes are accented in a highly effective way. When the chords of the last section have been compressed into the middle register, the percussion add a fleeting echo of the first part as a last touch.

Notice that, although the movements of *Livre* were to have been unrelated to one another, in fact they are not quite so. Compare the brass chord after 210 in the second movement to the one just before 109 in the first, for example. Notice, too, that the gesture of accenting single pitch classes (212) has been anticipated in the first movement (before 105). Similarly, the third movement is not entirely new; compare the brass texture at 302 with that at 108 in the first movement, or the woodwind texture at 304 with similar passages in the second movement.

In the opening section of the third movement, the placement of rhythmic attack points is governed by a simple three-measure *talea*. The technique is not properly isorhythmic, however, since the pattern governing pitch distribution is of the same three-measure length. This pitch pattern is subjected to inversion on the second playing, to permutation of register on the third, and to both operations on the fourth (incomplete) playing. Example 6.17 gives the rhythmic model and the first two versions of the pitch pattern. To uncover such technical details amounts to fascinating but essentially trivial detective work, though; what counts is the musical effect produced. Lutosławski uses these simple models to create a style we might call 'blurred pointillism': attack points are dispersed in time and register, but they represent not individual sounds but voice-bundles of three lines each. Each attack begins as a whole-tone trichord (2-2), but each (except the third, sixth, and eighth in each pattern) is then blurred by quarter-tones (in effect precisely written-out glissandi).

6.17   Rhythm and pitch models from the opening of the third movement of *Livre*

In its broadest aspect the structure of the third movement is two-part, the second large part being a variation of the first. The first part presents three musical ideas: the texture just described; after a brief interruption by the brass (302), a new melodic idea emphasizing the tritone; and finally a fluent woodwind texture (304). The second part begins as a reprise of the opening, now over a rumbling bass (305), but this is soon combined with the other ideas from the first part in a sort of development. There is some attempt at reaching a climax (310–13), but the attempt is frustrated by repeated pauses. The strings return briefly to the opening music as a little codetta.

Livre's third chapter is, like the others, followed by a tranquil interlude. In this case, however, the interlude gradually transforms itself into the final chapter; the listener is taken unawares and only slowly returns to concentrated listening as the piece itself gathers concentration. Each of the preceding movements has been captivating in its way, but none has demanded any real psychological involvement; gradually it becomes clear that this one will be very different. The finale is like the second movement of the Second Symphony in miniature. Beyond their similar psychological functions in the end-accented orchestral cycle, the similarity extends even to details of form. Like the symphony finale, the fourth movement of *Livre* unfolds in stages as it makes a long, carefully controlled approach to a climax, and the means used are remarkably parallel:

Stage 1	Number 404	a.	Expanding cantilena in the strings, later joined by winds;
	411	b.	faster passages for winds superimposed on cantilena;
	413	c.	culmination of cantilena.
Stage 2	419		Short episodes; macrorhythmic accelerando.
Stage 3	439		Metric notation; macrorhythmic accelerando merges with microrhythm; primitive unison rhythm emerges; pauses.
Stage 4	445		Climax.
Coda	446		Overlaps conclusion of climax.

It is not surprising to find that harmonic construction is intimately bound up with expressive function in the fleshing out of this formal scheme. As in the Second Symphony, the expanding cantilena uses a simplified, 'consonant' harmonic style emphasizing interval class 2. As other solo strings join the two cellists who began the cantilena, the number of pitches in use grows from two to four (two whole-tone dyads) to six (two whole-tone trichords) to eight (two whole-tone tetrachords) to ten (two whole-tone pentads); with the entry of the tutti strings at 409, a complete twelve-note chord is achieved (ex. 6.18). In the sonorous percussion accompaniment, the available complementary pitch classes are correspondingly reduced from ten to two. After the woodwinds and brass join this *cantabile* texture, the culminating phase of the cantilena is reached at 413 with a rich twelve-note chord built primarily of interval classes 3 and 4.

6.18   Harmonic summary of nos. 404–9, fourth movement of Livre

The second stage of the form produces a succession of twenty lively textural episodes, each shorter than the last (from eleven seconds at 419 to about half a second at 438). At first these episodes are wildly different from each other, but by number 425 the process has developed into a fierce battle between two textures: woodwinds (staccato) and strings (twelve-note chords). This stage of the form is given coherence and its quickening macrorhythm is made explicit by

the punctuating chord for brass, tom-tom, and doublebasses that
begins each episode (cf. the third Postlude). There is a succession of
ten such chords, which is then repeated (ex. 6.19). It is significant that
these chords provide the strongest possible harmonic contrast to the
preceding cantilena, since they are constructed exclusively of interval classes 1, 5, and 6 and hence are 'dissonant'. Moreover, the outer
voices proceed melodically only by the same three interval classes,
and they move consistently in contrary motion; evidently the sound
contrapuntal habits of a lifetime need not evaporate in a new stylistic
context. As the macrorhythm accelerates, the succession of these
punctuating chords emerges more clearly; at 439 the entire orchestra
takes up the chords (first the original ten and then a new sequence),
now transformed into microrhythm – quavers accelerating from
M.M. 120 to M.M. 160 and beyond. Suddenly the full orchestra stops
and then repeats the staccato chord at intervals of four, five, and seven
seconds. These are among the most intense silences in recent music;
indeed they are comparable in power to the celebrated crotchet rest in
the first movement of the 'Eroica' Symphony (m. 280). It is precisely
these inspired pauses that lift the music's acceleration above the
mechanical level of the last Postlude; for by interrupting the process
at the last moment, Lutosławski makes the arrival of the climax at 445
(*tutta forza ma cantabile*) genuinely exhilarating.

6.19   Punctuating brass chords in the fourth movement of *Livre*

Typically for Lutosławski, the way out of the climax is individual;
after a glorious explosion of brass sound, bells raised, one by one the
brass players relinquish their final phrase. Already the strings have
begun the revolving *ppp* chords of the coda. The work finishes with
an expressive duet for flutes, quite different in effect from the bass
duet that concludes the Second Symphony; and the string chords,
climbing ever higher, come to rest on a kind of cadence, the stable
tetrachord E, F-sharp, A, B. (The linear approach to this final chord,
incidentally, gives a particularly clear example of the auxiliary role
played by quarter-tones in Lutosławski's music; here they are simple
passing tones.)

The effect of stability produced by the climax and coda depends in part on the fact that, whether by design or not, the single pitch class E-natural assumes structural meaning. E is the bass (and the lower note of a perfect fifth) of the culmination of the cantilena (413) and of the climax chord (445); it is the highest note of the brass *furioso* passage that follows; the octave span e^2 to e^3 frames the flute duet; and e^3 is the goal to which the bass voice (i.e., fourth soloist, second violins) ascends at the close.

Livre pour orchestre magnifies every strength of the Second Symphony. Here the cantilena is truly rapturous, the ascent to the climax is exquisitely judged, the conclusion is satisfying, serene, and final. There is no hint of struggle with technique; every detail of the work is expressive. Having posed himself new questions in the symphony, in *Livre* Lutosławski attained a new certainty of purpose and mastery of technique to produce a masterpiece of the modern orchestral repertoire.

Cello Concerto

The soprano Galina Vishnevskaya (wife of Mstislav Rostropovich) refers to the Lutosławski Cello Concerto as 'the story of a twentieth-century Don Quixote'. Rostropovich himself, the work's dedicatee and its first and most famous exponent, has discussed it in similarly programmatic terms, and most outside observers have focused on its obviously dramatic qualities at the expense of its purely musical substance. This is only natural. The composer's tendency to instrumental characterization – the division of dramatic roles between double reeds and the other wind instruments in the first movement of the Second Symphony, for example – reaches a peak in the concerto, and extramusical interpretations become well nigh irresistible in the second and fourth movements. But taken as a whole the work refuses to support any detailed program from start to finish, and Lutosławski cautions against taking any such interpretation too seriously.[17]

That Lutosławski would occupy himself with such an old-fashioned and apparently unpromising genre at all was surprising; it was partly the happy coincidence of Rostropovich's interest in the late sixties that persuaded him to do so. And the work he composed is no ordinary concerto; he approached the form, as he had approached other large-scale closed forms before it, not to revive it but to reformulate its essential principles in an original way. Thus, although the solo writing does present formidable technical problems, it has none of that empty virtuosity that has burdened the genre in the past; every note is charged with musical purpose. There is no cadenza. And although the traditional three-movement pattern, fast–slow–fast, is perceptible in the Lutosławski concerto, the functions of these movements have been drastically altered in order to conform with Lutosławskian formal principles. Lutosławski's concerto is an invaluable addition to the solo cello repertoire and a convincing demonstration that, even in the late twentieth century, the solo concerto can be made a fit vehicle for original and cogent musical expression.

The work has four principal divisions, played without pause: an introduction for solo cello, a cycle of four episodes (occupying the position of first movement in the traditional scheme), a slow cantilena, and a finale with coda. The introduction, requiring more than four minutes to perform, is a peculiar affair unlike anything in Lutosławski's earlier works. The atmosphere is carefree, the sequence of events capricious. As if musing absent-mindedly, the soloist passes suddenly from moments of abstraction (the repeated D's, *indifferente*) to moments of concentration (*grazioso, un poco buffo*, etc.) and back again. One need not resort to a literary program to observe that the introduction's diffuse organization and its meandering exploration of quite unrelated materials create a characteristic 'low pressure', a kind of anxiety about the shape of the work to come. The introduction is *not* a repository of latent thematic ideas to be developed in later movements, though; with few exceptions (notably the repeated D's, which will return transformed to end the finale), its materials have little concrete relation to the rest of the work.

The cellist is brusquely interrupted by the entry of the trumpets playing what the composer has described as an 'irascible' phrase. (Note that the trumpets' c-sharp² has been prepared in the cello harmonics just preceding the interruption.) This first utterance from the ranks of the orchestra gives immediate notice of the hostile, disruptive role the orchestra will assume, a role that will be fully developed only in the dramatic confrontations of the finale. Though the cellist attempts to continue his soliloquy, the trumpets intrude again and again, erupting finally in an extended statement (ex. 6.20). These trumpet interruptions, and all such phrases later in the work, are based on the same hexachord for thirdless harmony that first appeared in the String Quartet and later made up the refrains of the Second Symphony (see ex. 5.7).

Having failed to sustain his monologue, it is as if the cellist now tries to engage the orchestra in dialogue. Each of the four episodes comprising the second movement unfolds in the same way: the soloist begins with isolated pizzicato notes, issuing a kind of invitation, and a colloquy between the cellist and small groups of orchestral

6.20   Trumpets, rehearsal no. 7, Cello Concerto

instruments ensues, at first haltingly, gradually becoming more
fluent. The cellist remains the leading voice throughout and continues, as in the introduction, to explore a kaleidoscopic range of
manners, by turns gentle, brilliant, playful, pathetic, lyrical, comic.
Even at their fullest moments the episodes are rather lightly scored
and subdued in dynamics. The brass, excluded from the orchestral
dialogue, continue to function as a disruptive force, breaking in *ff* to
cut short each episode before it has fully developed. The last such
intrusion (at 61), marking the end of the second movement, is an
extended, virulent statement like that which ended the introduction.

From a technical point of view the second movement's four
episodes exhibit some rather unexpected features. Much of the music
is metrical, and there are rhythmic complications of a kind that hark
back to the Concerto for Orchestra and even to the Two Etudes and the
Overture for Strings. The harmony is founded almost exclusively on
thirds, and the constant arpeggiation of 'seventh chords' and 'ninth
chords' – while nonfunctional, to be sure – creates a curiously Brit-
tenesque nostalgia for triadic tonality. Explicit twelve-note chords are
now more the exception than the rule; in their place are smaller
collections constantly forming and dissolving.

The orchestral strings play only a secondary role in the second
movement, but in the third they join with the cellist in an eloquent,
intensely beautiful cantilena. The sudden cooperation between cellist and orchestral strings is not intended to have any programmatic
meaning (for example, that the strings are taking sides with the soloist
against the winds and percussion), but is merely to take advantage of
their unexcelled capacity for lyricism. Indeed, this movement comes
closest of the four to its counterpart in a traditional concerto scheme,
the slow movement, and its character would be difficult to account for
in any programmatic reading of the whole work.

In form the cantilena is a distant relation of the da capo aria: three divisions, the first (from 64) and third (from 76) closely related, the second (from 69) contrasting. This simple plan is compelling partly because it projects simple, easily perceptible pitch relationships powerfully over a long span – relationships, moreover, of a sort that create a stable, almost tonal effect. In the first section the cellist intones his long-breathed melody, marked *molto espressivo, dolente*, against a long pedal point on E, which grows slowly to encompass the major third E/G-sharp and every quarter-tone between in six octave registers. The cello melody itself contains only two interval classes, 2 and 5; it is given a distinctive character by the sobbing rhythmic motive, grace note–quaver.

Typically, the contrast offered in the central section of the movement is rooted firmly in harmonic practice. The projection of pitch classes E and G-sharp gives way to complementary partitioning of the total chromatic between solo orchestral string players and the cellist. Neither E nor G-sharp is emphasized now. Though there can be no mistaking this for tonal music, it is telling that the projection of the ternary formal design depends, as in the da capo aria, not only on contrasting melodic gestures but even more importantly on harmonic contrast. Gradually the harmonic collections in the orchestra grow from six pitch classes to ten in a series of five clearly marked phrases; the cellist is accordingly restricted to smaller and smaller collections. At 75 the soloist reaches the summit of a long melodic ascent, the single pitch e^2, against which are eleven-note aggregates in the flutes, clarinets, celesta, harp, and piano. The effect is stunning, both because the primacy of the pitch class E has suddenly been restored and because the importance of this event is underscored by the sudden change to this new, shimmering color in the orchestra. At 76 the process underway in the first section of the movement is resumed at just the point it left off, the six-octave E to G-sharp clusters. The cellist ascends yet again from E to e^2, while the strings converge on unison g-sharp below middle c. At last soloist and orchestra unite to begin a unison statement of the cantilena on the a below middle c (ex. 6.21). Reduced to its bare essentials, the outline of the slow movement's principal pitches appears to suggest A as a 'tonic', E and G-sharp as protracted 'dominant' harmony. But the crucial test is whether such an association will suggest itself not to the eye but to the ear, and in fact it does not. The long maintenance of G-sharp and especially E as structurally significant pitches lends the movement an extraordinary clear and attractive, but not tonal, harmonic foundation.

The unison cantilena of the strings and soloist accelerates, becomes urgent, seems to bode a climax; but ruthlessly it is cut short by an ugly outburst in the brass – this time the entire brass section, not the

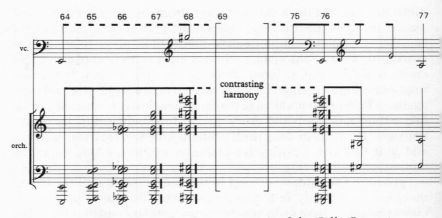

6.21   Structural pitches in the slow movement of the Cello Concerto

smaller groups that have interrupted the work earlier – and the finale, in which the real musical action of the concerto will transpire, has begun. Now the other orchestral groups join in the interruption music: after the brass the woodwinds, then strings, brass again, and percussion. Finally, at 86, the entire orchestra joins in a massive, savage statement, as if to attack the soloist and rebuke him for everything that has come before.[18] It is at this point that a dramatic view of the concerto's materials virtually forces itself upon the participants. Indeed the cellist interjects among the orchestral 'attacks' a puzzling little phrase (88), and during a rehearsal the afternoon of the first performance in 1970 Lutosławski advised Rostropovich to 'play this as if to say to the brasses, "Just you wait and see!"' The orchestra continues to attack, though, and from number 90 the cellist begins to reply in kind, *furioso*. This exchange marks the end of the first stage in the form of the finale.

Beginning at 96 the soloist mounts a vigorous countercharge, and a series of skirmishes follows in which various small groups of instruments taunt and assail him. The only relief from this wild atmosphere comes at 123, where the cellist pauses briefly to lament his situation. The battle resumes, and the orchestra, apparently victorious, reaches a climax at 133–4, delivering a series of eleven ferocious blows. Vanquished, the cellist replies with whimpering sounds. So deeply does Rostropovich identify with the dramatic persona of the solo part that before the première he confessed to the composer that he always wept during this passage. 'It is my death', he said. Lutosławski replied, 'But Sława, you will triumph in the end!'

So he shall. For in the short coda (from 137) the soloist rises, indomitable, ascending brilliantly from low C to a² to end the work alone, *tutta forza*, with insistent repetitions of the final pitch. Thus the Cello Concerto has two climaxes, the first collective, the second individual. The repeated-note gesture stems, of course, from the introduction, but its import has been radically transformed. Despite the mechanized, inhuman rhythmic assaults of the orchestra, the individual will has survived to proclaim a message of transcendent humanism.

Since much has been written about the tonal significance of the closing pitch, a final word on tonal organization in the concerto is in order. We have seen that the prevalence of harmonic collections rich in thirds creates a certain 'consonant' atmosphere in the second movement, and that the structural underpinnings of the third movement can be reduced to only two pitch classes. But it is untenable to infer some kind of crypto-tonal basis for the whole work from the mere circumstance that the piece opens with repeated D's and ends almost half an hour later with repeated A's. It cannot be denied that individual pitch classes are given local prominence through repetition; but the fact that the most obvious of these are D (first movement), E (third), and A (coda) is a coincidence brought about by the composer's natural desire to exploit the open strings and natural harmonics of the solo cello for expressive purposes, nothing more. The final A is no 'tonic' nor even 'dominant';[19] it is not a tonal but a dramatic resolution for this powerful, persuasive work.

Preludes and Fugue

Preludes and Fugue has enjoyed considerable success and has been rather frequently performed since its première in 1972. Like other late works of Lutosławski, it has impressed its admirers in no small part because of its composer's manifest commitment to unfashionable causes: the large-scale closed form, communication with the listener, and disciplined craftsmanship. After the first British performance in January 1973, Stanley Sadie noted that, though the preludes are in the familiar Lutosławski style, that style is 'treated more sparsely so far as actual notes are concerned and more richly and variously in ideas', and he found that in the fugue 'Lutosławski stretches his musical muscles and poses a challenge to the listener's intellect'.[20]

If Lutosławski's public had been surprised when he wrote a solo concerto, how must they have reacted to the news that he was working on a piece with an even more reactionary title? But in fact the name Preludes and Fugue does not refer to any neoclassic conception of form (nor, of course, of musical style) but rather to the same basic two-part, end-accented structure that marks most of the composer's recent music. The seven preludes are musical *hors d'œuvres*, like the preliminary movements of *Livre pour orchestre* enticing but not filling; the main course is the fugue, and only here is the grand gesture attempted. The title alludes, moreover, to a central issue in Lutosławski's work: the dialectical opposition and synthesis of freedom and discipline. Thus the preludes, averaging about two minutes each, represent fantasy, imprecision, impermanence, whimsy; while the fugue, which is as long as all the preludes together, embodies strict procedure, concentration of expression, and seriousness of purpose.

The instructions for performance reveal an uncharacteristic degree of concession to open form. If all seven preludes and the fugue are to be played, their original order must be observed. But a smaller number of preludes may be performed, alone or with a cut version of the fugue, in any order the performers choose. In any case, the end of one prelude always overlaps the beginning of another; thus Lutosławski had to foresee every possible order of performances for the preludes and compose their beginnings and endings so that every possible overlap would be acceptable to him. Harmonically this was made possible by fashioning all beginnings from a single hexachord and all endings from its complement (which is its inverted retrograde) (ex. 6.22). The challenge was to achieve the illusion of harmonic variety among the seven beginnings and endings and to arrange for each prelude to end naturally with the required pitch classes.

The preludes are little character pieces. Each is a jewel, but none is a completed musical statement. Pociej has aptly described them as 'dazzling eruptions of musical invention. Nothing is ever repeated, in every second something is going on, something is changing, there is unceasing movement. Perfect forms keep emerging as if for a moment only, then dissolve, evaporate, to give place to new structures.'[21] Reportedly the composer at one time considered making a second version of the whole work for symphony orchestra. If so, he must have come to see that a larger orchestra is unnecessary, for even from his modest ensemble of thirteen solo strings he has drawn a marvelous variety of arresting textures. The impression the preludes give of having been gleaned from accumulated sketches is reinforced by the fact that many passages are reminiscent of earlier works. Letter D in prelude 3 recalls parts of the String Quartet, for example, as does the end of prelude 7. The opening of prelude 1 brings to mind the introductory brass episode in the Second Symphony, and the contrabass solo in prelude 5 is very close kin to the cello writing in the concerto (cf. number 11 in the latter work, for example).

6.22 Hexachords for beginning and ending each prelude, Preludes and Fugue

The sketchbook impression is bolstered, too, by the large assortment of pitch-organizing methods to be found in the preludes. Note, for example, the technique at work in the second half of prelude 2: four solo violins in harmonics work their way through all three possible (3-3-3) tetrachords ('diminished-seventh chords'), accompanied by complementary nine-note chords. Or note the prominent 'triads' in the contrabass solo and its accompaniment. In prelude 6, the cello duet maintains one chromatic hexachord (A to D), the accompaniment the complement.[22] Viewing the seven preludes together as a single division of the overall form, prelude 7 can be seen as its culmination. Now the two hexachords restricted to beginning and ending the other preludes (ex. 6.22) are given a thorough thematic working out; and the vehement style of playing is both the most intense yet heard and an effective way of preparing the arrival of the fugue. As might be expected, the final prelude is not allowed to make a definitive climax but instead gives way suddenly to a soft, languid chorale rather like that after the climax of the String Quartet.

In what sense is Lutosławski's fugue a fugue? Certainly it does not recreate the high Baroque procedure; to cite only the most obvious deviations, Lutosławski uses six subjects, and he begins not with a subject exposition but with an episode. The critics have amused themselves proposing alternative genres; Marius Flothuis prefers the late Renaissance motet as a model, and others have suggested that 'canzona' or 'ricercar' would serve as a more accurate title. If one had to settle on an historical antecedent, either the polythematic keyboard ricercar of the sixteenth and seventeenth centuries or the so-called variation canzona of the seventeenth, in which the several expositions present melodic and rhythmic variants of a single theme, could probably be pressed into service. But it hardly seems credible that Lutosławski would suddenly resort simply to imitating an historical form. Rather this finale is called 'fugue' to underscore its serious, disciplined nature by contrast with the less concentrated preludes, and to indicate that it is devoted to polyphonic exposition and development.

The construction of the fugue depends principally on the juxtaposition of two radically different kinds of music, that of the subjects and that of the episodes. Their differences may be roughly summarized as follows:

Subject music	Episode music
Polyphonically combined voice-bundles	Monophonic polyphony
Collective ad libitum	A battuta; traditional meters
Sharply characterized microrhythms	Regular microrhythms
Static harmony	Mobile harmony
Interval classes 1, 6	Interval classes 2, 5
Distinct, contrasting characters	Uniform, undistinguished character

As the summary shows, two of Lutosławski's distinctive textural conceits play crucial roles in distinguishing the functions of the subject and episode musics: the bundle of voices and the technique of monophonic polyphony.

The subjects, though harmonically static, are harmonically intense, since they are based exclusively on tritones and semitones. (Indeed, the first subject is strongly reminiscent of the opening of *Muzyka żałobna*, although the composer denies any intentional allusion.) Each of the six subjects is associated with a characteristic style of expression and a small repertory of rhythmic gestures:

S_1	*cantabile*	♩. ♩ ♩ ♩ etc.
S_2	*grazioso*	etc.
S_3	*lamentoso*	♩ ♩ ♩. ♫ etc.
S_4	*misterioso*	etc.
S_5	*estatico*	gliss. ♩ etc.
S_6	*furioso*	gliss. etc.

As in the historical fugue, the subjects are exposed by imitative entries in several voices (two, three, or four); but here each contrapuntal voice is really a group of several instruments heterophonically playing the same pitches at different speeds.

The composer himself has noted that, like the episodes in traditional fugues, the episode music here is meant to provide moments of relaxation. It is also more active than the expositions harmonically (just as the traditional episodes are modulatory), continuously stating the total chromatic by means of a twelve-tone series whose construction exclusively in interval classes 2 and 5 ensures the placid effect the composer needed (ex. 6.23). Through transposition the series produces a 144-note model, which serves as the direct source of episode pitches. Each pitch is introduced as melody but sustained as harmony, producing the effect we have called monophonic polyphony: an apparently full, polyphonic texture that is, fundamentally, the expression of a single succession of attack points carrying one, occasionally two or more pitches. Thus, for example, the beginning of episode 6 (rehearsal number 20) can be reduced to the melody shown in example 6.24, except that the result is rather as if such a melody were played on the piano with the damper pedal depressed. The effect is peculiar, probably in part because of the incongruity between diatonic harmonic combinations and conventional rhythmic physiognomy on the one hand and the very disjunct character of the underlying melody on the other. Cadences are achieved by 'thickening' an attack point to three or more pitches.

6.23   Episode series from the Fugue

6.24   Attack points from the beginning of episode 6 (no. 20) in the Fugue

The episodes give structural definition to the first large section of the form by separating the expositions and by framing the whole with an introduction and a codetta. But they contribute to a sense of forward momentum as well, since they grow progressively shorter (macrorhythmic accelerando) and livelier (microrhythmic accelerando). Episode 7, which closes this first, expository section, is a kind of culmination of the episode music, much longer and more varied than the others and with many internal cadences and changes of tempo.

The expository section just described is the first of three large sections in the fugue. The entire scheme may be summarized as follows:

Fugue: Structural Synopsis

Rehearsal number	
	Exposition
	Episode 1 (introduction)
1	Exposition 1 (4-voice)
5	Episode 2
6	Exposition 2 (3-voice)
9	Episode 3
10	Exposition 3 (3-voice)
13	Episode 4
15	Exposition 4 (2-voice)
17	Episode 5
18	Exposition 5 (2-voice)
20	Episode 6
21	Exposition 6 (3-voice)
24	Episode 7 (codetta)
	Development
29	Stretto 1 (4-voice)
47	Episode 8
48	Stretto 2 (12-voice)
50	Stretto 3 (6-voice)
51	Stretto 4 (6-voice)
after 53	Climax
	Coda
54	Subsidence
after 60	Episode 9 (codetta)

Lutosławski authorizes four ways of shortening the fugue when it is performed with fewer than seven preludes: (1) to omit everything from episode 7 through stretto 2; (2) to omit episode 7 and stretto 1; (3) to omit stretto 1, episode 8, and stretto 2; or (4) to omit only stretto 1.

In the first part of the development (stretto 1 in our synopsis), the six subjects are contrapuntally combined for the first time. Each subject is represented only by its characteristic rhythms; since in their expositions the subjects were harmonically identical, their rhythms must now be furnished with new pitch patterns in order to achieve a varied harmonic palette. Four voice-bundles participate, their entries overlapping one another at shorter and shorter distances:

Stretto 1

```
vn 1–4       S₄            S₄          S₅          S₆            S₃
vn 5–7          S₁            S₅          S₅          S₆
vle 1–3             S₂          S₁          S₃          S₂
vc. 1–2, cb.      S₄       S₃          S₂          S₁       S₆
```

The dynamic is soft throughout this first stretto, but the quiet is suddenly broken by the *ff* insertion of the very brief episode 8, and the music will now continue *ff* as it pushes toward a climax. The second stretto presents the rhythms of subjects 4, 5, and 6 simultaneously in twelve individual voices (violin 7 is omitted); each voice is assigned a sequence of rhythms (e.g., S_4–S_5–S_6, S_5–S_6–S_4, etc.) and a single pitch class in a twelve-note chord. Stretto 3 comprises very close entries of six voice-bundles, to which are assigned the six subject rhythms from the lowest voice (S_1) to the highest (S_6); each voice-bundle contributes two pitches (with quarter-tone neighbors) to a twelve-note chord. The final stretto follows without pause; six voice-bundles are involved, each of them giving a succession of subject rhythms:

Stretto 4

vn 1–2	S_5	S_6	S_5	S_6
vn 3–4	S_6	S_5	S_6	S_5
vn 5–6	S_5	S_6	S_5	S_6
vn 7, vla 1	S_4	S_5	S_6	S_5
vle 2–3	S_3	S_4	S_5	S_6
vc. 1–2, cb.	S_2	S_3	S_4	S_5

At 53 the music passes directly into a frantic expanding texture rushing toward the climax, all the voices using either S_5 or S_6 rhythms.

Many of the intricacies of Lutosławski's fugal form will likely pass unnoticed by the unaided listener. What counts more heavily in creating a persuasive musical experience is the composer's unusually subtle adaptation of his technique of macrorhythmic control in the shaping of the fugue. We have seen that the expository first section is directional; that although two separate strands of continuity, the exposition music and the episode music, are continually interrupting each other, both participate in the gradual contraction of macrorhythmic intervals and the concomitant enlivening of microrhythmic character. Although this process seems to be brought to an end by the unexpectedly lengthy seventh episode, it will in fact resurface in the development – hence the accelerating entry points of the first stretto; the eighth episode, which is shorter and livelier than any in the first section; and the fact that in the development each stretto is shorter than the last.

As in many other Lutosławski works, the climax is a single twelve-note chord played *tutta forza*, creating a dense mass of sound. What is more interesting is its reflection of another fundamental trait of the composer: after the eminently rational development of the fugue, it is irrationality that triumphs at the climax. Neither the twelve-note chord nor the microrhythms through which it is projected have the slightest relation to the work's thematic materials.

As the individual players finish their climax phrase, they go on independently to the coda, in which a new twelve-note chord emerges to create a luminous, otherworldly atmosphere of whole-tone harmony. At number 54 begins a series of twelve imitative entries using augmented versions of S_5 rhythms, each statement falling gradually in register. The combined effect is of a wistful and very expressive echo of the fugue's former contrapuntal involvements. When all twelve entries have been completed, they are found to have created by octave transfers a new ten-note version of the whole-tone-dominated chord, which is then transformed again into the original twelve-note version (ex. 6.25).

6.25   Harmonic summary of the coda, Preludes and Fugue

The melancholy beauty of this coda is an unusually frank expression of emotion for the composer, a rare unguarded moment in which we are allowed to glimpse, undisguised, his deepest lyrical impulses. But it is not in Lutosławski's nature to let the work end in such an exposed state; he must append a brief but vigorous passage of episode music. This ninth episode is certainly logical; its opening dyad G/F ties it directly to the end of the preceding coda music (see the contrabass phrase at number 60), and as the shortest and most concentrated of all the episodes it is the natural consequence of the progressive changes marking the episodes in the expository section and surfacing again briefly during the development. But musically it is a mistake. It cannot seem natural here, because it is so distantly removed from the earlier appearances of the episode strand. As a closing gesture it is so brief as to be flippant, and its very artificiality seems to mock what has come before. One is reminded of the equally inappropriate ending of the Overture for Strings, written more than twenty years before.[23] Such cavils ought not to obscure the solid achievements of Preludes and Fugue, however: the brilliant coloration of the preludes, the ingenious architecture of the fugue, the splendid, dream-like coda, and above all the subtle musical wit that transforms and transcends dead convention to create a living art.

Les espaces du sommeil

In his first *Manifeste* (1924), André Breton, father of the surrealist movement, pronounced Robert Desnos the quintessential surrealist poet:

> he who, more than any of us, has perhaps got closest to the Surrealist truth, he who, in his still unpublished works and in the course of the numerous experiments he has been a party to, has fully justified the hope I placed in Surrealism and leads me to believe that a great deal more will still come of it. Desnos *speaks Surrealist* at will. His extraordinary agility in orally following his thought is worth as much to us as any number of splendid speeches which are lost, Desnos having better things to do than record them. He reads himself like an open book, and does nothing to retain the pages, which fly away in the windy wake of his life.[24]

Born in Paris in 1900, Desnos became a close friend of Breton and joined his artistic circle in 1922. He published his first volume of verse in 1924. Desnos displayed an unusual aptitude for the surrealist experiments to which Breton refers; he practiced automatic writing and developed the ability to fall asleep at will in order to enter his dreamscapes. The imagery of dreams, an important interest of the surrealists, became a central feature of his poetic style.

Around 1930 Desnos broke with Breton and the movement, but he continued to strive for a new poetic diction based in part on his earlier experiments. One of his aims was

> to fuse popular language, even the most colloquial, with an inexpressible 'atmosphere,' with a vital use of imagery so as to annex for ourselves those domains which – to this very day – remain incompatible with that famous goddamned poetic dignity which endlessly oozes from tongues once ripped from that scabrous Cerberus which still blocks the gateway to the domain of poetry.[25]

During the Second World War the poet was active in the French resistance. In 1944 he was arrested by the Gestapo and sent first to Auschwitz, then to Buchenwald, finally to the camp at Terezin, Czechoslovakia. There he contracted typhoid, and, although the Allies liberated the camp in May 1945, it was too late for Desnos. He died in June. His best work is generally thought to be found in *Corps et biens* (1930), which collects his verse of 1919–29. The language of these poems is distinguished by bizarre dream imagery and the hypnotic repetition of words and rhythms. It was in this collection that the prose poem 'Les espaces du sommeil', written in 1926, first appeared.

Given Lutosławski's deep-seated affinity for surrealist verse, it was only natural that he turn to Desnos in search of a text for Fischer-Dieskau. And given the criteria which had led him to the Michaux poems in 1961 and to those of Chabrun a few years later, it was equally natural that he be attracted specifically to 'Espaces', with its musically tempting imagery, its conveniently pliable structure, and its recurring textual elements. Exactly as in *Paroles tissées*, the structure of the poem afforded the composer a four-part musical design in which the first two parts are introductory, the third contains an orchestral climax, and the very brief fourth serves as coda to the whole work. The similarity to *Paroles tissées* extends further to the style of text setting for the solo voice (mainly with reciting tones and syllabic cantilena), and to the role of the orchestra, which 'surrounds the poem with a mysterious aura' of delicate sound in a 'wonderful tapestry of silken reflections'.[26] The full resources of the symphony orchestra come into play only in the climactic third section.

Parts 1 and 2 of Lutosławski's *Les espaces* establish a mysterious, nocturnal setting inhabited by dark rustlings, sudden, evanescent illuminations, eerie and evocative chirpings and twitterings. Their effect may be compared to Bartók's 'night-music' style, originating in *Out of Doors* and frequently returned to in later works (the Fourth and Fifth Quartets, *Music for Strings, Percussion, and Celesta*), though the actual musical substance here remains purely Lutosławskian. Part 1 makes a series of tiny gestures marked by frequent changes of texture and orchestration and frequent pauses, so that, like the poem's opening lines, it reflects a jumble of fragmentary, discontinuous images. Its pitch organization confirms that the composer has long since given up any symbolic allegiance to 'twelveness'; the special charm of the opening strings-and-percussion texture, for example, depends not only on instrumental timbre but also on the distinctive structure of its tetrachordal harmony. The total chromatic is completed only incidentally with the arrival of F-sharp in the fourth tetrachord (ex. 6.26). The second section of part 1 is divided into three phrases of parallel construction, corresponding to the division of the poem by the recurring line 'Il y a toi'. The phrase at number 10 is repeated, varied, at number 15; its third statement, at number 20, is cut short and gives way to a brief closing section, which presents a series of gliding nine-note chords to accompany the last lines of text:

> But myself as well, pursuing myself
> or ceaselessly overtaking myself.

6.26   Harmonic collections in the opening phrase of *Les espaces*

Part 2 (from number 24, *tranquillo*) is simpler in construction and more continuous in effect. It unfolds in a succession of five phrases, each of the same design. Each phrase begins with the introduction of sustained harmonies in the strings (cf. Postlude no. 1). The chords grow and change content under the influence of an informal twelve-tone series, emphasizing interval classes 2 and 5 and used in both prime and inverted forms (ex. 6.27). Against this gray, featureless background two wind instruments and one percussion produce fragmentary little wisps of sound, like the poem's 'strange shapes' that 'are born at the moment of sleep and disappear', 'phosphorescent flowers' that 'appear and wither and are reborn'. Each of the five phrases uses a different trio of instruments for this function, beginning with birdlike sounds in two piccolos and proceeding toward the middle register:

Number 24	2 piccolos, glockenspiel
33	2 oboes, piano
40	2 flutes, celesta
50	2 clarinets, piano
63	2 horns/2 trumpets, piano

The third element of texture is the baritone soloist, who recites the text simply, using mostly repeated notes. All of his principal pitches derive from the accompanying harmonic continuo.

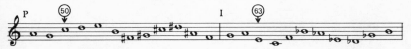

6.27   Excerpt of ordered pitch classes in the harmonic continuo, *Les espaces*

The third part of the work (from two measures before 83) brings the first lively tempo and agitated musical development in the orchestra, as well as the only sustained metrical notation in the work. Now the twelve-tone series used by the strings in part 2 returns to shape the baritone's lines, while the rest of the ensemble has a variety of (unrelated) twelve-note chords, many of them symmetrically constructed and emphasizing interval classes 3 and 5. The choice of this part of the text to support a musical climax was somewhat arbitrary, but, once chosen, the language lends itself to interpretation as a kind of cosmic dream, an escalating phantasmagoria leading to an agitated outcry:

You who are the root of my dreams
and who rouses my
metamorphosis-laden soul
and who leaves behind her glove
when I kiss her hand.

In the night
there are stars
and the shadowy motion of the sea
of rivers, forests, cities, grasses,
of the lungs of millions and millions of beings.

The vocal climax comes after number 94 with the highest pitch for the voice, f-sharp[1], which has been carefully led up to by step progression so as to serve convincingly as the melodic climax of the whole work. The orchestral climax follows shortly afterward, at 96.

But the most extraordinary passage in *Les espaces du sommeil* is not its rather predictable climax but its brief fourth part, the coda. In typical fashion it follows immediately from the climax. The harmonic basis of the coda is the combination of a whole-tone pentad and a minor third (i.e. the same harmonic structure that informs the coda of the fugue in Preludes and Fugue), which is allowed to generate chords of more than twelve notes (ex. 6.28). From these chords are drawn the pitches of the soloist's final melody. The ending is brilliant, surprising, and for Lutosławski unprecedented. The baritone sings the final phrases:

In the night there is you.
In the daytime, also.

Suddenly the orchestra enters with a forceful chord, which imme-

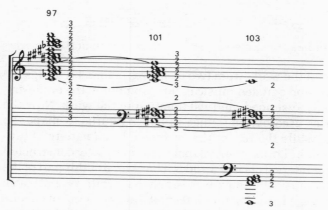

6.28 Harmonic summary of the coda (nos. 97–104 only), *Les espaces*

diately fractures into quickly dwindling splinters of sound, shattering the dream world in which poet, composer, and listener have been immersed together. The shocking light of day has intruded to break the nocturnal spell, and the fantastic visions of sleep vanish irretrievably.

Mi-parti

Mi-parti was the first purely symphonic composition to reach the public since *Livre pour orchestre* eight years before, and it stands with *Livre* among the most perfectly realized orchestral works of Lutosławski's career. Underlying the work's appeal are the composer's characteristically fastidious attention to detail and a new economy of means and subtlety of formal design unmatched in his earlier works. Yet so completely has the composer mastered the elements of his compositional technique that technique vanishes from the listener's perception and he is left to marvel at the sheer beauty of the orchestral sound.

The title is a French idiom, not readily translated, describing something divided into similar but not identical parts. This has nothing to do with the work's overall formal structure but refers instead to a compositional principle that affects the content of every stage of the form: the repetition of musical materials in subtle transformations. The work's single movement falls into two large divisions and a coda. Each of the two main divisions has a three-part structure: two introductory phrases followed by a third statement that leads to a culmination:

Mi-parti: Structural Synopsis

Rehearsal number	
	Part 1
	First phrase
8	Second phrase
14	Third (main) phrase, leading to
16	Culmination
	Part 2
20	First phrase
24	First brass interruption
25	Second phrase
28	Second brass interruption
29	Third (main) phrase, leading to
39	Climax
	Coda
40	'Icy' chord, gradually transformed
44	Cantilena, first phrase
49	second phrase

What is striking about this structure is that it owes nothing to histori-cal convention but manages nonetheless to organize a variety of smaller musical gestures into a single arch-like design of tension and relaxation.

Virtually all of the material in *Mi-parti* can be traced to one of three sources. The first of these is the cycle of eight twelve-note chords in the strings which underlies the whole of part 1. As we have already seen, each chord is derived from the preceding one by octave transfers (see ex. 5.6). The eight-chord cycle transposes itself systematically upward so that, beginning with the ninth chord, the cycle is repeated at transposition level 1. By the end of part 1 (i.e., by one measure after number 19), three cycles have been completed and the first chord of a fourth cycle (t = 3) has been reached. The outer voices have thus described a simple linear framework that gives coherence to the whole first division of the form (ex. 6.29). At the surface, however, it is not harmony but melody that reigns supreme: a gentle, five-voice woodwind polyphony gradually emerging from the strings' har-monic background. As regards pitch, the woodwind lines represent a simple composing-out of the eight-chord harmonic cycle, the chord tones being freely embellished with semitone neighbors (ex. 6.30).

6.29   Linear framework of *Mi-parti* (beginning to 1 m. after no. 19)

6.30   *Mi-parti*, rehearsal no. 2

The three large phrases that make up part 1 do not coincide exactly with the three transpositions of the harmonic 'color': thus, for example, phrase 2 starts with the eighth chord of the first cycle. The phrases are literally *mi-parti*: similarly but not identically constructed. Each begins tentatively with a few strings exploring some of the notes of the twelve-note chord; there are two such false starts before phrase 1 proper sets in and one such before phrase 2. Finally the whole chord is filled out and the woodwind soloists enter one by one, each with his own repertoire of distinctive rhythmic and melic gestures. The second phrase reverses the order of woodwind entries; the third combines the ordering of the first two and leads to the culmination of part 1, an ad libitum polyphony involving all the winds:

Phrase 1	Phrase 2	Phrase 3
bass clarinet	flute	flutes and bass clarinet
horn	oboe	oboes and horns
clarinet	clarinet	clarinets
oboe	horn	all winds (culmination)
flute	bass clarinet	

The structure of part 2 closely parallels that of part 1. As before, there are three large sections, each a transformation of the last, leading to a culmination point. But the characters of the two parts are radically different. Whereas the first was static, tranquil, and even idyllic, the second is active, dramatic, and exciting; and whereas the first led only to a culmination of restrained, lyrical playing, the second leads to a typical Lutosławskian climax (cf. the finales of the Second Symphony and *Livre*). Instead of a polyphony of soloists, the mode of discourse is now a polyphony of *textures*, the materials of each textural voice deriving in an ingenious way from the materials of part 1. From the characteristic melodic combinations of chord tones and neighbors in the earlier woodwind lines, Lutosławski extrapolates a very special twelve-tone set in which only intervals 1, 3, and 4 occur between adjacent order positions. The set is all-combinatorial, and the retrograde inversion is equivalent to the prime, the inversion equivalent to the retrograde (ex. 6.31). But the set is never stated in full; it serves merely as a source for unordered subsets that emphasize both linearly

order nos :   0   1   2   3   4   5   6   7   8   9   10   11

6.31   Source series for part 2 of *Mi-parti*

and harmonically the characteristic interval classes 1, 3, and 4. For example, the textural participants of the first two phrases use the following subsets:

		Unordered subsets (as order numbers of the source set)
	Phrase 1	
20	Piccolos, glockenspiel	0–4
	Violins 2	8–11
21	Piano	3–7
	Clarinets, marimba	11–2
22	Piccolos, glockenspiel	6–10
	Violins 2	2–5
23	Piano	9–1
	Phrase 2	
25	Clarinets, bassoons	10–2
	Celesta, harp, piano	5–9
	Violas, celli	0–3
26	Flutes, oboes	7–11
	Clarinets, bassoons	2–6
	Celesta, harp, piano	7, 10–1
	Violas, celli	4–8
27	Flutes, oboes	11–3
	Clarinets, bassoons	6–10
	Celesta, harp, piano	1–5

From this list it can be seen that the principle of *mi-parti* repetition is actually operating on several levels at once. In a sense part 2 is a vastly transformed repetition of part 1; phrase 2 is a transformation of phrase 1; and within an individual phrase the sequence of entering textural voices is repeated, but with new pitch-class collections. For example, when in phrase 1 the textural sequence piccolos–violins–piano is repeated, its pitch-class collections are found to have been advanced by six positions in the source set: 0–4 becomes 6–10, 8–11 becomes 2–5, 3–7 becomes 9–1.

One other element figures in part 2: a brass statement in the monophonic polyphony style that breaks in to separate phrase 1 from phrase 2 and again phrase 2 from phrase 3. The pitches of these brass episodes are generated by a simple set, just as in the episodes of Preludes and Fugue, except that this set has only nine members. It is used only in the prime form and in transpositions by descending whole-step (t = 10, t = 8, etc.) (ex. 6.32).[27] Both the episode at number

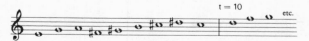

6.32   Nine-note series for the brass episodes of *Mi-parti*

24 and that at 28 exhaust five transpositions of the set and break off during a sixth (t = 2, incomplete).

In the first two phrases of part 2, the entries of the various textural voices have begun to come closer together. The third phrase, longer and more continuous than the others, continues this macrorhythmic accelerando beyond the point where the individual strands of texture can be kept separate by the ear. Rather they merge into a texture of truly symphonic, developmental character, surging toward the work's climax. In the midst of this developing energy is thrust the third brass episode, beginning three measures after number 35, and this time the transposition cycle of the nine-note series is completed (B-flat to B-flat). As in the finales of the Second Symphony and *Livre*, the approach to the climax is interrupted by dramatic pauses (two measures before 38), and at this moment the eight-chord harmonic cycle that was interrupted at the end of part 1 is resumed with chord 2 at t = 3. The climax chord at 39 is chord 7 of the cycle at t = 3.

The climax passes directly into the coda, according to Lutosławski's usual practice. As the individual players give up their *fff* playing, a chord in tritones and semitones is discovered in the winds, *pp* and without vibrato. Lutosławski has referred to this chord as 'a kind of "frozen" harmony . . . , a chord I can best describe as "cool", which contrasts with everything that has come before, all of which could be called quite "warm"'.[28] Gradually, almost imperceptibly, the chord contracts by a series of octave transfers toward a middle-register cluster, and the chill atmosphere warms once more. Some of the octave transfers are marked by puzzling, rather vulgar little fanfares in trombone and trumpet that represent, according to the composer, 'the real world outside' intruding, lest the music become 'too pretty, too idyllic, too naive'.

The work finishes with a long, slowly ascending cantilena played heterophonically by a voice-bundle of twelve intertwining violins. Their melody is in fact the nine-note brass series, now reincarnated in such changed circumstances that it will likely go unrecognized. And even here the *mi-parti* idea, the principle of similar but unequal phrase structure, operates. The first phrase of the cantilena extends from number 44 to 48, where the violinists reunite on unison a^2. Against this phrase are placed three fragmentary bits of commentary, splashes of color echoing the music's earlier, livelier moments: celesta, harp, and pizzicato strings; three oboes and chimes; and finally a fuller closing statement in timpani, celesta, harp, and strings. The design of the second phrase is parallel. As the violins continue their ascent into ethereal regions, there is brief commentary from three flutes and vibraphone and again from three flutes and glockenspiel.

When the final note of the cantilena, unison c^4, is reached, there comes again a fuller third statement. Timpani, celesta, harp, piano, and strings together create a wonderfully peaceful closing chord borrowed from the opening eight-chord cycle (chord 6, t = 0), and the music dies away.

Lutosławski's gift for creating living forms, his masterly handling of orchestral resources, the extreme economy of his musical materials – in *Mi-parti* all of the composer's refined technical skills go into fashioning a superbly made and utterly persuasive work of art. It is an essay no less symphonic for its lack of obvious symphonic form. It is, ultimately, a statement of faith that in the life of twentieth-century man there is and must be a place for beauty.

Catalog of works

Works are listed as nearly as possible in chronological order, except that all later versions of the same composition are grouped under the earliest version of the work. Uniform titles have been established according to the general rule that generic titles be given in English and all others be left in the original language, whether Polish or French; English and Polish translations are added as required.

The first extensive catalog of Lutosławski's works in English was compiled, with the composer's cooperation, by Ove Nordwall and published in his *Lutosławski* (Stockholm: Edition Wilhelm Hansen, 1968), pp. 127–34. The present catalog depends partly on Nordwall, but the information available there has been considerably amplified and many corrections have been introduced, again with the composer's help. Where Nordwall gives an incorrect or variant bit of information, his reading is identified by the symbol [N.:]. Similarly, where Library of Congress cataloging has established a misleading uniform title, it is given here preceded by the symbol [LC:].

Although the present catalog omits uncompleted works, the principal ones may be mentioned here. The *Suita kurpiowska* (Kurpian Suite) for orchestra was to have been Lutosławski's first attempt to draw on Polish folklore. He worked on the score in 1938 or 1939, following the completion of the Symphonic Variations, but he was dissatisfied and abandoned the project. The score was destroyed during the Second World War. The three movements for orchestra now known as Three Postludes (1958–60, rev. 1963; 1960; 1960) were to have led to a larger, climactic fourth movement, but that finale was abandoned at the sketch stage in 1960; some of the sketch material was later incorporated in the Second Symphony. The composer worked from 1972 at an orchestral composition to be called *A maiori . . .* (From Greater . . .) but abandoned it in 1974. *A maiori . . .* would have satisfied a commission from Zubin Mehta and the Los Angeles Philharmonic Orchestra. Another commission, this one from the Chicago Symphony Orchestra, prompted Lutosławski to plan a Third Symphony in four movements: Invocation, Cycle of Etudes, Toccata, and Hymn. Between 1977 and late 1978 he wrote and then rejected one version of the third movement; it appears that the project will remain unrealized.

Among the large quantity of functional music by which Lutosławski supported himself from 1945 to about 1960 were a great many incidental scores for radio and stage plays. It is no longer possible to give a faithful accounting of this music. Many of the manuscripts were kept by Polish Radio and have since disappeared; and the composer, attaching no artistic importance to such efforts, did not keep any careful record of his activity. The lists of sixty-six radio plays and fourteen stage plays offered by Nordwall (pp. 135–7) were reconstructed by the composer himself, but they are incomplete and not chronological. None of these scores is reflected in the present catalog.

Most works in manuscript (ms.) remain in the composer's possession in Warsaw, although a few manuscripts have passed into the collection of the Biblioteka Narodowa (National Library) in Warsaw. The following abbreviations are used for publishers:

PWM: Polskie Wydawnictwo Muzyczne, al. Krasińskiego 11a, 31-111 Cracow. Export distributor: Ars Polona-'Ruch', Krakowskie Przedmieście 7, 00-068 Warsaw 10.

Chester: Chester Music, J. & W. Chester/Edition Wilhelm Hansen London Ltd, Eagle

Court, London EC1M 5QD. US distributor: Magnamusic-Baton, Inc., 10370 Page Industrial Boulevard, St Louis, MO 63132.

Moeck: Moeck Verlag, Postfach 143, D 31 Celle, Federal Republic of Germany. Sole US agent: Belwin-Mills Publishing Corporation, 16 W. 61st Street, New York, NY 10023.

Prelude (1922) for piano
Ms. lost

[Juvenilia: small pieces for piano] (1923–6)
Mss. lost

Two Sonatas for Violin and Piano [N.: Sonata] (1927)
Mss. lost
Remarks: Played privately by Lutosławski (piano) and his violin teacher, Lidia Kmitowa

Poème (1928) for piano
Ms. lost

Taniec chimery (1930) for piano
Dance of the Chimera [N.: Chimera-Dance]
First performance: the composer; Warsaw Conservatory, 1932 [N.: 1930]
Ms. lost

Scherzo (1930) for orchestra
Ms. lost

Harun al Raszid (1931) for orchestra
Haroun al Rashid
First concert performance: Warsaw Phil. Orch., Józef Oziminski; Warsaw, 1933
Ms. lost
Remarks: Reorchestrated version of ballet music originally written for a stage production of a play by Janusz Makarczyk

Sonata for Piano (1934)
Sonata na fortepian, Sonata fortepianowa
3 movements, fast–slow–fast
Duration: 25 min.
First performance: the composer; Warsaw, 1935
Ms.

Wodnica and **Kołysanka lipowa** (1934) for voice and piano
Water Sprite, and Lullaby of the Linden [N.: Two Songs]
Texts: Kazimiera Iłłakowicz (1892–)
First performance: Ewa Bandrowska-Turska and the composer; Warsaw, 1941
Ms. lost

Uwaga (c. 1935–6), film score
Attention!

Zwarcie (c. 1935–6), film score
Contraction

Gore (c. 1935–6), film score
Fire!

Double Fugue (1936) for orchestra
First performance: Conservatory orch., Walerian Bierdiajew; Warsaw Conservatory, 1937
Ms. lost

Preludium i aria (1936) for piano
Prelude and Aria
Ms. lost

Requiem aeternam for chorus and orchestra, and **Lacrimosa** for soprano and orchestra (1937)
[N.: Two fragments of a Requiem]
Duration (Lacrimosa only): 3 min.
First performance (Lacrimosa only): Helena Warpechowska, sop., Warsaw Phil. Orch., Tadeusz Wilczak; Warsaw, 1938
Requiem aeternam, ms. lost; Lacrimosa, ms.; transcription for soprano and organ publ. PWM, 1948, ©1946
Remarks: Diploma composition, Warsaw Conservatory

Symphonic Variations (1936–8) [N.: 1938] for orchestra
[LC:] Variations symphoniques; Wariacje symfoniczne
Picc.-2-2-e.h.-3(b.)-2-cbsn; 4-3-3-1; timp.-perc.-cel.-hp-pf.; strings
Duration: 9 min.
First performance: Polish Radio broadcast, April 1939; first concert performance: Polish Radio Sym. Orch., Grzegorz Fitelberg; Cracow, 17 June 1939
Publisher: PWM, [1947]; 1966; 3d edn, 1978; subpubl. Chester, 1972

Two Etudes (1940–1) [N.: 1941] for piano
Dwa etiudy
I. *Allegro*; II. *Non troppo allegro*
Duration: I. 1 min. 50 sec.; II. 2 min. 30 sec.
First performance (no. 1 only): Maria Bilińska-Riegerowa; Cracow, 26 January 1948
Publisher: PWM, ©1946; republ. 1971; ©1974 Witold Lutosławski; repr. 1975 in Lutosławski, Album per pianoforte, PWM

Variations on a Theme of Paganini (1941) for two pianos
Wariacje na temat Paganiniego
Duration: 6 min.
First performance: the composer and Andrzej Panufnik; Warsaw, 1941; first performance abroad: G. Joy and J. Bonneau; Radio Paris, 1948
Publisher: PWM, ©1949; republ. 1970, 1971; subpubl. Chester, 1972: Moscow: Izdatel'stvo 'Muzyka', 1976, ed. Galina and Julia Turkinaia

Paganini Variations (1977–8) for piano and orchestra
2(picc.)-2-2-2(cbsn); 4-3-3-1; timp.-perc.-hp; strings
Duration: 11 min.
First performance: Felicja Blumental, pf., Florida Phil. Orch., Brian Priestman, Miami, 18 November 1979
Publisher: Chester, ©1978; PWM, ©1978
Remarks: A version by the composer, expanded by repeating variations with changes in instrumentation. Written for and dedicated to Felicja Blumental

Pieśni walki podziemnej (1942–4) for voice and piano
Songs of the Underground Struggle [N.: Songs of the Polish Underground]
Contents:
1. Żelazny marsz [Iron march], *Tempo marsza*
2. Do broni [To arms], *Tempo marsza*
3. Przed nami przestrzeń otwarta [An open stretch before us], *Tempo marsza*
4. Jedno słowo, jeden znak [One word, one sign], *Spokojnie* [calmly]; *żywiej (tempo mazurka)* [livelier]
5. Wesoły pluton [The merry platoon], *Tempo marsza*
Texts: No. 1 by Stanisław Ryszard Dobrowolski (1907–), an officer in the Armija Krajowa (underground Home Army); no. 2 by Aleksander Maliszewski (1901–); nos. 3 and 4 by Zofia Zawadzka; no. 5 anon.
Duration: 15 min.
Publisher: PWM, ©1948, as vol. 1 in the series Pieśni walki podziemnej
Remarks: 'Żelazny marsz' is also included in Seven Songs (1950–2)

[Thirty pieces for woodwinds] (1943–4)
[N.: Thirty small polyphonic pieces]
Contents: 10 canons for 2 cl., 10 canons for 3 cl., and 10 pieces for ob. and bsn
Ms.
Remarks: The oft-repeated but erroneous identification of these pieces as being for brass appears to stem from a mistranslation in Stefan Jarociński (ed.), *Polish Music* (Warsaw: Państwowe Wydawnictwo Naukowe, 1965), p. 195

Trio (late 1944–early 1945) [N.: 1945] for oboe, clarinet, and bassoon
I. *Allegro moderato*; II. [tempo unk.]; III. *Allegro giocoso*
Duration: 16 min.
First performance: Seweryn Śnieckowski, ob., Teofil Rudnicki, cl., and Bazyli Orłow, bsn; Cracow, Festival of Contemporary Polish Music, September 1945 [N.: 1946]
Ms.

Trzy kolędy (1945) for solo voices, unison chorus, and chamber ensemble
Three [N.: Polish] Carols
Publisher: Warsaw: Edition Czytelnik

Melodie ludowe
Folk Songs [N.: Folk Melodies]
Contents:
1. Ach, mój Jasienko (melodia łowicka) [Oh, my Johnny (Łowickian melody)], *Sostenuto*
2. Hej, od Krakowa jadę (melodia krakowska) [Hey, I come from Cracow (Cracovian melody)], *Allegretto*
3. Jest drożyna, jest (melodia podlaska) [There is a path, there is (Podlasian melody)], *Andantino*
4. Pastereczka (melodia podlaska) [The shepherd girl (Podlasian melody)], *Allegretto*
5. Na jabłoni jabłko wisi (melodia sieradzka) [An apple hangs on the apple tree (melody from Sieradz)], *Moderato*
6. Od Sieradza płynie rzeka (melodia sieradzka) [a river flows from Sieradz (melody from Sieradz)], *Allegretto*
7. Panie Michale (walc kurpiowski) [Master Michael (Kurpian waltz)], *Poco sostenuto*
8. W polu lipeńka (melodia mazurska) [The linden in the field (melody from Mazury)], *Sostenuto*
9. Zalotny (taniec śląski) [Flirting (Silesian dance)], *Allegretto*

10. Gaik (taniec śląski) [The grove (Silesian dance)], *Allegro vivace*
11. Gąsior (taniec śląski) [The gander (Silesian dance)], *Andantino*
12. Rektor (taniec śląski) [The schoolmaster (Silesian dance)], *Allegro*
Duration: 10 min.
First performance: Zbigniew Drzewiecki; Cracow, 1947
Publisher: PWM, ©1947; republ. 1959, 1964, 1971; repr. 1975 in Lutosławski, Album per pianoforte, PWM
Remarks: Commissioned by PWM. Melodies from an unpubl. collection by Jerzy Olszewski. Transcription by José de Azpiazu of all but nos. 6, 7, and 11 for guitar, publ. PWM, [1955?], 1971

Pięć melodii ludowych (1952) for string orchestra
Five Folk Songs [LC: Folk melodies for string orchestra]
Transcription by the composer of nos. 1, 2, 10, 11, and 12
Publisher: PWM, [1955?]; ©1968; in series Biblioteka Szkolnych Instrumentalnych

Cztery melodie śląski (1954) for 4 violins
Four Silesian Songs [N.: Four Silesian Folksongs]
Transcription by the composer of nos. 9–12
First performance: 22 October 1954, Warsaw
Publisher: PWM, [1955]

Dwadzieście kolęd (1946) for voice and piano
Twenty [N.: Polish] Carols
Contents:
1. Anioł pasterzom mówił [The angel said to the shepherds], *Con moto*
2. Gdy się Chrystus rodzi [When Christ was born], *Andante*
3. Przybieżeli do Betlejem [They hurried to Bethlehem], *Vivace*
4. Jezus malusieńki [Tiny Jesus], *Lento*
5. Bóg się rodzi [God is born], *Andante*
6. W żłobie leży [He is lying in a manger], *Andantino*
7. Północ już była [It was already midnight], *Allegro agitato*
8. Hej, weselmy się [Heigh, we rejoice], *Vivace*
9. Gdy śliczna Panna [When the lovely maiden], *Poco sostenuto*
10. Lulajże, Jezuniu [Sleep, little Jesus], *Andante*
11. My też pastuszkowie [We shepherds too], *Moderato*
12. Hej, w dzień narodzenia [Heigh, on the day of the Nativity], *Vivo*
13. Hola hola, pasterze z pola [Hola, hola, shepherds from the field], *Vivace*
14. Jezu, śliczny kwiecie [Jesus, lovely flower], *Andante con moto*
15. Z narodzenia Pana [Of the Lord's birth], *Allegro vivace*
16. Pasterze mili [The gentle shepherds], *Andante con moto*
17. A cóz z tą dzieciną [And what with this child], *Allegretto*
18. Dziecina mała [The little babe], *Andante con moto*
19. Hej hej, lelija Panna Maryja [Heigh, heigh, thou lily Virgin Mary], *Andante con moto*
20. Najświętsza Panienka po świecie chodziła [The most blessed maiden walked on earth], *Molto tranquillo*
Texts and melodies: Nos. 1, 5, and 6 from Michał Mioduszewski, Śpiewnik kościelny, czyli pieśni nabozne z melodyjami w kościele katolickum używane, a dla wygody kościołów parafijalnych (Cracow, 1838), respectively pp. 28, 45, and 30; nos. 14 and 15 from ibid., Suppl. I (Cracow, 1842), respectively pp. 434 and 433; nos. 2 and 16 from ibid., Suppl. II (Cracow, 1853), respectively pp. 772 and 778; nos. 2, 4, 7, 8, 9, 10, 11, 12, 13, 16, 17, and 18 from idem, Pastoralki i kolędy z melodyjami (Cracow: S. Gieszkowski, 1843), respectively pp. 56, 85, 138, 68, 57, 92, 99, 78, 81, 127, 29, and 53; no. 19

from Oskar Kolberg, *Lubelskie*, vol. 1 = *Lud* . . ., vol. 16 (Cracow, 1883), p. 108; and no. 20 from idem, *Łęczyckie* = *Lud* . . ., vol. 22 (Cracow, 1889), p. 20

First performance (nos. 11, 15, 17, 18, and 20 only): Aniela Szlemińska, sop., and Jan Hoffman, pf.; Cracow, 29 January 1947 (31 January according to Zygmunt Mycielski, 'Życie muzyczne w kraju: Kraków', *Ruch muzyczny* 3, no. 3–4 [1947]: 20; 19 January according to note by Jan Stęszewski in the PWM edition of 1974)
Publisher: PWM, ©1947; republ. 1974
Remarks: Commissioned by PWM

Odrą do Bałtyku (1946), film score
To the Baltic on the Oder

Symphony [No. 1] (1941–7) for orchestra
Symfonia [pierwsza]
Picc.-2(picc.2)-2-e.h.(ob.3)-3(picc.,b.)-2-cbsn; 4-3-3-1; timp.-perc.-cel.-hp-pf.; strings
I. *Allegro giusto*; II. *Poco adagio*; III. *Allegretto misterioso*; IV. *Allegro vivace*
Duration: 25 min.
First performance: Polish Radio Sym. Orch., Grzegorz Fitelberg; Katowice, 6 April 1948
Publisher: PWM, ©1957; min. score, 1973; subpubl. Chester, 1972

Sześć piosenek dziecinnych (1947) for [N.: female] voice and piano
Six Children's Songs
Contents:
1. Taniec [Dance], *Vivo*
2. Rok i bieda [Year and trouble], *Tranquillo*
3. Kotek [Kitten], *Andantino*
4. Idzie Grześ [Here comes Greg], *Tranquillo; allegretto*
5. Rzeczka [River], *Con moto*
6. Ptasie plotki [Birds' gossips], *Moderato; vivace*
Texts: Julian Tuwim (1894–1953), reprinted in *Dzieła*, vol. 1, pt 2 (4 vols.; Warsaw: Edition Czytelnik, 1955–9)
Duration: 8 min.
Publisher: PWM, ©1948; 2nd edn, 1974

> **Sześć piosenek dziecinnych** (1952) for children's choir and orchestra
> Arrangement by the composer
> First performance: Warsaw Children's Choir, Warsaw Phil. Orch., Witold Rowicki; Warsaw, 29 April 1954
> Ms.

> **Sześć piosenek dziecinnych** (1952–3) for mezzo-soprano and orchestra
> Orchestration by the composer
> First performance: Janina Godlewska, mezzo; Warsaw Radio Orch., the composer; Warsaw, Polish Radio, [1954?]
> Ms.

Suita warszawska (c. 1947), film score
Warsaw Suite

Spóźniony słowik [N.: slowik] and **O panu Tralalińskim** (1948), children's songs for [N.: female] voice and piano
The Belated Nightingale, and About Mr Tralaliński [N.: Two Children's Songs]

Texts: Julian Tuwim (1894–1953)
Duration: 5 min.
First performance: Irena Wiskida, sop., Jadwiga Szamotulska, pf.; Cracow, 26 January 1948
Publisher: PWM, ©1948
Remarks: Transcr. for SSA chorus and piano by Marie Pooler publ. separately in English transl. as Two Nightingales and About Mr Tralalinski; Chester, ©1977; PWM, ©1976

Spóźniony słowik and O panu Tralalińskim (1952) for voice and chamber orchestra
Orchestration by the composer
First performance: Maria Drewniakówna, sop., Polish Radio, Sym. Orch., Stefan Rachoń; Warsaw, [1953?]
Ms.

Overture for Strings (1949)
Uwertura smyczkowa, Uwertura na smyczki
Duration: 5 min.
First performance: Prague Radio Sym. Orch., Grzegorz Fitelberg; Prague, 9 November 1949
Publisher: PWM, ©1956; min. score, 1972; subpubl. Chester, 1972
Remarks: Dedicated to Mirko Očadlik

Lawina (1949) for soprano and piano
The Snowslide [N.: Lawina Avalanche]
Text: The poem 'Obval' (1829) by Aleksandr Pushkin
First performance: Lesław Finze, tenor; Cracow, 26 September 1950
Publisher: PWM
Remarks: Written for a competition for songs on texts of Pushkin on the 150th anniversary of the poet's birth, sponsored by the Union of Polish Composers, and awarded 2d prize

Mała suita (1950) for chamber orchestra
Little Suite
Contents:
1. Fujarka [Fife], *Allegretto*
2. Hurra polka, *Vivace*
3. Piosenka [Song], *Andante molto sostenuto*
4. Taniec [Dance], *Allegro molto*
Duration: 10 min.
First performance: Warsaw Radio Sym. Orch., Grzegorz Fitelberg; Warsaw, 20 April 1951
Ms.
Remarks: Commissioned by Polish Radio. Uses folk melodies from the village of Machów in the region of Rzeszów

Mała suita (1951) for orchestra
Revised by the composer and orchestrated for picc.-1-2-2-2; 4-3-3-1; timp.-sn.d.; strings
Duration: 11 min.
Publisher: PWM, ©1953; min. score, 1970; subpubl. Chester, 1972

Słomkowy łańcuszek i inne dziecinne utwory (1950–1), song cycle for soprano, mezzo-soprano, flute, oboe, 2 clarinets, and bassoon

Chain of Straw and Other Children's Pieces; Die Strohkette
Contents:
1. Wstęp instrumentalny [Instrumental introduction], *Allegro*
2. Chałupeczka niska [Low hut], *Andantino* (duet)
3. Była babuleńka [There was an old woman], *Allegro vivo* (mezzo)
4. Co tam w lesie huknęło [What went boom in the woods?], *Allegro vivo* (sop.)
5. W polu grusza stała [A pear tree stood in the field], *Andantino* (mezzo)
6. Rosła kalina [A guelder-rose grew], *Allegretto* (sop.)
7. Chciało się Zosi jagódek [Sophie wanted some berries], *Allegretto* (sop.)
8. [Theme and variations] Słomkowy łańcuszek [Chain of straw]
  a. Dzieci [Children], *Allegro* (duet)
  b. Studzienka [The pump], *Andantino* (sop.)
  c. Krzak róży [The rosebush], *Stesso tempo* (mezzo)
  d. Pies [The dog], *Allegretto* (mezzo)
  e. Kwiatek [Flower], *Andante* (sop.)
  f. Krowa [The cow], *Andante* (mezzo)
  g. Zakończenie [Finale], *Allegro non troppo* (duet)
Texts and melodies: No. 1: original. No. 2: text and melody from Oskar Kolberg, *Krakowskie*, vol. 2 = *Lud* . . . , vol. 6 (Cracow: Drukarnia Uniwersytetu Jagiełłońskiego, 1873), p. 512. No. 3: text and melody from ibid., p. 217. No. 4: text and melody from ibid. No. 5: text by Janina Porazińska (1888–1971); melody from unk. folk source. No. 6: text by Teofil Lenartowicz (1822–93); melody from unk. folk source. No. 7: text from Kolberg, p. 281; melody from unk. folk source. No. 8: text by Lucyna Krzemieniecka (1907–55); original music
Duration: 10 min.
First performance: Polish Radio; Warsaw, 1951
Publisher: PWM, 1952, ©1953; 2d edn, 1953; Chester, 1980, as Straw Chain, transl. Marie Pooler
Remarks: Commissioned by Polish Radio. Nos. 1–7 as a set were written and broadcast separately from no. 8, being combined later for publication.

Tryptyk śląski (1951) for soprano and orchestra
Silesian Triptych
Picc.-2(picc.2)-2-2-b.cl.(cl.3)-2; 4-3-3-1; timp.-perc.-cel.-hp; strings
I. *Allegro non troppo*; II. *Andante quieto*; III. *Allegro vivace*
Texts and melodies: Silesian folk texts and melodies from Jan Stanisław Bystroń [ed.], *Pieśni ludowe z polskiego Śląska*, vol. 1 in 2 pts (Cracow: Polska Akademia Umiejętności, 1927–34)
Duration: 9 min.
First performance: Eugenia Umińska, vn; Cracow, [1952?]
Fitelberg; Warsaw, 2 December 1951
Publisher: PWM, ©1953; 2d edn, 1974; min. score, ©1955, republ. 1973; subpubl. Chester, 1972
Remarks: First Prize, Festival of Polish Music, 16 December 1951; State Prize class II, 17 July 1952

Recitativo e arioso (1951) for violin and piano
Duration: 3 min.
First performance: Eugenia Umińska, vn; Cracow, [1952?]
Publisher: PWM, ©1953
Remarks: Written as a gift to Tadeusz Ochlewski, then director of PWM. Transcr. 1966 for violino grande and pf. by Bronisław Eichenholz; first performed in this version by Eichenholz, vn, and Herta Fischer, pf., Malmö, 30 September 1966; ms.

Wiosna (1951), children's song cycle for mezzo-soprano and chamber orchestra
Spring
Contents:
1. Już jest wiosna [Spring is here]
2. Piosenka o złotym listku [Song of the golden leaf]
3. Jak warszawski woźnica [Like a Warsaw driver]
4. Majowa nocka [May night]
Texts: No. 1 by Wł. Domeradzki; no. 2 by Jadwiga Korczakowska; no. 3 by Januszewska; no. 4 by Lucyna Krzemieniecka (1907–55)
First performance: Janina Godlewska, mezzo, Warsaw Radio Sym. Orch., the composer; Polish Radio, Warsaw, 1951
Ms.
Remarks: Transcr. of no. 4 for SSA chorus and piano by Marie Pooler publ. as A Night in May, no. 1 of Lutosławski, Three Children's Songs; Chester, ©1977; PWM, ©1976

Piosenka o złotym listku and **Majowa nocka** (1952) for mezzo-soprano and piano
Song of the Golden Leaf, and May Night [N.: Two Songs]
Transcription by the composer of nos. 2 and 4
Publisher: PWM, ©1954

Jesień (1951), children's song cycle for mezzo-soprano and chamber orchestra
Autumn
Contents:
1. W listopadzie [In October]
2. Świerszcz [The cricket]
3. Mgła [Fog]
4. Deszczyk jesienny [Little autumn rain]
Texts: Lucyna Krzemieniecka (1907–55)
First performance: Janina Godlewska, mezzo, Warsaw Radio Sym. Orch., the composer; Polish Radio, Warsaw, 1951
Ms.

Dziesięc polskich pieśni ludowych na tematy żołnierskie (1951) for men's chorus a cappella
Ten Popular Polish Songs on Soldiers' Themes [N.: Ten Polish Traditional Soldiers' Songs]
Contents:
1. Pod Krakowem czarna rola [A black field near Cracow], *Żywo; bardzo żywo* [Lively; very lively]
2. Nie będę łez ronić [No tear will be shed], *Spokojnie; trochę wolniej* [Calmly; a little slower]
3. A w Warszawie [And in Warsaw], *Żwawo* [Briskly]
4. Zachodzi słoneczko [The sun is setting], *Spokojnie* [Calmly]
5. Oj, i w polu jezioro [Oh! and in the field a lake], *Dość żywo; bardzo żywo* [Quite lively; very lively]
6. Jam kalinkę łamała [I broke the guelder-rose], *Bardzo żywo* [Very lively]
7. Gdzie to jedziesz, Jasiu? [Where are you going, Jack?], *Umiarkowanie; trochę wolniej* [Moderately; a little slower]
8. A na onej górze [And on that mountain], *Dość żywo* [Quite lively]
9. Już to mija siódmy roczek [The seventh year passes already]. *Żywo, wesoło* [Lively, gaily]

10. Małgorzatka [Maggie], *Bardzo żywo; znacznie wolniej; wolno* [Very lively; much slower; slowly]
Texts and melodies: Nos. 2, 4, 9 from Oskar Kolberg, *Krakowskie*, vol. 2 = *Lud* . . . , vol. 6 (Cracow: Drukarnia Uniwersytetu Jagiełłońskiego, 1873), respectively pp. 398, 179, and 166–7. No. 7 from idem, *Mazowsze*, vol. 3 = *Lud* . . . , vol. 26 (Cracow: Druk Wł. L. Anczyca i Spółki, 1887), p. 292. No. 8 from ibid., vol. 4 = *Lud* . . . , vol. 27 (Cracow: Wł. L. Anczyca i Spółki, 1888), p. 257. No. 10 from ibid., vol. 1 = *Lud* . . . , vol. 24 (Cracow: Druk Wł. L. Anczyca i Spółki, 1885), p. 86. Source for nos. 1, 3, 5, and 6 unk.
Publisher: Wydawnictwo Ministerstwa Obrony, [December 1951], series Dom Wojska Polskiego, Biblioteka muzyczna, vol. 31
Remarks: Commissioned by the Ministry of National Defense

Siedem pieśni (1950–2), [mass] songs for voice [or unison chorus] and piano
Seven Songs, mass songs
Contents:
1. Zwycieska droga [The road of victory]
2. Wyszłabym ja [I would marry]
3. Nowa Huta [literally 'new foundry', a city near Cracow]
4. Służba Polsce [Service to Poland]
5. Żelazny marsz [Iron march] = no. 1 of *Pieśni walki podziemnej* (1942–4)
6. Najpiękniejszy sen [The most beautiful dream]
7. Naprzód idziemy [We are going forward]
Texts: Nos. 1 and 6 by Tadeusz Urgacz (1926–); no. 2 by Leopold Lewin (1910–); nos. 3 and 4 by Stanisław Wygodzki; no. 5 by Stanisław Ryszard Dobrowolski (1907–); no. 7 by Jan Brzechwa (1900–66)
Publisher: PWM, 1950, 1951 in series Festiwal Muzyki Polskiej

Wyszłabym ja (1951) for mixed chorus a cappella
I Would Marry
Arrangement of no. 2 by the composer
Publisher: PWM, ©1951, Festiwal Muzyki Polskiej no. 4b

Służba Polsce (1951) for men's chorus and piano
Service to Poland
Arrangement of no. 4 by the composer
Publisher: PWM, ©1951, Festiwal Muzyki Polskiej no. 3e

Żelazny marsz (1951) for mixed chorus a cappella
Iron March
Arrangement of no. 5 by the composer
Publisher: PWM, ©1951, Festiwal Muzyki Polskiej no. 36b

Naprzód idziemy (1951) for mixed chorus a cappella
We Are Going Forward
Arrangement of no. 7 by the composer
Publisher: PWM, ©1951, Festiwal Muzyki Polskiej no. 35b

Bukoliki (1952) for piano
Bucolics
I. *Allegro vivace*; II. *Allegretto sostenuto*; III. *Allegro molto*; IV. *Andantino*; V. *Allegro marciale*
Duration: 5 min. 15 sec.
First performance: the composer; Warsaw, December 1953 [N.: April 1952]

Publisher: PWM, 1957, ©1954; republ. 1964, 1971; repr. 1975 in Lutosławski, Album per pianoforte
Remarks: Dedicated to Zbigniew Drzewiecki. Based on Kurpian folk melodies from Władysław Skierkowski, *Puszcza kurpiowska w pieśni* (Płock, 1928–34)

Bukoliki (1962) for viola and cello
Transcription by the composer
Publisher: PWM, ©1973, vla ed. by Stefan Kamasa, vc. by Andrzej Orkisz

Towarzysz (1952) for mixed chorus and orchestra
Comrade
Ms.

Srebrna szybka and **Muszelka** (1952) for voice and piano
Silver Pane and Little Seashell [N.: Two Children's Songs]
Texts: S. Barto
Publisher: PWM, ©1954
Remarks: Written for Polish Radio. Transcr. for SSA chorus and piano by Marie Pooler, publ. as In Every Little Seashell and Windowpanes of Ice, respectively nos. 3 and 2 of Lutosławski, Three Children's Songs; Chester, ©1977; PWM, ©1976

Srebrna szybka and **Muszelka** (1953) for mezzo-soprano and chamber orchestra
Transcription by the composer
Ms.

Trzy utwory dla młodzieży (1953) for piano
Three Pieces for Young People; [LC:] Utwory dla młodzieży
Contents:
1. Czteropalcówka [Four-finger exercise], *Allegro*
2. Melodia [Melody], *Andante con moto*
3. Marsz [March], *Allegro*
Publisher: PWM, ©1955; 2d edn, 1956; repr. 1964; and 1975 in Lutosławski, Album per pianoforte
Remarks: Commissioned by PWM

Pióreczko (1953), children's song for voice and piano
Little Feather
Text: J. Osińska
Publisher: PWM
Remarks: Written for Polish Radio

Pióreczko (1953) for voice and orchestra
Transcription by the composer
Ms.

Wróbelek (1953), children's song for voice and piano
The Little Sparrow
Text: Lucyna Krzemieniecka (1907–55)
Publisher: PWM
Remarks: Written for Polish Radio

Wróbelek (1953) for voice and orchestra
Transcription by the composer
Ms.

Wianki (1953), children's song for voice and piano
Wreaths
Text: Stefania Schuchowa
Publisher: PWM
Remarks: Written for Polish Radio

Pożegnanie wakacji (1953), children's song for voice and piano
Holiday Farewell
Text: Lucyna Krzemieniecka (1907–55)
Publisher: PWM
Remarks: Written for Polish Radio

Trzy pieśni (1953), soldier's songs for voice [or unison chorus] and piano
Three Songs
Contents:
1. Kto pierwszy [Who first]
2. Narciarski patrol [Ski patrol]
3. Skowronki [Larks]
Ms.
Texts: No. 1 by S. Czachowski; no. 2 by Aleksander Rymkiewicz (1913–); no. 3 by M. Dolęga

Dziesięć tańców polskich (1953) for chamber orchestra
Ten Polish Dances
Ms.
Remarks: Commissioned by Polskie Nagrania to accompany instructional materials on Polish folk dances. Based on folk materials of Silesia and Kashubia

Concerto for Orchestra (1950–4) [N.: 1951–4]
Koncert na orkiestrę
3(2picc.)-3(e.h.)-3(b.)-3(cbsn); 4-4-4-1; timp.-perc.-cel.-2hp-pf.; strings
1. Intrada, *Allegro maestoso*; II. Capriccio notturno e Arioso, *Vivace*; III. Passacaglia, Toccata e Corale, *Andante con moto*; *Allegro giusto*; *Presto*
Duration: 29 min.
First performance: Warsaw National Phil. Orch., Witold Rowicki; Warsaw, 26 November 1954
Publisher: PWM, ©1956, 1962; min. score 1956, 1957, 1969; Eulenburg (photorepr. from PWM), [1970?], Musik des zwanzigsten Jahrhunderts, Studien-Partitur 3006; subpubl. Chester, 1972; Moscow: Izdatel'stvo 'Muzyka', 1975
Remarks: Written at the invitation of Witold Rowicki (1950) for the Warsaw National Phil. Orch. and dedicated to him. Uses folk melodies from Oskar Kolberg, *Mazowsze*, vols. 2 and 5 = *Lud*..., vols. 25 and 28 (Cracow: Druk Wł. L. Anczyca i Spółki, 1886, and 1890)

Spijże, śpij [N.: Spijźe, śpij] (1954), children's song for soprano and chamber orchestra
Sleep, Sleep
Text: Lucyna Krzemieniecka (1907–55)
Ms.
Remarks: Written for Polish Radio

Idzie nocka (1954), children's song for soprano and chamber orchestra
Night Is Falling

Text: J. Osińska
Ms.
Remarks: Written for Polish Radio

Dmuchawce (1954) for orchestra
Dandelions
Ms.
Remarks: Based on Polish folk dances and intended to accompany a folk-dance ensemble

Warzywa and **Trudny rachunek** (1954) for voice and chamber orchestra
Vegetables, and Hard Arithmetic [N.: Two Children's Songs]
Texts: Julian Tuwim (1894–1953)
Ms.
Remarks: Written for Polish Radio

Preludia taneczne (1954) for clarinet in B-flat and piano
Dance Preludes; Préludes de danse; [LC: Preludia taneczne, clarinet and orchestra, arr.]
I. *Allegro molto*; II. *Andantino*; III. *Allegro giocoso*; IV. *Andante*; V. *Allegro molto*
Duration: 7 min.
First performance: Ludwik Kurkiewicz, cl., and Sergiusz Nadgryzowski, pf.; Warsaw, 15 February 1955
Publisher: PWM, ©1964; subpubl. Chester, 1972
Remarks: Result of a commission from PWM, originally for ten easy pieces for violin and piano. Based on folk melodies.

Preludia taneczne (1955) for clarinet in B-flat and chamber orchestra
Version by the composer scored for timp.-perc.-hp-pf.; strings
First performance: Alojzy Szulc, cl., Polish Radio Sym. Orch., Jan Krenz; Polish Radio, [1955?]; first concert performance: Gervase de Peyer, cl., English Ch. Orch., Benjamin Britten; Aldeburgh Festival, June 1963
Publisher: PWM, ©1957; repr. 1971, 1972; min. score 1968, repr. 1971; subpubl. Chester, 1972

Preludia taneczne (1959) for nine instruments
Version by the composer for fl., cl., ob., bsn, hn [N.: e.h.], vn, vla, vc., and cb.
First performance: Czech Nonet; Louny, 10 November 1959
Publisher: Chester, ©1970; PWM, ©1970

Four Fanfares (1954)
Ms.
Remarks: Written for the 2d Festival of Polish Music

Five Songs on Texts of Kazimiera Iłłakowicz (1956–7) [N.: 1957] for mezzo-soprano and piano
[LC: Songs (1963), arr.]; Pięć pieśni do słów Kazimiery Iłłakowiczówny
Contents:
1. Morze [The sea], *Con moto ma quieto*
2. Wiatr [The wind], *Furioso*
3. Zima [Winter], *Quieto*
4. Rycerze [Knights], *Impetuoso*
5. Dzwony cerkiewne [Church bells], *Soave*

Texts: Kazimiera Iłłakowicz (1892–   ), *Rymy dziecięce* (Cracow: Nakładem Spółki wydawniczej 'Fala', [1923])
Duration: 8 min. 35 sec.
First performance: Krystyna Szostek-Radkowa, mezzo; Katowice, 25 November 1959
Publisher: PWM, ©1963, 1969; Moeck, ©1963
Remarks: No. 1 dedicated to Marya Freund, nos. 2-5 to Nadia Boulanger

Five Songs on Texts of Kazimiera Iłłakowicz (1958) for mezzo-soprano and chamber orchestra
[LC: Songs (1963)]
Version by the composer scored for timp.-per.-2hp-pf.; strings
First performance: Krystyna Szostek-Radkowa, mezzo, Great Sym. Orch. of Polish Radio and Television, Jan Krenz; Katowice, 12 February 1960
Publisher: PWM, ©1963, 1969; Moeck, ©1963

Zasłyszana melodyjka (1957) for two pianos
An Overheard Tune
Publisher: PWM

Piosenka na prima aprilis (1958), children's song for voice and piano
Song on April Fools' Day
Text: Roman Pisarski (1912–69)
Ms.

Kuku, kuku (1958), children's song for voice and piano
Cuckoo! Cuckoo!
Text: Roman Pisarski (1912–69)
Ms.

Piosenki dziecinne (1958) for voice and piano
Children's Songs
Contents:
1. Siwy mróz [Grayhead frost]
2. Malowane miski [Painted bowls]
3. Kap, kap, kap [Drip, drip drip]
4. Bajki iskierki [The fairy-tale of the spark]
5. Butki za cztery dudki [Boots for four hoopoes]
6. Plama na podłodze [A stain on the floor]
Texts: Janina Porazińska (1888–1971)
Ms.

Na Wroniej ulicy w Warszawie (1958), children's song for voice and piano
On Wronia Street in Warsaw
Text: Roman Pisarski (1912–69)
Ms.

Muzyka żałobna (late 1954–8) [N.: 1958] for string orchestra
Music of Mourning [but usually] Funeral Music; [N.:] Musique funèbre; Trauermusik
In 1 movement of 4 sections: Prolog, Metamorfozy, Apogeum, Epilog
Duration: 13 min. 30 sec.
First performance: Great Sym. Orch. of Polish Radio and Television, Jan Krenz; Katowice, 26 March 1958
Publisher: PWM, ©1958; repr. 1965, 1969; Eulenburg (photorepr. from PWM), 1970, Musik des zwanzigsten Jahrhunderts, Studien-Partitur 3003; subpubl. Chester, 1972

Remarks: Written at the invitation of Jan Krenz (1954) to commemorate the 10th anniversary of Bartók's death, and dedicated 'à la mémoire de Béla Bartók'. Annual prize of the Union of Polish composers, 15 January 1959; first prize (shared with Tadeusz Baird), Tribune Internationale des Compositeurs, Paris, 12–15 May 1959

Sześć kolęd (1959) for 3 recorders
Six [N.: Polish] Christmas Carols
Publisher: Moeck

Trzy piosenki dziecinne (1959) for voice and piano
Three Children's Songs
Contents:
1. Trąbka [Trumpet]
2. Abecadło [ABC]
3. Lato [summer]
Texts: Benedykt Hertz (1872–1952)
Ms.

Three Postludes (1958–60, rev. 1963; 1960; 1960) for orchestra
Trzy postludia
Picc.-2(picc.2)-3-3(b.)-3(cbsn); 4-3-3-1; timp.-perc.-cel.-2hp-pf; strings 16-14-12-12-8
I. M.M. 80; II. M.M. 160; III. M.M. 150
Duration: I. 3 min. 30 sec.; II. 4 min. 50 sec.; III. 8 min. 40 sec. (total 17 min.)
First performance (no. 1): L'Orch. de la Suisse Romande, Ernest Ansermet; Geneva (Grand Théâtre), 1 September 1963, in a concert honoring the centenary of the International Red Cross; under the title *Per humanitatem ad pacem*; first performance (all 3 pieces together): Cracow Phil. Orch., Henryk Czyż; Cracow, 8 October 1965, in a concert honoring the 20th anniversary of PWM
Publisher (no. 1): PWM, ©1964, as Postludium na orkiestrę; (all 3 pieces together) PWM, ©1966; 2d ed. (min. score), 1970; 3d ed, 1974; subpubl. Chester, 1972
Remarks: No. 1 only inscribed 'Pour le centenaire de la Croix-Rouge'

Jeux vénitiens (1960–1) [N.: 1961] for chamber orchestra
Venetian Games; Gry weneckie
2(picc.)-1-3(b.)-1; 1-1-1-0; timp.-perc.-hp-pf.(2 players)(cel.); 4-3-3-2
I. [No tempo indicated]; II. M.M. 150; III. M.M. 60; IV. M.M. 60
Duration: 13 min.
First performance (movements 1, 2, and 4 in preliminary version): Ch. Orch. of Cracow Phil., Andrzej Markowski; Venice Biennale (Teatro la Fenice), 24 April 1961; first performance (revised and completed version): Warsaw National Phil. Orch., Witold Rowicki; Warsaw, 16 September 1961
Publisher: PWM, ©1962; 2d edn, 1973; 3d edn 1978; Moeck, ©1962
Remarks: Commissioned by Andrzej Markowski and the Ch. Orch. of the Cracow Phil. Orch. First prize of the Tribune Internationale des Compositeurs, Paris, May 1962

Trois poèmes d'Henri Michaux (late 1961–3) for mixed chorus and orchestra of winds and percussion
Three Poems of Henri Michaux; Trzy poematy Henri Michaux
5 sopranos, 5 altos, 5 tenors, 5 basses (all soloists); 3(2picc.)-2-3-2; 2-2-2-0; timp.-perc.-hp-2pf.
Contents:
1. Pensées, $\frac{1}{2} = \frac{3}{4} = \frac{5}{8} = 60 = 1$ sec.
2. Le grand combat [no tempo indication]
3. Repros dans le Malheur [no tempo indication]

Texts: Henri Michaux (1899–); nos. 1 and 3 from *Plume* (Paris: Editions de la Nouvelle Revue Française, Librairie Gallimard, 1938); no. 2 from *Qui je fus* (idem, 1928)
Duration: 20 min.
First performance: Zagreb Radio Orch., the composer; Zagreb Radio Choir, Slavko Zlatić; Muzički Biennale Zagreb, 9 May 1963
Remarks: Commissioned by Slavko Zlatić and the Zagreb Radio Choir. First prize of the Tribune Internationale des Compositeurs, Paris, May 1964

String Quartet (1964; 1st movement completed December, 2d completed November)
Kwartet smyczkowy
I. Introductory Movement; II. Main Movement
Duration: I. *c.* 8 min. 30 sec.; II. *c.* 15 min. (total *c.* 23 min. 30 sec.)
First performance: LaSalle Quartet; Stockholm, 12 March 1965
Publisher: Chester, ©1967; 2d ed, 1970; PWM, 1969, © 1968
Remarks: Commissioned by the Swedish Radio for the 10th anniversary of the concert series 'Nutida Musik'

Paroles tissées (1965) for tenor and chamber orchestra of 20 soloists
Woven Words
Perc.-hp.-pf.; strings 10-3-3-1
I. M.M. *c.* 84; II. *Quieto*, M.M. *c.* 120; III. *Allegro molto*, M.M. *c.* 160; IV. *Quieto*, M.M. 160
Text: 'Quatre tapisseries pour la Châtelaine de Vergi', by Jean-François Chabrun, publ. in *Poésie 47* (Paris: Seghers)
Duration: 15 min. [publ. score: 16 min.]
First performance: Peter Pears, tenor, Philomusica of London, the composer; Aldeburgh Festival, 20 June 1965
Publisher: Chester, ©1967; PWM, 1972, ©1967
Remarks: Written for and dedicated to Peter Pears

Symphony No. 2 (summer 1965–7) [N.: 1966–7] for orchestra
Symfonia druga
3(3picc.)-3(e.h.)-3(b.)-3; 4-3-3-1; timp.-perc.-hp-pf.(2 players)(cel.); strings 16-14-12-9-6
I. Hésitant, M.M. *c.* 132; II. Direct, M.M. *c.* 96
Duration: 30 min.
First performance (2d movement only): Sinf.-Orch. des Norddeutschen Rundfunks, Pierre Boulez; Hamburg, 18 October 1966; first performance (completed work): Great Sym. Orch. of Polish Radio and Television, the composer; Katowice, 9 June 1967
Publisher: Chester, ©1968; PWM, 1969, ©1968
Remarks: Commissioned by Norddeutscher Rundfunk, Hamburg, for the 100th concert of its series 'Das neue Werk'. First prize of the Tribune Internationale des Compositeurs, Paris, 20–24 May 1968

Livre pour orchestre (1968)
Książka na orkiestrę
3(2picc.)-3-3-3(cbsn); 4-3-3-1; timp.-perc.-cel.-hp-pf.; strings
Contents:
1er chapitre, M.M. 80
1er intermède
2me chapitre, M.M. 50
2me intermède
3me chapitre, M.M. 160
3me intermède et chapitre final

Duration: 20 min.
First performance: Städtisches Orch. Hagen, Berthold Lehmann; Hagen, 18 November 1968
Publisher: Chester, ©1969, 2d edn, 1970; PWM, 1970, ©1969
Remarks: Commissioned by the town of Hagen, West Germany, and dedicated to Berthold Lehmann

Inwencja (1968) for piano
Invention
Duration: 50 sec.
Publisher: PWM, ©1975, in Lutosławski, Album per pianoforte
Remarks: Dedicated to Stefan Śledziński on his 71st birthday

Concerto for Cello and Orchestra (1969–70)
Koncert wiolonczelowy
3(3picc.)-3-3(b.)-3(cbsn); 4-3-3-1; timp.-perc.-cel.-hp-pf.; strings
Duration: 24 min.
First performance: Mstislav Rostropovich, vc., Bournemouth Sym. Orch., Edward Downes; London (Royal Festival Hall), 14 October 1970
Publisher: Chester, ©1971; PWM, 1971, ©1972
Remarks: Commissioned by the Royal Philharmonic Society, London, supported by the Calouste Gulbenkian Foundation, 1968. Written for and dedicated to Mstislav Rostropovich. Annual award of the Union of Polish Composers, voted 21 December 1972, awarded January 1973

Preludes and Fugue (1970–2) for 13 solo strings
Preludia i fuga
7 vns., 3 vlas., 2 vc., 1 cb.
Contents:
Prelude 1, M.M. *c.* 120
Prelude 2, M.M. *c.* 152
Prelude 3, M.M. *c.* 132
Prelude 4, M.M. *c.* 72
Prelude 5, M.M. *c.* 160
Prelude 6, M.M. *c.* 144
Prelude 7, *Presto*
Fugue, M.M. *c.* 80
Duration: 34 min.
First performance: Ch. Orch. of Radio-Televizija Zagreb, Mario di Bonaventura; Graz, Steirischer Herbst Festival, 12 October 1972
Publisher: Chester, ©1973; PWM, ©1973
Remarks: Commissioned by Mario di Bonaventura [1970?] and dedicated to him. 'The work can be performed whole or in various shortened versions. In the case of performances of the whole, the indicated order of the Preludes is obligatory. Any number of the Preludes in any order can be performed with or without a shortened version of the Fugue.'

Les espaces du sommeil (1975) for baritone and orchestra
The Spaces of Sleep; Przestrzenie snu
3(2picc.)-3-3(b.)-3; 4-3-3-1; timp.-perc.-cel.-hp-pf.; strings
Text: From Robert Desnos, *Corps et biens* (1926) (Paris: Nouvelle Revue Française, 1930)
Duration: 15 min.
First performance: Dietrich Fischer-Dieskau, bari., Berlin Phil. Orch., the composer;

Berlin, 12 April 1978
Publisher: Chester, ©1978; PWM, ©1978
Remarks: Written for and dedicated to Dietrich Fischer-Dieskau

Sacher Variation (1975) for unaccompanied cello
Wariacja dla Paula Sachera
First performance: Mstislav Rostropovich, vc.; Zurich, 2 May 1976
Publisher: Chester, ©1979; PWM
Remarks: Commissioned by Rostropovich, and dedicated to Paul Sacher in honor of his 70th birthday

Mi-parti (1975–6) for orchestra
3(3picc.)-3-3(b.)-3; 4-3-3-1; timp.-perc.-cel.-hp-pf.; strings
Duration: 15 min.
First performance: Concertgebouw Orch., the composer; Amsterdam, 22 October 1976
Publisher: Chester, ©1976; PWM, ©1976
Remarks: Commissioned by the city of Amsterdam [1973?] for the Concertgebouw Orch.

Novelette (1978–5 May 1979) for orchestra
3(3picc.)-3-3(b.)-3; 4-3-3-1; timp.-perc.-cel.-2hp-pf.; strings
Announcement; 3 Events; Conclusion
Duration: 18 min.
First performance: Washington National Sym. Orch., Mstislav Rostropovich; Washington, 29 January 1980
Publisher: Chester; PWM
Remarks: Commissioned by the Washington National Sym. Orch. and dedicated to Mstislav Rostropovich

Discography

Alphabetical Listing by Label

Akkord GOST 5289–61. *Tryptyk śląski.*

Angel S–36045 (stereo). Concerto for Orchestra. Chicago Sym. Orch., Seiji Ozawa. With Janáček: Sinfonietta. Released c. January 1971. Equivalent release: EMI Electrola 1C 063–02118 (mono and stereo).

Angel S–37146 (quad). Concerto for Cello and Orchestra. Mstislav Rostropovich, vc.; Orchestre de Paris, Witold Lutosławski. With Dutilleux: *Tout un monde lointain . . .* Recorded December 1974, Paris; released c. February 1976. Koussevitzky Prix Mondial du Disque, Paris, 1977. Equivalent releases: EMI Electrola 1C 065-02687Q (quad); HMV ASD 3145 (quad).

Aurora 5059 (stereo) = Muza SXL 1145. Released c. March 1978.

Bis 0087. *Preludia taneczne* (nonet version). Vestjysk Kammerensemble. With Britten: Sinfonietta; Prokofiev; Quintet, op. 39.

Candide CE 11028 (stereo). Concerto for Orchestra. ORF Sym., Milan Horvat. With Schoenberg: Variations for Orchestra, op. 31.

Candide CE 31035 (stereo). *Mała suita; Słomkowy łańcuszek; Preludia taneczne* (chamber orchestra version); Overture for Strings. Josef Masseli, cl.; Barbara Miller, sop.; Oksana Sowlak, mezzo; Berlin Sym. Orch., Arthur Grüber. *Muzyka żałobna.* Hamburg Sym. Orch., Arthur Grüger. Released c. November 1970. Equivalent release: CBS (France) (30)34-61232 (stereo).

CBS (France) (30)34-61232 (stereo) = Candide CE 31035.

Columbia 33WSX 714 = Columbia C/STC 80816.

Columbia C 80816 (mono), STC 80816 (stereo). Variations on a Theme of Paganini. Liselotte Gierth and Gerd Lohmeyer, pf. With Bartók: *Mikrokosmos* excerpts; Clementi: Sonata No. 1; Milhaud: *Scaramouche*; Mozart: Sonata, K. 448; Poulenc: Sonata. Released c. early 1964. Equivalent releases: Columbia 33WSX 714; Mace MCS 9023 (stereo); Odeon 80816.

Coro CLP 929. Variations on a Theme of Paganini. Nelly and Jaime Ingram, pf.

Da Camera 91604 (stereo). Concerto for Orchestra. Landesjugendorchester Nordrheinland-Westfalen, Martin Stephani. With Hindemith: *Vorspiel zu einem Requiem.*

Da Camera 91605 (stereo). *Muzyka żałobna.* Landesjugendorchester Nordrheinland-Westfalen, Martin Stephani. With Klebe: *Orpheus*; Liszt: *Orpheus.*

Decca HEAD 3 (stereo). *Paroles tissées.* Peter Pears, tenor; London Sinfonietta, Witold Lutosławski. With Berkeley: *Four Ronsard Sonnets*; Bedford: *Tentacles of the Dark Nebula.* Recorded September 1972, Maltings, Snape; released in the UK c. April 1974, in the US c. December 1975.

Decca LXT 6158 (mono), SXL 6158 (stereo). Variations on a Theme of Paganini. Bracha Eden and Alexander Tamir, pf. With Milhaud: *Scaramouche*; Poulenc: Sonata; Rakhmaninov: Suite No. 2, op. 17. Music for Two Pianos. Released c. January 1965; in the US as London CM 9434 (mono), CS 6343 (stereo) c. October 1965.

Decca SXL 644 (mono or stereo). Concerto for Orchestra. L'Orchestre de la Suisse

214   Discography

Romande, Paul Kletzki. With Hindemith: Sinfonie Mathis der Maler. Released c.
December 1970; in the US as London CS 6665 (stereo) c. November 1971; deleted
1978.
DG 137001 (stereo). String Quartet. LaSalle Quartet. With Penderecki: Quartetto per
archi; Mayuzumi: Prelude for String Quartet. [Series] avant garde. Released c.
December 1968; deleted September 1974; rereleased c. January 1977 as DG 2530
735 (Stereo), with Cage: Quartet. (≠ Mace MXX 9104; Muza XL/SXL 0282; Wergo
60019)
DG 2530 735 (stereo). See DG 137001.
EMI Electrola 1C 063-02118 (stereo) = Angel S-36045.
EMI Electrola 1C 065-02687Q (quad) = Angel S-37146.
EMI Electrola 1C 165-03231/36Q (6 discs, quad). Preludes and Fugue; Symphony No. 1;
Symphony No. 2; Concerto for Cello and Orchestra; Livre pour orchestre; Concerto
for Orchestra; Muzyka żałobna; Five Songs (Iłłakowicz); Trois poèmes d'Henri
Michaux; Paroles tissées; Symphonic Variations; Three Postludes, no. 1; Jeux
vénitiens; Mi-parti. Halina Łukomska, sop.; Louis Devos, tenor; Roman Jabłoński,
vc.; Cracow Radio Chorus, Wojciech Michniewski; Polish Ch. Orch.; Polish
National Radio Sym. Orch., Witold Lutosławski. Werke für Orchester. Released
1978. International Record Critics' Award, 1979.
HMV ALP 2065 (stereo). Variations on a Theme of Paganini. Vitya Vronsky and Victor
Babin, pf. With Bizet: Jeux d'enfants; Rakhmaninov; Symphonic Dances, op. 45.
Released c. 1962; in the US as Seraphim S-60053 (stereo) c. October 1967. Equiva-
lent release: Odeon ASD 614 (stereo).
HMV ASD 3145 (quad) = Angel S-37146
Hungaroton SLPX 11749 (stereo). Concerto for Cello and Orchestra. Miklós Perényi,
vc.; Budapest Sym. Orch., György Lehel.
Hungaroton SLPX 11847 (stereo). String Quartet. New Budapest Quartet. With Petro-
vics: String Quartet.
London CM 9434 (mono), CS 6434 (stereo) = Decca LXT 6158 (mono), SXL 6158
(stereo)
London CS 6665 (stereo) = Decca SXL 644
Mace MCS 9023 (stereo) = Columbia STC 80816
Mace MXX 9104 (stereo) = Wergo 60019
Melodiya 33ts 015055/56. Muzyka żałobna. Moscow Radio Sym. Orch., Robert
Satanowski. With Szymanowski, Spisak, Moniuszko.
Mirasound 7024. Four songs from Dziesięć polskich pieśni ludowych na tematy
żołnierskie. Koninklijk Mannenkoor Die Haghe Sanghers, Rene Verhoff. With
Janequin, Lasso, Morley, et al.
MIR Calidad [no. unk.]. Variations on a Theme of Paganini.
Musical Heritage Society MHS 1473 (stereo). Preludia taneczne. Chester Milosovich,
cl.; William Dresden, pf. With Berg: Four Pieces, op. 5; Brahms: Sonata in F Minor,
op. 120, no. 1; Stravinsky: Three Pieces for Clarinet Solo. The Virtuoso Clarinet.
Released c. 1972.
Musicaphon (Bärenreiter) 1407 (stereo) = Muza SXL 0571.
Muza 2242/44 (78 rpm). Dziesięć tańców ludowych. Chamber Ensemble of Warsaw
Phil. Orch., Witold Lutosławski.
Muza 2246/47 (78 rpm). Mała suita (orchestral version). Warsaw Phil. Orch., Witold
Lutosławski. Rereleased in 33 rpm as Muza L 0002, side B.
Muza 2552/53a (78 rpm). Tryptyk śląski; Symphonic Variations. Maria Drewniakówna,
sop.; Polish Radio Sym. Orch., Grzegorz Fitelberg (Tryptyk) and Witold
Lutosławski (Variations). Rereleased in 33 rpm as Muza L 0009.
Muza 2577 (78 rpm). Bukoliki. Witold Lutosławski, pf.
Muza L 0002 (mono) = Muza 2246/47
Muza L 0009 (mono) = Muza 2552/53a

Muza L 0214 (mono). *Melodie ludowe*, nos. 1 and 4. Regina Smendzianka, pf.

Muza M3 XW 897/98 (mono). Symphony No. 2. Warsaw National Phil. Orch., Witold Lutosławski. Kronika dźwiękowa, 1967 Warsaw Autumn.

Muza M3 XW 1179 (mono). *Livre pour orchestre*. Warsaw National Phil. Orch., Jan Krenz. Kronika dźwiękowa, 1969 Warsaw Autumn.

Muza SX 1370 (stereo). *Livre pour orchestre*. Warsaw National Phil. Orch., Witold Rowicki. With Kilar: *Krzesany*.

Muza SXL 0786/87 (2 discs, stereo). Three Postludes, no. 1 = Muza XL 0237. Polska w muzyce i pieśni [Poland in music and song].

Muza SXL 1064 (stereo). Variations on a Theme of Paganini. Jacek and Marek Lukasz-czyk, pf. with Debussy: *En blanc et noir*; Infante: *Gracia – Danse andalouse No. 3*; Stravinsky: *Sonata*; Poulenc: *L'embarquement pour Cythère*.

Muza SXL 1145 (stereo). Preludes and Fugue. Ch. Orch. of National Phil., Witold Lutosławski. Equivalent release: Aurora 5059 (stereo).

Muza W 6 (mono). *Mała suita* (orchestral version). Witold Lutosawski.

Muza W 75-2 (mono). Tryptyk śląski.

Muza W 76-6 (mono). Symphonic Variations. Witold Lutosławski.

Muza W 176 (mono). Concerto for Orchestra, movements 1 and 2. Wiener Sym-phoniker, Michel Gielen. Kronika dźiękowa, 1956 Warsaw Autumn.

Muza W 514 (mono). *Muzyka żałobna*. Great Sym. Orch. of Polish Radio and Tele-vision, Katowice, Jan Krenz. Kronika dźwiękowa, 1958 Warsaw Autumn.

Muza W 681 (mono). Five Songs (Iłłakowicz), nos. 3-5. Krystyna Szostek-Radkowa, mezzo; Ch. Orch. of Polish Radio and Television, Jan Krenz. Kronika dźwiękowa, 1960 Warsaw Autumn.

Muza W 770 (mono). *Jeux vénitiens*, movement 1. Warsaw National Phil. Orch., Witold Rowicki. Kronika dźwiękowa, 1961 Warsaw Autumn.

Muza W 871/72 (mono). *Trois poèmes d'Henri Michaux*. Cracow Radio Chorus, Witold Lutosławski; Great Sym. Orch. of Polish Radio and Television, Jan Krenz. Kronika dźwiękowa, 1963 Warsaw Autumn.

Muza W 970 (mono). Three Postludes, no. 1. Great Sym. Orch. of Polish Radio and Television, Jan Krenz. Kronika dźwiękowa, 1964 Warsaw Autumn.

Muza XL 0072 (mono) = Muza XW 143.

Muza XL 0132 (mono) = Muza XW 263/64.

Muza XL 0237 (mono), SXL 0237 (stereo). *Trois poèmes d'Henri Michaux*; Three Postludes, no. 1, Symphony No. 1. Cracow Radio Chorus, Witold Lutosławski; Great Sym. Orch. of Polish Radio and Television, Jan Krenz. Released not later than 1967. *Trois poèmes* and Postlude released on Mace MXX 9104 (stereo) and Wergo 60019 (mono and stereo); Symphony on Wergo 60044 (mono and stereo).

Muza XL 0282 (mono), SXL 0282 (stereo). String Quartet. LaSalle Quartet. With Pen-derecki: *Quartetto per archi*; Webern: Five Movements for String Quartet, op. 5. Released not later than 1967. Lutosławski only also released on Mace MXX 9104 (mono); Wergo 60019 (mono and stereo). (≠ DG 137001, DG 2530 735).

Muza XL 0394 (mono), SXL 0394 (stereo). Five Songs (Iłłakowicz). Halina Łukomska, sop.; Warsaw National Phil. Orch., Andrzej Markowski. With A. Bloch: *Medytacje*; Serocki: *Oczy powietrza*.

Muza XL 0453 (mono), SXL 0453 (stereo). *Paroles tissées*; Symphony No. 2. Louis Devos, tenor; Warsaw National Phil. Orch., Witold Lutosławski.

Muza XL 0571 (mono), SXL 0571 (stereo). *Livre pour orchestre*. Warsaw National Phil. Orch., Jan Krenz. With Baird: Symphony No. 3. Released *c.* late 1970. Académie Charles Cros, Grand Prix du Disque for 1969, Paris, 1970; Złota Muza prize, Warsaw, 1971.

Muza XL 0827 (mono), SXL 0827 (stereo). *Bukoliki*. Andrzej Dutkiewicz, pf. With Borkowski: *Fragmenti*; Dutkiewicz: *Suita*; Kisielewski: *Danse vive*; Serocki: *A piacere*; Webern: Variations, op. 27.

Muza XW 143 (mono). *Muzyka żałobna*. Warsaw National Phil. Orch., Witold Rowicki. Also released on Muza XL 0072 (mono).

Muza XW 263/64 (mono). Concerto for Orchestra; *Jeux vénitiens*. Warsaw National Phil. Orch., Witold Rowicki. Koussevitzky Prix Mondial du Disque, Paris, 27 May 1964. Equivalent release: Muza XL 0132 (mono).

Muza XW 569 = Muza XL 0282 (mono), SXL 0282 (stereo).

Odeon 80816 = Columbia C 80816 (mono), STC 80816 (stereo).

Orion 76238 (stereo). Variations on a Theme of Paganini. Monique LeDuc and Charles Engel, pf. With Debussy: *Nocturnes*; Poulenc: Sonata; Ravel: *La Valse*. Released 1977.

Orion 78289 (stereo). Variations on a Theme of Paganini. Nancy and Neal O'Doan, pf. With Brahms: *Haydn Variations*; Britten: Two Compositions for Piano Duet, op. 23; Martinů: *Trois danses tchéques*. Released 1978.

Philips 835303 AY (mono), 839261 DSY (stereo) = Philips PHS 900159.

Philips 6500 628 (stereo). Modern Music Series. See Philips PHS 900159.

Philips A 02434 L = Philips PHS 900159.

Philips PHS 900159 (stereo) = Muza XW 143, XW 263/64. Released c. September 1967; deleted c. early 1972; rereleased as Philips 6500 628 c. March 1974.

Proprius [no. unk.]. *Recitativo e arioso*.

Radio Nederland Transcription Service 6808 332/34 (3 discs, stereo). *Preludia taneczne*. Herman Braune, cl.; Jan Gruithuyzen, pf. [Title] Prix d'excellence. Released 1975.

RBM Musikproduktion 3022. *Bukoliki*. Alex Blin, pf. With Ekier: *Humoreske, Preludium II*; Maciejewski: *Mazurkas, Berceuse*; Moszumańska-Nazar: *Constellations*; Rudziński: *Study on C*; Serocki: *Preludia*.

Seraphim S-60053 (stereo) = HMV ALP 2065.

Supraphon SUA 10694 (mono), SUA ST 50694 (stereo). Variations on a Theme of Paganini. Věra and Vlastimil Lejsek, pf. With Britten: Two Compositions for Piano Duet, op. 23; Stravinsky: Concerto for Two Pianos. Released 1965.

Telefunken 6.48066EK (2 discs, stereo). *Trois poèmes d'Henri Michaux*. Chorus and Sym. Orch. of Oesterreichischer Rundfunk, Vienna, Gottfried Preinfalk (chorus) and Bruno Maderna. With Boulez: *cummings ist der dichter*; Messiaen: *Et exspecto resurrectionem mortuorum*; Stravinsky: *Canticum sacrum*. Bruno Maderna: Ein Dokument. Recorded live, 29 July 1973, Salzburger Festspiel; released c. June 1975.

Vanguard VRS 6013 (mono). *Mała suita* (chamber orch. version); three songs from *Jesień*; three songs from *Wiosna*. Janina Godlewska, mezzo; Warsaw Radio Orch., J. Kolaczkowski (*Mała suita*) and Witold Lutosławski. Music of Poland, vol. 2. Released not later than 1958; deleted not later than 1963.

Veriton SXV 778 (stereo). *Dwadzieście kolęd*. Krystyna Szostek-Radkowa, mezzo; Andrzej Hiolski, baritone; J. Witkowski, pf.

Veriton SXV 811/12 (2 discs, stereo). String Quartet. Wilanowski Quartet. With: Baird, Meyer, Penderecki, Szymanowski. Polish Contemporary Music.

Wergo 0311. *Trois poèmes d'Henri Michaux*, movements 2 and 3 = Muza XL/SXL 0273.

Wergo 60019 (mono and stereo). *Trois poèmes d'Henri Michaux*; Three Postludes, no. 1 = Muza XL/SXL 0237; String Quartet = Muza XL/SXL 0282. Studio Reihe neuer Musik. Released c. 1968. Equivalent release: Mace MXX 9104 (stereo).

Wergo 60044 (mono and stereo). Symphony No. 1 = Muza XL/SXL 0237; Symphony No. 2. Orchester des Südwestfunks, Baden-Baden, Ernest Bour.

Wergo 60073 (stereo). Five Songs (Iłłakowicz) (texts in German). Roswitha Trexler, mezzo; Rundunk-Sinfonieorchester Leipzig, Witold Lutosławski. With Dessau: *Tierverse*; Eisler: *Elegien, Hölderlin-Fragmente, Taoteking-Legende, Zuchthaus-Kantate*. Recorded April 1972, Leipzig.

Label unknown. *Dziesięć polskich pieśni ludowych na tematy żołnierskie*, nos. 3, 4, 6, and 9. Rotte's Mannenkoor, Jos Vranken.
Label unknown. Concerto for Orchestra. Danish State Radio Orch. UNESCO International Music Council/Gesellschaft der Musikfreunde, first prize, November 1963.

Alphabetical Listing by Title

Bukoliki   Muza 2577, XL/SXL 0827; RBM 3022
Chain of Straw   See *Słomkowy łańcuszek*
Children's songs   See *Jesień; Sześć piosenek dziecinnych; Wiosna*
Concerto for Cello and Orchestra   Angel S-37146; EMI Electrola 1C 065-02687Q, 1C 165-03231/36Q; HMV   ASD 3145; Hungaroton SLPX 11749
Concerto for Orchestra   Angel S-36045; Candide CE 11028; Da Camera 91604; Decca SXL 644; EMI Electrola 1C 063-02118, 1C 165-03231/36Q; London CS 6665; Muza W 176, XL 0132, XW 263/64; Philips 835303 AY, 839261 DSY, 6500 628, A 02434 L, PHS 900159; label unknown (Danish State Radio Orchestra)
Dance Preludes   See *Preludia taneczne*
Dwadzieście kolęd   Veriton SXV 778
Dziesięc polskich pieśni ludowych na tematy żołnierskie   Mirasound 7024; label unknown (Rotte's Mannenkoor)
Dziesięć tańców ludowych   Muza 2242/44
Five Songs (Iłłakowicz)   EMI Electrola 1C 165-03231/36Q; Muza XL/SXL 0394, W 681; Wergo 60073
Folk Melodies, Folk Songs   See *Melodie ludowe*
Funeral Music   See *Muzya żałobna*
Iłłakowicz Songs   See Five Songs (Iłłakowicz)
Jesień   Vanguard VRS 6013
Jeux vénitiens   EMI Electrola 1C 165-03231/36Q; Muza W 770, XL 0132, XW 263/64; Philips 835303 AY, 839261 DSY, 6500 628, A 02434 L, PHS 900159
Kolędy   See *Dwadzieście kolęd*
Little Suite   See *Mała suita*
Livre pour orchestre   EMI Electrola 1C 165-03231/36Q; Musicaphon 1407; Muza SX 1370, XL/SXL 0571, M3 XW 1179
Mała suita   CBS (France) (30)34-61232; Candide CE 31035; Muza 2246/47, L 0002, W 6; Vanguard VRS 6013
Melodie ludowe   Muza L 0214
Mi-parti   EMI Electrola 1C 165-03231/36Q
Musique funèbre   See *Muzyka żałobna*
Muzyka żałobna   CBS (France) (30)34-61232; Candide CE 31035; Da Camera 91605; EMI Electrola 1C 165-03231/36Q; Melodiya 33ts 015055/56; Muza XL 0072, XW 143, W 514; Philips 835303 AY, 839261 DSY, 6500 628, A 02434 L; PHS 900159
Overture for Strings   CBS (France) (30)34-61232; Candide CE 31035
Paganini Variations   See Variations on a Theme of Paganini
Paroles tissées   Decca HEAD 3; EMI Electrola 1C 165-03231/36Q; Muza XL/SXL 0453
Postludium   See Three Postludes, no. 1
Preludes and Fugue   Aurora 5059; EMI Electrola 1C 165-03231/36Q; Muza SXL 1145
Preludia taneczne   Bis 0087; CBS (France) (30)34-61232; Candide CE 31035; Musical Heritage Society MHS 1473; Radio Nederland Transcription Service 6808 332/34   Proprius [no. unk.]
Recitativo e arioso   Proprius [no. unk.]
Silesian Triptych   See *Tryptyk śląski*
Słomkowy łańcuszek   CBS (France) (30)34-61232; Candide CE 31035
Soldiers' Songs   See *Dziesięc polskich pieśni ludowych na tematy żołnierskie*
String Quartet   DG 137001, 2530 735; Hungaroton SLPX 11847; Mace MXX 9104; Muza XL/SXL 0282, XW 569; Veriton SXV 811/12; Wergo 60019

Strohkette   See *Słomkowy łańcuszek*
Sześć piosenek dziecinnych   Muza Wa 95-6, Wa 96
Symphonic Variations   EMI Electrola 1C 165-03231/36Q; Muza 2552/53a, L 0009, W 76-6
Symphony No. 1   EMI Electrola 1C 165-03231/36Q; Muza XL/SXL 0237; Wergo 60044
Symphony No. 2   EMI Electrola 1C 165-03231/36Q; Muza M3 XW 897/98, XL/SXL 0453, Wergo 60044
Three Postludes, no. 1   EMI Electrola 1C 165-03231/36Q; Mace MXX 9104; Muza SXL 0786/87, XL/SXL 0237, W 970; Wergo 60019
Trois poèmes d'Henri Michaux   EMI Electrola 1C 165-03231/36Q; Mace MXX 9104; Muza XL/SXL 0237, W 871/72; Telefunken 6.48066EK; Wergo 0311, 60019
Tryptyk śląski   Akkord GOST 5289-61; Muza 2552/53a, L 0009, W 75-2
Variations on a Theme of Paganini   Columbia 33WSX 714, C/STC 80816; Coro CLP 929; Decca LXT/SXL 6158; HMV ALP 2065; London CM 9434, CS 6434; Mace MCS 9023; MIR Calidad [no. unk.]; Muza SXL 1064; Odeon 80816, ASD 614; Orion 76238, 78289; Seraphim S-60053; Supraphon SUA 10694, SUA ST 50694
Venetian Games   See *Jeux vénitiens*
Wiosna   Vanguard VRS 6013

Select bibliography

Because it is hoped that the present survey of available sources will be of use both to the scholar and to the general reader having only a casual interest in Lutosławski, differing standards of selection have been applied in the various sections of the bibliography. The first section, containing the composer's published writings, attempts to be exhaustive, while the remaining sections are quite selective. Thus interviews which do not offer much of substance have been excluded from the second section; and the great majority of concert and record reviews have been excluded from the last section. All dictionary and encyclopedia articles have been omitted.

When an article has been reprinted, translated, or revised, its earliest appearance is given as the main entry, with subsequent versions immediately following in chronological order of publication.

Titles in Slavonic and Scandinavian languages and in Hungarian are provided with English translations; but titles in French, German, and Italian (as well as titles in other languages whose meaning is easy for English-speaking readers to divine) are not translated.

Collected Writings of Lutosławski

Jarociński, Stefan (comp.). *Witold Lutosławski: Materiały do monografii* [WL: materials for a monograph]. Cracow: Polskie Wydawnictwo Muzyczne, 1967. Reprints fourteen writings, lectures, and interviews.

Individual Writings of Lutosławski

'Att spela ad libitum: Anteckningar kring framförandet av min nya stråkkvartett' [To play ad libitum: notes on the performance of my new string quartet]. Transl. Sven Hallenborg. *Nutida musik* 8 (1964–5): 124–7. Based partly on letters from the composer to Walter Levin, first violinist of the LaSalle Quartet.
    'Uwagi o sposobie wykonywanie mego Kwartetu smyczkowego' [Remarks on the method of performing my String Quartet]. *Ruch muzyczny*, n.s. 9, no. 17 (1965): 3–4.
    'Kwartet smyczkowy' [String Quartet]. In Jarociński, *Witold Lutosławski*, pp. 55–9.
    'String Quartet'. In Nordwall, *Lutosławski*, pp. 81–8.
'Une création fascinante – souvenir de l'an 1944'. Transl. Tadeusz Zawadzki. *Schweizerische Musikzeitung/Revue musicale suisse* 117 (1977); 69–70. About Constantin Regamey.
'Czy to jest muzyka?' [Is this music?]. A talk on BBC Radio, 1963. In Jarociński, *Witold Lutosławski*, pp. 22–8.
'Doctoral Speech', *Polish Music* 8, no. 3–4 (1973): 18–19. Delivered 30 June 1973 on receiving an honorary doctorate from Warsaw University. Also in German.
    Quoted in full in Maciejewski, *Twelve Polish Composers*, pp. 53–5.

220   Select bibliography

'Festiwal Mozartowski w Salzburgu' [The Mozart Festival in Salzburg]. *Przegląd kulturalny*, 5, no. 10 (1956): 6.
'Festiwal Sibeliusa w Helsinkach' [The Sibelius Festival in Helsinki]. *Przegląd kulturalny* 4, no. 28 (1955): 8.
'Festiwal współczesnej muzyki niemieckiej w Berlinie' [Festival of contemporary German music in Berlin]. *Muzyka* 4, 1–2 (1953): 38–41.
'Gedanken über das Ballett'. *Opera viva*, 1962, no. 3, [pp. unk.].
    'Rozmyślając o balecie' [Reflecting on ballet] In Jarociński, *Witold Lutosławski*, pp. 37–8.
'Improvisationer på ett givet tema' [Improvisations on a given theme]. *Nutida musik* 3, no. 2 (1959–60): 8–9. On *Muzyka żałobna*.
    'Musique funèbre'. Transl. Christopher Gibbs. In Nordwall, *Lutosławski*, pp. 49–56.
'In memoriam Witold Małcużyński'. *Polish Music* 12, no. 3 (1977): 3–5. Also in German.
'Jego muzyka żyje . . .' [His music lives on . . .]. *Ruch muzyczny*, n.s. 9, no. 14 (1965): 6. On the composer Michał Spisak, following his death.
'Kilka wrażeń z podróży do ZSRR' [Some impressions from a visit to the USSR]. *Muzyka* 2, no. 11 (1951): 6–7.
'Kompozytor a odbiorca' [The composer and the listener]. *Ruch muzyczny*, n.s. 8, no. 4 (1964): 3–4. Text delivered at a conference on music criticism organized by the Association of Polish Musical Artists (SPAM), 11 January 1964, Warsaw.
    Ibid. In *Krytycy przy okrągłym stole* [Critics at the roundtable], ed. Elżbieta Dziębowska, pp. 23–6. [Warsaw:] Wydawnictwo Artystyczne i Filmowe, 1966. Proceedings of the 1964 conference.
    'Komponisten og tilhøren – indlaeg ved et kritikseminar' [The composer and the listener – contribution to a criticism seminar]. Transl. Mogens Andersen. *Dansk musiktidsskrift* 41 (1966): 76–7.
    'Kompozytor a odbiorca'. In Jarociński, *Witold Lutosławski*, pp. 65–70.
    'Tonsätteren och lyssnaren' [The composer and the listener]. *Musikern* [59?] (February 1967): 13–14.
    'The Composer and the Listener'. In Nordwall, *Lutosławski*, pp. 119–24.
    'The Composer and His Audience'. *Polish Perspectives* 11 (August-September 1968): 39–42.
    'The Composer and the Listener'. *International Music Educator*, no. 1 (1969): 8, 45. Also in French and German.
'Koncert na orkiestrę' [Concerto for Orchestra]. Program note for Norddeutscher Rundfunk. In Jarociński, *Witold Lutosławski*, pp. 44–5.
'Concerto for Orchestra'. In Nordwall, *Lutosławski*, pp. 31–5.
'London Sinfonietta'. *Times* (London), 16 February 1973, p. 19. A letter to the editor. Quoted in full in E. M. Webster, 'The London Sinfonietta: A Study in Survival'. *Musical Opinion* 96 (1972–3): 409, 411.
'Musik i det tyvende århundrede' [Music in the twentieth century]. Transl. Niels Jørgen Steen. *Dansk musiktidsskrift* 39 (1964): 117–19. Text of a lecture originally delivered at the Zagreb Biennale, 19 May 1961.
'Nad grobem Grzegorza Fitelberga' [At the grave of Grzegorz Fitelberg]. *Przegląd kulturalny* 2, no. 24 (1953): 2.
'Nowy utwór na orkiestrę symfoniczną' [A new work for symphony orchestra]. *Res facta* 4 (1970): 6-13. On the Second Symphony.
    [On the Second Symphony.] In Robert Stephan Hines (ed.), *The Orchestral Composer's Point of View: Essays on Twentieth-Century Music by Those Who Wrote It*, pp. 128–51. Norman: University of Oklahoma Press, 1970.
'O Grzegorzu Fitelbergu' [About Grzegorz Fitelberg]. *Muzyka* 5, no. 7–8 (1954): 26–33.
'O J. S. Bachu' [About J. S. Bach]. In *Jan Sebastian Bach, 1750–1950: Almanach*, ed. Zofia Lissa, pp. 143–44. Warsaw: Edition Czytelnik, 1951.

'Okres rozkwitu: Co nowego widzę w muzyce Dwudziestolecia Polski Ludowej' [A period of flowering: what I see that is new in the music of twenty-year-old People's Poland]. *Życie Warszawy*, 5–6 April 1964, p. 3.

Ibid. In Jarociński, *Witold Lutosławski*, p. 64.

'Om det aleatoriske princip i musikken' [On the aleatory principle in music]. Transl. Birgit Giedekier. *Dansk musiktidsskrift* 40 (1965): 58–61. Text of a lecture originally delivered in English to the composition seminar of the Swedish Royal Academy of Music, Stockholm, March 1965.

'O roli elementu przypadku w technice komponowania' [On the role of the element of chance in compositional technique]. *Res facta* 1 (1967): 34–8.

Ibid. In Jarociński, *Witold Lutosławski*, pp. 29–36.

'About the Element of Chance in Music'. In György Ligeti et al., *Three Aspects of New Music*, pp. 45–53. Royal Academy of Music and Royal Swedish College of Music Publications, vol. 4. Stockholm: Nordiska Musikförlaget, 1968.

'Ueber das Element des Zufalls in der Musik'. Transl. Ken W. Bartlett. *Melos* 36 (1969): 457–60.

'O prvku náhody v hudbě' [About the element of chance in music]. *Hudební rozhledy* 23 (1970): 126–9.

[On conducting.] *Times* (London), 28 January 1973, p. 37a.

[On Five Songs on texts of Iłłakowicz.] In IVᵉ Festival International de Musique Contemporaine, *Automne varsovien* [program booklet], pp. 27–8. [Warsaw, 1960.] In French.

[On Grażyna Bacewicz.] *Ruch muzyczny*, n.s. 13, no. 7 (1969): 5. Contribution to a special number devoted to the composer Bacewicz following her death.

[On Igor Stravinsky.] *Die Welt* (Hamburg), 16 June 1962, [no p. no.]. A tribute on Stravinsky's eightieth birthday, appearing alongside statements from Hába, Carter, Boulez, Milhaud, Henze, and others.

'Strawiński'. In Jarociński, *Witold Lutosławski*, p. 39.

'On the Occasion of the Twentieth "Warsaw Autumn"'. *Polish Music* 11, no. 4 (1976): 5–7. Also in German.

'O radiu' [About radio]. *Radio i telewiżja* 15, no. 47 (1959): 24.

'Paroles tissées'. Program note for the Aldeburgh Festival, 1965. In Jarociński, *Witold Lutosławski*, p. 54.

'Reflections on the Future of Music'. *Polish Music* 7, no. 2 (1972): 3–6. Also in German.

'Z rozmyślań nad przyszłością muzyki' [Fom reflections on the future of music]. *Tygodnik powszechny*, 19 November 1972, p. 1.

'Lutoslawského úvahy o budoucnosti hudby' [L's reflections on the future of music]. *Hudební rozhledy* 26 (1973): 258.

'Gedanken über die Zukunft der Musik'. *Philharmonische Blätter* (Berlin) 5 (1974–5): [pp. unk.].

Ibid. *Das Orchester* 23 (1975): 478–80.

'The Role of Today's Graduates in the Musical Arena for the Years Ahead'. *Notes of the Cleveland Institute of Music* 9, no. 2 (1971): 1–4. Text of an address to the graduating class on receiving an honorary degree, 2 June 1971.

'Sur l'orchestre d'aujourd'hui'. *Ruch muzyczny*, n.s. 12, no. 17 (1968): 3–4. Compressed version of parts of 'Nowy utwór'. Also in Polish.

'Tchnienie wielkości' [The aura of greatness]. *Muzyka polska* 4 (1937): 169–70. On the death of Karol Szymanowski.

'Teoria a praktyka w pracy kompozytora' [Theory and practice in the work of the composer]. *Studia estetyczne* 2 (1965): 128–33. Reprints a Polish version of Musik i det tyvende århundrede', titled 'Z dziejów muzyki xx wieku' [About the history of twentieth-century music], along with a commentary on the original text. Summaries in Russian and English.

'Kommentar zur "Musikgeschichte des 20. Jahrhunderts"'. In *Parabeln*, Jahrbuch der Freien Akademie der Künste in Hamburg, pp. 18–23. Hamburg, 1966. Text delivered on the occasion of Lutosławski's election as an honorary member and the award of the academy's 1966 *Plakette* to him, October 1966.

Ibid. In *Profile*, Jahrbuch der Freien Akademie der Künste in Hamburg, pp. 41–6. Hamburg, 1967.

'Teoria a praktyka w pracy kompozytora'. In Jarociński, *Witold Lutosławski*, pp. 14–21.

'Trois poèmes d'Henri Michaux'. Program note for BBC Radio, 1965. In Jarociński, *Witold Lutosławski*, pp. 50–2.

Ibid. In Nordwall, *Lutosławski*, pp. 71–9.

'Vom Element des Zufalls'. In 'Komponist und Hörer: Komponisten und Musikwissenschaftler äussern sich zu Fragen des musikalischen Schaffens'. *Beiträge zur Musikwissenschaft* 16 (1974): 320–4.

'W xx-lecie PWM' [PWM at age twenty]. *Ruch muzyczny*, n.s. 9, no. 19 (1965):4.

'W pracowniach kompozytorów polskich: Witold Lutosławski' [In the studios of Polish composers: WL]. *Życie Warszawy*, 15–16 November 1953, p. 13.

'Webern a hudba dneška' [Webern and the music of today]. *Slovenské pohl'ady* 79, no. 12 (1963): 92–3. A brief statement solicited by the editors on the eightieth anniversary of Webern's birth.

'Webern'. In Jarociński, *Witold Lutosławski*, p. 42.

'Wspomnienie o Grzegorzu Fitelbergu' [Reminiscence of Grzegorz Fitelberg]. *Gazeta robotnicza* (Wrocław), 13–14 June 1953, [pp. unk.].

'Zagałenie dyskusji na walnym zjeździe Związku Kompozytorów Polskich' [Opening address of the discussion at the General Assembly of the Union of Polish Composers]. *Ruch muzyczny*, n.s. 1, no. 1 (1957): 2–3.

Interviews and Panel Discussions with Lutosławski

Bălan, Theodor. 'De vorbă cu W. Lutosławski' [Conversations with WL]. *Muzica* 21 (December 1971): 13–17.

Biegański, Krzysztof. 'Ilustracje muzyczne W. Lutosławskiego do audycji Polskiego Radia' [WL's musical illustrations for a Polish Radio broadcast]. *Antena*, 1956, no. 12, pp. 23–6; 1957, no. 1, pp. 8–10.

Blyth, Alan. 'Polish Composer on His Music'. *Times* (London) [early edn only], 11 March 1968, p. 6.

'Witold Lutosławski', *Times* (London), 9 February 1971, p. 10.

Cegiełła, Janusz. 'Autoportret polskiej muzyki: Lutosławski' [A self-portrait of Polish music: L]. *Współczesność* 16, no. 4 (1971): 3.

Chruściński, Czesław. 'Znakomity polski kompozytor opowiada o wrażeniach z USA' [A distinguished Polish composer reports his impressions of the USA]. *Siedem dni w Polsce* 6, no. 44 (1962): 7. Follows Lutosławski's first American visit, summer 1962.

DeJong, Janny. 'In gesprek met Lutoslawski' [In conversation with L] *Mens en melodie* 31 (1976): 365–6. Devoted chiefly to *Mi-parti*.

Drabarek, Stefan. 'Witold Lutosławski o wrażeniach z Biennale w Zagrzebiu' [WL on his impressions of the Zagreb Biennale]. *Kurier polski*, 29 May 1963, pp. 1–2.

Fleuret, Maurice. 'Le contrôle du hasard'. *France Observateur*, 5 November 1964, p. 21.

Hordyński, Jerzy. 'Polscy kompozytorzy współczesnej: Witold Lutosławski' [Contemporary Polish composers: WL]. *Życie literackie* 10, no. 42 (1960): 3.

Kaczyński, Tadeusz. 'Livre pour orchestre: Rozmowa z Witoldem Lutosławskim' [Conversation with WL]. *Ruch muzyczny*, n.s. 13, no. 17 (1969): 3–5, 18.

'O ii Symfonii z Witoldem Lutosławskim' [TK talks with WL about his Second Symphony]. *Ruch muzyczny*, n.s. 11, no. 21 (1967): 3–6.

'Symphony No. 2 (1966–67): Interview with Witold Lutosławski'. Transl. Krzysztof Klinger. In Nordwall, *Lutosławski*, pp. 103–18.

'Paroles tissées: Wywiad z Witoldem Lutosławskim' [Interview with WL]. Ruch muzyczny, n.s. 12, no. 4 (1968): 3–6.

Rozmowy z Witoldem Lutosławskim [Conversations with WL]. Cracow: Polskie Wydawnictwo Muzyczne, [1973]. Twelve conversations. Six are about individual works, of which five (on Livre, Second Symphony, Paroles, Trois poèmes, and Cello Concerto) are reprinted from Ruch muzyczny; the other is about the String Quartet.

    Kachin'skii, Tadeush. 'Iz besed s Vitol'dom Liutoslavskim' [From Conversations with WL]. Transl. K. Ivanov. Sovetskaia muzyka, 1975, no. 8, pp. 115–20. Abridged excerpts of pp. 146–61, 90–3, and 117–27 in Russian translation.

    Gespräche mit Witold Lutosławski; mit einem Anhang, Bálint András Varga, Neun Stunden bei Lutosławski. Transl. Lothar Fahlbusch and C. Rüger. Leipzig: P. Reclam jun., 1976.

    Conversations with Lutosławski. Transl. Yolanta May. London: Chester Music, 1980.

'Trzy poematy Henri Michaux: Rozmowa z Witoldem Lutosławskim' [Trois poèmes d'Henri Michaux: conversation with WL]. Ruch muzyczny, n.s. 7, no. 18 (1963): 3–6.

'Witold Lutosławski o swoim Koncercie wiolonczelowym' [WL on his Cello Concerto]. Ruch muzyczny, n.s. 17, no. 18 (1973); 3–5.

Klein, Howard. 'Notes from Underground'. New York Times, 7 August 1966, sec. 2, p. 13.

Levtonova, O. 'Nashi interviu s Vitol'dom Liutoslavskim' [Our interview with WL]. Sovetskaia muzyka, 1973, no. 7, pp. 127–8.

M[arek], T[adeusz]. 'Composer's Workshop: Witold Lutosławski, Preludes and Fugue'. Polish Music 7, no. 3 (1972): 18–22. Also in German.

    'A New Work by Lutosławski: Les espaces du sommeil for Baritone and Symphony Orchestra'. Polish Music 11, no. 1 (1976): 3–5. Also in German.

Marias, A. 'Susret sa Vitoldom Lutoslavskim' [Encounter with WL]. Zvuk (Sarajevo), no. 3 (Fall 1977): 55–7.

Nastulanka, Krystyna. 'O potrzebie i torturze słuchania muzyki: O Warszawskiej Jesieni oraz o wiele innych sprawach mówi Witold Lutosławski' [On the need and torture of listening to music: WL talks about the Warsaw Autumn as well as many other subjects]. Polityka 4, no. 46 (1960): 6.

Nikol'skaia, I[rena]. 'Vitol'd Liutoslavskii: Beseda posle kontserta' [WL: conversation after a concert]. Sovetskaia muzyka, 1979, no. 3, pp. 125–7.

Pilarski, Bohdan. 'Moja muzyka jest grą' [My music is a game]. Współczesność 6, no. 9 (1961): 15. On Jeux vénitiens.

    'Om Witold Lutoslawskis Jeux vénitiens'. Transl. Norbert Zaba. Nutida musik 6, no. 4 (1962–3): 32–5.

    'Witold Lutosławski odpowiada na pytania' [WL replies to questions]. Ruch muzyczny, n.s. 2, no. 7 (1958): 2–5 On Muzyka żałobna.

    'Muzyka żałobna'. In Jarociński, Witold Lutosławski, pp. 47–8 (excerpts). Reprinted in Bohdan Pilarski, Szkice o muzyce (Warsaw: Pax, 1969).

Pociej, Bohdan. 'O roli słowa, teatralności i tradycji w muzyce mówi Witold Lutosławski' [WL talks about the role of text, drama, and tradition in music]. Poezja 9 (October 1973): 78–81. Ibid. In Pociej, Lutosławski a wartość muzyki, pp. 128–33.

Rich, Alan. 'Poland's Far-Out Is Finding an Audience'. New York Times, 12 August 1962, sec. 2, p. 9.

S[ierpiński], Z. 'O syntezatore i muzyce polskiej w USA rozmawiamy z Witoldem Lutosławskim' [We talk with WL about the synthesizer and about Polish music in the USA]. Życie Warszawy, 14–15 October 1962, p. 3. Follows Lutosławski's first American visit, summer 1962.

'Stan i potrzeby kultury w Polsce: Brahms czy Penderecki? . . . ' [The condition and

224   *Select bibliography*

needs of culture in Poland: Brahms or Penderecki?...], *Nowa kultura* 13, no. 51–2
(1962): 3, 13. Transcript of a panel discussion.
'Discussion on Music Today'. *Polish Perspectives* 6 (March 1963): 23–9.
Abridged.
'Stan i potrzeby kultury w Polsce'. In Jarociński, *Witold Lutosławski*, pp. 61–3.
Reprints only Lutosławski's statements
'Trzy pracowite miesiące Witolda Lutosławskiego za oceanem' [WL's three busy
months overseas]. *Kurier polski*, 11 October 1962, p. 4. Follows the composer's first
American visit, summer 1962.
Varga, Bálint András. *Beszélgetések Witold Lutosławskival* [Conversations with WL]
Budapest: Zeneműkiado, Zeneműny, 1974. Transcript of nine hours of conversa-
tion conducted (in English) at the composer's home in Warsaw, March 1973.
Lutosławski Profile. London: Chester Music, 1976.
Neun Stunden bei Lutosławski. In Kaczyński, *Gespräche.*
'Witold Lutosławski: Odpowiedź na ankietę na temat twórczości Igora Strawińskiego'
[WL: reply to an inquiry on the works of Igor Stravinsky]. *Ruch muzyczny*, n.s. 1,
no. 7 (1957): 6.

General Sources on the Composer and his Music

Błaszkiewicz, Teresa. *Aleatoryzm w twórczości Witolda Lutosławskiego* [Aleatorism
in the works of WL]. Prace specjalne Państwowej Wyższej Szkoły Muzycznej w
Gdańsku, ed. J. Krassowski, vol. 3. Gdańsk: State Higher School of Music, 1973.
Butsko, Iurii. 'Vitol'd Liutoslavskii: Zametki o tekhnike instrumental'noi kompozitsii'
[WL: notes on his technique of instrumental composition]. *Sovetskaia muzyka*,
1972, no. 8, pp. 111–19.
Chylińska, Teresa, Stanisław Haraschin, and Bogusław Schäffer. *Przewodnik koncer-
towy* [Concert guide]. New edn. Cracow: Polskie Wydawnictwo Muzyczne, 1971.
See pp. 452–60.
Cieślak, Elżbieta. 'Kształtowanie języka muzycznego w twórczości symfonicznej
Witolda Lutosławskiego' [The moulding of musical language in the symphonic
works of WL]. M.A. thesis, State Higher School of Music, Gdańsk, 1968.
Cowie, Edward. 'Mobiles of Sound'. *Music and Musicians* 20 (October 1971): 34–40.
Entelis, Leonid. *Vstrekhi s sovremennoi pol'skoi muzykoi.* Leningrad: Izdatel'stvo
'Muzyka', 1978.
Häusler, Josef. 'Einheit in der Mannigfaltigkeit: Skizze über Lutosławski'. *Neue
Zeitschrift für Musik* 134 (1973): 23–6.
——. *Musik im 20. Jahrhundert: Von Schönberg zu Penderecki.* Bremen: Carl
Schünemann, 1969. See pp. 269–74.
Jarociński, Stefan. 'Biographical Data'. Transl. George Simpson. In Nordwall,
Lutosławski, pp. 143–6.
——. 'The Music of Witold Lutosławski'. *Polish Perspectives* 1 (October 1958): 29–34.
'Witold Lutosławski'. *Fono Forum* 6 (June 1961): 10–11.
——. 'La musica polacca dopo Szymanowski'. *Rassegna musicale* 30 (1960): 216–29.
See esp. pp. 223–5.
'Polish Music after Szymanowski'. In *Polish Music*, ed. Stefan Jarociński,
pp.168–90. Warsaw: Polish Scientific Publishers, 1965.
'Polish Music after World War II'. *Musical Quarterly* 51 (1965): 244–58.
——. 'Sylwetki twórców: Witold Lutosławski' [Outlines of creative artists: WL]. *Prze-
gląd kulturalny* 1, no. 2 (1952): 6.
——. 'Trends in Music'. *Polish Perspectives* 13 (March 1970): 49–51.
——. 'Witold Lutosławski'. In Jarociński, *Polish Music*, pp. 191–9.
Konold, Wulf. 'Zwischen Folklore und Aleatorik: Der Komponist Witold Lutosławski'.
Musica 27 (1973): 438–44.

[Ligeti, György.] 'Ligeti über Lutosławski'. *Musica* 22 (1968): 453. A letter to Ove Nordwall expressing Ligeti's admiration for Lutosławski and discussing limited aleatorism.

Maciejewski, B. M. *Twelve Polish Composers.* London: Allegro Press, 1976. See pp. 36–56. Valuable source, despite many errors.

Mainka, Jürgen. 'Zum Werk Witold Lutosławskis'. *Musik und Gesellschaft* 21 (1971): 344–8.

Niewadomska, Barbara. 'Przejawy aleatoryzmu w polskiej muzyce współczesnej' [Manifestations of aleatorism in contemporary Polish music]. M.A. thesis, State Higher School of Music, Warsaw, 1968.

Nordwall, Ove (comp.). 'Förteckning över Witold Lutoslawskis viktigaste verk 1934–1964' [Catalog of WL's principal works 1934–64]. *Nutida musik* 8 (1964–5): 128–9.

—— (ed.). *Lutosławski.* Transl. Christopher Gibbs et al. Stockholm: Edition Wilhelm Hansen, 1968. Includes an introduction by the editor treating the composer's stylistic development (pp. 7–30), translated writings and program notes by the composer, chronological and systematic catalogs of works (pp. 125–40), and a biographical sketch (Jarociński, 'Biographical Data').

   Witold Lutosławski och hans musik [WL and his music]. Stockholm: Norstedt, 1969. [Rev. edn]

——. '"Pour enchainer": Introduktion til Lutoslawskis musik'. *Dansk musiktidsskrift* 42 (1967): 62–4, 107–10. Danish version of Nordwall, *Lutosławski*, pp. 7–30.

Pociej, Bohdan. 'Kompozytor i działanie' [The composer and the action]. *Ruch muzyczny,* n.s. 18, no. 4 (1974): 6–8. Fragment of Pociej, *Lutosławski a wartość muzyki.*

——. *Lutosławski a wartość muzyki* [L and the value of music]. Cracow: Polskie Wydawnictwo Muzyczne, 1976.

——. 'Lutosławski i wartość muzyki'. *Ruch muzyczny,* n.s. 13, no. 22 (1969): 7–9. Ibid. In Pociej, *Idea, dźwięk, forma: Szkice o muzyce* (Cracow: Polskie Wydawnictwo Muzyczne, 1972), pp. 314–22.

——. 'The Music of Witold Lutosławski'. *Polish Perspectives* 15 (July-August 1972): 24–31.

Piotrowska, Maria. 'Aleatoryzm Witolda Lutosławskiego na tle genezy tego kierunku w muzyce współczesnej' [The aleatorism of WL against the background of the origins of this tendency in contemporary music]. *Muzyka* 14, no. 3 (1969): 67–86. Extracted from Piotrowska, 'Wybrane aspekty'.

Rappoport, Lidiia Grigor'evna. *Vitol'd Liutoslavskii.* Moscow: Izdatel'stvo 'Muzyka', 1976.

——. 'Vydaiushchiisia master' [A distinguished master]. *Sovetskaia muzyka,* 1969, no. 7, pp. 114–20.

Regamey, Konstanty. 'Uwagi o uwagach w sprawie aleatoryzmu' [Remarks on remarks in the matter of aleatorism]. *Ruch muzyczny,* n.s. 11, no. 12 (1967): 8–10; no. 13, pp. 17–19; no. 16, pp. 3–8.

Schaefer, Hansjürgen. 'Konsequenz und Klarheit: Bemerkungen zum Schaffen Witold Lutosławskis'. *Musik und Gesellschaft* 25 (1975): 82–6.

Schäffer, Bogusław. 'Dotychczasowa twórczość Witolda Lutosławskiego' [WL's works to date]. M.A. thesis, Jagiellonian University of Cracow, [c. 1954?].

Shaltuper, Iu. 'O stile Liutoslavskogo 60-kh godov' [On L's style of the 1960s]. In *Problemy muzykal'noi nauki,* no. 3, ed. I. Prudnikova, pp. 238–79. Moscow: Sovetskii Kompozitor, 1975.

Stucky, Steven. 'The Music of Witold Lutosławski: A Style-Critical Survey'. D.Mus.A. thesis, Cornell University, 1978.

Thomas, Adrian T. 'Rhythmic Articulation in the Music of Lutosławski'. M.A. thesis, University of Cardiff, 1970.

226   *Select bibliography*

Whittall, Arnold. *Music since the First World War*. London: J. M. Dent and Sons, 1977. See pp. 235–9.
Zieliński, Tadeusz A. 'Droga twórcza Witolda Lutosławskiego' [The creative path of WL]. *Ruch muzyczny*, n.s. 12, no. 20 (1968): 3–6; no. 21, pp. 11–13.
Zvereva, Iu. 'Vitol'd Liutoslavskii'. *Muzykal'naia zhizn'* 16 (March 1973): 18–20.

Sources on Individual Works

Bukoliki

Jarociński, Stefan. 'Nowe utwory fortepianowe Lutosławskiego' [New works for piano by L]. *Muzyka* 4, no. 9–10 (1953): 71–6.
See also Chodkowski, 'Miniatura fortepianowa', pp. 77–8; Schäffer, 'Polskie melodie ludowe', pp. 346–54; Stucky, 'The Music of Witold Lutosławski', pp. 165–71.

Chain of Straw

See *Słomkowy łańcuszek*

Children's songs

Haubenstock[-Ramati]. Roman. 'Pieśni dziecinne Witolda Lutosławskiego' [WL's songs for children]. *Ruch muzyczny* 4, no. 1 (1948): 14. On 'Spóźniony słowik' and 'O panu Tralalińskim'.
———. 'Piosenki dziecinne W. Lutosławskiego' [WL's songs for children]. *Ruch muzyczny* 4, no. 2 (1948): 14. On *Sześć piosenek dziecinnych*.
I[waszkiewicz], J[arosław]. 'Piosenki Lutosławskiego i kolędy Ekiera' [L's songs and Ekier's carols]. *Nowiny literackie* 2, no. 7 (1948): 7.
See also Kaczyński, 'Lutosławski's Music for Children'; Stucky, 'The Music of Witold Lutosławski', pp. 154–6.

Concerto for Cello and Orchestra

Bradshaw, Susan. 'Lutoslawski for Cello'. *Music and Musicians* 19 (October 1970): 34, 62.
Crichton, Ronald. 'Music in London'. *Musical Times* 111 (1970): 1239. Review of the world première.
Dale, S. S. 'Contemporary Cello Concerti X: Witold Lutosławski'. *Strad* 84 (1973–4): 147–51.
Heyworth, Peter. 'Three Outlooks from Three Moderns'. *New York Times*, 6 December 1970, sec. 2, pp. 37, 42. Review of the world première.
Huber, Alfred. 'Witold Lutosławski: Cellokonzert'. *Melos* 40 (1973): 229–36. Useful analytical notes.
Kaczyński, Tadeusz. 'Rostropowicz o Lutosławskim' [Rostropovich on L]. *Ruch muzyczny*, n.s. 21, no. 20 (1977): 8–9. Interview.
Lawson, Stephen Peter. 'First Performances'. *Tempo*, Winter 1970–1, pp. 34–6. Review of the world première.
'Musikalische Neuheiten-Messe: Eindrücke vom 46. Weltmusikfest der IGNM in Graz'. *Musikhandel* 23 (1972): 340. Review of the Austrian première with Schiff.
Orga, Ates. 'Lutoslawski's Cello Concerto'. *Music and Musicians* 19 (December 1970): 81. Review of the world première.
Schiffer, Brigitte. 'London hört Lutoslawskis neues Cellokonzert'. *Melos* 38 (1971): 74–5. Review of the world première.
Schonberg, Harold C. 'Music: A Century in Polish Perspective'. *New York Times*, 1 October 1976, sec. 3, p. 16.

Simmons, David. 'London Music'. *Musical Opinion* 94 (1970): 119–20. Review of the world première.
Webster, E. M. 'London: Lutoslawski, Gerhard and Tippett – Communication Clear and Confused'. *Musical Opinion* 94 (1970): 64–5. Review of the world première.
See also Chylińska et al., *Przewodnik koncertowy*; Kaczyński, *Rozmowy*; idem, 'Witold Lutosławski o swoim Koncercie'; Pociej, *Lutosławski a wartość muzyki*, esp. pp. 121–3; Stucky, 'The Music of Witold Lutosławski', pp. 261–2.

Concerto for Orchestra

Jarociński, Stefan. 'Wielka muzyka' [Great music]. *Przegląd kulturalny* 3, no. 49 (1954): 2. Review of the world première.
Koszewski, Andrzej. 'Koncert na orkiestrę Witolda Lutosławskiego' [WL's Concerto for Orchestra]. *Ruch muzyczny*, n.s. 2, no. 21 (1958): 15–18.
Kuźniak, Henryk. 'Koncert na orkiestrę Witolda Lutosławskiego: Problemy kolorystyki orkiestrowej' [WL's Concerto for Orchestra: problems of orchestral color]. M.A. thesis, Institute of Musicology, Warsaw University, 1960.
Lissa, Zofia. 'Koncert na orkiestrę Witolda Lutosławskiego (szkic analityczny)' [An analytical sketch]. *Muzyka* 6, no. 3–4 (1955): 25–52.
   'Het Concert voor orkest van Witold Lutosławski.' *Preludium*, 1960, no. 2, [pp. unk.].
   'Witold Lutosławskis Konzert für Orchester (analytische Skizze)'. Transl. Edda Werfel. In *Zur musikalischen Analyse*, ed. Gerhard Schuhmacher, pp. 282–322. Wege der Forschung, vol. 257. Darmstadt: Wissenschaftlicher Buchgesellschaft, 1974.
——. 'Koncert na orkiestrę Witolda Lutosławskiego' [WL's Concerto for Orchestra]. *Studia muzykologiczne* 5 (1956): 196–299. Greatly expanded version of the preceding with important new material.
Sannemüller, Gerd. 'Das Konzert für Orchester von Witold Lutosławski'. *Schweizerische Musikzeitung* 107 (1967): 258–64.
Schäffer, Bogusław. 'Najnowsze dzieło Witolda Lutosławskiego' [WL's newest work]. *Tygodnik powszechny* 11, no. 1 (1955): 10–11. Review of the world première.
—— and Mieczysława Schäffer. 'Życie muzyczne w kraju: Koncerty Filharmonii Krakowskiej' [Musical life at home: concerts of the Cracow Philharmonic]. *Muzyka* 6, no. 5–6 (1955): 99–101.
See also Chylińska et al., *Przewodnik koncertowy*; Lutosławski, 'Koncert na orkiestrę'; Nordwall, *Lutosławski*, pp. 32–5; Rappoport, *Vitol'd Liutoslavskii*, pp. 33–40; Stucky, 'The Music of Witold Lutosławski', pp. 176–97.

Dance Preludes

See *Preludia taneczne*

Dwadzieście kolęd

See Rappoport, *Vitol'd Liutoslavskii*, pp. 19–20; Schäffer, 'Polskie melodie ludowe', pp. 324–6; Stucky, 'The Music of Witold Lutosławski', pp. 147–53.

Dziesięć polskich pieśni ludowych na tematy żołnierskie

See Stucky, 'The Music of Witold Lutosławski', pp. 160–3.

Les espaces du sommeil

Zieliński, Tadeusz A. 'Przestrzenie snu Witolda Lutosławskiego' [*Les espaces du sommeil* by WL]. *Ruch muzyczny*, n.s. 22, no. 12 (1978): 3–5.
See also Marek, 'A New Work'.

228   *Select bibliography*

Five Songs on Texts of Iłłakowicz

Chlopicka, Regina. 'Pięć pieśni Lutosłwskiego do słów Iłłakowiczówny' [L's Five Songs on Texts of Iłłakowiczówna]. *Ruch muzyczny*, n.s. 21, no. 20 (1977): 4–6.

Markiewicz, Leon. 'Pięć pieśni Witolda Lutosławskiego' [Five Songs by WL]. *Ruch muzyczny*, n.s. 4, no. 5–6 (1960): 24–5.

Nordwall, Ove. 'Fünf Illakowicz-Lieder von Witold Lutoslawski'. *Melos* 33 (1966): 212–16.

See also Lutosławski, [On Five Songs]; Nordwall, *Lutosławski*, pp. 37–47; Stucky, 'The Music of Witold Lutosławski', pp. 201–10; Thomas, 'A Deep Resonance'.

Folk Melodies, Folk Songs

See *Melodie ludowe*

Funeral Music

See *Muzyka żałobna*

Iłłakowicz Songs

See Five Songs on Texts of Iłłakowicz

Jeux vénitiens

Carter, Elliott. 'Letter from Europe'. *Perspectives of New Music* 1 (Spring 1963): 199.

Helm, Everett. 'Autumn Music'. *Musical America* 81 (November 1961): 23–4. Review of the world première of the final version.

——. 'Nine-Day Festival'. *New York Times*, 8 October 1961, sec. 2, p. 13. Review of the world première of the final version.

——. 'Warschauer Herbst 1961: Die neue polnische Schule'. *Neue Zeitschrift für Musik* 122 (1961): 468–9. Review of the world première of the final version.

Jarociński, Stefan. 'Indywidualność Lutosławskiego' [L's individuality]. *Ruch muzyczny*, n.s. 5, no. 21 (1961): 5–6.

Piotrowska, Maria. 'Wybrane aspekty problematyki *Jeux vénitiens* jako wstęp do badań strukturalnych nad twórczością Witolda Lutosławskiego' [Selected problematic aspects of *Jeux vénitiens* as an introduction to structural studies of the works of WL]. M.A. thesis, Institute of Musicology, Warsaw University, 1968. Computer-assisted statistical analysis of various parameters.

Pociej, Bohdan. 'Gry weneckie: Nowy utwór Witolda Lutosławskiego' [*Jeux vénitiens*: a new work by WL]. *Ruch muzyczny*, n.s. 5, no. 10 (1961): 4.

Podhajski, Marek. 'Formy aleatoryzmu w *Grach weneckich* Witolda Lutosławskiego: Próba typizacji' [Types of aleatorism in WL's *Jeux vénitiens*: an attempt to classify them]. In *Z dziejów muzyki polskiej*, no. 15, pp. 59–78. Bydgoszcz: Bydgoskie Towarzystwo Naukowe, 1971.

Rogge, Wolfgang. 'Die *Jeux vénitiens* von Witold Lutoslawski im Schulfunk: Ein Beitrag zum Thema "Oeffentliche Konzerte für Schüler"'. *Music und Bildung* 5 (1973): 24–9.

Sadie, Stanley. 'Musical "Games" from Poland'. *Times* (London), 24 July 1967, p. 7.

——. 'The Proms'. *Musical Times* 108 (1967): 820.

Schiller, Henryk. 'Percussione batteria we współczesnej muzyce polskiej' [The percussion battery in contemporary Polish music]. *Res facta* 1 (1967): 41–3.

See also Błaszkiewicz, *Aleatoryzm*; Chylińska et al., *Przewodnik koncertowy*; Nordwall, *Lutosławski*, pp. 20–1, 68–9; Pilarski, 'Witold Lutosławski odpowiada na pytania'; Rappoport, *Vitol'd Liutoslavskii*, pp. 57–63; Stucky, 'The Music of Witold Lutosławski', p. 265.

Kolędy

See *Dwadzieście kolęd*

Lacrimosa

Dobrowolski, Andrzej. 'Lacrimosa Lutosławskiego'. *Ruch muzyczny* 4, no. 18 (1948): 16–17.
See also Rappoport, *Vitol'd Liutoslavskii*, pp. 8–9; Stucky, 'The Music of Witold Lutosławski', pp. 78–82.

Little Suite

See *Mała suita*

Livre pour orchestre

Balkanskii, L. 'Varshavska esen 1969' [Warsaw Autumn 1969]. *Bulgarska muzika* 21, no. 3 (1970): 90–1.
Frank, Andrew. 'Music Reviews'. *Notes* 31 (1974–5): 393.
Kirchberg, Klaus. 'Lutoslawskis *Livre pour orchestre*'. *Musica* 23 (1969): 30–1. Review of the world première.
Kniese, Horst. 'Lutoslawski schreibt für Hagen ein Meisterwerk'. *Melos* 36 (1969): 22. Review of the world première.
Murray, Bain. 'Adventures in Poland'. *High Fidelity/Musical America* 19 (December 1969): MA26–7. Review of the 1969 Warsaw Autumn.
Pociej, Bohdan. 'Dźwiękowa sublimacja świata' [Sound sublimation of the world]. *Polska*, 1970, no. 7, pp. 31–2.
Slonimskii, S[ergei], and V. Fere. '"Varshavska osen" – 69' [Warsaw Autumn – 69]. *Sovetskaia muzyka*, 1970, no. 1, pp. 125, 127–8.
Zieliński, Tadeusz A. 'Die polnische Musik tritt auf der Stelle'. *Melos* 37 (1970): 61–4. Review of the 1969 Warsaw Autumn.
———. 'Jesienne konfrontacje' [Autumn confrontations]. *Ruch muzyczny*, n.s. 13, no. 23 (1969): 10–13.
See also Chylińska et al., *Przewodnik koncertowy*; Kaczyński, 'Livre'; idem, *Rozmowy*; Rappoport, *Vitol'd Liutoslavskii*, pp. 106–17; Stucky, 'The Music of Witold Lutosławski', pp. 261, 268–70, 274, 279–81.

Mała suita

Broszkiewicz, Jerzy. 'Śliczna czy piękna?' [Lovely or beautiful?] *Przegląd kulturalny* 3, no. 21 (1954): 5.
Lissa, Zofia. 'Mała suita i Tryptyk Witolda Lutosławskiego'. *Muzyka* 3, no. 5–6 (1952): 7–56.
Łobaczewska, Stefania. 'Próba zbadania realizmu socjalistycznego w muzyce na podstawie polskiej twórczości 10-lecia' [An attempt to investigate Socialist realism in music on the basis of the Polish works of the last decade]. *Studia muzykologiczne* 5 (1956): 7–195. See pp. 114–32.
Michałowski, M. Józef. 'Pierwszy etap festiwalu muzyki polskiej w Katowicach' [The first stage of the Festival of Polish Music in Katowice]. *Muzyka* 2, no. 7 (1951): 38–9.
Swolkień, Henryk. 'Po pierwszym etapie festiwalu muzyki polskiej w Warszawie' [After the first stage of the Festival of Polish Music in Warsaw]. *Muzyka* 2, no. 7 (1951): 35–7.

230   *Select bibliography*

See also Chylińska et al., *Przewodnik koncertowy*; Lissa, 'Die Folklore'; idem and Chomiński, 'Zagadnienie folkloru'; Rappoport, *Vitol'd Liutoslavskii*, pp. 20–2; Schäffer, 'Polskie melodie ludowe', pp. 328–45; Stucky, 'The Music of Witold Lutosławski', pp. 172–4.

Mass songs

Dziębowska, Elżbieta. 'Pieśń masowa w twórczości W. Lutosławskiego' [The mass song in the works of WL]. *Muzyka* 5, no. 7–8 (1954): 38–44.
See also Stucky, 'The Music of Witold Lutosławski', pp. 163–5.

Melodie ludowe

Chodkowski, Andrzej. 'Miniatura fortepianowa dziesięciolecia 1945–1955' [Piano miniatures of the decade 1945–55]. M.A. thesis, Institute of Musicology, Warsaw University, 1958. See esp. pp. 74–6.
Lissa, Zofia. 'Die Folklore im Schaffen zeitgenössischer polnischer Komponisten'. *Kulturprobleme des Neuen Polens* 3, no. 10 (1951): 1–8.
—— and Józef M. Chomiński. 'Zagadnienie folkloru w twórczości współczesnych kompozytorów polskich' [The problem of folklore in the works of contemporary Polish composers]. *Muzyka* 2, no. 5–6 (1951): 3–24. See esp. p. 17.
Schäffer, Bogusław. 'Polskie melodie ludowe w twórczości Witolda Lutosławskiego' [Polish folk songs in the works of WL]. *Studia muzykologiczne* 5 (1956): 300–56. See esp. 301–23.
See also Lissa, 'Muzyka jako czynnik'; Rappoport, *Vitol'd Liutoslavskii*, pp. 19–20; Stucky, 'The Music of Witold Lutosławski', pp. 141–7.

Mi-parti

Erhardt, Ludwik, et al. 'Z sal koncertowych – Lutosławski: *Mi-parti*' [From the concert halls]. *Ruch muzyczny*, n.s. 21, no. 23 (1977): 12.
Griffiths, Paul. 'New Music'. *Musical Times* 119 (1978): 159. Review of the London première.
Hanson, Robert. 'Lutoslawski's *Mi-parti*'. *Tempo*, March 1978, pp. 30–1.
Marek, Tadeusz. 'Witold Lutosławski: *Mi-parti*'. *Polish Music* 12, no. 2 (1977): 3–4.
Millington, Barry. 'Edinburgh'. *Musical Times* 118 (1977): 941–2.
Pociej, Bohdan. 'Symphonicism Redivivus'. *Polish Perspectives* 20 (May 1977): 44–51.
Von Rhein, John. 'Barenboim, Chicago Symphony Ring Out Old Year in Vigorous Style'. *Chicago Tribune*, 17 December 1977, sec. 1, p. 13. Review of the American première.
Zieliński, Tadeusz A. '*Mi-parti* Witolda Lutosławskiego'. *Ruch muzyczny*, n.s. 21, no. 19 (1977): 4–5.
See also DeJong, 'In gesprek met Lutoslawski'.

Musique funèbre

See *Muzyka żałobna*

Muzyka żałobna

Brennecke, Wilfried. 'Die Trauermusik von Witold Lutosławski'. In *Festschrift Friedrich Blume zum 70. Geburtstag*, ed. Anna Amalie Abert and Wilhelm Pfannkuch, pp. 60–73. Kassel: Bärenreiter, 1963.

In *Studia Hieronymo Feicht septuagenario dedicata*, ed. Zofia Lissa, pp. 457–71. Cracow: Polskie Wydawnictwo Muzyczne, 1967. In Polish.

Helm, Everett. 'Current Chronicle: Poland'. *Musical Quarterly* 45 (1959): 112–13. Review of the 1958 Warsaw Autumn.

Jarociński, Stefan. 'Nowa muzyka Lutosławskiego' [New music by L]. *Przegląd kulturalny* 7, no. 22 (1958): 7. Review of the Warsaw première.
'Podwójny sukces' [Twofold success]. *Antena* 2, no. 6 (1958): 13.

Mycielski, Zygmunt. 'O Muzyce żałobnej Lutosławskiego' [On L's *Muzyka żałobna*]. *Przegląd kulturalny* 7, no. 16 (1958): 7.

Nikol'skaia, Irena. 'Traurnaia muzyka Vitol'da Liutoslavskogo i ee mesto v evoliutsii simfonicheskogo tvorchestva kompozitora' [The *Muzyka żałobna* of WL and its place in the evolution of the composer's symphonic works]. Diploma thesis, Gnesin Institute, Moscow, [1975?].

——. 'Traurnaia muzyka Vitol'da Liutoslavskogo i problemy zvukovysotnoi organizatsii v muzyka xx veka' [The *Muzyka żałobna* of WL and problems of pitch organization in twentieth-century music]. In *Muzyka i sovremennost'*, no. 10, ed. D. V. Frishman, pp. 187–206. Moscow: Izdatel'stvo 'Muzyka', 1976.

Pilarski, Bohdan. 'Nowe święto muzyki polskiej – po prawykonaniu Muzyki żałobnej Witolda Lutosławskiego [The new Festival of Polish Music – after the première of WL's *Muzyka żałobna*]. *Ruch muzyczny*, n.s. 2, no. 9 (1958): 2–7.

Schäffer, Bogusław. 'Nowy kierunek w twórczości Witolda Lutosławskiego' [A new direction in the works of WL]. *Życie literackie* 8, no. 20 (1958): 10.
In Bogusław Schäffer, *W. kręgu nowej muzyki*, pp. 238–43. Cracow: Wydawnictwo Literackie, 1967.

Smith Brindle, Reginald. 'Current Chronicle: Italy'. *Musical Quarterly* 46 (1960): 86–8. Review of the 1959 Venice Biennale.

Stanilewicz. Maria. 'Organizacja materiału dźwiękowego w Muzyce żałobnej Witolda Lutosławskiego' [The organization of sound material in WL's *Muzyka żałobna*]. *Muzyka*, n.s. 20, no. 4 (1975): 3–27.

——. 'Problem formy w Muzyce żałobnej Witolda Lutosławskiego' [The question of form in WL's *Muzyka żałobna*]. *Muzyka*, n.s. 23, no. 1 (1978): 33–44.

See also Chylińska et al., *Przewodnik koncertowy*; Lutosławski, 'Improvisationer på ett givet tema': Nordwall, *Lutosławski*, pp. 50–8; Pilarski, 'Witold Lutoslawski odpowiada na pytania'; Pociej, *Lutosławski a wartość muzyki*, esp. pp. 13–16, 52–4, 62, 68–9, 113–14; Rappoport, *Vitol'd Liutoslavskii*, pp. 45–51; Stucky, 'The Music of Witold Lutosławski', pp. 210–22.

Overture for Strings

Pociej, Bohdan. 'Uwertura na smyczki Witolda Lutosławskiego' [WL's Overture for Strings]. *Ruch muzyczny*, n.s. 2, no. 4 (1958): 23–8.

See also Chylińska et al., *Przewodnik koncertowy*; Pociej, *Lutosławski a wartość muzyki*, esp. pp. 48–51; Stucky, 'The Music of Witold Lutosławski', pp. 134–40.

Paroles tissées

Bäck, Sven-Erik. 'Uttryck i det abstrakta: Kring förhållandet ord-ton i tre aktuelle verk' [Expression in the abstract: on the relation of word to tone in three current works]. *Nutida musik* 13, no. 4 (1969–70): 10.

Goodwin, Noël. 'Suffolk Constellation'. *Music and Musicians* 13 (August 1965): 17. Review of the world première.

Sadie, Stanley. 'Aldeburgh'. *Musical Times* 106 (1965): 616–17. Review of the world première.

'Wit and Resource in New Britten Variation [sic]'. Times (London), 21 June 1965, p. 6. Review of the world première.
See also Kaczyński, 'Paroles tissées'; idem, Rozmowy; Lutosławski, 'Paroles tissées; Nordwall, Lutosławski, pp. 90–102; Rappoport, Vitol'd Liutoslavskii, pp. 77–86.

Pieśni or piosenki dziecinne

See Children's songs

Pieśni masowe

See Mass songs

Pieśni walki podziemnej

G.M. 'Pesni pol'skikh partizan' [Songs of the Polish guerillas]. Sovetskaia muzyka, 1949, no. 8, pp. 110–11.
    'Pieśni polskich partyzantów' [Songs of the Polish guerillas]. Ruch muzyczny 5, no. 15 (1949): 37.
Levtonova, O. 'Pesni khudozhnika-patriota' [Songs of an artist-patriot]. Sovetskaia muzyka, 1973, no. 3, pp. 119–21.
See also Dziębowska, 'Pieśń masowa'; Rappoport, Vitol'd Liutoslavskii, p. 12; Stucky, 'The Music of Witold Lutosławski', pp. 101–5.

Postludium

See Three Postludes

Preludes and Fugue

Bachmann, Claus-Henning. 'Graz: Eine überwiegend bedrückende Bestandsaufnahme; Das 46. Weltmusikfest'. Neue Zeitschrift für Musik 133 (1972): 710. Review of the world première.
    'Notizen zum 46. Weltmusikfest in Graz'. Das Orchester 21 (1973): 89.
Flothuis, Marius. 'Het musiekfest der ISCM te Graz'. Mens en melodie 27 (1972): 357–60. Review of the world première.
Griffiths, Paul. 'Music in London: Lutoslawski'. Musical Times 114 (1973): 285. Review of the British première.
Heijne, Ingemar von. 'Det dålige samvetets världmusikfest: Ett slags rapport från 1972 års ISCM-fest i Graz' [The bad-conscience world music festival: one kind of account from the 1972 ISCM festival in Graz]. Nutida musik 16, no. 2 (1972–3): 60–1. Review of the world première.
Jack, Adrian. 'Composers'. Music and Musicians 21 (April 1973): 64, 66.
Pociej, Bohdan. 'Fugue and Copernicus'. Polish Perspectives 16 (October 1973): 68–70. Review of the 1973 Warsaw Autumn.
——. 'Thought and Inspiration'. Poland, January 1974, pp. 41–3.
Restagna, E. 'Da Graz'. Rassegna musicale italiana 6 (1972): 596–8. Review of the world première.
Sadie, Stanley. 'Lutoslawski'. Times (London), 22 January 1973, p. 10. Review of the British première.
Zieliński, Tadeusz A. 'Perspektywy piękna, wyrazu i formy' [Vistas of beauty, expression, and form]. Ruch muzyczny, n.s. 17, no. 18 (1973): 4–6.
See also Marek, 'Composer's Workshop'; Pociej, Lutosławski a wartość muzyki, esp. pp. 27–31; Stucky, 'The Music of Witold Lutosławski', pp. 258–60, 267–8.

Preludia taneczne
See Konold, 'Zwischen Folklore und Aleatorik'.

Requiem
See *Lacrimosa*

Resistance songs
See *Pieśni walki podziemnej*

Sacher Variation
See Stucky, 'The Music of Witold Lutosławski', p. 258.

Silesian Triptych
See *Tryptyk śląski*

Słomkowy łańcuszek
Kaczyński, Tadeusz. 'Lutosławski's Music for Children'. *Polish Music* 9, no. 4 (1974): 9–11. Also in German.

Soldiers' songs
See *Dziesięć polskich pieśni ludowych na tematy żołnierskie*

Sonata for Piano
See Rappoport, *Vitol'd Liutoslavskii*, pp. 7–8; Schäffer, 'Polskie melodie ludowe', pp. 354–5; Stucky, 'The Music of Witold Lutosławski', pp. 75–8.

Songs of the Polish Underground
See *Pieśni walki podziemnej*

String Quartet
Hansberger, Joachim. 'Begrenzte Aleatorik: Das Streichquartett Witold Lutosławskis'. *Musica* 25 (1971): 248–57.

Helm, Everett. 'Warschauer Herbst 1965'. *Neue Zeitschrift für Musik* 126 (1965): 482–3.

Joachim, Heinz. 'Die moderne Tonsprache konsolidiert sich'. *Die Welt* (Hamburg), 19 March 1965, p. 7. Review of the world première.

Müry, Albert, Robert Suter, and Rudolph Häusler. 'Das Weltmusikfest der IGNM in Basel'. *Schweizerische Musikzeitung* 110 (1970): 240, 244–5.

Mycielski, Zygmunt. 'Do przyjaciół: ix Międzynarodowy Festiwal Muzyki Współczesnej "Warszawska Jesień"' [To my friends: the ninth International Festival of Contemporary Music 'Warsaw Autumn']. *Ruch muzyczny*, n.s. 9, no. 21 (1965): 13.

Payne, Anthony. 'Music in London: New Music'. *Musical Times* 109 (1968): 531–2. Review of the British première.

——. 'New Sound Worlds'. *Times* (London), 2 March 1968, p. 19. Review of the British première.

234   Select bibliography

Schiller, Henryk. 'Kwartet smyczkowy Witolda Lutosławskiego' [WL's String Quartet]. *Res facta* 2 (1968): 15–29.
Schmidt, Christian Martin. 'Witold Lutosławski: Streichquartett'. In *Die Musik der sechziger Jahre*, ed. Rudolph Stephan, pp. 154–62. Veröffentlichungen des Institute für neue Musik und Musikerziehung Darmstadt, vol. 12. Mainz: B. Schott's Söhne, 1972.
Selleck, John. 'Pitch and Duration as Textural Elements in Lutosławski's String Quartet'. *Perspectives of New Music* 13 (Spring-Summer 1975): 150–61.
Stucky, Steven. 'The String Quartet of Witold Lutosławski'. M.F.A. thesis, Cornell University, 1973.
See also Jarociński, *Witold Lutosławski*, pp. 4–5; Kaczyński, *Rozmowy*; Lutosławski. 'Att spela ad libitum'; Nordwall, *Lutosławski*, pp. 83–8; Rappoport, *Vitol'd Liutoslavskii*, pp. 86–94; Stucky, 'The Music of Witold Lutosławski', pp. 237–9, 255–7.

Symphonic Variations

Broszkiewicz, Jerzy. 'Życie muzyczne w kraju: Kraków' [Musical life at home: Cracow]. *Ruch muzyczny* 3, no. 21 (1947): 22; no. 22, p. 20.
Richards, Denby. 'The Contemporary Scene (and Some Twentieth Century Operas)'. *Musical Opinion* 98 (1975): 504–5.
See also Chylińska et al., *Przewodnik koncertowy*; Pociej, *Lutosławski a wartość muzyki*, esp. pp. 41–5; Rappoport, *Vitol'd Liutoslavskii*, pp. 9–10; Stucky, 'The Music of Witold Lutosławski', pp. 82–92.

Symphony [No. 1]

F[ord], C[hristopher]. 'Lutoslawski's First'. *Music and Musicians* 25 (May 1977): 4–5.
Haubenstock[-Ramati], Roman. 'Życie muzyczne w kraju: Kraków' [Musical life at home: Cracow]. *Ruch muzyczny* 4, no. 18 (1948): 21.
Kisielewski, Stefan. 'Życie muzyczne' [Musical life]. *Tygodnik powszechny*, 4 July 1948, p. 11.
Mycielski, Zygmunt. 'Najlepsza orkiestra w Polsce' [The best orchestra in Poland]. *Odrodzenie* (Lublin), 11 April 1948, p. 8. Review of the world première.
——. 'Stokowski in Warsaw'. *Polish Perspectives* 2 (October 1959): 93–4.
See also Chylińska et al., *Przewodnik koncertowy*; Rappoport, *Vitol'd Liutoslavskii*, pp. 12, 26–33; Stucky, 'The Music of Witold Lutosławski', pp. 108–32.

Symphony No. 2

Bowen, Meirion. 'Lutoslawski 2 in London'. *Music and Musicians* 17 (August 1969): 50–1.
Daniel, Oliver. 'More from Poland'. *Saturday Review* 52 (28 June 1969): 54–5.
Dibelius, Ulrich. 'Die Wellen haben sich gelegt – Das XI. Festival für zeitgenössische Musik in Warschau'. *Musikalische Jugend* 16, no. 5 (1967): 2. Review of the 1967 Warsaw Autumn.
Erhardt, Ludwik. 'Autumn XI'. *Polish Perspectives* 10 (December 1967): 80–1. Review of the 1967 Warsaw Autumn.
——. 'Dziewięć bogatych dni' [Nine rich days]. *Ruch muzyczny*, n.s. 11, no. 21 (1967): 13–14. Review of the 1967 Warsaw Autumn.
Lück, Hartmut. 'Xenakis und Lutoslawski setzten die Maßstäbe: Eindrücke vom "Warschauer Herbst 1967"'. *Neue Zeitschrift für Musik* 128 (1967): 443–4.
Markiewicz, Leon. 'II Symfonia Witolda Lutosławskiego'. *Muzyka*, n.s. 13, no. 2 (1968): 67–76.

Nest'ev, I[zrail']. 'Varshavskie melodii' [Warsaw melodies]. *Sovetskaia muzyka*, 1968, no. 3, pp. 116–21.
Orga, Ates. 'Liverpool: Lutoslawski's Second'. *Music and Musicians* 17 (July 1969): 60–1.
Paap, Wouter. 'Tweede Symfonie van Witold Lutoslawski'. *Mens en melodie* 24 (1968): 146–8.
Pociej, Bohdan, 'Order is Born of Chaos'. *Poland*, July 1968, pp. 13–15, 38.
Sannemüller, Gerd. 'Witold Lutoslawskis 2. Sinfonie'. *Musik und Bildung* 10 (1978): 588–95.
Schwinger, Wolfram. 'Lutoslawskis zweite Sinfonie'. *Melos* 22 (1968): 445. Review of the West German première of the complete work.
Trumpff, G. A. 'Lutoslawskis zweite Sinfonie: Deutsche Erstaufführung unter Ernest Bour'. *Neue Zeitschrift für Musik* 129 (1968): 415–16. Review of the West German première of the complete work.
Várnai, Péter, 'Szemle: Varsói Osz, 1967' [Review: Warsaw Autumn, 1967]. *Magyar zene* 8 (1967): 635.
See also Chylińska et al., *Przewodnik koncertowy*; Kaczyński, 'O II Symfonii'; idem, *Rozmowy*; Lutosławski, 'Nowy utwór'; idem, 'Sur l'orchestre d'aujourd'hui'; Nordwall, *Lutosławski*, pp. 105–18; Pociej, *Lutosławski a wartość muzyki*, esp. pp. 89–90, 117–18; Rappoport, *Vitol'd Liutoslavskii*, pp. 94–106; Stucky, 'The Music of Witold Lutosławski', pp. 253–4, 256–7, 277–8, 281.

Thirty pieces for woodwinds

See Rappoport, *Vitol'd Liutoslavskii*, p. 12.

Three Postludes

Ehinger, Hans. 'Für das Rote Kreuz komponiert'. *Neue Zeitschrift für Musik* 124 (1963): 491. Review of the world première of no. 1.
Klein, Howard. 'Congregation of Arts Offers Works by Lutoslawski, Top Polish Composer'. *New York Times*, 26 July 1966, sec. 1, p. 26.
Peiko, N. 'Dve instrumental'nye miniatury (kompozitsionnyi analiz p'es O. Messiana i V. Liutoslavskogo)' [Two instrumental miniatures (compositional analysis of works by O. Messiaen and W. Lutosławski)]. In *Muzyka i sovremennost'*, no. 9, ed. D. V. Frishman, pp. 282–308. Moscow: Izdatel'stvo 'Muzyka', 1975.
Schulé, Bernard. 'Zeitgenössische Musik im Dienst des Roten Kreuzes'. *Schweizerische Musikzeitung* 103 (1963): 302. Review of the world première of no. 1.
Thiele, Siegfried. 'Zeitstrukturen in den Motetten des Philippe de Vitry und ihre Bedeutung für zeitgenössisches Komponieren'. *Neue Zeitschrift für Musik* 135 (1974): 426–33. Pp. 431–3 are devoted to rhythmic structures in Postlude no. 1.
See also Nordwall, *Lutosławski*, pp. 60–5; Rappoport, *Vitol'd Liutoslavskii*, pp. 51–3; Stucky, 'The Music of Witold Lutosławski', pp. 222–7.

Trio for Woodwinds

Kisielewski, Stefan. 'Festival Polskiej Muzyki Współczesnej w Krakowie (1–4 IX 1945)' [Festival of Contemporary Polish Music in Cracow (1–4 September 1945)]. *Ruch muzyczny* 1, no. 1 (1945): 25. Review of the world première.
See also Rappoport, *Vitol'd Liutoslavskii*, p. 13.

236   Select bibliography

Trois poèmes d'Henri Michaux

Bachmann, Claus-Henning. 'Ein Musikprotokoll – über Boulez, Eisler und den Realismus'. *Neue Zeitschrift für Musik* 133 (1972): 31–6.
Cvetko, Dragotin. 'Yugoslavia: Picture in Depth'. *Musical America* 83 (July 1963): 16. Review of the world première.
Goodwin, Noël. 'Commentary: Zagreb'. *Music and Musicians* 11 (July 1963): 16–17. On the world première.
[Hartzell, Eugene?] 'Modern Vocal Music from Schoenberg to Nono'. *Times* (London), 14 October 1963, p. 14. Review of the 1963 Warsaw Autumn.
Jarociński, Stefan. 'O paru festiwalowych wydarzeniach' [On a couple of festival events]. *Ruch muzyczny*, n.s. 7, no. 21 (1963): 7–8. Review of the 1963 Warsaw Autumn.
Laaban, Ilmar. 'Michaux och musiken' [Michaux and music]. *Nutida musik* 12, no. 3 (1968–9): 19–27.
Merkù, Pavle. 'Misli o novi glasbi (po letošnjem zagrebškim bienalu)' [Thoughts on new music (after this summer's Zagreb Biennale)]. *Sodobnost* (Ljubljana) 11 (1963): 815. Review of the world première.
Pensdorfova, Eva. 'Tři poemata Witolda Lutoslavského'. *Hudební rozhledy* 18 (1965): 106–8.
Riis-Vestergaard, Hans. 'Trois poèmes d'Henri Michaux'. *Dansk musiktidsskrift* 41 (1966): 3–4.
Stadlen, Peter. 'Welcome for "New Trend" Music: Michaux Poems'. *Daily Telegraph*, 24 September 1963, [pp. unk.].
Stone, Kurt. 'Reviews of Records'. *Musical Quarterly* 50 (1964): 265–6. After the 1963 Warsaw Autumn.
Stuckenschmidt, H. H. 'Zagreber Biennale zwischen Schostakowitsch und Cage'. *Melos* 30 (1963): 257–8. Review of the world première.
Thomas, Adrian. 'A Deep Resonance: Lutosławski's Trois poèmes d'Henri Michaux'. *Soundings*, no. 1 (Autumn 1970): 58–70.
Wallek-Walewski, Marian. 'Uwagi o Trois poèmes d'Henri Michaux' [Remarks on Trois poèmes d'Henri Michaux]. *Ruch muzyczny*, n.s. 13, no. 3 (1969): 6–9.
Zieliński, Tadeusz A. 'Internationales Panorama beim Warschauer Herbst 1963'. *Melos* 31 (1964): 32–4.
———. 'Poland: The Latest Styles'. *Musical America* 84 (January 1964): 27, 57. Review of the 1963 Warsaw Autumn.
See also Chylińska et al., *Przewodnik koncertowy*; Kaczyński, 'Trzy poematy'; idem, *Rozmowy*; Lutosławski, 'Trois poèmes'; Nordwall, *Lutosławski*, pp. 26–30; Rappoport, *Vitol'd Liutoslavskii*, pp. 64–77; Schiller, 'Percussione batteria'.

Tryptyk śląski

Lissa, Zofia. 'Muzyka jako czynnik integracji narodowej' [Music as a factor of national integration]. *Kwartalnik historyczny* 76 (1969): 376–94.
See also Lissa, 'Mała suita'; Rappoport, *Vitol'd Liutoslavskii*, pp. 22–4; Stucky, 'The Music of Witold Lutosławski', pp. 174–5.

Trzy utwory dla młodzieży

Wobozil, Jadwiga. 'Twórczość fortepianowa dla dzieci kompozytorów polskich w latach 1945–1957' [Piano works for children by Polish composers during the years 1945–57]. M.A. thesis, Institute of Musicology, Warsaw University, 1959. See esp. pp. 119–21.
See also Stucky, 'The Music of Witold Lutosławski', pp. 158–60.

Two Etudes

See Rappoport, *Vitol'd Liutoslavskii*, pp. 11–12; Stucky, 'The Music of Witold Lutosławski', pp. 92–7.

Variations on a Theme of Paganini

Cieślak-Łastowiecka, Maria. 'Fortepianowe wersje 24 kaprysu Paganiniego' [Piano versions of Paganini's 24th Caprice]. M.A. thesis, Institute of Musicology, Warsaw University, 1964.

Łobaczewska, Stefania. 'Życie muzyczne w kraju: Kraków' [Musical life at home: Cracow]. *Odrodzenie* (Lublin), 1 December 1946, p. 11.

See also Rappoport, *Vitol'd Liutoslavskii*, p. 11; Stucky, 'The Music of Witold Lutosławski', pp. 97–101.

Venetian Games

See *Jeux vénitiens*

Notes

1 The early years

1. Wincenty Lutosławski, *Sur une nouvelle méthode pour déterminer la chronologie des dialogues de Platon* (Paris: H. Welter, 1896); idem, *The Origin and Growth of Plato's Logic, with an Account of Plato's Style and the Chronology of His Writings* (London: Longmans, Green, 1897).
2. Biographies of Józef, his brothers, and Sofía are to be found in *Polski słownik biograficzny* (Cracow: Zakład Narodowy im. Ossolińskich, Wydawnictwo Polskiej Akademii Nauk, 1935–), 8:148–56. Additional details of Józef's life are available in Zygmunt Wasilewski's biographical sketch in Józef Lutosławski, *Chleb i ojczyzna* (Warsaw: E. Wende i Spółka, 1919), pp. vii–xii.
3. Bálint András Varga, *Lutosławski Profile* (London: Chester Music, 1976), p. 1.
4. Bohdan Pilarski, 'Witold Lutosławski odpowiada na pytania', *Ruch muzyczny*, n.s. 2, no. 7 (1958): 2 (my translation).
5. *Vitol'd Liutoslavskii* (Moscow: Izdatel'stvo 'Muzyka', 1976), p. 8.
6. Stefan Jarociński (ed.), *Polish Music* (Warsaw: Polish Scientific Publishers, 1965), p. 171.
7. Varga, pp. 4–5.
8. Tadeusz Kaczyński, *Rozmowy z Witoldem Lutosławskim* (Cracow: Polskie Wydawnictwo Muzyczne, 1972), p. 125 (my translation).
9. Quoted in Lidiia Rappoport, 'Vydaiushchiisia master', *Sovetskaia muzyka*, 1969, no. 7, p. 114 (my translation).
10. Rappoport, *Vitol'd Liutoslavskii*, p. 9.
11. Varga, p. 7.
12. 'The Polish Intelligentsia: Past and Present', in *Poland since 1956: Readings and Essays on Government and Politics* (New York: Twayne Publishers, 1972), p. 111.
13. Grzegorz Michałski et al., *Dzieje muzyki polskiej w zarysie* (Warsaw: Interpress, 1976), p. 130.
14. Quoted in Howard Klein, 'Notes from Underground', *New York Times*, 7 August 1966, sec. 2, p. 13. See further Tadeusz Ochlewski, 'Muzyka w Warszawie podczas okupacji', *Ruch muzyczny*, n.s. 14, no. 11 (1970): 16–17; and Krystyna Michalska, 'O życiu muzycznym w latach okupacji', *Ruch muzyczny*, n.s. 19, no. 10 (1975): 4–5.
15. For a reprint of no. 2 see O. Levtonova, 'Pesni khudozhnika-patriota', *Sovetskaia muzyka*, 1973, no. 3, pp. 120–1. No. 4 is quoted in full in Steven Stucky, 'The Music of Witold Lutosławski: A Style-Critical Survey' (D.Mus.A. thesis, Cornell University, 1978), pp. 104–5.
16. For an excellent scholarly account of the background of the Polish resistance movement and the Warsaw Rising, see Jan A. Ciechanowski, *The Warsaw Rising of 1944* (Cambridge: Cambridge University Press, 1974).
17. Varga, p. 29.
18. *Twelve Polish Composers* (London: Allegro Press, 1976), p. 44.
19. A partial list of incidental music for radio and stage plays composed 1946–60 is

238

given in Ove Nordwall (ed.), *Lutosławski* (Stockholm: Edition Wilhelm Hansen, 1968), pp. 135–7.
20. 'Festival Polskiej Muzyki Współczesnej w Krakowie (1–4 IX 1945)', *Ruch muzyczny* 1, no. 1 (1945): 25 (my translation).
21. 'Najlepsza orkiestra w Polsce', *Odrodzenie* (Lublin), 11 April 1948, p. 8 (my translation).
22. 'Życie muzyczne w kraju: Kraków', *Ruch muzyczny* 4, no. 18 (1948): 21 (my translation).
23. *Polish Music*, p. 181.
24. 'Życie muzyczne', *Tygodnik powszechny*, 4 July 1948, p. 11 (my translation).
25. *Polish Music*, p. 181.
26. But striking as this chord may be, it is by no means 'the sound source for all subsequent themes, harmonies and section cadences', as Edward Cowie has asserted in 'Mobiles of Sound', *Music and Musicians* 20 (October 1971): 34.
27. *Vitol'd Liutoslavskii*, p. 29.
28. Ibid., pp. 12–13.
29. Ibid., pp. 26–7, 31.
30. Varga, p. 9.
31. *Twentieth-Century Music: An Introduction*, 2d edn. (Englewood Cliffs: Prentice-Hall, 1974), p. 44.

2   The dark years

1. 'Ob opere *Velikaia druzhba* V. Muradeli'. The complete text was published in *Sovetskaia muzyka*, 1948, no. 1, pp. 3–8; a translation is given in Nicolas Slonimsky, *Music since 1900*, 4th edn (New York: Charles Scribner's Sons, 1971), pp. 1358–62. See also Alexander Werth, *Musical Uproar in Moscow* (London: Turnstile Press, [1949]).
2. Quoted in Izrail' Vladimirovich Nest'ev, *Prokofiev*, transl. Florence Jonas (Stanford: Stanford University Press, 1960), p. 278.
3. See Ludwik Erhardt, *Music in Poland*, transl. Jan Aleksandrowicz (Warsaw: Interpress, 1975), p. 79.
4. See, for example, Józef M. Chomiński, 'Zagadnienia formalizmu i tendencje idealogiczne w polskiej muzyce współczesnej na tle rozwoju muzyki światowej', *Ruch muzyczny* 4, no. 20 (1948): 2–6.
5. The complete text is given in Slonimsky, pp. 1378–9.
6. *Ruch muzyczny* 5, no. 14 (1949) is devoted to the proceedings of the Łagów conference, including the remarks of Sokorski (pp. 3–6) and Mycielski (pp. 6–10) and a transcript of the discussions (pp. 12–31). (It is telling that the very next issue of this periodical was wholly given over to Russian music and translations of articles by Soviet authors.) See also Zygmunt Mycielski, 'Wrażenie ze zjazdu kompozytorów w Łagowie', *Życie śpiewacze*, 1949, no. 9; and Witold Rudziński, 'Zjazd kompozytorów w Łagowie', *Odrodzenie* (Lublin), 1949, no. 35.
7. Stefan Jarociński (ed.), *Polish Music* (Warsaw: Polish Scientific Publishers, 1965), pp. 182–3. Stanisław Moniuszko (1819–72) composed in many genres, but he is remembered principally for national operas and songs.
8. Bálint András Varga, *Lutosławski Profile* (London: Chester Music, 1976), p. 8.
9. Details of the published sources for these and the other folklore-related works may be found in Catalog of Works.
10. For a detailed examination of these features in the *Melodie* and *Kolędy*, see Steven Stucky, 'The Music of Witold Lutosławski: A Style-Critical Survey' (D.Mus.A. thesis, Cornell University, 1978), pp. 142–53.
11. (Vienna: Universal Edition, 1935); reprinted as Béla Bartók, *Ethnomusikologische Schriften*, ed. D[enijs] Diller, vol. 4 (Mainz: B. Schott's Söhne, [1968]).

12. See Béla Bartók, 'Der Einfluss der Volksmusik auf die heutige Kunstmusik', *Melos* 1 (1920): 386.
13. *Dzieje muzyki polskiej w zarysie* (Warsaw: Interpress, 1976), p. 145.
14. 'Pieśń masowa w twórczości W. Lutosławskiego', *Muzyka* 5, no. 7–8 (1954): 39 (my translation).
15. The smaller functional pieces mentioned above are discussed more fully in Stucky, pp. 154–65.
16. See 'Kilka wrażeń z podróży do ZSRR', *Muzyka* 2, no. 11 (1951): 6–7; and 'Festiwal współczesnej muzyki niemieckiej w Berlinie', *Muzyka* 4, no. 1–2 (1953): 38–41.
17. See 'Nad grobem Grzegorza Fitelberga', *Przegląd kulturalny* 2, no. 24 (1953): 2; and 'O Grzegorzu Fitelbergu', *Muzyka* 5, no. 7–8 (1954): 26–33.
18. Ove Nordwall (ed.), *Lutosławski* (Stockholm: Edition Wilhelm Hansen, 1968), pp. 33–5.
19. Zofia Lissa, 'Mała suita i Tryptyk Witolda Lutosławskiego', *Muzyka* 3, no. 5–6 (1952): 14–15.
20. Varga, pp. 8–9.
21. See Bohdan Pociej, 'Uwertura na smyczki Witolda Lutosławskiego', *Ruch muzyczny*, n.s. 2, no. 4 (1958): 24.
22. Lissa, pp. 14–15 (my translation).
23. See Iu. Paisov, 'Politonal'nost' i muzykal'naia forma', in *Muzyka i sovremennost'*, no. 10, ed. D. V. Frishman (Moscow: Izdatel'stvo 'Muzyka', 1976), p. 244.
24. 'Wielka muzyka', *Przegląd kulturalny* 3, no. 49 (1954): 2.
25. 'Witold Lutosławskis Konzert für Orchester (Analytische Skizze)', transl. Edda Werfel, in *Zur musikalischen Analyse*, ed. Gerhard Schumacher (Darmstadt: Wissenschaftlicher Buchgesellschaft, 1974), pp. 285, 290.
26. *The Life and Music of Béla Bartók*, rev. edn (London: Oxford University Press, 1964), p. 129.
27. Volume and page numbers in the example refer to Oskar Kolberg, *Mazowsze*, vols. 2 and 5 = *Lud . . .* , vols. 25 and 28 (Cracow: Druk Wł. L. Anczyca i Spółki, 1886, 1890). The identification of folk sources in the discussion to follow is based on Zofia Lissa, 'Koncert na orkiestrę Witolda Lutosławskiego', *Studia muzykologiczne* 5 (1956): 241–5, and partly on information supplied by the composer.
28. Bohdan Pilarski, 'Witold Lutosławski odpowiada na pytania', *Ruch muzyczny*, n.s. 2, no. 7 (1958): 4 (my translation).
29. Erhardt, p. 86.
30. Pilarski, pp. 2–3 (my translation).

3   The years of transition

1. Scarlett Panufnik, the composer's wife, provides a self-indulgent but intermittently fascinating account of her husband's escape in *Out of the City of Fear* (London: Hodder and Stoughton, 1956).
2. 'O twórczości muzycznej dziesięciolecia', *Muzyka* 6, no. 7–8 (1955): 20–2 (my translation).
3. A number of excellent accounts of the Polish October are available in English. The following are recommended: Nicholas Bethell, *Gomułka: His Poland. His Communism* (New York: Holt, Rinehart, and Winston, 1969), pp. 212–28; Tadeusz N. Cieplak (ed.), *Poland since 1956: Readings and Essays on Government and Politics* (New York: Twayne Publishers, 1972), pp. 1–6; M. K. Dziewanowski, *Poland in the Twentieth Century* (New York: Columbia University Press, 1977), pp. 173–85; and Konrad Syrop, *Spring in October: The Polish Revolution of 1956* (London: Weidenfeld and Nicolson, 1957). A glance backward to the Polish October in music is given in Józef M. Chomiński, 'Przełom w muzyce polskiej', *Ruch muzyczny*, n.s. 18, no. 15 (1974): 8–9.

4. Z.S., '"Warsaw Autumn" – A Musical Spring', *Polish Perspectives* 1 (July-August 1958): 104–5.
5. *Sławetny*, a stilted form used ironically.
6. 'Zagajenie dyskusji na walnym zjeździe Związku Kompozytorów Polskich', *Ruch muzyczny*, n.s. 1, no. 1 (1957): 2–3 (my translation).
7. Witold Lutosławski, 'Webern a hudba dneška', *Slovenské pohl'ady* 79, no. 12 (1963): 92–3 (my translation).
8. Bálint András Varga, *Lutosławski Profile* (London: Chester Music, 1976), p. 11.
9. IVᵉ Festival International de Musique Contemporaine, *Automne varsovien* [Warsaw, 1960], p. 27 (my translation).
10. The twelve simple intervals, containing from 0 to 11 semitones ('unison' to 'major seventh'), may be reduced to seven *interval classes*, numbered 0 to 6, by considering an interval and its octave complement to be equivalent. Thus, for example, intervals 1 and 11 ('minor second' and 'major seventh') are both representatives of interval class 1, as are intervals 13 ('minor ninth'), 23 ('major fourteenth'), etc.
11. Measure numbers run continuously through the five songs and follow the barring of the orchestral version, which is slightly changed from the piano version.
12. 'Mobiles of Sound', *Music and Musicians* 20 (October 1971): 35.
13. *Muzyka żałobna* has attracted more intensive analytical attention than perhaps any other work of Lutosławski save the String Quartet (though unfortunately none of the analyses is in English). The present discussion relies heavily on Wilfried Brennecke, 'Die Trauermusik von Witold Lutosławski', in *Festschrift Friedrich Blume zum 70. Geburtstag* (Kassel: Bärenreiter, 1963), pp. 60–73. Brennecke's analysis, in turn, had the benefit of the composer's assistance (without which it seems unlikely that the construction of the Metamorphoses in particular could ever have been penetrated).
14. Quoted by Stefan Jarociński in Ove Nordwall (ed.), *Lutosławski* (Stockholm: Edition Wilhelm Hansen, 1968), pp. 145–6.
15. Varga, p. 11.
16. This process is carried out with almost complete strictness. Brennecke, p. 67n, lists six instances in which slight liberties are taken with the modal segments.
17. Maria Stanilewicz, 'Organizacja materiału dźwiękowego w Muzyce żałobnej Witolda Lutosławskiego', *Muzyka*, n.s. 20, no. 4 (1975): 14–20, provides an extraordinarily detailed analysis of the vertical intervallic content of the Apogeum, demonstrating statistically the predominance of interval classes 3 and 6.
18. Stefan Jarociński, 'Nowa muzyka Lutosławskiego', *Przegląd kulturalny* 7, no. 22 (1958): 7 (my translation).
19. Reginald Smith Brindle, 'Current Chronicle: Italy', *Musical Quarterly* 46 (1960): 86.
20. 'Polish–Hungarian Relations in Music – Yesterday and Today', *Polish Music* 10, no. 2 (1975): 38.
21. Robert Sabin, 'Skrowaczewski Conducts Lutoslawski Concerto', *Musical America* 81 (February 1961): 43.
22. In Robert Stephan Hines (ed.), *The Orchestral Composer's Point of View: Essays on Twentieth-Century Music by Those Who Wrote It* (Norman: University of Oklahoma Press, 1970), pp. 132–3.
23. The flute and piccolo figure which begins in m. 87 is placed one quaver too early in the published score. See Siegfried Thiele, 'Zeitstrukturen in den Motetten des Philippe de Vitry und ihre Bedeutung für zeitgenössisches Komponieren', *Neue Zeitschrift für Musik* 135 (1974): 432n.
24. Iurii Butsko, 'Vitol'd Liutoslavskii: Zametki o tekhnike instrumental'noi kompozitsii', *Sovetskaia muzyka*, 1979, no. 8, p. 113.
25. Nordwall, pp. 61, 65.

4 The years of maturity

1. Bálint András Varga, *Lutosławski Profile* (London: Chester Music, 1976), p. 12. A competing story that Lutosławski met Cage in Darmstadt in 1961 and was impressed by what he heard there stems from an inaccurate quotation in a newspaper interview: Howard Klein, 'Notes from Underground', *New York Times*, 7 August 1966, sec. 2, p. 13. In fact neither Cage nor Lutosławski was in Darmstadt in 1961.
2. Published in Polish as 'Z dziejów muzyki xx wieku', in Witold Lutosławski, 'Teoria a praktyka w pracy kompozytora,' *Studia estetyczne* 2 (1965): 128–33.
3. Published in Polish as 'Czy to jest muzyka?' in Stefan Jarociński (ed.), *Witold Lutosławski: Materiały do monografii* (Cracow: Polskie Wydawnictwo Muzyczne, 1967), pp. 22–8.
4. Noël Goodwin, 'Commentary: Zagreb', *Music and Musicians* 11 (July 1963): 17.
5. Robert Craft, *Stravinsky: Chronicle of a Friendship, 1948–1972* (New York: Alfred A. Knopf, 1972), p. 275.
6. Heinz Joachim, 'Die moderne Tonsprache konsolidiert sich', *Die Welt* (Hamburg), 19 March 1965, p. 7 (my translation).
7. Published as 'About the Element of Chance in Music', in György Ligeti et al., *Three Aspects of New Music* (Stockholm: Nordiska Musikförlaget, 1968), pp. 45–53.
8. In Robert Stephan Hines (ed.), *The Orchestral Composer's Point of View: Essays on Twentieth-Century Music by Those Who Wrote It* (Norman: University of Oklahoma Press, 1970), p. 149.
9. Published as 'Kommentar zur "Musikgeschichte des 20. Jahrhunderts"', in *Parabeln*, Jahrbuch der Freien Akademie der Künste in Hamburg (Hamburg, 1966), pp. 18–23.
10. Varga, p. 27.
11. Ibid., p. 41.
12. 'Lutosławski schreibt für Hagen ein Meisterwerk', *Melos* 36 (1969): 22.
13. Wilfried Brennecke, 'Berichte: Das 44. Weltmusikfest der IGNM', *Musica* 24 (1970): 460 (my translation).
14. Tadeusz Kaczyński, *Rozmowy z Witoldem Lutosławskim* (Cracow: Polskie Wydawnictwo Muzyczne, 1973), pp. 127–8 (my translation).
15. Ibid., pp. 76–7 (my translation).
16. Ibid., p. 129 (my translation).
17. Published in the *New York Times*, 13 November 1970, p. 1; and in *Saturday Review* 53 (28 November 1970): 28.
18. Letter to the author, 11 October 1977.
19. E. M., 'Composers Talk and Talk', *Music and Musicians* 19 (February 1971): 4.
20. Published as 'The Role of Today's Graduates in the Musical Arena for the Years Ahead', *Notes of the Cleveland Institute of Music* 9, no. 2 (1971): 1–4.
21. Varga, p. 50.
22. Ibid., p. 49.
23. Kaczyński, pp. 123–4 (my translation).
24. Tadeusz Marek, 'The 10th Festival of Contemporary Polish Music in Wrocław', *Polish Music* 9, no. 2 (1974): 32.
25. Arrand Parsons, 'The Warsaw Autumn 1972', *Polish Music* 7, no. 4 (1972): 7.
26. *Times* (London), 16 February 1973, p. 19.
27. Published as 'Doctoral Speech', *Polish Music* 8, no. 3–4 (1973): 18–19.
28. *Proceedings of the American Academy of the Arts and Letters and the National Institute of Arts and Letters*, 2d ser., no. 26 (1976): 5.
29. *Musical Times* 119 (1978): 159.
30. Quoted in Alan Blyth, 'Witold Lutosławski', *Times* (London), 9 February 1971, p. 10.
31. Varga, p. 35.

32. Ibid., p. 36.
33. Kaczyński, p. 160 (my translation).
34. Alan Blyth, 'Polish Composer on His Music', *Times* (London), early edn, 11 March 1968, p. 10.
35. Quoted in Blyth, 'Witold Lutosławski'.
36. O. Levtonova, 'Nashi interviu s Vitol'dom Liutoslavskim', *Sovetskaia muzyka*, 1973, no. 7, p. 128.
37. Kaczyński, p. 159 (my translation).
38. 'Mobiles of Sound', *Music and Musicians* 20 (October 1971): 34.
39. Quoted in Tadeusz Kaczyński, 'Olivier Messiaen o swojej *Transfiguracji* i o muzyce polskiej', *Ruch muzyczny*, n.s. 22, no. 18–19 (1978): 4 (my translation).
40. 'Tchnienie wielkości', *Muzyka polska* 4 (1937): 169, quoted in Stefan Jarociński, 'Sylwetki twórców: Witold Lutosławski', *Przegląd kulturalny* 1, no. 2 (1952): 6 (my translation).
41. 'Paris: Journées internationales de musique contemporaine', *Courier musical de France* 28 (1969): 222–4.
42. 'Composers', *Music and Musicians* 21 (April 1973): 64, 66.
43. See, for example, 'Musical "Games" from Poland', *Times* (London), 24 July 1967, p. 7.
44. Varga, pp. 42–3.

5 The late style

1. *Muzyka xx wieku: Twórcy i problemy* (Cracow: Wydawnictwo Literackie, 1975), p. 220 (my translation).
2. 'Chamber Music', *Polish Perspectives* 16 (November 1973): 69.
3. Bálint András Varga, *Lutosławski Profile* (London: Chester Music, 1976), p. 17.
4. 'The Composer and the Listener', in Ove Nordwall (ed.), *Lutosławski* (Stockholm: Edition Wilhelm Hansen, 1968), pp. 121–2. In the Polish original of this text, Lutosławski refers explicitly to Stockhausen to exemplify a 'cabalistic faith in numbers' to which he is opposed (apparently Lutosławski has in mind the *Elektronische Studien* of the early fifties, where numerical orderings determine the basic sound material).
5. 'The Music of Witold Lutosławski', *Polish Perspectives* 15 (July-August 1972): 25.
6. In Polish *ograniczowy, kierowany*, or *kontrolowany aleatoryzm*. He has also described the technique as 'collective ad libitum' (*zbiorowo ad libitum*) and 'aleatorism of texture'. Limited aleatorism, which deals with rhythmic organization, is related to but distinct from aleatory counterpoint, which deals with the organization of pitch.
7. Quoted in Stefan Jarociński (ed.), *Polish Music* (Warsaw: Polish Scientific Publishers, 1965), p. 199.
8. 'Ligeti über Lutoslawski', *Musica* 22 (1968): 453.
9. 'About the Element of Chance in Music', in György Ligeti et al., *Three Aspects of New Music* (Stockholm: Nordiska Musikförlaget, 1968), pp. 52–3.
10. 'Statistic and Psychologic Problems of Sound', *Die Reihe* 1 (English edition, 1958): 55.
11. 'About the Element of Chance in Music', p. 52.
12. In Robert Stephan Hines (ed.), *The Orchestral Composer's Point of View: Essays on Twentieth-Century Music by Those Who Wrote It* (Norman: University of Oklahoma Press, 1970), pp. 130–1.
13. The following rhythmic analysis of this section relies in part on Christian Martin Schmidt, 'Witold Lutosławski: Streichquartett', in *Die Musik der sechziger Jahre*, ed. Rudolph Stephan (Mainz: B. Schott's Söhne, 1972), pp. 158–9.
14. Hines, p. 131.

15. Varga, pp. 16–17.
16. First quoted by Stefan Jarociński in 'Indywidualność Lutosławskiego', Ruch muzyczny, n.s. 5, no. 21 (1961): 5–6; this translation from Nordwall, pp. 145–146.
17. Although Lutosławski has used quarter-tones frequently, they are not discussed here because their role is invariably melodic; they function solely as auxiliaries (passing, neighboring tones) to the twelve chromatic pitch classes and take no essential part in harmonic practice.
18. Varga, pp. 24–5.
19. Nordwall, p. 19.
20. Quoted in Tadeusz Marek, 'A New Work by Lutosławski: Les espaces du sommeil', Polish Music 11, no. 1 (1976): 4–5.
21. 'Mobiles of Sound', Music and Musicians 20 (October 1971): 34.
22. International Cyclopedia of Music and Musicians, 10th edn, ed. Bruce Bobek (New York: Dodd, Mead, 1975), p. 1287.
23. 'The Composer and the Listener', in Nordwall, p. 121.
24. See Leonard B. Meyer, Emotion and Meaning in Music (Chicago: University of Chicago Press, 1956), pp. 22–69; and idem, Music, the Arts, and Ideas (Chicago: University of Chicago Press, 1967), pp. 5–21.
25. Hines, pp. 133–4.
26. Der Begriff der musikalischen Form in der Wiener Klassik: Versuch einer Grundlegung der Theorie der musikalischen Formung, 2d edn (Giebing über Prien am Chiemsee: Musikverlag Emil Katzbichler, 1971), pp. 47–57.
27. Quoted in Nordwall, p. 95.
28. The Polish terms are Lutosławski's, in Bohdan Pociej, 'O roli słowa, teatralność i tradycji w muzyce mówi Witold Lutosławski', Poezja 9 (October 1973): 80.
29. Schlegel's description was called to the author's attention by an unpublished lecture of Charles Rosen.

6 The late works

1. Marek Podhajski gives a detailed analysis of the microrhythmic structure of this percussion passage in 'Formy aleatoryzmu w Grach weneckich Witolda Lutosławskiego: Próba typizacji', in Z dziejów muzyki polskiej, no. 15 (Bydgoszcz: Bydgoskie Towarzystwo Naukowe, 1971), p. 66.
2. See Malcolm Bowie, Henri Michaux: A Study of His Literary Works (Oxford: Clarendon Press, 1973), pp. 103, 140–2.
3. Ibid., p. 101.
4. Henri Michaux, Selected Writings: The Space Within (New York: New Directions, 1951), p. 7.
5. Aleatoryzm w twórczości Witolda Lutosławskiego (Gdańsk: State Higher School of Music, 1973), p. 97. See also p. 107 for an analysis of microrhythm in the second part of the first movement.
6. 'Begrenzte Aleatorik: Das Streichquartett Witold Lutosławskis', Musica 25 (1971): 248.
7. A detailed motivic analysis is given in Steven Stucky, 'The String Quartet of Witold Lutosławski' (M.F.A. thesis, Cornell University, 1973), pp. 13–35 passim. See also ex. 5.9, above.
8. Christian Martin Schmidt, 'Witold Lutosławski: Streichquartett', in Die Musik der sechziger Jahre, ed. Rudolph Stephan (Mainz: B. Schott's Söhne, 1972), p. 157; Hansberger, p. 250.
9. Schmidt's suggestion (p. 161) that sections 47, 48 and 50 refer to sections 1 and 2 is misleading, however. The connection is motive y, but the manner in which that motive is stated near the end refers specifically to section 15.

10. Tadeusz Kaczyński, *Rozmowy z Witoldem Lutosławskim* (Cracow: Polskie Wydawnictwo Muzyczny, 1972), p. 36 (my translation).

11. Ibid., pp. 37–8 (my translation).

12. *Gramophone* 51 (1974): 2063.

13. In Robert Stephan Hines (ed.), *The Orchestral Composer's Point of View: Essays on Twentieth-Century Music by Those Who Wrote It* (Norman: University of Oklahoma Press, 1970), pp. 128–51.

14. The following summary is adapted from ibid., pp. 139–41. Cf. the version given by Leon Markiewicz in 'II Symfonia Witolda Lutosławskiego', *Muzyka*, n.s. 13, no. 2 (1968): 72.

15. Details of the microrhythmic structure at number 125 are analyzed in Błaszkiewicz, pp. 94–5.

16. *High Fidelity/Musical America* 24 (June 1974): MA30.

17. See Kaczyński, p. 82.

18. Alfred Huber offers an analysis of the microrhythmic construction of two of these orchestral statements (numbers 82 and 86) in 'Witold Lutosławski: Cellokonzert', *Melos* 40 (1973): 232–4.

19. Stephen Peter Lawson, for example, calls the final A an 'imperfect cadence', in *Tempo* 95 (Winter 1970–1): 36.

20. *Times* (London), 22 January 1973, p. 10.

21. Bohdan Pociej, 'Fugue and Copernicus', *Polish Perspectives* 16 (October 1973): 68–9.

22. At letter L in prelude 6, the cellists' pitches are indeterminate. This is exceedingly rare for Lutosławski, though it does happen briefly at 128 in the Second Symphony and 109 in *Livre* (both for xylophone). In all three passages the situation is such that the precise identity of pitches has no effect on the aural result anyway.

23. Adrian Jack in *Music and Musicians* 21 (April 1973): 66 agrees: 'So far the only real miscalculation I have spotted in Preludes and Fugue is the inappropriately chirpy ending.'   -

24. *Manifestoes of Surrealism*, transl. Richard Seaver and Helen R. Lane (Ann Arbor: University of Michigan Press, 1969), p. 29.

25. Quoted in Robert Desnos, *22 Poems*, transl. Michael Benedikt (Santa Cruz, Calif.: Kayak Books, 1971), p. 6.

26. Jacques Doucelin, 'Fischer-Dieskau, le poète', *Figaro*, 30 October 1979 (review of the French première; my translation).

27. It has been claimed that even this set derives from the material of part 1. See Robert Hanson, 'Lutoslawski's *Mi-parti*', *Tempo*, March 1978, p. 31.

28. Quoted in Janny DeJong, 'In gesprek met Lutoslawski', *Mens en melodie* 31 (1976): 365 (my translation).

Index